The Head of the House of Coombe

Frances Hodgson Burnett

Contents

THE HEAD OF THE HOUSE
OF COOMBE

BY

Frances Hodgson Burnett

CHAPTER I

The history of the circumstances about to be related began many years ago--or so it seems in these days. It began, at least, years before the world being rocked to and fro revealed in the pause between each of its heavings some startling suggestion of a new arrangement of its kaleidoscopic particles, and then immediately a re-arrangement, and another and another until all belief in a permanency of design seemed lost, and the inhabitants of the earth waited, helplessly gazing at changing stars and colours in a degree of mental chaos.

Its opening incidents may be dated from a period when people still had reason to believe in permanency and had indeed many of them--sometimes through ingenuousness, sometimes through stupidity of type--acquired a singular confidence in the importance and stability of their possessions, desires, ambitions and forms of conviction.

London at the time, in common with other great capitals, felt itself rather final though priding itself on being much more fluid and adaptable than it had been fifty years previously. In speaking of itself it at least dealt with fixed customs, and conditions and established facts connected with them--which gave rise to brilliant--or dull--witticisms.

One of these, heard not infrequently, was to the effect that--in London--one might live under an umbrella if one lived under it in the right neighbourhood and on the right side of the street, which axiom is the reason that a certain child through the first six years of her life sat on certain days staring out of a window in a small, dingy room on the top floor of a slice of a house on a narrow but highly fashionable London street and looked on at the passing of motors, carriages and people in the dull afternoon grayness.

The room was exalted above its station by being called The Day Nursery and another room equally dingy and uninviting was known as The Night Nursery. The slice of a house was inhabited by the very pretty Mrs. Gareth-Lawless, its inordinate rent being reluctantly paid by her--apparently with the assistance of those "ravens" who are expected to supply the truly deserving. The rent was inordinate only from the standpoint of one regarding it soberly in connection with the character of the house itself which was a gaudy little kennel crowded between two comparatively stately mansions. On one side lived an inordinately rich South African millionaire, and on the other an inordinately exalted person of title, which facts combined to form sufficient grounds for a certain inordinateness of rent.

Mrs. Gareth-Lawless was also, it may be stated, of the fibre which must live on the right side of the street or dissolve into nothingness--since as nearly nothingness as an embodied entity can achieve had Nature seemingly created her at the outset. So light and airy was the fair, slim, physical presentation of her being to the earthly vision, and so almost impalpably diaphanous the texture and form of mind and character to be observed by human perception, that among such friends--and enemies--as so slight a thing could claim she was prettily known as "Feather". Her real name, "Amabel", was not half as charming and whimsical in its appropriateness. "Feather" she adored being called and as it was the fashion among the amazing if amusing circle in which she spent her life, to call its acquaintances fantastic pet names selected from among the world of birds, beasts and fishes or inanimate objects--"Feather" she floated through her curious existence. And it so happened that she was the mother of the child who so often stared out of the window of the dingy and comfortless Day Nursery, too much a child to be more than vaguely conscious in a chaotic way that a certain feeling which at times raged within her and made her little body hot and restless was founded on something like actual hate for a special man who had certainly taken no deliberate steps to cause her detestation.

*   *   *   *   *

"Feather" had not been called by that delicious name when she married Robert Gareth-Lawless who was a beautiful and irresponsibly rather than deliberately bad young man. She was known as Amabel Darrel and the loveliest girl in the lovely corner of the island of Jersey where her father, a country doctor, had begotten a large family of lovely creatures and brought them up on the appallingly inadequate proceeds of his totally inadequate practice. Pretty female things must be disposed of early lest their market value decline. Therefore a well-born young man even without obvious resources represents a sail in the offing which is naturally welcomed as possibly belonging to a bark which may at least bear away a burden which the back carrying it as part of its pack will willingly shuffle on to other shoulders. It is all very well for a man with six lovely daughters to regard them as capital if he has money or position or generous relations or if he has energy and an ingenious unfatigued mind. But a man who is tired and neither clever nor important in any degree and who has reared his brood in one of the Channel Islands with a faded, silly, unattractive wife as his only aid in any difficulty, is wise in leaving the whole hopeless situation to chance and luck. Sometimes luck comes without assistance but--almost invariably--it does not.

"Feather"--who was then "Amabel"--thought Robert Gareth-Lawless incredible good luck. He only drifted into her summer by merest chance because a friend's yacht in which he was wandering about "came in" for supplies. A girl Ariel in a thin white frock and with big larkspur blue eyes yearning at you under her flapping hat as she answers your questions about the best road to somewhere will not be too difficult about showing the way herself. And there you are at a first-class beginning.

The night after she met Gareth-Lawless in a lane whose banks were thick with bluebells, Amabel and her sister Alice huddled close together in bed and talked almost pantingly in whispers over the possibilities which might reveal themselves--God willing--through a further acquaintance with Mr. Gareth-Lawless. They were eager and breathlessly anxious but they were young--YOUNG in their eagerness and Amabel was full of delight in his good looks.

"He is SO handsome, Alice," she whispered actually hugging her, not with affection but exultation. "And he can't be more than twenty-six or seven. And I'm SURE he liked me. You know that way a man has of looking at you--one sees it even in a place like this where there are only curates and things. He has brown eyes--like dark bright water in pools. Oh, Alice, if he SHOULD!"

Alice was not perhaps as enthusiastic as her sister. Amabel had seen him first and in the Darrel household there was a sort of unwritten, not always observed code flimsily founded on "First come first served." Just at the outset of an acquaintance one might say "Hands off" as it were. But not for long.

"It doesn't matter how pretty one is they seldom do," Alice grumbled. "And he mayn't have a farthing."

"Alice," whispered Amabel almost agonizingly, "I wouldn't CARE a farthing--if only he WOULD! Have I a farthing--have you a farthing--has anyone who ever comes here a farthing? He lives in London. He'd take me away. To live even in a back street IN LONDON would be Heaven! And one MUST--as soon as one possibly can.--One MUST! And Oh!" with another hug which this time was a shudder, "think of what Doris Harmer had to do! Think of his thick red old neck and his horrid fatness! And the way he breathed through his nose. Doris said that at first it used to make her ill to look at him."

"She's got over it," whispered Alice. "She's almost as fat as he is now. And she's loaded with pearls and things."

"I shouldn't have to 'get over' anything," said Amabel, "if this one WOULD. I could fall in love with him in a minute."

"Did you hear what Father said?" Alice brought out the words rather slowly and reluctantly. She was not eager on the whole to yield up a detail which after all added glow to possible prospects which from her point of view were already irritatingly glowing. Yet she could not resist the impulse of excitement. "No, you didn't hear. You were out of the room."

"What about? Something about HIM? I hope it wasn't horrid. How could it be?"

"He said," Alice drawled with a touch of girlishly spiteful indifference, "that if he was one of the poor Gareth-Lawlesses he hadn't much chance of succeeding to the title. His uncle--Lord Lawdor--is only forty-five and he has four splendid healthy boys--perfect little giants."

"Oh, I didn't know there was a title. How splendid," exclaimed Amabel rapturously. Then after a few moments' innocent maiden reflection she breathed with sweet hopefulness from under the sheet, "Children so often have scarlet fever or diphtheria, and you know they say those very strong ones are more likely to die than the other kind. The Vicar of Sheen lost FOUR all in a week. And the Vicar died too. The doctor said the diphtheria wouldn't have killed him if the shock hadn't helped."

Alice--who had a teaspoonful more brain than her sister--burst into a fit of giggling it was necessary to smother by stuffing the sheet in her mouth.

"Oh! Amabel!" she gurgled. "You ARE such a donkey! You would have been silly enough to say that even if people could have heard you. Suppose HE had!"

"Why should he care," said Amabel simply. "One can't help thinking things. If it happened he would be the Earl of Lawdor and--"

She fell again into sweet reflection while Alice giggled a little more. Then she herself stopped and thought also. After all perhaps--! One had to be practical. The tenor of her thoughts was such that she did not giggle again when Amabel broke the silence by whispering with tremulous, soft devoutness.

"Alice--do you think that praying REALLY helps?"

"I've prayed for things but I never got them," answered Alice. "But you know what the Vicar said on Sunday in sermon about 'Ask and ye shall receive'."

"Perhaps you haven't prayed in the right spirit," Amabel suggested with true piety. "Shall we--shall we try? Let us get out of bed and kneel down."

"Get out of bed and kneel down yourself," was Alice's sympathetic rejoinder. "You wouldn't take that much trouble for ME."

Amabel sat up on the edge of the bed. In the faint moonlight and her white night-gown she was almost angelic. She held the end of the long fair soft plait hanging over her shoulder and her eyes were full of reproach.

"I think you ought to take SOME interest," she said plaintively. "You know there would be more chances for you and the others--if I were not here."

"I'll wait until you are not here," replied the unstirred Alice.

But Amabel felt there was no time for waiting in this particular case. A yacht which "came in" might so soon "put out". She knelt down, clasping her slim young hands and bending her forehead upon them. In effect she implored that Divine Wisdom might guide Mr. Robert Gareth-Lawless in the much desired path. She also made divers promises because nothing is so easy as to promise things. She ended with a gently fervent appeal that--if her prayer were granted--something "might happen" which would result in her becoming a Countess of Lawdor. One could not have put the request with greater tentative delicacy.

She felt quite uplifted and a trifle saintly when she rose from her knees. Alice had actually fallen asleep already and she sighed quite tenderly as she slipped into the place beside her. Almost as her lovely little head touched the pillow her own eyes closed. Then she was asleep herself--and in the faintly moonlit room with the long soft plait trailing over her shoulder looked even more like an angel than before.

Whether or not as a result of this touching appeal to the Throne of Grace, Robert Gareth-Lawless DID. In three months there was a wedding at the very ancient village church, and the flowerlike bridesmaids followed a flower of a bride to the altar and later in the day to the station from where Mr. and Mrs. Robert Gareth-Lawless went on their way to London. Perhaps Alice and Olive also knelt by the side of their white beds the night after the wedding, for on that propitious day two friends of the bridegroom's--one of them the owner of the yacht--decided to return again to the place where there were to be found the most nymphlike of pretty creatures a man had ever by any chance beheld. Such delicate little fair crowned heads, such delicious little tip-tilted noses and slim white throats, such ripples of gay chatter and nonsense! When a man has fortune enough of his own why not take the prettiest thing he sees? So Alice and Olive were borne away also and poor Mr. and Mrs. Darrel breathed sighs of relief and there were not only more chances but causes for bright hopefulness in the once crowded house which now had rooms to spare. A certain inattention on the part of the Deity was no doubt responsible for the fact that "something" did not "happen" to the family of Lord Lawdor. On the contrary his four little giants of sons throve astonishingly and a few months after the Gareth-Lawless wedding Lady Lawdor--a trifle effusively, as it were--presented her husband with twin male infants so robust that they were humorously known for years afterwards as the "Twin Herculeses."

By that time Amabel had become "Feather" and despite Robert's ingenious and carefully detailed method of living upon nothing whatever, had many reasons for knowing that "life is a back street in London" is not a matter of beds of roses. Since the back street must be the "right street" and its accompaniments must wear an aspect of at least seeming to belong to the right order of detachment and fashionable ease, one was always in debt and forced to keep out of the way of duns, and obliged to pretend things and tell lies with aptness and outward gaiety. Sometimes one actually was so far driven to the wall that one could not keep most important engagements and the invention of plausible excuses demanded absolute genius. The slice of a house between the two big ones was a rash feature of the honeymoon but a year of giving smart little dinners in it and going to smart big dinners from it in a smart if small brougham ended in a condition somewhat akin to the feat of balancing oneself on the edge of a sword.

Then Robin was born. She was an intruder and a calamity of course. Nobody had contemplated her for a moment. Feather cried for a week when she first announced the probability of her advent. Afterwards however she managed to forget the approaching annoyance and went to parties and danced to the last hour continuing to be a great success because her prettiness was delicious and her diaphanous mentality was no train upon the minds of her admirers male and female.

That a Feather should become a parent gave rise to much wit of light weight when Robin in the form of a bundle of lace was carried down by her nurse to be exhibited in the gaudy crowded little drawing-room in the slice of a house in the Mayfair street.

It was the Head of the House of Coombe who asked the first question about her.

"What will you DO with her?" he inquired detachedly.

The frequently referred to "babe unborn" could not have presented a gaze of purer innocence than did the lovely Feather. Her eyes of larkspur blueness were clear of any thought or intention as spring water is clear at its unclouded best.

Her ripple of a laugh was clear also--enchantingly clear.

"Do!" repeated. "What is it people 'do' with babies? I suppose the nurse knows. I don't. I wouldn't touch her for the world. She frightens me."

She floated a trifle nearer and bent to look at her.

"I shall call her Robin," she said. "Her name is really Roberta as she couldn't be called Robert. People will turn round to look at a girl when they hear her called Robin. Besides she has eyes like a robin. I wish she'd open them and let you see."

By chance she did open them at the moment--quite slowly. They were dark liquid brown and seemed to be all lustrous iris which gazed unmovingly at the object in of focus. That object was the Head of the House of Coombe.

"She is staring at me. There is antipathy in her gaze," he said, and stared back unmovingly also, but with a sort of cold interest.

CHAPTER II

The Head of the House of Coombe was not a title to be found in Burke or Debrett. It was a fine irony of the Head's own and having been accepted by his acquaintances was not infrequently used by them in their light moments in the same spirit. The peerage recorded him as a Marquis and added several lesser attendant titles.

"When English society was respectable, even to stodginess at times," was his point of view, "to be born 'the Head of the House' was a weighty and awe-inspiring thing. In fearful private denunciatory interviews with one's parents and governors it was brought up against one as a final argument against immoral conduct such as debt and not going to church. As the Head of the House one was called upon to be an Example. In the country one appeared in one's pew and announced oneself a 'miserable sinner' in loud tones, one had to invite the rector to dinner with regularity and 'the ladies' of one's family gave tea and flannel petticoats and baby clothes to cottagers. Men and women were known as 'ladies' and 'gentlemen' in those halcyon days. One Represented things--Parties in Parliament--Benevolent Societies, and British Hospitality in the form of astounding long dinners at which one drank healths and made speeches. In roseate youth one danced the schottische and the polka and the round waltz which Lord Byron denounced as indecent. To recall the vigour of his poem gives rise to a smile--when one chances to sup at a cabaret."

He was considered very amusing when he analyzed his own mental attitude towards his world in general.

"I was born somewhat too late and somewhat too early," he explained in his light, rather cold and detached way. "I was born and educated at the closing of one era and have to adjust myself to living in another. I was as it were cradled among treasured relics of the ethics of the Georges and Queen Charlotte, and Queen Victoria in her bloom. *I* was in my bloom in the days when 'ladies' were reproved for wearing dresses cut too low at Drawing Rooms. Such training gives curious interest to fashions in which bodices are unconsidered trifles and Greek nymphs who dance with bare feet and beautiful bare legs may be one's own relations. I trust I do not seem even in the shadowiest way to comment unfavourably. I merely look on at the rapidities of change with unalloyed interest. As the Head of the House of Coombe I am not sure WHAT I am an Example of--or to. Which is why I at times regard myself in that capacity with a slightly ribald lightness."

The detachment of his question with regard to the newborn infant of the airily irresponsible Feather was in entire harmony with his attitude towards the singular incident of Life as illustrated by the World, the Flesh and the Devil by none of which he was--as far as could be observed--either impressed, disturbed or prejudiced. His own experience had been richly varied and practically unlimited in its opportunities for pleasure, sinful or unsinful indulgence, mitigated or unmitigated wickedness, the gathering of strange knowledge, and the possible ignoring of all dull boundaries. This being the case a superhuman charity alone could have forborne to believe that his opportunities had been neglected in the heyday of his youth. Wealth and lady of limitations in themselves would have been quite enough to cause the Nonconformist Victorian mind to regard a young--or middle-aged--male as likely to represent a fearsome moral example, but these three temptations combined with good looks and a certain mental brilliance were so inevitably the concomitants of elegant iniquity that the results might be taken for granted.

That the various worlds in which he lived in various lands accepted him joyfully as an interesting and desirable of more or less abominably sinful personage, the Head of the House of Coombe--even many years before he became its head--regarded with the detachment which he had, even much earlier, begun to learn. Why should it be in the least matter what people thought of one? Why should it in the least matter what one thought of oneself--and therefore--why should one think at all? He had begun at the outset a brilliantly happy young pagan with this simple theory. After the passing of some years he had not been quite so happy but had remained quite as pagan and retained the theory which had lost its first fine careless rapture and gained a secret bitterness. He had not married and innumerable stories were related to explain the reason why. They were most of them quite false and none of them quite true. When he ceased to be a young man his delinquency was much discussed, more especially when his father died and he took his place as the head of his family. He was old enough, rich enough, important enough for marriage to be almost imperative. But he remained unmarried. In addition he seemed to consider his abstinence entirely an affair of his own.

"Are you as wicked as people say you are?" a reckless young woman once asked him. She belonged to the younger set which was that season trying recklessness, in a tentative way, as a new fashion.

"I really don't know. It is so difficult to decide," he answered. "I could tell better if I knew exactly what wickedness is. When I find out I will let you know. So good of you to take an interest."

Thirty years earlier he knew that a young lady who had heard he was wicked would have perished in flames before immodestly mentioning the fact to him, but might have delicately attempted to offer "first aid" to reformation, by approaching with sweetness the subject of going to church.

The reckless young woman looked at him with an attention which he was far from being blind enough not to see was increased by his answer.

"I never know what you mean," she said almost wistfully.

"Neither do I," was his amiable response. "And I am sure it would not be worth while going into. Really, we neither of us know what we mean. Perhaps I am as wicked as I know how to be. And I may have painful limitations--or I may not."

After his father's death he spent rather more time in London and rather less in wandering over the face of the globe. But by the time he was forty he knew familiarly far countries and near and was intimate with most of the peoples thereof. He could have found his way about blind-folded in the most distinctive parts of most of the great cities. He had seen and learned many things. The most absorbing to his mind had been the ambitions and changes of nations, statesmen, rulers and those they ruled or were ruled by. Courts and capitals knew him, and his opportunities were such as gave him all ease as an onlooker. He was outwardly of the type which does not arouse caution in talkers and he heard much which was suggestive even to illumination, from those to whom he remained unsuspected of being a man who remembered things long and was astute in drawing conclusions. The fact remained however that he possessed a remarkable memory and one which was not a rag-bag filled with unassorted and parti-coloured remnants, but a large and orderly space whose contents were catalogued and filed and well enclosed from observation. He was also given to the mental argument which follows a point to its conclusion as a mere habit of mind. He saw and knew well those who sat and pondered with knit brows and cautiously hovering hand at the great chess-board which is formed by the Map of Europe. He found an enormous interest in watching their play. It was his fortune as a result of his position to know persons who wore crowns and a natural incident in whose lives it was to receive the homage expressed by the uncovering of the head and the bending of the knee. At forty he looked back at the time when the incongruousness, the abnormality and the unsteadiness of the foundations on which such personages stood first struck him. The realization had been in its almost sacrilegious novelty and daring, a sort of thunderbolt passing through his mind. He had at the time spoken of it only to one person.

"I have no moral or ethical views to offer," he had said. "I only SEE. The thing--as it is--will disintegrate. I am so at sea as to what will take its place that I feel as if the prospect were rather horrible. One has had the old landmarks and been im-pressed by the old pomp and picturesqueness so many centuries, that one cannot see the earth without them. There have been kings even in the Cannibal Islands."

As a statesman or a diplomat he would have seen far but he had been too much occupied with Life as an entertainment, too self-indulgent for work of any order. He freely admitted to himself that he was a worthless person but the fact did not disturb him. Having been born with a certain order of brain it observed and worked in spite of him, thereby adding flavour and interest to existence. But that was all.

It cannot be said that as the years passed he quite enjoyed the fact that he knew he was rarely spoken of to a stranger without its being mentioned that he was the most perfectly dressed man in London. He rather detested the idea though he was aware that the truth was unimpeachable. The perfection of his accompaniments had arisen in his youth from a secret feeling for fitness and harmony. Texture and colour gave him almost abnormal pleasure. His expression of this as a masculine creature had its limits which resulted in a concentration on perfection. Even at five-and-twenty however he had never been called a dandy and even at five-and-forty no one had as yet hinted at Beau Brummel though by that time men as well as women frequently described to each other the cut and colour of the garments he wore, and tailors besought him to honour them with crumbs of his patronage in the ambitious hope that they might mention him as a client. And the simple fact that he appeared in a certain colour or cut set it at once on its way to become a fashion to be seized upon, worn and exaggerated until it was dropped suddenly by its originator and lost in the oblivion of cheap imitations and cheap tailor shops. The first exaggeration of the harmony he had created and the original was seen no more.

Feather herself had a marvellous trick in the collecting of her garments. It was a trick which at times barely escaped assuming the proportions of absolute creation. Her passion for self-adornment expressed itself in ingenious combination and quite startling uniqueness of line now and then. Her slim fairness and ash-gold gossamer hair carried airily strange tilts and curves of little or large hats or daring tints other women could not sustain but invariably strove to imitate however disastrous the results. Beneath soft drooping or oddly flopping brims hopelessly unbecoming to most faces hers looked out quaintly lovely as a pictured child's wearing its grandmother's bonnet. Everything draped itself about or clung to her in entrancing folds which however whimsical were never grotesque.

"Things are always becoming to me," she said quite simply. "But often I stick a few pins into a dress to tuck it up here and there, or if I give a hat a poke somewhere to make it crooked, they are much more becoming. People are always asking me how I do it but I don't know how. I bought a hat from Cerise last week and I gave it two little thumps with my fist--one in the crown and one in the brim and they made it wonderful. The maid of the most grand kind of person tried to find out from my maid where I bought it. I wouldn't let her tell of course."

She created fashions and was imitated as was the Head of the House of Coombe but she was enraptured by the fact and the entire power of such gray matter as was held by her small brain cells was concentrated upon her desire to evolve new fantasies and amazements for her world.

Before he had been married for a year there began to creep into the mind of Bob Gareth-Lawless a fearsome doubt remotely hinting that she might end by becoming an awful bore in the course of time--particularly if she also ended by being less pretty. She chattered so incessantly about nothing and was such an empty-headed, extravagant little fool in her insistence on clothes--clothes--clothes--as if they were the breath of life. After watching her for about two hours one morning as she sat before her mirror directing her maid to arrange and re-arrange her hair in different styles--in delicate puffs and curls and straying rings--soft bands and loops--in braids and coils--he broke forth into an uneasy short laugh and expressed himself--though she did not know he was expressing himself and would not have understood him if she had.

"If you have a soul--and I'm not at all certain you have--" he said, "it's divided into a dressmaker's and a hairdresser's and a milliner's shop. It's full of tumbled piles of hats and frocks and diamond combs. It's an awful mess, Feather."

"I hope it's a shoe shop and a jeweller's as well," she laughed quite gaily. "And a lace-maker's. I need every one of them."

"It's a rag shop," he said. "It has nothing but CHIFFONS in it."

"If ever I DO think of souls I think of them as silly gauzy things floating about like little balloons," was her cheerful response.

"That's an idea," he answered with a rather louder laugh. "Yours might be made of pink and blue gauze spangled with those things you call paillettes."

The fancy attracted her.

"If I had one like that"--with a pleased creative air, "it would look rather ducky floating from my shoulder--or even my hat--or my hair in the evenings, just held by a tiny sparkling chain fastened with a diamond pin--and with lovely little pink and blue streamers." With the touch of genius she had at once relegated it to its place in the scheme of her universe. And Robert laughed even louder than before.

"You mustn't make me laugh," she said holding up her hand. "I am having my hair done to match that quakery thin pale mousey dress with the tiny poke bonnet--and I want to try my face too. I must look sweet and demure. You mustn't really laugh when you wear a dress and hat like that. You must only smile."

Some months earlier Bob would have found it difficult to believe that she said this entirely without any touch of humour but he realized now that it was so said. He had some sense of humour of his own and one of his reasons for vaguely feeling that she might become a bore was that she had none whatever.

It was at the garden party where she wore the thin quakery mousey dress and tiny poke bonnet that the Head of the House of Coombe first saw her. It was at the place of a fashionable artist who lived at Hampstead and had a garden and a few fine old trees. It had been Feather's special intention to strike this note of delicate dim colour. Every other woman was blue or pink or yellow or white or flowered and she in her filmy coolness of unusual hue stood out exquisitely among them. Other heads wore hats broad or curved or flopping, hers looked like a little nun's or an imaginary portrait of a delicious young great-grandmother. She was more arresting than any other female creature on the emerald sward or under the spreading trees.

When Coombe's eyes first fell upon her he was talking to a group of people and he stopped speaking. Someone standing quite near him said afterwards that he had for a second or so become pale--almost as if he saw something which frightened him.

"Who is that under the copper beech--being talked to by Harlow?" he inquired.

Feather was in fact listening with a gentle air and with her eyelids down drooped to the exact line harmonious with the angelic little poke bonnet.

"It is Mrs. Robert Gareth-Lawless--'Feather' we call her," he was answered. "Was there ever anything more artful than that startling little smoky dress? If it was flame colour one wouldn't see it as quickly."

"One wouldn't look at it as long," said Coombe. "One is in danger of staring. And the little hat--or bonnet--which pokes and is fastened under her pink ear by a satin bow held by a loose pale bud! Will someone rescue me from staring by leading me to her. It won't be staring if I am talking to her. Please."

The paleness appeared again as on being led across the grass he drew nearer to the copper beech. He was still rather pale when Feather lifted her eyes to him. Her eyes were so shaped by Nature that they looked like an angel's when they were lifted. There are eyes of that particular cut. But he had not talked to her fifteen minutes before he knew that there was no real reason why he should ever again lose his colour at the sight of her. He had thought at first there was. With the perception which invariably marked her sense of fitness of things she had begun in the course of the fifteen minutes--almost before the colour had quite returned to his face--the story of her husband's idea of her soul, as a balloon of pink and blue gauze spangled with paillettes. And of her own inspiration of wearing it floating from her shoulder or her hair by the light sparkling chain--and with delicate ribbon streamers. She was much delighted with his laugh--though she thought it had a rather cracked, harsh sound. She knew he was an important person and she always felt she was being a success when people laughed.

"Exquisite!" he said. "I shall never see you in the future without it. But wouldn't it be necessary to vary the colour at times?"

"Oh! Yes--to match things," seriously. "I couldn't wear a pink and blue one with this--" glancing over the smoky mousey thing "--or paillettes."

"Oh, no--not paillettes," he agreed almost with gravity, the harsh laugh having ended.

"One couldn't imagine the exact colour in a moment. One would have to think," she reflected. "Perhaps a misty dim bluey thing--like the edge of a rain-cloud--scarcely a colour at all."

For an instant her eyes were softly shadowed as if looking into a dream. He watched her fixedly then. A woman who was a sort of angel might look like that when she was asking herself how much her pure soul might dare to pray for. Then he laughed again and Feather laughed also.

Many practical thoughts had already begun to follow each other hastily through her mind. It would be the best possible thing for them if he really admired her. Bob was having all sorts of trouble with people they owed money to. Bills were sent in again and again and disagreeable letters were written. Her dressmaker and milliner had given her most rude hints which could indeed be scarcely considered hints at all. She scarcely dared speak to their smart young footman who she knew had only taken the place in the slice of a house because he had been told that it might be an opening to better things. She did not know the exact summing up at the agency had been as follows:

"They're a good looking pair and he's Lord Lawdor's nephew. They're bound to have their fling and smart people will come to their house because she's so pretty. They'll last two or three years perhaps and you'll open the door to the kind of people who remember a well set-up young fellow if he shows he knows his work above the usual."

The more men of the class of the Head of the House of Coombe who came in and out of the slice of a house the more likely the owners of it were to get good invitations and continued credit, Feather was aware. Besides which, she thought ingenuously, if he was rich he would no doubt lend Bob money. She had already known that certain men who liked her had done it. She did not mind it at all. One was obliged to have money.

This was the beginning of an acquaintance which gave rise to much argument over tea-cups and at dinner parties and in boudoirs--even in corners of Feather's own gaudy little drawing-room. The argument regarded the degree of Coombe's interest in her. There was always curiosity as to the degree of his interest in any woman--especially and privately on the part of the woman herself. Casual and shallow observers said he was quite infatuated if such a thing were possible to a man of his temperament; the more concentrated of mind said it was not possible to a man of his temperament and that any attraction Feather might have for him was of a kind special to himself and that he alone could explain it--and he would not.

Remained however the fact that he managed to see a great deal of her. It might be said that he even rather followed her about and more than one among the specially concentrated of mind had seen him on occasion stand apart a little and look at her--watch her--with an expression suggesting equally profound thought and the profound intention to betray his private meditations in no degree. There was no shadow of profundity of thought in his treatment of her. He talked to her as she best liked to be talked to about herself, her successes and her clothes which were more successful than anything else. He went to the little but exceedingly lively dinners the Gareth-Lawlesses gave and though he was understood not to be fond of dancing now and then danced with her at balls.

Feather was guilelessly doubtless concerning him. She was quite sure that he was in love with her. Her idea of that universal emotion was that it was a matter of clothes and propinquity and loveliness and that if one were at all clever one got things one wanted as a result of it. Her overwhelming affection for Bob and his for her had given her life in London and its entertaining accompaniments. Her frankness in the matter of this desirable capture when she talked to her husband was at once light and friendly.

"Of course you will be able to get credit at his tailor's as you know him so well," she said. "When I persuaded him to go with me to Madame Helene's last week she was quite amiable. He helped me to choose six dresses and I believe she would have let me choose six more."

"Does she think he is going to pay for them?" asked Bob.

"It doesn't matter what she thinks"; Feather laughed very prettily.

"Doesn't it?"

"Not a bit. I shall have the dresses. What's the matter, Rob? You look quite red and cross."

"I've had a headache for three days," he answered, "and I feel hot and cross. I don't care about a lot of things you say, Feather."

"Don't be silly," she retorted. "I don't care about a lot of things you say--and do, too, for the matter of that."

Robert Gareth-Lawless who was sitting on a chair in her dressing-room grunted slightly as he rubbed his red and flushed forehead.

"There's a--sort of limit," he commented. He hesitated a little before he added sulkily "--to the things one--SAYS."

"That sounds like Alice," was her undisturbed answer. "She used to squabble at me because I SAID things. But I believe one of the reasons people like me is because I make them laugh by SAYING things. Lord Coombe laughs. He is a very good person to know," she added practically. "Somehow he COUNTS. Don't you recollect how before we knew him--when he was abroad so long--people used to bring him into their talk as if they couldn't help remembering him and what he was like. I knew quite a lot about him--about his cleverness and his manners and his way of keeping women off without being rude--and the things he says about royalties and the aristocracy going out of fashion. And about his clothes. I adore his clothes. And I'm convinced he adores mine."

She had in fact at once observed his clothes as he had crossed the grass to her seat under the copper beech. She had seen that his fine thinness was inimitably fitted and presented itself to the eye as that final note of perfect line which ignores any possibility of comment. He did not wear things--they were expressions of his mental subtleties. Feather on her part knew that she wore her clothes--carried them about with her--however beautifully.

"I like him," she went on. "I don't know anything about political parties and the state of Europe so I don't understand the things he says which people think are so brilliant, but I like him. He isn't really as old as I thought he was the first day I saw him. He had a haggard look about his mouth and eyes then. He looked as if a spangled pink and blue gauze soul with little floating streamers was a relief to him."

The child Robin was a year old by that time and staggered about uncertainly in the dingy little Day Nursery in which she passed her existence except on such occasions as her nurse--who had promptly fallen in love with the smart young footman--carried her down to the kitchen and Servants' Hall in the basement where there was an earthy smell and an abundance of cockroaches. The Servants' Hall had been given that name in the catalogue of the fashionable agents who let the home and it was as cramped and grimy as the two top-floor nurseries.

The next afternoon Robert Gareth-Lawless staggered into his wife's drawing-room and dropped on to a sofa staring at her and breathing hard.

"Feather!" he gasped. "Don't know what's up with me. I believe I'm--awfully ill! I can't see straight. Can't think."

He fell over sidewise on to the cushions so helplessly that Feather sprang at him.

"Don't, Rob, don't!" she cried in actual anguish. "Lord Coombe is taking us to the opera and to supper afterwards. I'm going to wear--" She stopped speaking to shake him and try to lift his head. "Oh! do try to sit up," she begged pathetically. "Just try. DON'T give up till afterwards." But she could neither make him sit up nor make him hear. He lay back heavily with his mouth open, breathing stertorously and quite insensible. It happened that the Head of the House of Coombe was announced at that very moment even as she stood wringing her hands over the sofa.

He went to her side and looked at Gareth-Lawless.

"Have you sent for a doctor?" he inquired.

"He's--only just done it!" she exclaimed. "It's more than I can bear. You said the Prince would be at the supper after the opera and--"

"Were you thinking of going?" he put it to her quietly.

"I shall have to send for a nurse of course--" she began. He went so far as to interrupt her.

"You had better not go--if you'll pardon my saying so," he suggested.

"Not go? Not go at all?" she wailed.

"Not go at all," was his answer. And there was such entire lack of encouragement in it that Feather sat down and burst into sobs.

In few than two weeks Robert was dead and she was left a lovely penniless widow with a child.

CHAPTER III

Two or three decades earlier the prevailing sentiment would have been that "poor little Mrs. Gareth-Lawless" and her situation were pathetic. Her acquaintances would sympathetically have discussed her helplessness and absolute lack of all resource. So very pretty, so young, the mother of a dear little girl--left with no income! How very sad! What COULD she do? The elect would have paid her visits and sitting in her darkened drawing-room earnestly besought her to trust to her Maker and suggested "the Scriptures" as suitable reading. Some of them--rare and strange souls even in their time--would have known what they meant and meant what they said in a way they had as yet only the power to express through the medium of a certain shibboleth, the rest would have used the same forms merely because shibboleth is easy and always safe and creditable.

But to Feather's immediate circle a multiplicity of engagements, fevers of eagerness in the attainment of pleasures and ambitions, anxieties, small and large terrors, and a whirl of days left no time for the regarding of pathetic aspects. The tiny house up whose staircase--tucked against a wall--one had seemed to have the effect of crowding even when one went alone to make a call, suddenly ceased to represent hilarious little parties which were as entertaining as they were up to date and noisy. The most daring things London gossiped about had been said and done and worn there. Novel social ventures had been tried--dancing and songs which seemed almost startling at first--but which were gradually being generally adopted. There had always been a great deal of laughing and talking of nonsense and the bandying of jokes and catch phrases. And Feather fluttering about and saying delicious, silly things at which her hearers shouted with glee. Such a place could not suddenly become pathetic. It seemed almost indecent for Robert Gareth-Lawless to have dragged Death nakedly into their midst--to have died in his bed in one of the little bedrooms, to have been put in his coffin and carried down the stairs scraping the wall, and sent away in a hearse. Nobody could bear to think of it.

Feather could bear it less than anybody else. It seemed incredible that such a trick could have been played her. She shut herself up in her stuffy little bedroom with its shrimp pink frills and draperies and cried lamentably. At first she cried as a child might who was suddenly snatched away in the midst of a party. Then she began to cry because she was frightened. Numbers of cards "with sympathy" had been left at the front door during the first week after the funeral, they had accumulated in a pile on the salver but very few people had really come to see her and while she knew they had the excuse of her recent bereavement she felt that it made the house ghastly. It had never been silent and empty. Things had always been going on and now there was actually not a sound to be heard--no one going up and down stairs--Rob's room cleared of all his belongings and left orderly and empty--the drawing-room like a gay little tomb without an occupant. How long WOULD it be before it would be full of people again--how long must she wait before she could decently invite anyone?--It was really at this point that fright seized upon her. Her brain was not given to activities of reasoning and followed no thought far. She had not begun to ask herself questions as to ways and means. Rob had been winning at cards and had borrowed some money from a new acquaintance so no immediate abyss had yawned at her feet. But when the thought of future festivities rose before her a sudden check made her involuntarily clutch at her throat. She had no money at all, bills were piled everywhere, perhaps now Robert was dead none of the shops would give her credit. She remembered hearing Rob come into the house swearing only the day before he was taken ill and it had been because he had met on the door-step a collector of the rent which was long over-due and must be paid. She had no money to pay it, none to pay the servants' wages, none to pay the household bills, none to pay for the monthly hire of the brougham! Would they turn her into the street--would the servants go away--would she be left without even a carriage? What could she do about clothes! She could not wear anything but mourning now and by the time she was out of mourning her old clothes would have gone out of fashion. The morning on which this aspect of things occurred to her, she was so terrified that she began to run up and down the room like a frightened little cat seeing no escape from the trap it is caught in.

"It's awful--it's awful--it's awful!" broke out between her sobs. "What can I do? I can't do anything! There's nothing to do! It's awful--it's awful--it's awful!" She ended by throwing herself on the bed crying until she was exhausted. She had no mental resources which would suggest to her that there was anything but crying to be done. She had cried very little in her life previously because even in her days of limitation she had been able to get more or less what she wanted--though of course it had generally been less. And crying made one's nose and eyes red. On this occasion she actually forgot her nose and eyes and cried until she scarcely knew herself when she got up and looked in the glass.

She rang the bell for her maid and sat down to wait her coming. Tonson should bring her a cup of beef tea.

"It's time for lunch," she thought. "I'm faint with crying. And she shall bathe my eyes with rose-water."

It was not Tonson's custom to keep her mistress waiting but today she was not prompt. Feather rang a second time and an impatient third and then sat in her chair and waited until she began to feel as she felt always in these dreadful days the dead silence of the house. It was the thing which most struck terror to her soul--that horrid stillness. The servants whose place was in the basement were too much closed in their gloomy little quarters to have made themselves heard upstairs even if they had been inclined to. During the last few weeks feather had even found herself wishing that they were less well trained and would make a little noise--do anything to break the silence.

The room she sat in--Rob's awful little room adjoining--which was awful because of what she had seen for a moment lying stiff and hard on the bed before she was taken away in hysterics--were dread enclosures of utter silence. The whole house was dumb--the very street had no sound in it. She could not endure it. How dare Tonson? She sprang up and rang the bell again and again until its sound came back to her pealing through the place.

Then she waited again. It seemed to her that five minutes passed before she heard the smart young footman mounting the stairs slowly. She did not wait for his knock upon the door but opened it herself.

"How dare Tonson!" she began. "I have rung four or five times! How dare she!"

The smart young footman's manner had been formed in a good school. It was attentive, impersonal.

"I don't know, ma'am," he answered.

"What do you mean? What does SHE mean? Where is she?" Feather felt almost breathless before his unperturbed good style.

"I don't know, ma'am," he answered as before. Then with the same unbiassed bearing added, "None of us know. She has gone away."

Feather clutched the door handle because she felt herself swaying.

"Away! Away!" the words were a faint gasp.

"She packed her trunk yesterday and carried it away with her on a four-wheeler. About an hour ago, ma'am." Feather dropped her hand from the knob of the door and trailed back to the chair she had left, sinking into it helplessly.

"Who--who will dress me?" she half wailed.

"I don't know, ma'am," replied the young footman, his excellent manner presuming no suggestion or opinion whatever. He added however, "Cook, ma'am, wishes to speak to you."

"Tell her to come to me here," Feather said. "And I--I want a cup of beef tea."

"Yes, ma'am," with entire respect. And the door closed quietly behind him.

It was not long before it was opened again. "Cook" had knocked and Feather had told her to come in. Most cooks are stout, but this one was not. She was a thin, tall woman with square shoulders and a square face somewhat reddened by constant proximity to fires. She had been trained at a cooking school. She carried a pile of small account books but she brought nothing else.

"I wanted some beef tea, Cook," said Feather protestingly.

"There is no beef tea, ma'am," said Cook. "There is neither beef, nor stock, nor Liebig in the house."

"Why--why not?" stammered Feather and she stammered because even her lack of perception saw something in the woman's face which was new to her. It was a sort of finality.

She held out the pile of small books.

"Here are the books, ma'am," was her explanation. "Perhaps as you don't like to be troubled with such things, you don't know how far behind they are. Nothing has been paid for months. It's been an every-day fight to get the things that was wanted.

It's not an agreeable thing for a cook to have to struggle and plead. I've had to do it because I had my reputation to think of and I couldn't send up rubbish when there was company."

Feather felt herself growing pale as she sat and stared at her. Cook drew near and laid one little book after another on the small table near her.

"That's the butcher's book," she said. "He's sent nothing in for three days. We've been living on leavings. He's sent his last, he says and he means it. This is the baker's. He's not been for a week. I made up rolls because I had some flour left. It's done now--and HE'S done. This is groceries and Mercom & Fees wrote to Mr. Gareth-Lawless when the last month's supply came, that it would BE the last until payment was made. This is wines--and coal and wood--and laundry--and milk. And here is wages, ma'am, which CAN'T go on any longer."

Feather threw up her hands and quite wildly.

"Oh, go away!--go away!" she cried. "If Mr. Lawless were here--"

"He isn't, ma'am," Cook interposed, not fiercely but in a way more terrifying than any ferocity could have been--a way which pointed steadily to the end of things. "As long as there's a gentleman in a house there's generally a sort of a prospect that things MAY be settled some way. At any rate there's someone to go and speak your mind to even if you have to give up your place. But when there's no gentleman and nothing--and nobody--respectable people with their livings to make have got to protect themselves."

The woman had no intention of being insolent. Her simple statement that her employer's death had left "Nothing" and "Nobody" was prompted by no consciously ironic realization of the diaphanousness of Feather. As for the rest she had been professionally trained to take care of her interests as well as to cook and the ethics of the days of her grandmother when there had been servants with actual affections had not reached her.

"Oh! go away! Go AWA-AY!" Feather almost shrieked.

"I am going, ma'am. So are Edward and Emma and Louisa. It's no use waiting and giving the month's notice. We shouldn't save the month's wages and the trades-people wouldn't feed us. We can't stay here and starve. And it's a time of the year when places has to be looked for. You can't hold it against us, ma'am. It's better for you to have us out of the house tonight--which is when our boxes will be taken away."

Then was Feather seized with a panic. For the first time in her life she found herself facing mere common facts which rose before her like a solid wall of stone--not to be leapt, or crept under, or bored through, or slipped round. She was so overthrown and bewildered that she could not even think of any clever and rapidly constructed lie which would help her; indeed she was so aghast that she did not remember that there were such things as lies.

"Do you mean," she cried out, "that you are all going to LEAVE the house--that there won't be any servants to wait on me--that there's nothing to eat or drink--that I shall have to stay here ALONE--and starve!"

"We should have to starve if we stayed," answered Cook simply. "And of course there are a few things left in the pantry and closets. And you might get in a woman by the day. You won't starve, ma'am. You've got your family in Jersey. We waited because we thought Mr. and Mrs. Darrel would be sure to come."

"My father is ill. I think he's dying. My mother could not leave him for a moment. Perhaps he's dead now," Feather wailed.

"You've got your London friends, ma'am--"

Feather literally beat her hands together.

"My friends! Can I go to people's houses and knock at their front door and tell them I haven't any servants or anything to eat! Can I do that? Can I?" And she said it as if she were going crazy.

The woman had said what she had come to say as spokeswoman for the rest. It had not been pleasant but she knew she had been quite within her rights and dealt with plain facts. But she did not enjoy the prospect of seeing her little fool of a mistress raving in hysterics.

"You mustn't let yourself go, ma'am," she said. "You'd better lie down a bit and try to get quiet." She hesitated a moment looking at the pretty ruin who had risen from her seat and stood trembling.

"It's not my place of course to--make suggestions," she said quietly. "But--had you ever thought of sending for Lord Coombe, ma'am?"

Feather actually found the torn film of her mind caught for a second by something which wore a form of reality. Cook saw that her tremor appeared to verge on steadying itself.

"Coombe," she faintly breathed as if to herself and not to Cook. "Coombe."

"His lordship was very friendly with Mr. Lawless and he seemed fond of--coming to the house," was presented as a sort of added argument. "If you'll lie down I'll bring you a cup of tea, ma'am--though it can't be beef."

Feather staggered again to her bed and dropped flat upon it--flat as a slim little pancake in folds of thin black stuff which hung and floated.

"I can't bring you cream," said Cook as she went out of the room. "Louisa has had nothing but condensed milk--since yesterday--to give Miss Robin."

"Oh-h!" groaned Feather, not in horror of the tea without cream though that was awful enough in its significance, but because this was the first time since the falling to pieces of her world that she had given a thought to the added calamity of Robin.

CHAPTER IV

If one were to devote one's mental energies to speculation as to what is going on behind the noncommittal fronts of any row of houses in any great city the imaginative mind might be led far.

Bricks, mortar, windows, doors, steps which lead up to the threshold, are what are to be seen from the outside. Nothing particular may be transpiring within the walls, or tragedies, crimes, hideous suffering may be enclosed. The conclusion is obvious to banality--but as suggestive as banal--so suggestive in fact that the hypersensitive and too imaginative had better, for their own comfort's sake, leave the matter alone. In most cases the existing conditions would not be altered even if one knocked at the door and insisted on entering with drawn sword in the form of attendant policeman The outside of the slice of a house in which Feather lived was still rather fresh from its last decorative touching up. It had been painted cream colour and had white and windows and green window boxes with variegated vinca vines trailing from them and pink geraniums, dark blue lobelia and ferns filling the earth stuffed in by the florist who provided such adornments. Passers-by frequently glanced at it and thought it a nice little house whose amusing diminutiveness was a sort of attraction. It was rather like a new doll's house.

No one glancing at it in passing at the closing of this particular day had reason to suspect that any unaccustomed event was taking place behind the cream-coloured front. The front door "brasses" had been polished, the window-boxes watered and no cries for aid issued from the rooms behind them. The house was indeed quiet both inside and out. Inside it was indeed even quieter than usual. The servants' preparation for departure had been made gradually and undisturbedly. There had been exhaustive quiet discussion of the subject each night for weeks, even before Robert Gareth-Lawless' illness. The smart young footman Edward who had means of gaining practical information had constituted himself a sort of private detective. He had in time learned all that was to be learned. This, it had made itself clear to him on investigation, was not one of those cases when to wait for evolutionary family events might be the part of discretion. There were no prospects ahead--none at all. Matters would only get worse and the whole thing would end in everybody not only losing their unpaid back wages but having to walk out into the street through the door of a disgraced household whose owners would be turned out into the street also when their belongings were sold over their heads. Better get out before everything went to pieces and there were unpleasantnesses. There would be unpleasantnesses because there was no denying that the trades-people had been played tricks with. Mrs. Gareth-Lawless was only one of a lot of pretty daughters whose father was a poor country doctor in Jersey. He had had "a stroke" himself and his widow would have nothing to live on when he died. That was what Mrs. Lawless had to look to. As to Lord Lawdor Edward had learned from those who DID know that he had never approved of his nephew and that he'd said he was a fool for marrying and had absolutely refused to have anything to do with him. He had six boys and a girl now and big estates weren't what they had been, everyone knew. There was only one thing left for Cook and Edward and Emma and Louisa to do and that was to "get out" without any talk or argument.

"She's not one that won't find someone to look after her," ended Edward. "Somebody or other will take her up because they'll be sorry for her. But us lot aren't widows and orphans. No one's going to be sorry for us or care a hang what we've been let in for. The longer we stay, the longer we won't be paid." He was not a particularly depraved or cynical young footman but he laughed a little at the end of his speech. "There's the Marquis," he added. "He's been running in and out long enough to make a good bit of talk. Now's his time to turn up."

After she had taken her cup of tea without cream Feather had fallen asleep in reaction from her excited agitation. It was in accord with the inevitable trend of her being that even before her eyes closed she had ceased to believe that the servants were really going to leave the house. It seemed too ridiculous a thing to happen. She was possessed of no logic which could lead her to a realization of the indubitable fact that there was no reason why servants who could neither be paid nor provided with food should remain in a place. The mild stimulation of the tea also gave rise to the happy thought that she would not give them any references if they "behaved badly". It did not present itself to her that references from a house of cards which had ignominiously fallen to pieces and which henceforth would represent only shady failure, would be of no use. So she fell asleep.

*   *   *   *   *

When she awakened the lights were lighted in the streets and one directly across the way threw its reflection into her bedroom. It lit up the little table near which she had sat and the first thing she saw was the pile of small account books. The next was that the light which revealed them also fell brightly on the glass knob of the door which led into Robert's room.

She turned her eyes away quickly with a nervous shudder. She had a horror of the nearness of Rob's room. If there had been another part of the house in which she could have slept she would have fled to it as soon as he was taken ill. But the house was too small to have "parts". The tiny drawing-rooms piled themselves on top of the dining-room, the "master's bedrooms" on top of the drawing-rooms, and the nurseries and attics where Robin and the servants slept one on the other at the top of the house. So she had been obliged to stay and endure everything. Rob's cramped quarters had always been full of smart boots and the smell of cigars and men's clothes. He had moved about a good deal and had whistled and laughed and sworn and grumbled. They had neither of them had bad tempers so that they had not quarrelled with each other. They had talked through the open door when they were dressing and they had invented clever tricks which helped them to get out of money scrapes and they had gossiped and made fun of people. And now the door was locked and the room was a sort of horror. She could never think of it without seeing the stiff hard figure on the bed, the straight close line of the mouth and the white hard nose sharpened and narrowed as Rob's had never been. Somehow she particularly could not bear the recollection of the sharp unnatural modeling of the hard, white nose. She could not BEAR it! She found herself recalling it the moment she saw the light on the door handle and she got up to move about and try to forget it.

It was then that she went to the window and looked down into the street, probably attracted by some slight noise though she was not exactly aware that she had heard anything.

She must have heard something however. Two four-wheeled cabs were standing at the front door and the cabman assisted by Edward were putting trunks on top of them. They were servants' trunks and Cook was already inside the first cab which was filled with paper parcels and odds and ends. Even as her mistress watched Emma got in carrying a sedate band-box. She was the house-parlourmaid and a sedate person. The first cab drove away as soon as its door was closed and the cabman mounted to his seat. Louisa looking wholly unprofessional without her nurse's cap and apron and wearing a tailor-made navy blue costume and a hat with a wing in it, entered the second cab followed by Edward intensely suggesting private life and possible connection with a Bank. The second cab followed the first and Feather having lost her breath looked after them as they turned the corner of the street.

When they were quite out of sight she turned back into the room. The colour had left her skin, and her eyes were so wide stretched and her face so drawn and pinched with abject terror that her prettiness itself had left her.

"They've gone--all of them!" she gasped. She stopped a moment, her chest rising and falling. Then she added even more breathlessly, "There's no one left in the house. It's--empty!"

This was what was going on behind the cream-coloured front, the white windows and green flower-boxes of the slice of a house as motors and carriages passed it that evening on their way to dinner parties and theatres, and later as the policeman walked up and down slowly upon his beat.

Inside a dim light in the small hall showed a remote corner where on a peg above a decorative seat hung a man's hat of the highest gloss and latest form; and on the next peg a smart evening overcoat. They had belonged to Robert Gareth-Lawless who was dead and needed such things no more. The same dim light showed the steep narrowness of the white-railed staircase mounting into gruesome little corners of shadows, while the miniature drawing-rooms illumined only from the street seemed to await an explanation of dimness and chairs unfilled, combined with unnatural silence.

It would have been the silence of the tomb but that it was now and then broken by something like a half smothered shriek followed by a sort of moaning which made their way through the ceiling from the room above.

Feather had at first run up and down the room like a frightened cat as she had done in the afternoon. Afterwards she had had something like hysterics, falling face downward upon the carpet and clutching her hair until it fell down. She was not a person to be judged--she was one of the unexplained incidents of existence. The hour has passed when the clearly moral can sum up the responsibilities of a creature born apparently without brain, or soul or courage. Those who aspire to such morals as are expressed by fairness--mere fairness--are much given to hesitation. Courage had never been demanded of Feather so far. She had none whatever and now she only felt panic and resentment. She had no time to be pathetic about Robert, being too much occupied with herself. Robert was dead--she was alive--here--in an empty house with no money and no servants. She suddenly and rather awfully realized that she did not know a single person whom it would not be frantic to expect anything from.

Nobody had money enough for themselves, however rich they were. The richer they were the more they needed. It was when this thought came to her that she clutched her hands in her hair. The pretty and smart women and agreeable more or less good looking men who had chattered and laughed and made love in her drawing-rooms were chattering, laughing and making love in other houses at this very moment--or they were at the theatre applauding some fashionable actor-manager. At this very moment--while she lay on the carpet in the dark and every little room in the house had horror shut inside its closed doors--particularly Robert's room which was so hideously close to her own, and where there seemed still to lie moveless on the bed, the stiff hard figure. It was when she recalled this that the unnatural silence of the drawing-rooms was intruded upon by the brief half-stifled hysteric shriek, and the moaning which made its way through the ceiling. She felt almost as if the door handle might turn and something stiff and cold try to come in.

So the hours went on behind the cream-coloured outer walls and the white windows and gay flower-boxes. And the street became more and more silent--so silent at last that when the policeman walked past on his beat his heavy regular footfall seemed loud and almost resounding.

To even vaguely put to herself any question involving would not have been within the scope of her mentality. Even when she began to realize that she was beginning to feel faint for want of food she did not dare to contemplate going downstairs to look for something to eat. What did she know about downstairs? She had never there and had paid no attention whatever to Louisa's complaints that the kitchen and Servants' Hall were small and dark and inconvenient and that cockroaches ran about. She had cheerfully accepted the simple philosophy that London servants were used to these things and if they did their work it did not really matter. But to go out of one's room in the horrible stillness and creep downstairs, having to turn up the gas as one went, and to face the basement steps and cockroaches scuttling away, would be even more impossible than to starve. She sat upon the floor, her hair tumbling about her shoulders and her thin black dress crushed.

"I'd give almost ANYTHING for a cup of coffee," she protested feebly. "And there's no USE in ringing the bell!"

Her mother ought to have come whether her father was ill or not. He wasn't dead. Robert was dead and her mother ought to have come so that whatever happened she would not be quite alone and SOMETHING could be done for her. It was probably this tender thought of her mother which brought back the recollection of her wedding day and a certain wedding present she had received. It was a pretty silver travelling flask and she remembered that it must be in her dressing-bag now, and there was some cognac left in it. She got up and went to the place where the bag was kept. Cognac raised your spirits and made you go to sleep, and if she could sleep until morning the house would not be so frightening by daylight--and something might happen. The little flask was almost full. Neither she nor Robert had cared much about cognac. She poured some into a glass with water and drank it.

Because she was unaccustomed to stimulant it made her feel quite warm and in a few minutes she forgot that she had been hungry and realized that she was not so frightened. It was such a relief not to be terrified; it was as if a pain had stopped. She actually picked up one or two of the account books and glanced at the totals. If you couldn't pay bills you couldn't and nobody was put in prison for debt in these days. Besides she would not have been put in prison--Rob would--and Rob was dead. Something would happen--something.

As she began to arrange her hair for the night she remembered what Cook had said about Lord Coombe. She has cried until she did not look as lovely as usual, but after she had bathed her eyes with cold rose-water they began to seem only shadowy and faintly flushed. And her fine ash-gold hair was wonderful when it hung over each shoulder in wide, soft plaits. She might be a school-girl of fifteen. A delicate lacy night-gown was one of the most becoming things one wore. It was a pity one couldn't wear them to parties. There was nothing the least indecent about them. Millicent Hardwicke had been photographed in one of hers and no one had suspected what it was. Yes; she would send a little note to Coombe. She knew Madame Helene had only let her have her beautiful mourning because--. The things she had created were quite unique--thin, gauzy, black, floating or clinging. She had been quite happy the morning she gave Helene her orders. Tomorrow when she had slept through the night and it was broad daylight again she would be able to think of things to say in her letter to Lord Coombe. She would have to be a little careful because he did not like things to bore him.--Death and widows might--a little--at first. She had heard him say once that he did not wish to regard himself in the light of a charitable institution. It wouldn't do to frighten him away. Perhaps if he continued coming to the house and seemed very intimate the trades-people might be managed.

She felt much less helpless and when she was ready for bed she took a little more cognac. The flush had faded from her eye-lids and bloomed in delicious rose on her cheeks. As she crept between the cool sheets and nestled down on her pillow she had a delightful sense of increasing comfort--comfort. What a beautiful thing it was to go to sleep!

And then she was disturbed-started out of the divine doze stealing upon her-by a shrill prolonged wailing shriek!

It came from the Night Nursery and at the moment it seemed almost worse than anything which had occurred all through the day. It brought everything back so hideously. She had of course forgotten Robin again-and it was Robin! And Louisa had gone away with Edward. She had perhaps put the child to sleep discreetly before she went. And now she had wakened and was screaming. Feather had heard that she was a child with a temper but by fair means or foul Louisa had somehow managed to prevent her from being a nuisance.

The shrieks shocked her into sitting upright in bed. Their shrillness tearing through the utter soundlessness of the empty house brought back all her terrors and set her heart beating at a gallop.

"I--I WON'T!" she protested, fairly with chattering teeth. "I won't! I WON'T!"

She had never done anything for the child since its birth, she did not know how to do anything, she had not wanted to know. To reach her now she would be obliged to go out in the dark-the gas-jet she would have to light was actually close to the outer door of Robert's bedroom--THE room! If she did not die of panic while she was trying to light it she would have to make her way almost in the dark up the steep crooked little staircase which led to the nurseries. And the awful little creature's screams would be going on all the time making the blackness and dead silence of the house below more filled with horror by contrast-more shut off and at the same time more likely to waken to some horror which was new.

"I-I couldn't-even if I wanted to!" she quaked. "I daren't! I daren't! I wouldn't do it--for A MILLION POUNDS?" And she flung herself down again shuddering and burrowing her head under the coverings and pillows she dragged over her ears to shut out the sounds.

The screams had taken on a more determined note and a fiercer shrillness which the still house heard well and made the most of, but they were so far deadened for Feather that she began beneath her soft barrier to protest pantingly.

"I shouldn't know what to do if I went. If no one goes near her she'll cry herself to sleep. It's--it's only temper. Oh-h! what a horrible wail! It--it sounds like a--a lost soul!"

But she did not stir from the bed. She burrowed deeper under the bed clothes and held the pillow closer to her ears.

*   *   *   *   *

It did sound like a lost soul at times. What panic possesses a baby who cries in the darkness alone no one will ever know and one may perhaps give thanks to whatever gods there be that the baby itself does not remember. What awful woe of sudden unprotectedness when life exists only through protection--what piteous panic in the midst of black unmercifulness, inarticulate sound howsoever wildly shrill can neither explain nor express.

Robin knew only Louisa, warmth, food, sleep and waking. Or if she knew more she was not yet aware that she did. She had reached the age when she generally slept through the night. She might not have disturbed her mother until daylight but Louisa had with forethought given her an infant sleeping potion. It had disagreed with and awakened her. She was uncomfortable and darkness enveloped her. A cry or so and Louisa would ordinarily have come to her sleepy, and rather out of temper, but knowing what to do. In this strange night the normal cry of warning and demand produced no result.

No one came. The discomfort continued--the blackness remained black. The cries became shrieks--but nothing followed; the shrieks developed into prolonged screams. No Louisa, no light, no milk. The blackness drew in closer and became a thing to be fought with wild little beating hands. Not a glimmer--not a rustle--not a sound! Then came the cries of the lost soul--alone--alone--in a black world of space in which there was not even another lost soul. And then the panics of which there have been no records and never will be, because if the panic stricken does not die in mysterious convulsions he or she grows away from the memory of a formless past-- except that perhaps unexplained nightmares from which one wakens quaking, with cold sweat, may vaguely repeat the long hidden thing.

What the child Robin knew in the dark perhaps the silent house which echoed her might curiously have known. But the shrieks wore themselves out at last and sobs came--awful little sobs shuddering through the tiny breast and shaking the baby body. A baby's sobs are unspeakable things--incredible things. Slower and slower Robin's came--with small deep gasps and chokings between--and when an uninfantile druglike sleep came, the bitter, hopeless, beaten little sobs went on.

But Feather's head was still burrowed under the soft protection of the pillow.

CHAPTER V

The morning was a brighter one than London usually indulges in and the sun made its way into Feather's bedroom to the revealing of its coral pink glow and comfort. She had always liked her bedroom and had usually wakened in it to the sense of luxuriousness it is possible a pet cat feels when it wakens to stretch itself on a cushion with its saucer of cream awaiting it.

But she did not awaken either to a sense of brightness or luxury this morning. She had slept it was true, but once or twice when the pillow had slipped aside she had found herself disturbed by the far-off sound of the wailing of some little animal which had caused her automatically and really scarcely consciously to replace the pillow. It had only happened at long intervals because it is Nature that an exhausted baby falls asleep when it is worn out. Robin had probably slept almost as much as her mother.

Feather staring at the pinkness around her reached at last, with the assistance of a certain physical consciousness, a sort of spiritless intention.

"She's asleep now," she murmured. "I hope she won't waken for a long time. I feel faint. I shall have to find something to eat--if it's only biscuits." Then she lay and tried to remember what Cook had said about her not starving. "She said there were a few things left in the pantry and closets. Perhaps there's some condensed milk. How do you mix it up? If she cries I might go and give her some. It wouldn't be so awful now it's daylight."

She felt shaky when she got out of bed and stood on her feet. She had not had a maid in her girlhood so she could dress herself, much as she detested to do it. After she had begun however she could not help becoming rather interested because the dress she had worn the day before had become crushed and she put on a fresh one she had not worn at all. It was thin and soft also, and black was quite startlingly becoming to her. She would wear this one when Lord Coombe came, after she wrote to him. It was silly of her not to have written before though she knew he had left town after the funeral. Letters would be forwarded.

"It will be quite bright in the dining-room now," she said to encourage herself. "And Tonson once said that the only places the sun came into below stairs were the pantry and kitchen and it only stayed about an hour early in the morning. I must get there as soon as I can."

When she had so dressed herself that the reflection the mirror gave back to her was of the nature of a slight physical stimulant she opened her bedroom door and faced exploration of the deserted house below with a quaking sense of the proportions of the inevitable. She got down the narrow stairs casting a frightened glance at the emptiness of the drawing-rooms which seemed to stare at her as she passed them. There was sun in the dining-room and when she opened the sideboard she found some wine in decanters and some biscuits and even a few nuts and some raisins and oranges. She put them on the table and sat down and ate some of them and began to feel a little less shaky.

If she had been allowed time to sit longer and digest and reflect she might have reached the point of deciding on what she would write to Lord Coombe. She had not the pen of a ready writer and it must be thought over. But just when she was beginning to be conscious of the pleasant warmth of the sun which shone on her shoulders from the window, she was almost startled our of her chair by hearing again stealing down the staircase from the upper regions that faint wail like a little cat's.

"Just the moment--the very MOMENT I begin to feel a little quieted--and try to think--she begins again!" she cried out. "It's worse then ANYTHING!"

Large crystal tears ran down her face and upon the polished table.

"I suppose she would starve to death if I didn't give her some food--and then *I* should be blamed! People would be horrid about it. I've got nothing to eat myself."

She must at any rate manage to stop the crying before she could write to Coombe. She would be obliged to go down into the pantry and look for some condensed milk. The creature had no teeth but perhaps she could mumble a biscuit or a few raisins. If she could be made to swallow a little port wine it might make her sleepy. The sun was paying its brief morning visit to the kitchen and pantry when she reached there, but a few cockroaches scuttled away before her and made her utter a hysterical little scream. But there WAS some condensed milk and there was a little warm water in a kettle became the fire was not quite out. She imperfectly mixed a decoction and filled a bottle which ought not to have been downstairs but had been brought and left there by Louisa as a result of tender moments with Edward.

When she put the bottle and some biscuits and scraps of cold ham on a tray because she could not carry them all in her hands, her sense of outrage and despair made her almost sob.

"I am just like a servant--carrying trays upstairs," she wept. "I--I might be Edward--or--or Louisa." And her woe increased when she added in the dining-room the port wine and nuts and raisins and macaroons as viands which MIGHT somehow add to infant diet and induce sleep. She was not sure of course--but she knew they sucked things and liked sweets.

A baby left unattended to scream itself to sleep and awakening to scream itself to sleep again, does not present to a resentful observer the flowerlike bloom and beauty of infancy. When Feather carried her tray into the Night Nursery and found herself confronting the disordered crib on which her offspring lay she felt the child horrible to look at. Its face was disfigured and its eyes almost closed. She trembled all over as she put the bottle to its mouth and saw the fiercely hungry clutch of its hands. It was old enough to clutch, and clutch it did, and suck furiously and starvingly--even though actually forced to stop once or twice at first to give vent to a thwarted remnant of a scream.

Feather had only seen it as downy whiteness and perfume in Louisa's arms or in its carriage. It had been a singularly vivid and brilliant-eyed baby at whom people looked as they passed.

"Who will give her a bath?" wailed Feather. "Who will change her clothes? Someone must! Could a woman by the day do it? Cook said I could get a woman by the day."

And then she remembered that one got servants from agencies. And where were the agencies? And even a woman "by the day" would demand wages and food to eat.

And then the front door bell rang.

What could she do--what could she do? Go downstairs and open the door her-self and let everyone know! Let the ringer go on ringing until he was tired and went away? She was indeed hard driven, even though the wail had ceased as Robin clutched her bottle to her breast and fed with frenzy. Let them go away--let them! And then came the wild thought that it might be Something--the Something which must happen when things were at their worst! And if it had come and the house seemed to be empty! She did not walk down the stairs, she ran. Her heart beat until she reached the door out of breath and when she opened it stood their panting.

The people who waited upon the steps were strangers. They were very nice looking and quite young--a man and a woman very perfectly dressed. The man took a piece of paper out of his pocketbook and handed it to her with an agreeable apologetic courtesy.

"I hope we have not called early enough to disturb you," he said. "We waited until eleven but we are obliged to catch a train at half past. It is an 'order to view' from Carson & Bayle." He added this because Feather was staring at the paper.

Carson & Bayle were the agents they had rented the house from. It was Carson & Bayle's collector Robert had met on the threshold and sworn at two days before he had been taken ill. They were letting the house over her head and she would be turned out into the street?

The young man and woman finding themselves gazing at this exquisitely pretty creature in exquisite mourning, felt themselves appallingly embarrassed. She was plainly the widow Carson had spoken of. But why did she open the door herself? And why did she look as if she did not understand? Indignation against Carson & Bayle began to stir the young man.

"Beg pardon! So sorry! I am afraid we ought not to have come," he protested. "Agents ought to know better. They said you were giving up the house at once and we were afraid someone might take it."

Feather held the "order to view" in her hand and snared at them quite help-lessly.

"There--are no--no servants to show it to you," she said. "If you could wait--a few days--perhaps--"

She was so lovely and Madame Helene's filmy black creation was in itself such an appeal, that the amiable young strangers gave up at once.

"Oh, certainly--certainly! Do excuse us! Carson and Bayle ought not to have--! We are so sorry. Good morning, GOOD morning," they gave forth in discomfited sympathy and politeness, and really quite scurried away.

Having shut the door on their retreat Feather stood shivering.

"I am going to be turned out of the house! I shall have to live in the street!" she thought. "Where shall I keep my clothes if I live in the street!"

Even she knew that she was thinking idiotically. Of course if everything was taken from you and sold, you would have no clothes at all, and wardrobes and drawers and closets would not matter. The realization that scarcely anything in the house had been paid for came home to her with a ghastly shock. She staggered upstairs to the first drawing-room in which there was a silly pretty little buhl writing table.

She felt even more senseless when she sank into a chair before it and drew a sheet of note-paper towards her. Her thoughts would not connect themselves with each other and she could not imagine what she ought to say in her letter to Coombe. In fact she seemed to have no thoughts at all. She could only remember the things which had happened, and she actually found she could write nothing else. There seemed nothing else in the world.

"Dear Lord Coombe," trailed tremulously over the page--"The house is quite empty. The servants have gone away. I have no money. And there is not any food. And I am going to be turned out into the street--and the baby is crying because it is hungry."

She stopped there, knowing it was not what she ought to say. And as she stopped and looked at the words she began herself to wail somewhat as Robin had wailed in the dark when she would not listen or go to her. It was like a beggar's letter--a beggar's! Telling him that she had no money and no food--and would be turned out for unpaid rent. And that the baby was crying because it was starving!

"It's a beggar's letter--just a beggar's," she cried out aloud to the empty room. "And it's tru-ue!" Robin's wail itself had not been more hopeless than hers was as she dropped her head and let it lie on the buhl table.

She was not however even to be allowed to let it lie there, for the next instant there fell on her startled ear quite echoing through the house another ring at the doorbell and two steely raps on the smart brass knocker. It was merely because she did not know what else to do, having just lost her wits entirely that she got up and trailed down the staircase again.

When she opened the door, Lord Coombe--the apotheosis of exquisite fitness in form and perfect appointment as also of perfect expression--was standing on the threshold.

CHAPTER VI

If he had meant to speak he changed his mind after his first sight of her. He merely came in and closed the door behind him. Curious experiences with which life had provided him had added finish to an innate aptness of observation, and a fine readiness in action.

If she had been of another type he would have saved both her and himself a scene and steered ably through the difficulties of the situation towards a point where they could have met upon a normal plane. A very pretty woman with whose affairs one has nothing whatever to do, and whose pretty home has been the perfection of modern smartness of custom, suddenly opening her front door in the unexplained absence of a footman and confronting a visitor, plainly upon the verge of hysteria, suggests the necessity of promptness.

But Feather gave him not a breath's space. She was in fact not merely on the verge of her hysteria. She had gone farther. And here he was. Oh, here he was! She fell down upon her knees and actually clasped his immaculateness.

"Oh, Lord Coombe! Lord Coombe! Lord Coombe!" She said it three times because he presented to her but the one idea.

He did not drag himself away from her embrace but he distinctly removed himself from it.

"You must not fall upon your knees, Mrs. Lawless," he said. "Shall we go into the drawing-room?"

"I--was writing to you. I am starving--but it seemed too silly when I wrote it. And it's true!" Her broken words were as senseless in their sound as she had thought them when she saw them written.

"Will you come up into the drawing-room and tell me exactly what you mean," he said and he made her release him and stand upon her feet.

As the years had passed he had detached himself from so many weaknesses and their sequelae of emotion that he had felt himself a safely unreachable person. He was not young and he knew enough of the disagreeableness of consequences to be adroit in keeping out of the way of apparently harmless things which might be annoying. Yet as he followed Mrs. Gareth-Lawless and watched her stumbling up the stairs like a punished child he was aware that he was abnormally in danger of pitying her as he did not wish to pity people. The pity was also something apart from the feeling that it was hideous that a creature so lovely, so shallow and so fragile should have been caught in the great wheels of Life.

He knew what he had come to talk to her about but he had really no clear idea of what her circumstances actually were. Most people had of course guessed that her husband had been living on the edge of his resources and was accustomed to debt and duns, but a lovely being greeting you by clasping your knees and talking about "starving"--in this particular street in Mayfair, led one to ask oneself what one was walking into. Feather herself had not known, in fact neither had any other human being known, that there was a special reason why he had drifted into seeming rather to allow her about--why he had finally been counted among the frequenters of the narrow house--and why he had seemed to watch her a good deal sometimes with an expression of serious interest--sometimes with an air of irritation, and sometimes with no expression at all. But there existed this reason and this it was and this alone which had caused him to appear upon her threshold and it had also been the power which had prevented his disengaging himself with more incisive finality when he found himself ridiculously clasped about the knees as one who played the part of an obdurate parent in a melodrama.

Once in the familiar surroundings of her drawing-room her ash-gold blondness and her black gauzy frock heightened all her effects so extraordinarily that he frankly admitted to himself that she possessed assets which would have modified most things to most men.

As for Feather, when she herself beheld him against the background of the same intimate aspects, the effect of the sound of his voice, the manner in which he sat down in a chair and a certain remotely dim hint in the hue of his clothes and an almost concealed note of some touch of colour which scarcely seemed to belong to anything worn--were so reminiscent of the days which now seemed past forever that she began to cry again.

He received this with discreet lack of melodrama of tone.

"You mustn't do that, Mrs. Lawless," he said, "or I shall burst into tears myself. I am a sensitive creature."

"Oh, DO say 'Feather' instead of Mrs. Lawless," she implored. "Sometimes you said 'Feather'."

"I will say it now," he answered, "if you will not weep. It is an adorable name."

"I feel as if I should never hear it again," she shuddered, trying to dry her eyes. "It is all over!"

"What is all over?"

"This--!" turning a hopeless gaze upon the two tiny rooms crowded with knick-knacks and nonsense. "The parties and the fun--and everything in the world! I have only had some biscuits and raisins to eat today--and the landlord is going to turn me out."

It seemed almost too preposterous to quite credit that she was uttering naked truth.--And yet--! After a second's gaze at her be repeated what he had said below stairs.

"Will you tell me exactly what you mean?"

Then he sat still and listened while she poured it all forth. And as he listened he realized that it was the mere every day fact that they were sitting in the slice of a house with the cream-coloured front and the great lady in her mansion on one side and the millionaire and his splendours on the other, which peculiarly added to a certain hint of gruesomeness in the situation.

It was not necessary to add colour and desperation to the story. Any effort Feather had made in that direction would only have detracted from the nakedness of its stark facts. They were quite enough in themselves in their normal inevitable-ness. Feather in her pale and totally undignified panic presented the whole thing with clearness which had--without being aided by her--an actual dramatic value. This in spite of her mental dartings to and from and dragging in of points and bits of scenes which were not connected with each other. Only a brain whose processes of inclusion and exclusion were final and rapid could have followed her. Coombe watched her closely as she talked. No grief-stricken young widowed loneliness and heart-break were the background of her anguish. She was her own background and also her own foreground. The strength of the fine body laid prone on the bed of the room she held in horror, the white rigid face whose good looks had changed to something she could not bear to remember, had no pathos which was not concerned with the fact that Robert had amazingly and unnaturally failed her by dying and leaving her nothing but unpaid bills. This truth indeed made the situation more poignantly and finally squalid, as she brought forth one detail after another. There were bills which had been accumulating ever since they began their life in the narrow house, there had been trades-people who had been juggled with, promises made and supported by adroit tricks and cleverly invented misrepresentations and lies which neither of the pair had felt any compunctions about and had indeed laughed over. Coombe saw it all though he also saw that Feather did not know all she was telling him. He could realize the gradually increasing pressure and anger at tricks which betrayed themselves, and the gathering determination on the part of the creditors to end the matter in the only way in which it could be ended. It had come to this before Robert's illness, and Feather herself had heard of fierce interviews and had seen threatening letters, but she had not believed they could mean all they implied. Since things had been allowed to go on so long she felt that they would surely go on longer in the same way. There had been some serious threatening about the rent and the unpaid-for furniture. Robert's supporting idea had been that he might perhaps "get something out of Lawdor who wouldn't enjoy being the relation of a fellow who was turned into the street!"

"He ought to have done something," Feather plained. "Robert would have been Lord Lawdor himself if his uncle had died before he had all those disgusting children."

She was not aware that Coombe frequently refrained from saying things to her--but occasionally allowed himself NOT to refrain. He did not refrain now from making a simple comment.

"But he is extremely robust and he has the children. Six stalwart boys and a stalwart girl. Family feeling has apparently gone out of fashion."

As she wandered on with her story he mentally felt himself actually dragged into the shrimp-pink bedroom and standing an onlooker when the footman outside the door "did not know" where Tonson had gone. For a moment he felt conscious of

the presence of some scent which would have been sure to exhale itself from draperies and wardrobe. He saw Cook put the account books on the small table, he heard
her, he also comprehended her. And Feather at the window breathlessly watching
the two cabs with the servants' trunks on top, and the servants respectably unprofessional in attire and going away quietly without an unpractical compunction--he
saw these also and comprehended knowing exactly why compunctions had no part
in latter-day domestic arrangements. Why should they?

When Feather reached the point where it became necessary to refer to Robin
some fortunate memory of Alice's past warnings caused her to feel--quite suddenly-
-that certain details might be eliminated.

"She cried a little at first," she said, "but she fell asleep afterwards. I was glad
she did because I was afraid to go to her in the dark."

"Was she in the dark?"

"I think so. Perhaps Louisa taught her to sleep without a light. There was none
when I took her some condensed milk this morning. There was only c-con-d-densed
milk to give her."

She shed tears and choked as she described her journey into the lower regions
and the cockroaches scuttling away before her into their hiding-places.

"I MUST have a nurse! I MUST have one!" she almost sniffed. "Someone must
change her clothes and give her a bath!"

"You can't?" Coombe said.

"I!" dropping her handkerchief. "How--how CAN I?"

"I don't know," he answered and picked up the handkerchief with an aloof
grace of manner.

It was really Robin who was for Feather the breaking-point.

He thought she was in danger of flinging herself upon him again. She caught at
his arm and her eyes of larkspur blue were actually wild.

"Don't you see where I am! How there is nothing and nobody--Don't you
SEE?"

"Yes, I see," he answered. "You are quite right. There is nothing AND nobody.
I have been to Lawdor myself."

"You have been to TALK to him?"

"Yesterday. That was my reason for coming here. He will not see you or be written to. He says he knows better to begin that sort of thing. It may be that family feeling has not the vogue it once had, but you may recall that your husband infuriated him years ago. Also England is a less certain quantity than it once was--and the man has a family. He will allow you a hundred a year but there he draws the line."

"A hundred a year!" Feather breathed. From her delicate shoulders hung floating scarf-like sleeves of black transparency and she lifted one of them and held it out like a night moth's wing--"This cost forty pounds," she said, her voice quite faint and low. "A good nurse would cost forty! A cook--and a footman and a maid--and a coachman--and the brougham--I don't know how much they would cost. Oh-h!"

She drooped forward upon her sofa and laid face downward on a cushion--slim, exquisite in line, lost in despair.

The effect produced was that she gave herself into his hands. He felt as well as saw it and considered. She had no suggestion to offer, no reserve. There she was.

"It is an incredible sort of situation," he said in an even, low-pitched tone rather as if he were thinking aloud, "but it is baldly real. It is actually simple. In a street in Mayfair a woman and child might--" He hesitated a second and a wailed word came forth from the cushion.

"Starve!"

He moved slightly and continued.

"Since their bills have not been paid the trades-people will not send in food. Servants will not stay in a house where they are not fed and receive no wages. No landlord will allow a tenant to occupy his property unless he pays rent. It may sound inhuman--but it is only human."

The cushion in which Feather's face was buried retained a faint scent of Robert's cigar smoke and the fragrance brought back to her things she had heard him say dispassionately about Lord Coombe as well as about other men. He had not been a puritanic or condemnatory person. She seemed to see herself groveling again on the floor of her bedroom and to feel the darkness and silence through which she had not dared to go to Robin.

Not another night like that! No! No!

"You must go to Jersey to your mother and father," Coombe said. "A hundred a year will help you there in your own home."

Then she sat upright and there was something in her lovely little countenance he had never seen before. It was actually determination.

"I have heard," she said, "of poor girls who were driven--by starvation to--to go on the streets. I--would go ANYWHERE before I would go back there."

"Anywhere!" he repeated, his own countenance expressing--or rather refusing to express something as new as the thing he had seen in her own.

"Anywhere!" she cried and then she did what he had thought her on the verge of doing a few minutes earlier--she fell at his feet and embraced his knees. She clung to him, she sobbed, her pretty hair loosened itself and fell about her in wild but enchanting disorder.

"Oh, Lord Coombe! Oh, Lord Coombe! Oh, Lord Coombe!" she cried as she had cried in the hall.

He rose and endeavoured to disengage himself as he had done before. This time with less success because she would not let him go. He had the greatest possible objection to scenes.

"Mrs. Lawless--Feather--I beg you will get up," he said.

But she had reached the point of not caring what happened if she could keep him. He was a gentleman--he had everything in the world. What did it matter?

"I have no one but you and--and you always seemed to like me, I would do anything--ANYONE asked me, if they would take care of me. I have always liked you very much--and I did amuse you--didn't I? You liked to come here."

There was something poignant about her delicate distraught loveliness and, in the remoteness of his being, a shuddering knowledge that it was quite true that she would do anything for any man who would take care of her, produced an effect on him nothing else would have produced. Also a fantastic and finely ironic vision of Joseph and Potiphar's wife rose before him and the vision of himself as Joseph irked a certain complexness of his mentality. Poignant as the thing was in its modern way, it was also faintly ridiculous.

Then Robin awakened and shrieked again. The sound which had gained strength through long sleep and also through added discomfort quite rang through the house. What that sound added to the moment he himself would not have been able to explain until long afterwards. But it singularly and impellingly added.

"Listen!" panted Feather. "She has begun again. And there is no one to go to her."

"Get up, Mrs. Lawless," he said. "Do I understand that you are willing that *I* arrange this for you!"

He helped her to her feet.

"Do you mean--really!" she faltered. "Will you--will you--?"

Her uplifted eyes were like a young angel's brimming with crystal drops which slipped--as a child's tears slip--down her cheeks. She clasped her hands in exquisite appeal. He stood for a moment quite still, his mind fled far away and he forgot where he was. And because of this the little simpleton's shallow discretion deserted her.

"If you were a--a marrying man--?" she said foolishly--almost in a whisper.

He recovered himself.

"I am not," with a finality which cut as cleanly as a surgical knife.

Something which was not the words was of a succinctness which filled her with new terror.

"I--I know!" she whimpered, "I only said if you were!"

"If I were--in this instance--it would make no difference." He saw the kind of slippery silliness he was dealing with and what it might transform itself into if allowed a loophole. "There must be no mistakes."

In her fright she saw him for a moment more distinctly than she had ever seen him before and hideous dread beset her lest she had blundered fatally.

"There shall be none," she gasped. "I always knew. There shall be none at all."

"Do you know what you are asking me?" he inquired.

"Yes, yes--I'm not a girl, you know. I've been married. I won't go home. I can't starve or live in awful lodgings. SOMEBODY must save me!"

"Do you know what people will say?" his steady voice was slightly lower.

"It won't be said to me." Rather wildly. "Nobody minds--really."

He ceased altogether to look serious. He smiled with the light detached air his world was most familiar with.

"No--they don't really," he answered. "I had, however, a slight preference for knowing whether you would or not. You flatter me by intimating that you would not."

He knew that if he had held out an arm she would have fallen upon his breast and wept there, but he was not at the moment in the mood to hold out an arm. He merely touched hers with a light pressure.

"Let us sit down and talk it over," he suggested.

A hansom drove up to the door and stopped before he had time to seat himself. Hearing it he went to the window and saw a stout businesslike looking man get out, accompanied by an attendant. There followed a loud, authoritative ringing of the bell and an equally authoritative rap of the knocker. This repeated itself. Feather, who had run to the window and caught sight of the stout man, clutched his sleeve.

"It's the agent we took the house from. We always said we were out. It's either Carson or Bayle. I don't know which."

Coombe walked toward the staircase.

"You can't open the door!" she shrilled.

"He has doubtless come prepared to open it himself." he answered and proceeded at leisure down the narrow stairway.

The caller had come prepared. By the time Coombe stood in the hall a latchkey was put in the keyhole and, being turned, the door opened to let in Carson--or Bayle--who entered with an air of angered determination, followed by his young man.

The physical presence of the Head of the House of Coombe was always described as a subtly impressive one. Several centuries of rather careful breeding had resulted in his seeming to represent things by silent implication. A man who has never found the necessity of explaining or excusing himself inevitably presents a front wholly unsuggestive of uncertainty. The front Coombe presented merely awaited explanations from others.

Carson--or Bayle--had doubtless contemplated seeing a frightened servant trying to prepare a stammering obvious lie. He confronted a tall, thin man about whom--even if his clothes had been totally different--there could be no mistake. He stood awaiting an apology so evidently that Carson--or Bayle--began to stammer himself even before he had time to dismiss from his voice the suggestion of bluster. It would have irritated Coombe immensely if he had known that he--and a certain overcoat--had been once pointed out to the man at Sandown and that--in consequence of the overcoat--he vaguely recognized him.

"I--I beg pardon," he began.

"Quite so," said Coombe.

"Some tenants came to look at the house this morning. They had an order to view from us. They were sent away, my lord--and decline to come back. The rent has not been paid since the first half year. There is no one now who can even PRE-TEND it's going to be paid. Some step had to be taken."

"Quite so," said Coombe. "Suppose you step into the dining-room."

He led the pair into the room and pointed to chairs, but neither the agent nor his attendant was calm enough to sit down.

Coombe merely stood and explained himself.

"I quite understand," he said. "You are entirely within your rights. Mrs. Gareth-Lawless is, naturally, not able to attend to business. For the present--as a friend of her late husband's--I will arrange matters for her. I am Lord Coombe. She does not wish to give up the house. Don't send any more possible tenants. Call at Coombe House in an hour and I will give you a cheque."

There were a few awkward apologetic moments and then the front door opened and shut, the hansom jingled away and Coombe returned to the drawing-room. Robin was still shrieking.

"She wants some more condensed milk," he said. "Don't be frightened. Go and give her some. I know an elderly woman who understands children. She was a nurse some years ago. I will send her here at once. Kindly give me the account books. My housekeeper will send you some servants. The trades-people will come for orders."

Feather was staring at him.

"W-will they?" she stammered. "W-will everything--?"

"Yes--everything," he answered. "Don't be frightened. Go upstairs and try to stop her. I must go now. I never heard a creature yell with such fury."

She turned away and went towards the second flight of stairs with a rather dazed air. She had passed through a rather tremendous crisis and she WAS dazed. He made her feel so. She had never understood him for a moment and she did not understand him now--but then she never did understand people and the whole situation was a new one to her. If she had not been driven to the wall she would have been quite as respectable as she knew how to be.

Coombe called a hansom and drove home, thinking of many things and looking even more than usually detached. He had remarked the facial expression of the short and stout man as he had got into his cab and he was turning over mentally his own exact knowledge of the views the business mind would have held and what the business countenance would have decently covered if he--Coombe--had explained in detail that he was so far--in this particular case--an entirely blameless character.

CHAPTER VII

The slice of a house from that time forward presented the external aspect to which the inhabitants of the narrow and fashionable street and those who passed through it had been accustomed. Such individuals as had anticipated beholding at some early day notices conspicuously placed announcing "Sale by Auction. Elegant Modern Furniture" were vaguely puzzled as well as surprised by the fact that no such notices appeared even inconspicuously. Also there did not draw up before the door--even as the weeks went on--huge and heavy removal vans with their resultant litter, their final note of farewell a "To Let" in the front windows.

On the contrary, the florist came and refilled the window boxes with an admirable arrangement of fresh flowers; new and even more correct servants were to be seen ascending and descending the area step; a young footman quite as smart as the departed Edward opened the front door and attended Mrs. Gareth-Lawless to her perfect little brougham. The trades-people appeared promptly every day and were obsequiously respectful in manner. Evidently the household had not disintegrated as a result of the death of Mr. Gareth-Lawless.

As it became an established fact that the household had not fallen to pieces its frequenters gradually returned to it, wearing indeed the air of people who had never really remained away from it. There had been natural reasons enough for considerate absence from a house of bereavement and a desolate widow upon whose grief it would have been indelicate to intrude. As Feather herself had realized, the circle of her intimates was not formed of those who could readily adjust themselves to entirely changed circumstances. If you dance on a tight rope and the rope is unexpectedly withdrawn, where are you? You cannot continue dancing until the rope is restrung.

The rope, however, being apparently made absolutely secure, it was not long before the dancing began again. Feather's mourning, wonderfully shading itself from month to month, was the joy of all beholders. Madame Helene treated her as a star gleaming through gradually dispersing clouds. Her circle watched her with secretly humorous interest as each fine veil of dimness was withdrawn.

"The things she wears are priceless," was said amiably in her own drawing-room. "Where does she get them? Figure to yourself Lawdor paying the bills."

"She gets them from Helene," said a long thin young man with a rather good-looking narrow face and dark eyes, peering through pince nez, "But I couldn't."

In places where entertainment as a means of existence proceed so to speak, fast and furiously, questions of taste are not dwelt upon at leisure. You need not hesitate before saying anything you liked in any one's drawing-room so long as it was amusing enough to make somebody--if not everybody--laugh. Feather had made people laugh in the same fashion in the past. The persons she most admired were always making sly little impudent comments and suggestions, and the thwarted years on the island of Jersey had, in her case, resulted in an almost hectic desire to keep pace. Her efforts had usually been successes because Nature's self had provided her with the manner of a silly pretty child who did not know how far she went. Shouts of laughter had often greeted her, and the first time she had for a moment doubted her prowess was on an occasion when she had caught a glimpse of Coombe who stared at her with an expression which she would--just for one second--have felt might be horror, if she had not been so sure it couldn't be, and must of course be something else--one of the things nobody ever understood in him.

By the time the softly swathing veils of vaporous darkness were withdrawn, and the tight rope assuring everyone of its permanent security became a trusted support, Feather at her crowded little parties and at other people's bigger ones did not remain wholly unaware of the probability that even people who rather liked her made, among themselves, more or less witty comments upon her improved fortunes. They were improved greatly. Bills were paid, trades-people were polite, servants were respectful; she had no need to invent excuses and lies. She and Robert had always kept out of the way of stodgy, critical people, so they had been intimate with none of the punctilious who might have withdrawn themselves from a condition of things they chose to disapprove: accordingly, she found no gaps in her circle.

Those who had formed the habit of amusing themselves at her house were as ready as before to amuse themselves again.

The fact remained, however,--curiously, perhaps, in connection with the usual slightness of all impressions made on her--that there was a memory which never wholly left her. Even when she tried to force it so far into the background of her existence that it might almost be counted as forgotten, it had a trick of rising before her. It was the memory of the empty house as its emptiness had struck to the centre of her being when she had turned from her bedroom window after watching the servants drive away in their cabs. It was also the memory of the hours which had followed--the night in which nobody had been in any of the rooms--no one had gone up or down the stairs--when all had seemed dark and hollow--except the Night Nursery where Robin screamed, and her own room where she herself cowered under the bed clothes and pulled the pillow over her head. But though the picture would not let itself be blotted out, its effect was rather to intensify her sense of relief because she had slipped so safely from under the wheels of destiny.

"Sometimes," she revealed artlessly to Coombe, "while I am driving in the park on a fine afternoon when every one is out and the dresses look like the flower beds, I let myself remember it just to make myself enjoy everything more by contrast."

The elderly woman who had been a nurse in her youth and who had been sent by Lord Coombe temporarily to replace Louisa had not remained long in charge of Robin. She was not young and smart enough for a house on the right side of the right street, and Feather found a young person who looked exactly as she should when she pushed the child's carriage before her around the square.

The square--out of which the right street branches--and the "Gardens" in the middle of the square to which only privileged persons were admitted by private key, the basement kitchen and Servants' Hall, and the two top floor nurseries represented the world to the child Robin for some years. When she was old enough to walk in the street she was led by the hand over the ground she had travelled daily in her baby carriage. Her first memory of things was a memory of standing on the gravel path in the Square Gardens and watching some sparrows quarrel while Andrews, her nurse, sat on a bench with another nurse and talked in low tones. They were talking in a way Robin always connected with servants and which she naturally accepted as being the method of expression of their species--much as she accepted the mewing of cats and the barking of dogs. As she grew older, she reached the stage of knowing that they were generally saying things they did not wish her to hear.

She liked watching the sparrows in the Gardens because she liked watching sparrows at all times. They were the only friends she had ever known, though she was not old enough to call them friends, or to know what friends meant. Andrews had taught her, by means of a system of her own, to know better than to cry or to make any protesting noise when she was left alone in her ugly small nursery. Andrews' idea of her duties did not involve boring herself to death by sitting in a room on the top floor when livelier entertainment awaited her in the basement where the cook was a woman of wide experience, the housemaid a young person who had lived in gay country houses, and the footman at once a young man of spirit and humour. So Robin spent many hours of the day--taking them altogether--quite by herself. She might have more potently resented her isolations if she had ever known any other condition than that of a child in whom no one was in the least interested and in whom "being good" could only mean being passive under neglect and calling no one's attention to the fact that she wanted anything from anybody. As a bird born in captivity lives in its cage and perhaps believes it to be the world, Robin lived in her nursery and knew every square inch of it with a deadly if unconscious sense of distaste and fatigue. She was put to bed and taken up, she was fed and dressed in it, and once a day--twice perhaps if Andrews chose--she was taken out of it downstairs and into the street. That was all. And that was why she liked the sparrows so much.

And sparrows are worth watching if you live in a nursery where nothing ever happens and where, when you look out, you are so high up that it is not easy to see the people in the world below, in addition to which it seems nearly always raining. Robin used to watch them hopping about on the slate roofs of the homes on the other side of the street. They fluttered their wings, they picked up straws and carried them away. She thought they must have houses of their own among the chimneys--in places she could not see. She fancied it would be nice to hop about on the top of a roof oneself if one were not at all afraid of falling. She liked the chippering and chirping sounds the birds made became it sounded like talking and laughing--like the talking and laughing she sometimes wakened out of her sleep to lie and listen to when the Lady Downstairs had a party. She often wondered what the people were doing because it sounded as if they liked doing it very much.

Sometimes when it had rained two or three days she had a feeling which made her begin to cry to herself--but not aloud. She had once had a little black and blue mark on her arm for a week where Andrews had pinched her because she had cried loud enough to be heard. It had seemed to her that Andrews twisted and pinched the bit of flesh for five minutes without letting it go and she had held her large hand over her mouth as she did it.

"Now you keep that in your mind," she had said when she had finished and Robin had almost choked in her awful little struggle to keep back all sound.

The one thing Andrews was surest of was that nobody would come upstairs to the Nursery to inquire the meaning of any cries which were not unearthly enough to disturb the household. So it was easy to regulate the existence of her charge in such a manner as best suited herself.

"Just give her food enough and keep her from making silly noises when she wants what she doesn't get," said Andrews to her companions below stairs. "That one in the drawing-room isn't going to interfere with the Nursery. Not her! I know my business and I know how to manage her kind. I go to her politely now and then and ask her permission to buy things from Best's or Liberty's or some other good place. She always stares a minute when I begin, as if she scarcely understood what I was talking about and then she says 'Oh, yes, I suppose she must have them.' And I go and get them. I keep her as well dressed as any child in Mayfair. And she's been a beauty since she was a year old so she looks first rate when I wheel her up and down the street, so the people can see she's well taken care of and not kept hidden away. No one can complain of her looks and nobody is bothered with her. That's all that's wanted of ME. I get good wages and I get them regular. I don't turn up my nose at a place like this, whatever the outside talk is. Who cares in these days anyway? Fashionable people's broader minded than they used to be. In Queen Victoria's young days they tell me servants were no class that didn't live in families where they kept the commandments."

"Fat lot the commandments give any one trouble in these times," said Jennings, the footman, who was a wit. "There's one of 'em I could mention that's been broken till there's no bits of it left to keep. If I smashed that plate until it was powder it'd have to be swept into the dust din. That's what happened to one or two commandments in particular."

"Well," remarked Mrs. Blayne, the cook, "she don't interfere and he pays the bills prompt. That'll do ME instead of commandments. If you'll believe me, my mother told me that in them Queen Victoria days ladies used to inquire about cold meat and ask what was done with the dripping. Civilisation's gone beyond that--commandments or no commandments."

"He's precious particular about bills being paid," volunteered Jennings, with the air of a man of the world. "I heard him having a row with her one day about some bills she hadn't paid. She'd spent the money for some nonsense and he was pretty stiff in that queer way of his. Quite right he was too. I'd have been the same myself," pulling up his collar and stretching his neck in a manner indicating exact knowledge of the natural sentiments of a Marquis when justly annoyed. "What he intimated was that if them bills was not paid with the money that was meant to pay them, the money wouldn't be forthcoming the next time." Jennings was rather pleased by the word "forthcoming" and therefore he repeated it with emphasis, "It wouldn't be FORTHCOMING."

"That'd frighten her," was Andrews' succinct observation.

"It did!" said Jennings. "She'd have gone in hysterics if he hadn't kept her down. He's got a way with him, Coombe has."

Andrews laughed, a brief, dry laugh.

"Do you know what the child calls her?" she said. "She calls her the Lady Downstairs. She's got a sort of fancy for her and tries to get peeps at her when we go out. I notice she always cranes her little neck if we pass a room she might chance to be in. It's her pretty clothes and her laughing that does it. Children's drawn by bright colours and noise that sounds merry."

"It's my belief the child doesn't know she IS her mother!" said Mrs. Blayne as she opened an oven door to look at some rolls.

"It's my belief that if I told her she was she wouldn't know what the word meant. It was me she got the name from," Andrews still laughed as she explained. "I used to tell her about the Lady Downstairs would hear if she made a noise, or I'd say I'd let her have a peep at the Lady Downstairs if she was very good. I saw she had a kind of awe of her though she liked her so much, so it was a good way of managing her. You mayn't believe me but for a good bit I didn't take in that she didn't know there was such things as mothers and, when I did take it in, I saw there wasn't any use in trying to explain. She wouldn't have understood."

"How would you go about to explain a mother, anyway?" suggested Jennings. "I'd have to say that she was the person that had the right to slap your head if you didn't do what she told you."

"I'd have to say that she was the woman that could keep you slaving at kitchen maid's work fifteen hours a day," said Mrs. Blayne; "My mother was cook in a big house and trained me under her."

"I never had one," said Andrews stiffly. The truth was that she had taken care of eight infant brothers and sisters, while her maternal parent slept raucously under the influence of beer when she was not quarrelling with her offspring.

Jane, the housemaid, had passed a not uncomfortable childhood in the country and was perhaps of a soft nature.

"I'd say that a mother's the one that you belong to and that's fond of you, even if she does keep you straight," she put in.

"Her mother isn't fond of her and doesn't keep herself straight," said Jennings. "So that wouldn't do."

"And she doesn't slap her head or teach her to do kitchen maid's work," put in Mrs. Blayne, "so yours is no use, Mr. Jennings, and neither is mine. Miss Andrews 'll have to cook up an explanation of her own herself when she finds she has to."

"She can get it out of a Drury Lane melodrama," said Jennings, with great humour. "You'll have to sit down some night, Miss Andrews, and say, 'The time has come, me chee-ild, when I must tell you All'."

In this manner were Mrs. Gareth-Lawless and her maternal affections discussed below stairs. The interesting fact remained that to Robin the Lady Downstairs was merely a radiant and beautiful being who floated through certain rooms laughing or chattering like a bird, and always wearing pretty clothes, which were different each time one beheld her. Sometimes one might catch a glimpse of her through a door, or, if one pressed one's face against the window pane at the right moment, she might get into her bright little carnage in the street below and, after Jennings had shut its door, she might be seen to give a lovely flutter to her clothes as she settled back against the richly dark blue cushions.

It is a somewhat portentous thing to realize that a newborn human creature can only know what it is taught. The teaching may be conscious or unconscious, intelligent or idiotic, exquisite or brutal. The images presented by those surrounding it, as its perceptions awaken day by day, are those which record themselves on its soul, its brain, its physical being which is its sole means of expressing, during physical life, all it has learned. That which automatically becomes the Law at the dawning of newborn consciousness remains, to its understanding, the Law of Being, the Law of the Universe. To the cautious of responsibility this at times wears the aspect of an awesome thing, suggesting, however remotely, that it might seem well, perhaps, to remove the shoes from one's feet, as it were, and tread with deliberate and delicate considering of one's steps, as do the reverently courteous even on the approaching of an unknown altar.

This being acknowledged a scientific, as well as a spiritual truth, there remains no mystery in the fact that Robin at six years old--when she watched the sparrows in the Square Gardens--did not know the name of the feeling which had grown within her as a result of her pleasure in the chance glimpses of the Lady Downstairs. It was a feeling which made her eager to see her or anything which belonged to her; it made her strain her child ears to catch the sound of her voice; it made her long to hear Andrews or the other servants speak of her, and yet much too shy to dare to ask any questions. She had found a place on the staircase leading to the Nursery, where, by squeezing against the balustrade, she could sometimes see the Lady pass in and out of her pink bedroom. She used to sit on a step and peer between the railing with beating heart. Sometimes, after she had been put to bed for the night and Andrews was safely entertained downstairs, Robin would be awakened from her first sleep by sounds in the room below and would creep out of bed and down to her special step and, crouching in a hectic joy, would see the Lady come out with sparkling things in her hair and round her lovely, very bare white neck and arms, all swathed in tints and draperies which made her seem a vision of colour and light. She was so radiant a thing that often the child drew in her breath with a sound like a little sob of ecstasy, and her lip trembled as if she were going to cry. But she did not know that what she felt was the yearning of a thing called love--a quite simple and natural common thing of which she had no reason for having any personal knowledge. As she was unaware of mothers, so she was unaware of affection, of which Andrews would have felt it to be superfluously sentimental to talk to her.

On the very rare occasions when the Lady Downstairs appeared on the threshold of the Day Nursery, Robin--always having been freshly dressed in one of her nicest frocks--stood and stared with immense startled eyes and answered in a whisper the banal little questions put to her. The Lady appeared at such rare intervals and remained poised upon the threshold like a tropic plumaged bird for moments so brief, that there never was time to do more than lose breath and gaze as at a sudden vision. Why she came--when she did come--Robin did not understand. She evidently did not belong to the small, dingy nurseries which grew shabbier every year as they grew steadily more grimy under the persistent London soot and fogs.

Feather always held up her draperies when she came. She would not have come at all but for the fact that she had once or twice been asked if the child was growing pretty, and it would have seemed absurd to admit that she never saw her at all.

"I think she's rather pretty," she said downstairs. "She's round and she has a bright colour--almost too bright, and her eyes are round too. She's either rather stupid or she's shy--and one's as bad as the other. She's a child that stares."

If, when Andrews had taken her into the Gardens, she had played with other children, Robin would no doubt have learned something of the existence and normal attitude of mothers through the mere accident of childish chatter, but it somehow happened that she never formed relations with the charges of other nurses. She took it for granted for some time that this was because Andrews had laid down some mysterious law. Andrews did not seem to form acquaintances herself. Sometimes she sat on a bench and talked a little to another nurse, but she seldom sat twice with the same person. It was indeed generally her custom to sit alone, crocheting or sewing, with a rather lofty and exclusive air and to call Robin back to her side if she saw her slowly edging towards some other child.

"My rule is to keep myself to myself," she said in the kitchen. "And to look as if I was the one that would turn up noses, if noses was to be turned up. There's those that would snatch away their children if I let Robin begin to make up to them. Some wouldn't, of course, but I'm not going to run risks. I'm going to save my own pride."

But one morning when Robin was watching her sparrows, a nurse, who was an old acquaintance, surprised Andrews by appearing in the Gardens with two little girls in her charge. They were children of nine and eleven and quite sufficient for themselves, apart from the fact that they regarded Robin as a baby and, therefore, took no notice of her. They began playing with skipping ropes, which left their nurse free to engage in delighted conversation with Andrews.

It was conversation so delightful that Robin was forgotten, even to the extent of being allowed to follow her sparrows round a clump of shrubbery and, therefore, out of Andrews' sight, though she was only a few yards away. The sparrows this morning were quarrelsome and suddenly engaged in a fight, pecking each other furiously, beating their wings and uttering shrill, protesting chipperings. Robin did not quite understand what they were doing and stood watching them with spell-bound interest.

It was while she watched them that she heard footsteps on the gravel walk which stopped near her and made her look up to see who was at her side. A big boy in Highland kilts and bonnet and sporan was standing by her, and she found herself staring into a pair of handsome deep blue eyes, blue like the waters of a hillside tarn. They were wide, glowing, friendly eyes and none like them had ever looked into hers before. He seemed to her to be a very big boy indeed, and in fact, he was unusually tall and broad for his age, but he was only eight years old and a simple enough child pagan. Robin's heart began to beat as it did when she watched the Lady Downstairs, but there was something different in the beating. It was something which made her red mouth spread and curve itself into a smile which showed all her small teeth.

So they stood and stared at each other and for some strange, strange reason--created, perhaps, with the creating of Man and still hidden among the deep secrets of the Universe--they were drawn to each other--wanted each other--knew each other. Their advances were, of course, of the most primitive--as primitive and as much a matter of instinct as the nosing and sniffing of young animals. He spread and curved his red mouth and showed the healthy whiteness of his own handsome teeth as she had shown her smaller ones. Then he began to run and prance round in a circle, capering like a Shetland pony to exhibit at once his friendliness and his prowess. He tossed his curled head and laughed to make her laugh also, and she not only laughed but clapped her hands. He was more beautiful than anything she had ever seen before in her life, and he was plainly trying to please her. No child creature had ever done anything like it before, because no child creature had ever been allowed by Andrews to make friends with her. He, on his part, was only doing what any other little boy animal would have done--expressing his child masculinity by "showing off" before a little female. But to this little female it had never happened before.

It was all beautifully elemental. As does not too often happen, two souls as well as two bodies were drawn towards each other by the Magnet of Being. When he had exhibited himself for a minute or two he came back to her, breathing fast and glowing.

"My pony in Scotland does that. His name is Chieftain. He is a Shetland pony and he is only that high," he measured forty inches from the ground. "I'm called Donal. What are you called?"

"Robin," she answered, her lips and voice trembling with joy. He was so beautiful. His hair was bright and curly. His broad forehead was clear white where he had pushed back his bonnet with the eagle feather standing upright on it. His strong legs and knees were white between his tartan kilt and his rolled back stockings. The clasps which held his feather and the plaid over his shoulder were set with fine stones in rich silver. She did not know that he was perfectly equipped as a little Highland chieftain, the head of his clan, should be.

They began to play together, and the unknown Fates, which do their work as they choose, so wrought on this occasion as to cause Andrews' friend to set forth upon a journey through a story so exciting in its nature that its hearer was held spellbound and oblivious to her surroundings themselves. Once, it is true, she rose as in a dream and walked round the group of shrubs, but the Fates had arranged for that moment also. Robin was alone and was busily playing with some leaves she had plucked and laid on the seat of a bench for some mysterious reason. She looked good for an hour's safe occupation, and Andrews returned to her friend's detailed and intimate version of a great country house scandal, of which the papers were full because it had ended in the divorce court.

Donal had, at that special moment, gone to pick some of the biggest leaves from the lilac bush of which the Gardens contained numerous sooty specimens. The leaves Robin was playing with were some he had plucked first to show her a wonderful thing. If you laid a leaf flat on the seat of the bench and were fortunate enough to possess a large pin you could prick beautiful patterns on the leaf's green-ness--dots and circles, and borders and tiny triangles of a most decorative order. Neither Donal nor Robin had a pin but Donal had, in his rolled down stocking, a little dirk the point of which could apparently be used for any interesting purpose. It was really he who did the decoration, but Robin leaned against the bench and looked on enthralled. She had never been happy before in the entire course of her brief existence. She had not known or expected and conditions other than those she was familiar with--the conditions of being fed and clothed, kept clean and exer-cised, but totally unloved and unentertained. She did not even know that this near-ness to another human creature, the exchange of companionable looks, which were like flashes of sunlight, the mutual outbreaks of child laughter and pleasure were happiness. To her, what she felt, the glow and delight of it, had no name but she wanted it to go on and on, never to be put an end to by Andrews or anyone else.

The boy Donal was not so unconscious. He had been happy all his life. What he felt was that he had liked this little girl the minute he saw her. She was pretty, though he thought her immensely younger than himself, and, when she had looked up at him with her round, asking eyes, he had wanted to talk to her and make friends. He had not played much with boys and he had no haughty objection to girls who liked him. This one did, he saw at once.

Through what means children so quickly convey to each other--while seeming scarcely to do more than play--the entire history of their lives and surroundings, is a sort of occult secret. It is not a matter of prolonged conversation. Perhaps images created by the briefest of unadorned statements produce on the unwritten tablets of the child mind immediate and complete impressions. Safe as the locked garden was, Andrews cannot have forgotten her charge for any very great length of time and yet before Donal, hearing his attendant's voice from her corner, left Robin to join her and be taken home, the two children knew each other intimately. Robin knew that Donal's home was in Scotland--where there are hills and moors with stags on them. He lived there with "Mother" and he had been brought to London for a visit. The person he called "Mother" was a woman who took care of him and he spoke of her quite often. Robin did not think she was like Andrews, though she did not in the least know why. On his part Donal knew about the nurseries and the sparrows who hopped about on the slates of the houses opposite. Robin did not describe the nurseries to him, but Donal knew that they were ugly and that there were no toys in them and nothing to do. Also, in some mystic fashion, he realized that Andrews would not let Robin play with him if she saw them together, and that, therefore, they must make the most of their time. Full of their joy in each other, they actually embarked upon an ingenious infant intrigue, which involved their trying to meet behind the shrubs if they were brought to the Gardens the next day. Donal was sure he could come because his nurse always did what he asked of her. He was so big now that she was not a real nurse, but she had been his nurse when he was quite little and "Mother" liked her to travel with them. He had a tutor but he had stayed behind in Scotland at Braemarnie, which was their house. Donal would come to-morrow and he would look for Robin and when she saw him she must get away from Andrews and they would play together again.

"I will bring one of my picture books," he said grandly. "Can you read at all?"

"No," answered Robin adoring him. "What are picture books?"

"Haven't you any?" he blurted out.

"No," said Robin. She looked at the gravel walk, reflecting a moment thoughtfully on the Day Nursery and the Night Nursery. Then she lifted her eyes to the glowing blueness of his and said quite simply, "I haven't anything."

He suddenly remembered things his Mother had told him about poor people. Perhaps she was poor. Could she be poor when her frock and hat and coat were so pretty? It was not polite to ask. But the thought made him love her more. He felt something warm rush all over his body. The truth, if he had been old enough to be aware of it, was that the entire simpleness of her acceptance of things as they were, and a something which was unconsciousness of any cause for complaint, moved his child masculinity enormously. His old nurse's voice came from her corner again.

"I must go to Nanny," he said, feeling somehow as if he had been running fast. "I'll come tomorrow and bring two picture books."

He was a loving, warm blooded child human thing, and the expression of affection was, to him, a familiar natural impulse. He put his strong little eight-year-old arms round her and kissed her full on her mouth, as he embraced her with all his strength. He kissed her twice.

It was the first time for Robin. Andrews did not kiss. There was no one else. It was the first time, and Nature had also made her a loving, warm blooded, human thing. How beautiful he was--how big--how strong his arms were--and how soft and warm his mouth felt. She stood and gazed at him with wide asking eyes and laughed a little. She had no words because she did not know what had happened.

"Don't you like to be kissed?" said Donal, uncertain because she looked so startled and had not kissed him back.

"Kissed," she repeated, with a small, caught breath, "ye-es." She knew now what it was. It was being kissed. She drew nearer at once and lifted up her face as sweetly and gladly, as a flower lifts itself to the sun. "Kiss me again," she said quite eagerly. As ingenuously and heartily as before, he kissed her again and, this time, she kissed too. When he ran quickly away, she stood looking after him with smiling, trembling lips, uplifted, joyful--wondering and amazed.

CHAPTER VIII

When she went back to Andrews she carried the pricked leaves with her. She could not have left them behind. From what source she had drawn a characterizing passionate, though silent, strength of mind and body, it would be difficult to explain. Her mind and her emotions had been left utterly unfed, but they were not of the inert order which scarcely needs feeding. Her feeling for the sparrows had held more than she could have expressed; her secret adoration of the "Lady Downstairs" was an intense thing. Her immediate surrender to the desire in the first pair of human eyes--child eyes though they were--which had ever called to her being for response, was simple and undiluted rapture. She had passed over her little soul without a moment's delay and without any knowledge of the giving. It had flown from her as a bird might fly from darkness into the sun. Eight-year-old Donal was the sun.

No special tendency to innate duplicity was denoted by the fact that she had acquired, through her observation of Andrews, Jennings, Jane and Mrs. Blayne, the knowledge that there were things it was best not to let other people know. You were careful about them. From the occult communications between herself and Donal, which had resulted in their intrigue, there had of course evolved a realizing sense of the value of discretion. She did not let Andrews see the decorated leaves, but put them into a small pocket in her coat. Her Machiavellian intention was to slip them out when she was taken up to the Nursery. Andrews was always in a hurry to go downstairs to her lunch and she would be left alone and could find a place where she could hide them.

Andrews' friend started when Robin drew near to them. The child's cheeks and lips were the colour of Jacqueminot rose petals. Her eyes glowed with actual rapture.

"My word! That's a beauty if I ever saw one," said the woman. "First sight makes you jump. My word!"

Robin, however, did not know what she was talking about and in fact scarcely heard her. She was thinking of Donal. She thought of him as she was taken home, and she did not cease thinking of him during the whole rest of the day and far into the night. When Andrews left her, she found a place to hide the pricked leaves and before she put them away she did what Donal had done to her--she kissed them. She kissed them several times because they were Donal's leaves and he had made the stars and lines on them. It was almost like kissing Donal but not quite so beautiful.

After she was put to bed at night and Andrews left her she lay awake for a long time. She did not want to go to sleep because everything seemed so warm and wonderful and she could think and think and think. What she thought about was Donal's face, his delightful eyes, his white forehead with curly hair pushed back with his Highland bonnet. His plaid swung about when he ran and jumped. When he held her tight the buttons of his jacket hurt her a little because they pressed against her body. What was "Mother" like? Did he kiss her? What pretty stones there were in his clasps and buckles! How nice it was to hear him laugh and how fond he was of laughing. Donal! Donal! Donal! He liked to play with her though she was a girl and so little. He would play with her tomorrow. His cheeks were bright pink, his hair was bright, his eyes were bright. He was all bright. She tried to see into the blueness of his eyes again as it seemed when they looked at each other close to. As she began to see the clear colour she fell asleep.

The power which had on the first morning guided Robin to the seclusion behind the clump of shrubs and had provided Andrews with an enthralling companion, extended, the next day, an even more beneficent and complete protection. Andrews was smitten with a cold so alarming as to confine her to bed. Having no intention of running any risks, whatsoever, she promptly sent for a younger sister who, temporarily being "out of place", came into the house as substitute. She was a pretty young woman who assumed no special responsibilities and was fond of reading novels.

"She's been trained to be no trouble, Anne. She'll amuse herself without bothering you as long as you keep her out," Andrews said of Robin.

Anne took "Lady Audley's Secret" with her to the Gardens and, having led her charge to a shady and comfortable seat which exactly suited her, she settled herself for a pleasant morning.

"Now, you can play while I read," she said to Robin.

As they had entered the Gardens they had passed, not far from the gate, a bench on which sat a highly respectable looking woman who was hemming a delicate bit of cambric, and evidently in charge of two picture books which lay on the seat beside her. A fine boy in Highland kilts was playing a few yards away. Robin felt something like a warm flood rush over her and her joy was so great and exquisite that she wondered if Anne felt her hand trembling. Anne did not because she was looking at a lady getting into a carriage across the street.

The marvel of that early summer morning in the gardens of a splendid but dingy London square thing was not a thing for which human words could find expression. It was not an earthly thing, or, at least, not a thing belonging to an earth grown old. A child Adam and Eve might have known something like it in the Garden of Eden. It was as clear and simple as spring water and as warm as the sun.

Anne's permission to "play" once given, Robin found her way behind the group of lilacs and snowballs. Donal would come, not only because he was so big that Nanny would let him do what he wanted to do, but because he would do everything and anything in the world. Donal! Donal! Her heart was a mere baby's heart but it beat as if she were seventeen--beat with pure rapture. He was all bright and he would laugh and laugh.

The coming was easy enough for Donal. He had told his mother and Nanny rejoicingly about the little girl he had made friends with and who had no picture books. But he did not come straight to her. He took his picture books under his arm, and showing all his white teeth in a joyous grin, set out to begin their play properly with a surprise. He did not let her see him coming but "stalked" her behind the trees and bushes until he found where she was waiting, and then thrust his face between the branches of a tall shrub near her and laughed the outright laugh she loved. And when she turned she was looking straight into the clear blue she had tried to see when she fell asleep. "Donal! Donal!" she cried like a little bird with but one note.

The lilac and the snowball were in blossom and there was a big hawthorn tree which smelt sweet and sweet. They could not see the drift of smuts on the blossoms, they only smelled the sweetness and sat under the hawthorn and sniffed and sniffed. The sun was deliciously warm and a piano organ was playing beautifully not far away. They sat close to each other, so close that the picture book could lie open on both pairs of knees and the warmth of each young body penetrated the softness of the other. Sometimes Donal threw an arm around her as she bent over the page. Love and caresses were not amazements to him; he accepted them as parts of the normal joy of life. To Robin they were absolute wonder. The pictures were delight and amazement in one. Donal knew all about them and told her stories. She felt that such splendour could have emanated only from him. It could not occur to her that he had not invented them and made the pictures. He showed her Robinson Crusoe and Robin Hood. The scent of the hawthorn and lilac intoxicated them and they laughed tremendously because Robin Hood's name was like Robin's own and he was a man and she was a girl. They could scarcely stop laughing and Donal rolled over and over on the grass, half from unconquerable high spirits and half to make Robin laugh still more.

He had some beautiful coloured glass marbles in his pocket and he showed her how to play with them, and gave her two of the prettiest. He could shoot them over the ground in a way to thrill the beholder. He could hop on one leg as far as he liked. He could read out of books.

"Do you like me?" he said once in a pause between displays of his prowess.

Robin was kneeling upon the grass watching him and she clasped her little hands as if she were uttering a prayer.

"Oh, yes, yes!" she yearned. "Yes! Yes!"

"I like you," he answered; "I told my mother all about you."

He came to her and knelt by her side.

"Have you a mother?" he asked.

"No," shaking her head.

"Do you live with your aunt?"

"No, I don't live with anybody."

He looked puzzled.

"Isn't there any lady in your house?" he put it to her. She brightened a little, relieved to think she had something to tell him.

"There's the Lady Downstairs," she said. "She's so pretty--so pretty."

"Is she----" he stopped and shook his head. "She couldn't be your mother," he corrected himself. "You'd know about HER."

"She wears pretty clothes. Sometimes they float about and sparkle and she wears little crowns on her head--or flowers. She laughs," Robin described eagerly. "A great many people come to see her. They all laugh. Sometimes they sing. I lie in bed and listen."

"Does she ever come upstairs to the Nursery?" inquired Donal with a somewhat reflective air.

"Yes. She comes and stands near the door and says, 'Is she quite well, Andrews?' She does not laugh then. She--she LOOKS at me."

She stopped there, feeling suddenly that she wished very much that she had more to tell. What she was saying was evidently not very satisfactory. He seemed to expect more--and she had no more to give. A sense of emptiness crept upon her and for no reason she understood there was a little click in her throat.

"Does she only stand near the door?" he suggested, as one putting the situation to a sort of crucial test. "Does she never sit on a big chair and take you on her knee?"

"No, no," in a dropped voice. "She will not sit down. She says the chairs are grubby."

"Doesn't she LOVE you at all?" persisted Donal. "Doesn't she KISS you?"

There was a thing she had known for what seemed to her a long time--God knows in what mysterious fashion she had learned it, but learned it well she had. That no human being but herself was aware of her knowledge was inevitable. To whom could she have told it? But Donal--Donal wanted to know all about her. The little click made itself felt in her throat again.

"She--she doesn't LIKE me!" Her dropped voice was the whisper of one humbled to the dust by confession, "She--doesn't LIKE me!" And the click became another thing which made her put up her arm over her eyes--her round, troubled child eyes, which, as she had looked into Donal's, had widened with sudden, bewildered tears.

Donal flung his arms round her and squeezed his buttons into her tender chest. He hugged her close; he kissed her; there was a choking in his throat. He was hot all over.

"She does like you. She must like you. I'll make her!" he cried passionately. "She's not your mother. If she was, she'd LOVE you! She'd LOVE you!"

"Do Mothers l-love you?" the small voice asked with a half sob. "What's--what's LOVE you?" It was not vulgar curiosity. She only wanted to find out.

He loosed his embrace, sitting back on his heels to stare.

"Don't you KNOW?"

She shook her head with soft meekness.

"N-no," she answered.

Big boys like himself did not usually play with such little girls. But something had drawn him to her at their first moment of encounter. She wasn't like any other little girls. He felt it all the time and that was part of the thing which drew him. He was not, of course, aware that the male thrill at being regarded as one who is a god had its power over the emotions. She wasn't making silly fun and pretending. She really didn't know--because she was different.

"It's liking very much. It's more," he explained. "My mother loves ME. I--I LOVE you!" stoutly. "Yes, I LOVE you. That's why I kissed you when you cried."

She was so uplifted, so overwhelmed with adoring gratitude that as she knelt on the grass she worshipped him.

"I love YOU," she answered him. "I LOVE you--LOVE you!" And she looked at him with such actual prayerfulness that he caught at her and, with manly promptness, kissed her again-this being mere Nature.

Because he was eight years old and she was six her tears flashed away and they both laughed joyously as they sat down on the grass again to talk it over.

He told her all the pleasant things he knew about Mothers. The world was full of them it seemed--full. You belong to them from the time you were a baby. He had not known many personally because he had always lived at Braemarnie, which was in the country in Scotland. There were no houses near his home. You had to drive miles and miles before you came to a house or a castle. He had not seen much of other children except a few who lived at the Manse and belonged to the minister. Children had fathers as well as mothers. Fathers did not love you or take care of you quite as much as Mothers--because they were men. But they loved you too. His own father had died when he was a baby. His mother loved him as much as he loved her. She was beautiful but--it seemed to reveal itself--not like the Lady Downstairs. She did not laugh very much, though she laughed when they played together. He was too big now to sit on her knee, but squeezed into the big chair beside her when she read or told him stories. He always did what his mother told him. She knew everything in the world and so knew what he ought to do. Even when he was a big man he should do what his mother told him.

Robin listened to every word with enraptured eyes and bated breath. This was the story of Love and Life and it was the first time she had ever heard it. It was as much a revelation as the Kiss. She had spent her days in the grimy Nursery and her one close intimate had been a bony woman who had taught her not to cry, employing the practical method of terrifying her into silence by pinching her--knowing it was quite safe to do it. It had not been necessary to do it often. She had seen people on the streets, but she had only seen them in passing by. She had not watched them as she had watched the sparrows. When she was taken down for a few minutes into the basement, she vaguely knew that she was in the way and that Mrs. Blayne's and Andrews' and Jennings' low voices and occasional sidelong look meant that they were talking about her and did not want her to hear.

"I have no mother and no father," she explained quite simply to Donal. "No one kisses me."

"No one!" Donal said, feeling curious. "Has no one ever kissed you but me?"

"No," she answered.

Donal laughed--because children always laugh when they do not know what else to do.

"Was that why you looked as if you were frightened when I said good-bye to you yesterday?"

"I-I didn't know," said Robin, laughing a little too--but not very much, "I wasn't frightened. I liked you."

"I'll kiss you as often as you want me to," he volunteered nobly. "I'm used to it--because of my mother. I'll kiss you again now." And he did it quite without embarrassment. It was a sort of manly gratuity.

Once Anne, with her book in her hand, came round the shrubs to see how her charge was employing herself, and seeing her looking at pictures with a handsomely dressed companion, she returned to "Lady Audley's Secret" feeling entirely safe.

The lilac and the hawthorn tree continued to breathe forth warmed scents of paradise in the sunshine, the piano organ went on playing, sometimes nearer, sometimes farther away, but evidently finding the neighbourhood a desirable one. Sometimes the children laughed at each other, sometimes at pictures Donal showed, or stories he told, or at his own extreme wit. The boundaries were removed from Robin's world. She began to understand that there was another larger one containing wonderful and delightful things she had known nothing about. Donal was revealing it to her in everything he said even when he was not aware that he was telling her anything. When Eve was formed from the rib of Adam the information it was necessary for him to give her regarding her surroundings must have filled her with enthralling interest and a reverence which adored. The planted enclosure which was the central feature of the soot sprinkled, stately London Square was as the Garden of Eden.

*   *   *   *   *

The Garden of Eden it remained for two weeks. Andrews' cold was serious enough to require a doctor and her sister Anne continued to perform their duties. The weather was exceptionally fine and, being a vain young woman, she liked to dress Robin in her pretty clothes and take her out because she was a beauty and attracted attention to her nurse as well as to herself. Mornings spent under the trees reading were entirely satisfactory. Each morning the children played together and each night Robin lay awake and lived again the delights of the past hours. Each day she learned more wonders and her young mind and soul were fed. There began to stir in her brain new thoughts and the beginning of questioning. Scotland, Braemarnie, Donal's mother, even the Manse and the children in it, combined to form a world of enchantment. There were hills with stags living in them, there were moors with purple heather and yellow brome and gorse; birds built their nests under the bushes and Donal's pony knew exactly where to step even in the roughest places. There were two boys and two girls at the Manse and they had a father and a mother. These things were enough for a new heaven and a new earth to form themselves around. The centre of the whole Universe was Donal with his strength and his laugh and his eyes which were so alive and glowing that she seemed always to see them. She knew nothing about the thing which was their somehow--not-to-be-denied allure. They were ASKING eyes--and eyes which gave. The boy was in truth a splendid creature. His body and beauty were perfect life and joyous perfect living. His eyes asked other eyes for everything. "Tell me more," they said. "Tell me more! Like me! Answer me! Let us give each other everything in the world." He had always been well, he had always been happy, he had always been praised and loved. He had known no other things.

During the first week in which the two children played together, his mother, whose intense desire it was to understand him, observed in him a certain absorption of mood when he was not talking or amusing himself actively. He began to fall into a habit of standing at the windows, often with his chin in his hand, looking out as if he were so full of thought that he saw nothing. It was not an old habit, it was a new one.

"What are you thinking about, Donal?" she asked one afternoon.

He seemed to awaken, as it were, when he heard her. He turned about with his alluring smile.

"I am thinking it is FUNNY," he said. "It is funny that I should like such a little girl such a lot. She is years and years younger than I am. But I like her so. It is such fun to tell her things." He marched over to his mother's writing table and leaned against it. What his mother saw was that he had an impassioned desire to talk about this child. She felt it was a desire even a trifle abnormal in its eagerness.

"She has such a queer house, I think," he explained. "She has a nurse and such pretty clothes and she is so pretty herself, but I don't believe she has any toys or books in her nursery."

"Where is her mother?"

"She must be dead. There is no lady in her house but the Lady Downstairs. She is very pretty and is always laughing. But she is not her mother because she doesn't like her and she never kisses her. I think that's the queerest thing of all. No one had EVER kissed her till I did."

His mother was a woman given to psychological analysis. Her eyes began to dwell on his face with slightly anxious questioning.

"Did you kiss her?" she inquired.

"Yes. I kissed her when I said good morning the first day. I thought she didn't like me to do it but she did. It was only because no one had ever done it before. She likes it very much."

He leaned farther over the writing table and began to pour forth, his smile growing and his eyes full of pleasure. His mother was a trifle alarmedly struck by the feeling that he was talking like a young man in love who cannot keep his tongue still, though in his case even the youngest manhood was years away, and he made no effort to conceal his sentiments which a young man would certainly have striven to do.

"She's got such a pretty little face and such a pretty mouth and cheeks," he touched a Jacqueminot rose in a vase. "They are the colour of that. Today a robin came with the sparrows and hopped about near us. We laughed and laughed because her eyes are like the robin's, and she is called Robin. I wish you would come into the Gardens and see her, mother. She likes everything I do."

"I must come, dear," she answered.

"Nanny thinks she is lovely," he announced. "She says I am in love with her. Am I, mother?"

"You are too young to be in love," she said. "And even when you are older you must not fall in love with people you know nothing about."

It was an unconscious bit of Scotch cautiousness which she at once realized was absurd and quite out of place. But--!

She realized it because he stood up and squared his shoulders in an odd young-mannish way. He had not flushed even faintly before and now a touch of colour crept under his fair skin.

"But I DO love her," he said. "I DO. I can't stop." And though he was quite simple and obviously little boy-like, she actually felt frightened for a moment.

CHAPTER IX

On the afternoon of the day upon which this occurred, Coombe was standing in Feather's drawing room with a cup of tea in his hand and wearing the look of a man who is given up to reflection.

"I saw Mrs. Muir today for the first time for several years," he said after a silence. "She is in London with the boy."

"Is she as handsome as ever?"

"Quite. Hers is not the beauty that disappears. It is line and bearing and a sort of splendid grace and harmony."

"What is the boy like?"

Coombe reflected again before he answered.

"He is--amazing. One so seldom sees anything approaching physical perfection that it strikes one a sort of blow when one comes upon it suddenly face to face."

"Is he as beautiful as all that?"

"The Greeks used to make statues of bodies like his. They often called them gods--but not always. The Creative Intention plainly was that all human beings should be beautiful and he is the expression of it."

Feather was pretending to embroider a pink flower on a bit of gauze and she smiled vaguely.

"I don't know what you mean," she admitted with no abasement of spirit, "but if ever there was any Intention of that kind it has not been carried out." Her smile broke into a little laugh as she stuck her needle into her work. "I'm thinking of Henry," she let drop in addition.

"So was I, it happened," answered Coombe after a second or so of pause.

Henry was the next of kin who was--to Coombe's great objection--his heir presumptive, and was universally admitted to be a repulsive sort of person both physically and morally. He had brought into the world a weakly and rickety framework and had from mere boyhood devoted himself to a life which would have undermined a Hercules. A relative may so easily present the aspect of an unfortunate incident over which one has no control. This was the case with Henry. His character and appearance were such that even his connection with an important heritage was not enough to induce respectable persons to accept him in any form. But if Coombe remained without issue Henry would be the Head of the House.

"How is his cough?" inquired Feather.

"Frightful. He is an emaciated wreck and he has no physical cause for remaining alive."

Feather made three or four stitches.

"Does Mrs. Muir know?" she said.

"If Mrs. Muir is conscious of his miserable existence, that is all," he answered. "She is not the woman to inquire. Of course she cannot help knowing that--when he is done with--her boy takes his place in the line of succession."

"Oh, yes, she'd know that," put in Feather.

It was Coombe who smiled now--very faintly.

"You have a mistaken view of her," he said.

"You admire her very much," Feather bridled. The figure of this big Scotch creature with her "line" and her "splendid grace and harmony" was enough to make one bridle.

"She doesn't admire me," said Coombe. "She is not proud of me as a connection. She doesn't really want the position for the boy, in her heart of hearts."

"Doesn't want it!" Feather's exclamation was a little jeer only because she would not have dared a big one.

"She is Scotch Early Victorian in some things and extremely advanced in others," he went on. "She has strong ideas of her own as to how he shall be brought up. She's rather Greek in her feeling for his being as perfect physically and mentally as she can help him to be. She believes things. It was she who said what you did not understand--about the Creative Intention."

"I suppose she is religious," Feather said. "Scotch people often are but their religion isn't usually like that. Creative Intention's a new name for God, I suppose. I ought to know all about God. I've heard enough about Him. My father was not a clergyman but he was very miserable, and it made him so religious that he was ALMOST one. We were every one of us christened and catechized and confirmed and all that. So God's rather an old story."

"Queer how old--from Greenland's icy mountains to India's coral strand," said Coombe. "It's an ancient search--that for the Idea--whether it takes form in metal or wood or stone."

"Well," said Feather, holding her bit of gauze away from her the better to criticize the pink flower. "As ALMOST a clergyman's daughter I must say that if there is one tiling God didn't do, it was to fill the world with beautiful people and things as if it was only to be happy in. It was made to-to try us by suffering and-that sort of thing. It's a-a-what d'ye call it? Something beginning with P."

"Probation," suggested Coombe regarding her with an expression of speculative interest. Her airy bringing forth of her glib time-worn little scraps of orthodoxy--as one who fished them out of a bag of long-discarded remnants of rubbish--was so true to type that it almost fascinated him for a moment.

"Yes. That's it--probation," she answered. "I knew it began with a P. It means 'thorny paths' and 'seas of blood' and, if you are religious, you 'tread them with bleeding feet--' or swim them as the people do in hymns. And you praise and glorify all the time you're doing it. Of course, I'm not religious myself and I can't say I think it's pleasant--but I do KNOW! Every body beautiful and perfect indeed! That's not religion--it's being irreligious. Good gracious, think of the cripples and lepers and hunchbacks!"

"And the idea is that God made them all--by way of entertaining himself?" he put it to her quietly.

"Well, who else did?" said Feather cheerfully.

"I don't know," he said. "Certain things I heard Mrs. Muir say suggested to one that it might be interesting to think it out."

"Did she talk to you about God at afternoon tea?" said Feather. "It's the kind of thing a religious Scotch woman might do."

"No, she did not talk to me. Perhaps that was her mistake. She might have reformed me. She never says more to me than civility demands. And it was not at tea. I accidentally dropped in on the Bethunes and found an Oriental had been lecturing there. Mrs. Muir was talking to him and I heard her. The man seemed to be a scholar and a deep thinker and as they talked a group of us stood and listened or asked questions."

"How funny!" said Feather.

"It was not funny at all. It was astonishingly calm and serious--and logical. The logic was the new note. I had never thought of reason in that connection."

"Reason has nothing to do with it. You must have faith. You must just believe what you're told not think at all. Thinking is wickedness--unless you think what you hear preached." Feather was even a trifle delicately smug as she rattled off her orthodoxy--but she laughed after she had done with it. "But it MUST have been funny--a Turk or a Hindoo in a turban and a thing like a tea gown and Mrs. Muir in her Edinburgh looking clothes talking about God."

"You are quite out of it," Coombe did not smile at all as he said it. "The Oriental was as physically beautiful as Donal Muir is. And Mrs. Muir--no other woman in the room compared with her. Perhaps people who think grow beautiful."

Feather was not often alluring or coquettish in her manner to Coombe but she tilted her head prettily and looked down at her flower through lovely lashes.

"I don't think," she said. "And I am not so bad looking."

"No," he answered coldly. "You are not. At times you look like a young angel."

"If Mrs. Muir is like that," she said after a brief pause, "I should like to know what she thinks of me?"

"No, you would not--neither should I--if she thinks at all," was his answer. "But you remember you said you did not mind that sort of thing."

"I don't. Why should I? It can't harm me." Her hint of a pout made her mouth entrancing. "But, if she thinks good looks are the result of religiousness I should like to let her see Robin--and compare her with her boy. I saw Robin in the park last week and she's a perfect beauty."

"Last week?" said Coombe.

"She doesn't need anyone but Andrews. I should bore her to death if I went and sat in the Nursery and stared at her. No one does that sort of thing in these days. But I should like to see Mrs. Muir to see the two children together!" "That could not easily be arranged, I am afraid," he said.

"Why not?"

His answer was politely deliberate.

"She greatly disapproves of me, I have told you. She is not proud of the relationship."

"She does not like ME you mean?"

"Excuse me. I mean exactly what I said in telling you that she has her own very strong views of the boy's training and surroundings. They may be ridiculous but that sort of thing need not trouble you."

Feather held up her hand and actually laughed.

"If Robin meets him in ten years from now-THAT for her very strong views of his training and surroundings!"

And she snapped her fingers.

Mrs. Muir's distaste for her son's unavoidable connection the man he might succeed had a firm foundation. She had been brought up in a Scottish Manse where her father dominated as an omnipotent and almost divine authority. As a child of imagination she had not been happy but she had been obedient. In her girlhood she had varied from type through her marriage with a young man who was a dreamer, an advanced thinker, an impassioned Greek scholar and a lover of beauty. After he had from her terrors of damnation, they had been profoundly happy. They were young and at ease and they read and thought together ardently. They explored new creeds and cults and sometimes found themselves talking nonsense and sometimes discovering untrodden paths of wisdom. They were youthful enough to be solemn about things at times, and clever enough to laugh at their solemnity when they awakened to it. Helen Muir left the reverent gloom of the life at the Manse far behind despite her respect for certain meanings they beclouded.

"I live in a new structure," she said to her husband, "but it is built on a foundation which is like a solid subterranean chamber. I don't use the subterranean chamber or go into it. I don't want to. But now and then echoes--almost noises--make themselves heard in it. Sometimes I find I have listened in spite of myself."

She had always been rather grave about her little son and when her husband's early death left him and his dignified but not large estate in her care she realized that there lay in her hands the power to direct a life as she chose, in as far as was humanly possible. The pure blood and healthy tendencies of a long and fine ancestry expressing themselves in the boy's splendid body and unusual beauty had set the minds of two imaginative people working from the first. One of Muir's deepest interests was the study of development of the race. It was he who had planted in her mind that daringly fearless thought of a human perfection as to the Intention of the Creative Cause. They used to look at the child as he lay asleep and note the beauty of him--his hands, his feet, his torso, the tint and texture and line of him.

"This is what was MEANT--in the plan for every human being--How could there be scamping and inefficiency in Creation. It is we ourselves who have scamped and been incomplete in our thought and life. Here he is. Look at him. But he will only develop as he is--if living does not warp him." This was what his father said. His mother was at her gravest as she looked down at the little god in the crib.

"It's as if some power had thrust a casket of loose jewels into our hands and said, 'It is for you to see that not one is lost'," she murmured. Then the looked up and smiled.

"Are we being solemn--over a baby?" she said.

"Perhaps," he was always even readier to smile than she was. "I've an idea, however, that there's enough to be solemn about--not too solemn, but just solemn enough. You are a beautiful thing, Fair Helen! Why shouldn't he be like you? Neither of us will forget what we have just said."

Through her darkest hours of young bereavement she remembered the words many times and felt as if they were a sort of light she might hold in her hand as she trod the paths of the "Afterwards" which were in the days before her. She lived with Donal at Braemarnie and lived FOR him without neglecting her duty of being the head of a household and an estate and also a good and gracious neighbour to things and people. She kept watch over every jewel in his casket, great and small. He was so much a part of her religion that sometimes she realized that the echoes from the subterranean chamber were perhaps making her a little strict but she tried to keep guard over herself.

He was handsome and radiant with glowing health and vitality. He was a friendly, rejoicing creature and as full of the joy of life as a scampering moor pony. He was clever enough but not too clever and he was friends with the world. Braemarnie was picturesquely ancient and beautiful. It would be a home of sufficient ease and luxury to be a pleasure but no burden. Life in it could be perfect and also supply freedom. Coombe Court and Coombe Keep were huge and castellated and demanded great things. Even if the Head of the House had been a man to like and be proud of--the accession of a beautiful young Marquis would rouse the hounds of war, so to speak, and set them racing upon his track. Even the totally unalluring "Henry" had been beset with temptations from his earliest years. That he promptly succumbed to the first only brought forth others. It did not seem fair that a creature so different, a splendid fearless thing, should be dragged from his hills and moors and fair heather and made to breathe the foul scent of things, of whose poison he could know nothing. She was not an ignorant childish woman. In her fine aloof way she had learned much in her stays in London with her husband and in their explorings of foreign cities.

This was the reason for her views of her boy's training and surroundings. She had not asked questions about Coombe himself, but it had not been necessary. Once or twice she had seen Feather by chance. In spite of herself she had heard about Henry. Now and then he was furbished up and appeared briefly at Coombe Court or at The Keep. It was always briefly because he inevitably began to verge on misbehaving himself after twenty-four hours had passed. On his last visit to Coombe House in town, where he had turned up without invitation, he had become so frightfully drunk that he had been barely rescued from the trifling faux pas of attempting to kiss a very young royal princess. There were quite definite objections to Henry.

Helen Muir was NOT proud of the Coombe relationship and with unvaried and resourceful good breeding kept herself and her boy from all chance of being drawn into anything approaching an intimacy. Donal knew nothing of his prospects. There would be time enough for that when he was older, but, in the meantime, there should be no intercourse if it could be avoided.

She had smiled at herself when the "echo" had prompted her to the hint of a quaint caution in connection with his little boy flame of delight in the strange child he had made friends with. But it HAD been a flame and, though she, had smiled, she sat very still by the window later that night and she had felt a touch of weight on her heart as she thought it over. There were wonderful years when one could give one's children all the things they wanted, she was saying to herself--the desires of their child hearts, the joy of their child bodies, their little raptures of delight. Those were divine years. They were so safe then. Donal was living through those years now. He did not know that any happiness could be taken from him. He was hers and she was his. It would be horrible if there were anything one could not let him keep--in this early unshadowed time!

She was looking out at the Spring night with all its stars lit and gleaming over the Park which she could see from her window. Suddenly she left her chair and rang for Nanny.

"Nanny," she said when the old nurse came, "tell me something about the little girl Donal plays with in the Square gardens."

"She's a bonny thing and finely dressed, ma'am," was the woman's careful answer, "but I don't make friends with strange nurses and I don't think much of hers. She's a young dawdler who sits novel reading and if Master Donal were a young pickpocket with the measles, the child would be playing with him just the same as far as I can see. The young woman sits under a tree and reads and the pretty little thing may do what she likes. I keep my eye on them, however, and they're in no mischief. Master Donal reads out of his picture books and shows himself off before her grandly and she laughs and looks up to him as if he were a king. Every lad child likes a woman child to look up to him. It's pretty to see the pair of them. They're daft about each other. Just wee things in love at first sight."

"Donal has known very few girls. Those plain little things at the Manse are too dull for him," his mother said slowly.

"This one's not plain and she's not dull," Nanny answered. "My word! but she's like a bit of witch fire dancing--with her colour and her big silk curls in a heap. Donal stares at her like a young man at a beauty. I wish, ma'am, we knew more of her forbears."

"I must see her," Mrs. Muir said. "Tomorrow I'll go with you both to the Gardens."

Therefore the following day Donal pranced proudly up the path to his trysting place and with him walked a tall lady at whom people looked as she passed. She was fair like Donal and had a small head softly swathed with lovely folds of hair. Also her eyes were very clear and calm. Donal was plainly proud and happy to be with her and was indeed prancing though his prance was broken by walking steps at intervals.

Robin was waiting behind the lilac bushes and her nurse was already deep in the mystery of Lady Audley.

"There she is!" cried Donal, and he ran to her. "My mother has come with me. She wants to see you, too," and he pulled her forward by her hand. "This is Robin, Mother! This is Robin." He panted with elation and stood holding his prize as if she might get away before he had displayed her; his eyes lifted to his tall mother's were those of an exultant owner.

Robin had no desire to run away. To adore anything which belonged to Donal was only nature. And this tall, fair, wonderful person was a Mother. No wonder Donal talked of her so much. The child could only look up at her as Donal did. So they stood hand in hand like little worshippers before a deity.

Andrews' sister in her pride had attired the small creature like a flower of Spring. Her exquisiteness and her physical brilliancy gave Mrs. Muir something not unlike a slight shock. Oh! no wonder--since she was like that. She stooped and kissed the round cheek delicately.

"Donal wanted me to see his little friend," she said. "I always want to see his playmates. Shall we walk round the Garden together and you shall show me where you play and tell me all about it."

She took the small hand and they walked slowly. Robin was at first too much awed to talk but as Donal was not awed at all and continued his prancing and the Mother lady said pretty things about the flowers and the grass and the birds and even about the pony at Braemarnie, she began now and then to break into a little hop herself and presently into sudden ripples of laughter like a bird's brief bubble of song. The tall lady's hand was not like Andrews, or the hand of Andrews' sister. It did not pull or jerk and it had a lovely feeling. The sensation she did not know was happiness again welled up within her. Just one walk round the Garden and then the tall lady sat down on a seat to watch them play. It was wonderful. She did not read or work. She sat and watched them as if she wanted to do that more than anything else. Donal kept calling out to her and making her smile: he ran backwards and forwards to her to ask questions and tell her what they were "making up" to play. When they gathered leaves to prick stars and circles on, they did them on the seat on which she sat and she helped them with new designs. Several times, in the midst of her play, Robin stopped and stood still a moment with a sort of puzzled expression. It was because she did not feel like Robin. Two people--a big boy and a lady--

letting her play and talk to them as if they liked her and had time!

The truth was that Mrs. Muir's eyes followed Robin more than they followed Donal. Their clear deeps yearned over her. Such a glowing vital little thing! No wonder! No wonder! And as she grew older she would be more vivid and compelling with every year. And Donal was of her kind. His strength, his beauty, his fearless happiness-claiming temperament. How could one--with dignity and delicacy--find out why she had this obvious air of belonging to nobody? Donal was an exact little lad. He had had foundation for his curious scraps of her story. No mother--no playthings or books--no one had ever kissed her! And she dressed and soignee like this! Who was the Lady Downstairs?

A victoria was driving past the Gardens. It was going slowly because the two people in it wished to look at the spring budding out of hyacinths and tulips. Suddenly one of the pair--a sweetly-hued figure whose early season attire was hyacinth-like itself--spoke to the coachman.

"Stop here!" she said. "I want to get out."

As the victoria drew up near a gate she made a light gesture.

"What do you think, Starling," she laughed. "The very woman we are talking about is sitting in the Gardens there. I know her perfectly though I only saw her portrait at the Academy years ago. Yes, there she is. Mrs. Muir, you know." She clapped her hands and her laugh became a delighted giggle. "And my Robin is playing on the grass near her--with a boy! What a joke! It must be THE boy! And I wanted to see the pair together. Coombe said couldn't be done. And more than anything I want to speak to HER. Let's get out."

They got out and this was why Helen Muir, turning her eyes a moment from Robin whose hand she was holding, saw two women coming towards her with evident intention. At least one of them had evident intention. She was the one whose light attire produced the effect of being made of hyacinth petals.

Because Mrs. Muir's glance turned towards her, Robin's turned also. She started a little and leaned against Mrs. Muir's knee, her eyes growing very large and round indeed and filling with a sudden worshipping light.

"It is--" she ecstatically sighed or rather gasped, "the Lady Downstairs!"

Feather floated near to the seat and paused smiling.

"Where is your nurse, Robin?" she said.

Robin being always dazzled by the sight of her did not of course shine.

"She is reading under the tree," she answered tremulously.

"She is only a few yards away," said Mrs. Muir. "She knows Robin is playing with my boy and that I am watching them. Robin is your little girl?" amiably.

"Yes. So kind of you to let her play with your boy. Don't let her bore you. I am Mrs. Gareth-Lawless."

There was a little silence--a delicate little silence.

"I recognized you as Mrs. Muir at once," said Feather. unperturbed and smiling brilliantly, "I saw your portrait at the Grosvenor."

"Yes," said Mrs. Muir gently. She had risen and was beautifully tall,--"the line" was perfect, and she looked with a gracious calm into Feather's eyes.

Donal, allured by the hyacinth petal colours, drew near. Robin made an unconscious little catch at his plaid and whispered something.

"Is this Donal?" Feather said.

"ARE you the Lady Downstairs, please?" Donal put in politely, because he wanted so to know.

Feather's pretty smile ended in the prettiest of outright laughs. Her maid had told her Andrews' story of the name.

"Yes, I believe that's what she calls me. It's a nice name for a mother, isn't it?"

Donal took a quick step forward.

"ARE you her mother?" he asked eagerly.

"Of course I am."

Donal quite flushed with excitement.

"She doesn't KNOW," he said.

He turned on Robin.

"She's your Mother! You thought you hadn't one! She's your Mother!"

"But I am the Lady Downstairs, too." Feather was immensely amused. She was not subtle enough to know why she felt a perverse kind of pleasure in seeing the Scotch woman standing so still, and that it led her into a touch of vulgarity. "I wanted very much to see your boy," she said.

"Yes," still gently from Mrs. Muir.

"Because of Coombe, you know. We are such old friends. How queer that the two little things have made friends, too. I didn't know. I am so glad I caught a glimpse of you and that I had seen the portrait. GOOD morning. Goodbye, children."

While she strayed airily away they all watched her. She picked up her friend, the Starling, who, not feeling concerned or needed, had paused to look at daffodils. The children watched her until her victoria drove away, the chiffon ruffles of her flowerlike parasol fluttering in the air.

Mrs. Muir had sat down again and Donal and Robin leaned against her. They saw she was not laughing any more but they did not know that her eyes had something like grief in them.

"She's her Mother!" Donal cried. "She's lovely, too. But she's--her MOTHER!" and his voice and face were equally puzzled.

Robin's little hand delicately touched Mrs. Muir.

"IS--she?" she faltered.

Helen Muir took her in her arms and held her quite close. She kissed her.

"Yes, she is, my lamb," she said. "She's your mother."

She was clear as to what she must do for Donal's sake. It was the only safe and sane course. But--at this age--the child WAS a lamb and she could not help holding her close for a moment. Her little body was deliciously soft and warm and the big silk curls all in a heap were a fragrance against her breast.

CHAPTER X

Donal talked a great deal as he pranced home. Feather had excited as well as allured him. Why hadn't she told Robin she was her mother? Why did she never show her pictures in the Nursery and hold her on her knee? She was little enough to be held on knees! Did some mothers never tell their children and did the children never find out? This was what he wanted to hear explained. He took the gloved hand near him and held it close and a trifle authoritatively.

"I am glad I know you are my mother," he said, "I always knew."

He was not sure that the matter was explained very clearly. Not as clearly as things usually were. But he was not really disturbed. He had remembered a book he could show Robin tomorrow and he thought of that. There was also a game in a little box which could be easily carried under his arm. His mother was "thinking" and he was used to that. It came on her sometimes and of his own volition he always, on such occasion, kept as quiet as was humanly possible.

After he was asleep, Helen sent for Nanny.

"You're tired, ma'am," the woman said when she saw her, "I'm afraid you've a headache."

"I have had a good deal of thinking to do since this afternoon," her mistress answered, "You were right about the nurse. The little girl might have been playing with any boy chance sent in her way--boys quite unlike Donal."

"Yes, ma'am." And because she loved her and knew her face and voice Nanny watched her closely.

"You will be as--startled--as I was. By some queer chance the child's mother was driving by and saw us and came in to speak to me. Nanny--she is Mrs. Gareth-Lawless."

Nanny did start; she also reddened and spoke sharply.

"And she came in and spoke to you, ma'am!"

"Things have altered and are altering every day," Mrs. Muir said. "Society is not at all inflexible. She has a smart set of her own--and she is very pretty and evidently well provided for. Easy-going people who choose to find explanations suggest that her husband was a relation of Lord Lawdor's."

"And him a canny Scotchman with a new child a year. Yes, my certie," offered Nanny, with an acrid grimness. Mrs. Muir's hands clasped strongly as they lay on the table before her.

"That doesn't come within my bailiewick," she said in her quiet voice. "Her life is her own and not mine. Words are the wind that blows." She stopped just a moment and began again. "We must leave for Scotland by the earliest train."

"What'll he do?" the words escaped from the woman as if involuntarily. She even drew a quick breath. "He's a strong feeling bairn--strong!"

"He'll be stronger when he is a young man, Nanny!" desperately. "That is why I must act now. There is no half way. I don't want to be hard. Oh, am I hard--am I hard?" she cried out low as if she were pleading.

"No, ma'am. You are not. He's your own flesh and blood." Nanny had never before seen her mistress as she saw her in the next curious almost exaggerated moment.

Her hand flew to her side.

"He's my heart and my soul--" she said, "--he is the very entrails of me! And it will hurt him so and I cannot explain to him because he is too young to understand. He is only a little boy who must go where he is taken. And he cannot help himself. It's--unfair!"

Nanny was prone to become more Scotch as she became moved. But she still managed to look grim.

"He canna help himsel," she said, "an waur still, YOU canna."

There was a moment of stillness and then she said:

"I must go and pack up." And walked out of the room.

    *   *   *   *   *

Donal always slept like a young roe in the bracken, and in deep and rapturous ease he slept this night. Another perfectly joyful day had passed and his Mother had liked Robin and kissed her. All was well with the world. As long as he had remained awake--and it had not been long--he had thought of delightful things unfeverishly. Of Robin, somehow at Braemarnie, growing bigger very quickly--big enough for all sorts of games--learning to ride Chieftain, even to gallop. His mother would buy another pony and they could ride side by side. Robin would laugh and her hair would fly behind her if they went fast. She would see how fast he could go--she would see him make Chieftain jump. They would have picnics--catch sight of deer and fawns delicately lifting their feet as they stepped. She would always look at him with that nice look in her eyes and the little smile which came and went in a second. She was quite different from the minister's little girls at the Manse. He liked her--he liked her!

*   *   *   *   *

He was wakened by a light in his room and by the sound of moving about. He sat up quickly and found his Mother standing by his bed and Nanny putting things into a travelling bag. He felt as if his Mother looked taller than she had looked yesterday--and almost thin--and her face was anxious and--shy.

"We let you sleep as late as we could, Donal," she said. "You must get up quickly now and have breakfast. Something has happened. We are obliged to go back to Scotland by very early train. There is not a minute to waste."

At first he only said:

"Back!"

"Yes, dear. Get up."

"To Braemarnie?"

"Yes, dear laddie!"

He felt himself grow hot and cold.

"Away! Away!" he said again vaguely.

"Yes. Get up, dear."

He was as she had said only a little boy and accustomed to do as he was told. He was also a fine, sturdy little Scot with a pride of his own. His breeding had been of the sort which did not include insubordinate scenes, so he got out of bed and began to dress. But his mother saw that his hands shook.

"I shall not see Robin," he said in a queer voice. "She won't find me when she goes behind the lilac bushes. She won't know why I don't come."

He swallowed very hard and was dead still for a few minutes, though he did not linger over his dressing. His mother felt that the whole thing was horrible. He was acting almost like a young man even now. She did not know how she could bear it. She spoke to him in a tone which was actually rather humble.

"If we knew where she lived you--you could write a little letter and tell her about it. But we do not where she lives."

He answered her very low.

"That's it. And she's little--and she won't understand. She's very little--really." There was a harrowingly protective note in his voice. "Perhaps--she'll cry."

Helen looking down at him with anguished eyes--he was buttoning his shoes--made an unearthly effort to find words, but, as she said them, she knew they were not the right ones.

"She will be disappointed, of course, but she is so little that she will not feel it as much as if she were bigger. She will get over it, darling. Very little girls do not remember things long." Oh, how coarse and crass and stupid it sounded--how course and crass and stupid to say it to this small defiant scrap of what seemed the inevitable suffering of the world!

The clear blue of the eyes Robin had dwelt in, lifted itself to her. There was something almost fierce in it--almost like impotent hatred of something.

"She won't," he said, and she actually heard him grind his little teeth after it.

He did not look like Donal when he was dressed and sat at the breakfast table. He did not eat much of his porridge, but she saw that he determinedly ate some. She felt several times as if he actually did not look like anybody she had ever seen. And at the same time his fair hair, his fair cheeks, and the fair sturdy knees beneath his swinging kilt made him seem as much a little boy as she had ever known him. It was his hot blue eyes which were different.

He obeyed her every wish and followed where she led. When the train laboured out of the big station he had taken a seat in a corner and sat with his face turned to the window, so that his back was towards her. He stared and stared at the passing country and she could only see part of his cheek and the side of his neck. She could not help watching them and presently she saw a hot red glow under the skin as if a flood had risen. It subsided in a few moments, but presently she saw it rise again. This happened several times and he was holding his lip with, his teeth. Once she saw his shoulders more and he coughed obstinately two or three times. She knew that he would die before he would let himself cry, but she wished he would descend to it just this once, as the fields and hedges raced past and he was carried "Away! Away!" It might be that it was all his manhood she was saving for him.

He really made her heart stand still for a moment just as she was thinking this and saying it to herself almost fiercely. He suddenly turned on her; the blue of his eyes was flaming and the tide had risen again in his cheeks and neck. It was a thing like rage she saw before her--a child's rage and impotently fierce. He cried out as if he were ending a sentence he had not finished when he spoke as he sat on the floor buttoning his shoes.

"She has no one but me to remember!" he said. "No one but me had ever even kissed her. She didn't know!"

To her amazement he clenched both his savage young fists and shook them before him.

"It'll kill me!" he raged.

She could not hold herself back. She caught at him with her arms and meant to drag him to her breast. "No! No! Donal!" she cried. "Darling! No--No!" But, as suddenly as the queer unchildish thing had broken out, did he remember himself and boy shame at his fantastic emotion overtook him. He had never spoken like that to anyone before! It was almost as bad as bursting out crying! The red tide ebbed away and he withdrew himself awkwardly from her embrace. He said not another word and sat down in his corner with his back turned toward the world.

*   *   *   *   *

That the Lady Downstairs, who was so fond of laughing and who knew so many persons who seemed to laugh nearly all the time, might have been joking about being her mother presented itself to Robin as a vague solution of the problem. The Lady had laughed when she said it, as people so often laughed at children. Perhaps she had only been amusing herself as grown-up persons were apparently entitled to do. Even Donal had not seemed wholly convinced and though his mother had said the Lady Downstairs WAS--somehow the subject had been changed at once. Mrs. Muir had so soon begun to tell them a story. Robin was not in the least aware that she had swiftly distracted their attention from a question, any discussion of which would have involved explanations she could not have produced. It would have been impossible to make it clear to any child. She herself was helpless before the situation and therefore her only refuge was to make the two think of other things. She had so well done this that Robin had gone home later only remembering the brightly transitory episode as she recalled others as brief and bright, when she had stared at a light and lovely figure standing on the nursery threshold and asking careless questions of Andrews, without coming in and risking the freshness of her draperies by contact with London top-floor grubbiness. The child was, in fact, too full of the reality of her happiness with Donal and Donal's mother to be more than faintly bewildered by a sort of visionary conundrum.

Robin, like Donal, slept perfectly through the night. Her sleep was perhaps made more perfect by fair dreams in which she played in the Gardens and she and Donal ran to and from the knees of the Mother lady to ask questions and explain their games. As the child had often, in the past, looked up at the sky, so she had looked up into the clear eyes of the Mother lady. There was something in them which she had never seen before but which she kept wanting to see again. Then there came a queer bit of a dream about the Lady Downstairs. She came dancing towards them dressed in hyacinths and with her arms full of daffodils. She danced before Donal's Mother--danced and laughed as if she thought they were all funny. She threw a few daffodils at them and then danced away. The daffodils lay on the gravel walk and they all looked at them but no one picked them up. Afterwards--in the dream--Mrs. Muir suddenly caught her in her arms and kissed her and Robin was glad and felt warm all over--inside and out.

She wakened smiling at the dingy ceiling of the dingy room. There was but one tiny shadow in the world, which was the fear that Andrews would get well too quickly. She was no longer in bed but was well enough to sit up and sew a little before the tiny fire in the atom of a servant's room grate. The doctor would not let her go out yet; therefore, Anne still remained in charge. Founding one's hope on previous knowledge of Anne's habits, she might be trusted to sit and read and show no untoward curiosity.

From her bed Robin could see the sky was blue. That meant that she would be taken out. She lay as quiet as a mouse and thought of the joy before her, until Anne came to dress her and give her her breakfast.

"We'll put on your rose-coloured smock this morning," the girl said, when the dressing began. "I like the hat and socks that match."

Anne was not quite like Andrews who was not talkative. She made a conversational sort of remark after she had tied the white shoes.

"You've got pretty little aristocratic legs of your own," she said amiably. "I like my children to have nice legs."

Robin was uplifted in spirit by the commendation, but she hoped Anne would put on her own things quickly. Sometimes she was rather a long time. The one course, however, towards which discretion pointed as entirely safe was the continuance of being as quiet as a mouse--even quieter, if such thing might be--so that nothing might interfere with anything any one wanted to do. To interfere would have been to attract attention and might lead to delay. So she stood and watched the sparrows inoffensively until Anne called her.

When she found herself out on the street her step was so light on the pavement that she was rather like a rose petal blown fluttering along by soft vagrant puffs of spring air. Under her flopping hat her eyes and lips and cheeks were so happy that more than one passer-by turned head over shoulder to look after her.

"Your name ought to be Rose," Anne giggled involuntarily as she glanced down at her because someone had stared. She had not meant to speak but the words said themselves.

Because the time was young June even London sky and air were wonderful. Stray breaths of fragrance came and went. The green of the trees in the Gardens was light and fresh and in the bedded-out curves and stars and circles there were more flowers every hour, so that it seemed as if blooming things with scents grew thick about one's feet. It was no wonder one felt light and smiled back at nurses and governesses who looked up. Robin drew eyes became she was like a summer bloom suddenly appearing in the Spring Garden.

Nanny was not sitting on the bench near the gate and Donal was not to be seen amusing himself. But he was somewhere just out of sight, or, if he had chanced to be late, he would come very soon even if his Mother could not come with him--though Robin could not believe she would not. To a child thing both happiness and despair cannot be conceived of except as lasting forever.

Anne sat down and opened her book. She had reached an exciting part and looked forward to a thoroughly enjoyable morning.

Robin hopped about for a few minutes. Donal had taught her to hop and she felt it an accomplishment. Entangled in the meshes of the feathery, golden, if criminal, ringlets of Lady Audley, Anne did not know when she hopped round the curve of the walk behind the lilac and snowball bushes.

Once safe in her bit of enchanted land, the child stood still and looked about her. There was no kilted figure to be seen, but it would come towards her soon with swinging plaid and eagle's feather standing up grandly in its Highland bonnet. He would come soon. Perhaps he would come running--and the Mother lady would walk behind more slowly and smile. Robin waited and looked--she waited and looked.

She was used to waiting but she had never watched for anyone before. There had never been any one or anything to watch for. The newness of the suspense gave it a sort of deep thrill at first. How long was "at first"? She did not know. She stood--and stood--and stood--and looked at every creature who entered the gate. She did not see any one who looked in the least like Donal or his Mother or Nanny. There were nurses and governesses and children and a loitering lady or two. There were never many people in the Gardens--only those who had keys. She knew nothing about time but at length she knew that on other mornings they had been playing together before this.

The small rose-coloured figure stood so still for so long that it began to look rigid and a nurse sitting at some distance said to another,

"What is that child waiting for?"

What length of time had passed before she found herself looking slowly down at her feet because of something. The "something" which had drawn her eyes downward was that she had stood so long without moving that her tense feet had begun vaguely to hurt her and the ache attracted her attention. She changed her position slightly and turned her eyes upon the gate again. He was coming very soon. He would be sure to run fast now and he would be laughing. Donal! Donal! She even laughed a little low, quivering laugh herself.

"What is that child waiting for? I should really like to know," the distant nurse said again curiously.

If she had been eighteen years old she would have said to herself that she was waiting hours and hours. She would have looked at a little watch a thousand times; she would have walked up and down and round and round the garden never losing sight of the gate--or any other point for that matter--for more than a minute. Each sound of the church clock striking a few streets away would have brought her young heart thumping into her throat.

But a child has no watch, no words out of which to build hopes and fears and reasons, arguments battling against anguish which grows--palliations, excuses. Robin, could only wait in the midst of a slow dark, rising tide of something she had no name for. This slow rising of an engulfing flood she felt when pins and needles began to take possession of her feet, when her legs ached, and her eyes felt as if they had grown big and tightly strained. Donal! Donal! Donal!

Who knows but that some echo of the terror against which she had fought and screamed on the night when she had lain alone in the dark in her cradle and Feather had hid her head under the pillow--came back and closed slowly around and over her, filling her inarticulate being with panic which at last reached its unbearable height? She had not really stood waiting the entire morning, but she was young enough to think that she had and that at any moment Anne might come and take her away. He had not come running--he had not come laughing--he had not come with his plaid swinging and his feather standing high! There came a moment when her strained eyes no longer seemed to see clearly! Something like a big lump crawled up into her throat! Something of the same sort happened the day she had burst into a wail of loneliness and Andrews had pinched her. Panic seized her; she clutched the breast of her rose-coloured frock and panic-driven turned and fled into a thick clump of bushes where there was no path and where even Donal had never pierced.

"That child has run away at last," the distant nurse remarked, "I'd like to find out what she WAS waiting for."

The shrubs were part of the enclosing planting of the Gardens. The children who came to play on the grass and paths felt as if they formed a sort of forest. Because of this, Robin had made her frantic dash to their shelter. No one would come--no one would see her--no one would hear her, beneath them it was almost dark. Bereft, broken and betrayed, a little mad thing, she pushed her way into their shadow and threw herself face downward, a small, writhing, rose-coloured heap, upon the damp mould. She could not have explained what she was doing or why she had given up all, as if some tidal wave had overwhelmed her. Suddenly she knew that all her new world had gone--forever and ever. As it had come so it had gone. As she had not doubted the permanence of its joy, so she KNEW that the end had come. Only the wisdom of the occult would dare to suggest that from her child mate, squaring his sturdy young shoulders against the world as the flying train sped on its way, some wave of desperate, inchoate thinking rushed backward. There was nothing more. He would not come back running. He was GONE!

There was no Andrews to hear. Hidden in the shadow under the shrubs, the rattle and roar of the street outside the railing drowned her mad little cries. All she had never done before, she did then. Her hands beat on the damp mould and tore at it--her small feet beat it and dug into it. She cried, she sobbed; the big lump in her throat almost strangled her--she writhed and did not know she was writhing. Her tears pouring forth wet her hair, her face, her dress. She did not cry out, "Donal! Donal!" because he was nowhere--nowhere. If Andrews had seen her she would have said she was "in a tantrum," But she was not. The world had been torn away.

A long time afterwards, as it seemed to her, she crawled out from under the shrubs, carrying her pretty flopping hat in her earth-stained hand. It was not pretty any more. She had been lying on it and it was crushed and flat. She crept slowly round the curve to Anne.

Seeing her, Anne sprang to her feet. The rose was a piteous thing beaten to earth by a storm. The child's face was swollen and stained, her hair was tangled and damp there were dark marks of mould on her dress, her hat, her hands, her white cheeks; her white shoes were earth-stained also, and the feet in the rose-coloured socks dragged themselves heavily--slowly.

"My gracious!" the young woman almost shrieked. "What's happened! Where have you been? Did you fall down? Ah, my good gracious! Mercy me!"

Robin caught her breath but did not say a word.

"You fell down on a flower bed where they'd been watering the plants!" almost wept Anne. "You must have. There isn't that much dirt anywhere else in the Gardens."

And when she took her charge home that was the story she told Andrews. Out of Robin she could get nothing, and it was necessary to have an explanation.

The truth, of which she knew nothing, was but the story of a child's awful dismay and a child's woe at one of Life's first betrayals. It would be left behind by the days which came and went--it would pass--as all things pass but the everlasting hills--but in this way it was that it came and wrote itself upon the tablets of a child's day.

CHAPTER XI

The child's always been well, ma'am," Andrews was standing, the image of exact correctness, in her mistress' bedroom, while Feather lay in bed with her breakfast on a convenient and decorative little table. "It's been a thing I've prided myself on. But I should say she isn't well now."

"Well, I suppose it's only natural that she should begin sometime," remarked Feather. "They always do, of course. I remember we all had things when we were children. What does the doctor say? I hope it isn't the measles, or the beginning of anything worse?"

"No, ma'am, it isn't. It's nothing like a child's disease. I could have managed that. There's good private nursing homes for them in these days. Everything taken care of exactly as it should be and no trouble of disinfecting and isolating for the family. I know what you'd have wished to have done, ma'am."

"You do know your business, Andrews," was Feather's amiable comment.

"Thank you, ma'am," from Andrews. "Infectious things are easy managed if they're taken away quick. But the doctor said you must be spoken to because perhaps a change was needed."

"You could take her to Ramsgate or somewhere bracing." said Feather. "But what did he SAY?"

"He seemed puzzled, ma'am. That's what struck me. When I told him about her not eating--and lying awake crying all night--to judge from her looks in the morning--and getting thin and pale--he examined her very careful and he looked queer and he said, 'This child hasn't had a SHOCK of any kind, has she? This looks like what we should call shock--if she were older'."

Feather laughed.

"How could a baby like that have a shock?"

"That's what I thought myself, ma'am," answered Andrews. "A child that's had her hours regular and is fed and bathed and sleeps by the clock, and goes out and plays by herself in the Gardens, well watched over, hasn't any chance to get shocks. I told him so and he sat still and watched her quite curious, and then he said very slow: 'Sometimes little children are a good deal shaken up by a fall when they are playing. Do you remember any chance fall when she cried a good deal?'"

"But you didn't, of course," said Feather.

"No, ma'am, I didn't. I keep my eye on her pretty strict and shouldn't encourage wild running or playing. I don't let her play with other children. And she's not one of those stumbling, falling children. I told him the only fall I ever knew of her having was a bit of a slip on a soft flower bed that had just been watered--to judge from the state her clothes were in. She had cried because she's not used to such things, and I think she was frightened. But there wasn't a scratch or a shadow of a bruise on her. Even that wouldn't have happened if I'd been with her. It was when I was ill and my sister Anne took my place. Ann thought at first that she'd been playing with a little boy she had made friends with--but she found out that the boy hadn't come that morning--"

"A boy!" Andrews was sharp enough to detect a new and interested note. "What boy?"

"She wouldn't have played with any other child if I'd been there" said Andrews, "I was pretty sharp with Anne about it. But she said he was an aristocratic looking little fellow--"

"Was he in Highland costume?" Feather interrupted.

"Yes, ma'am. Anne excused herself by saying she thought you must know something about him. She declares she saw you come into the Gardens and speak to his Mother quite friendly. That was the day before Robin fell and ruined her rose-coloured smock and things. But it wasn't through playing boisterous with the boy--because he didn't come that morning, as I said, and he never has since."

Andrews, on this, found cause for being momentarily puzzled by the change of expression in her mistress' face. Was it an odd little gleam of angry spite she saw?

"And never has since, has he?" Mrs. Gareth-Lawless said with a half laugh.

"Not once, ma'am," answered Andrews. "And Anne thinks it queer the child never seemed to look for him. As if she'd lost interest. She just droops and drags about and doesn't try to play at all."

"How much did she play with him?"

"Well, he was such a fine little fellow and had such a respectable, elderly, Scotch looking woman in charge of him that Anne owned up that she hadn't thought there was any objections to them playing together. She says they were as well behaved and quiet as children could be." Andrews thought proper to further justify herself by repeating, "She didn't think there could be any objection."

"There couldn't," Mrs. Gareth-Lawless remarked. "I do know the boy. He is a relation of Lord Coombe's."

"Indeed, ma'am," with colourless civility, "Anne said he was a big handsome child."

Feather took a small bunch of hothouse grapes from her breakfast tray and, after picking one off, suddenly began to laugh.

"Good gracious, Andrews!" she said. "He was the 'shock'! How perfectly ridiculous! Robin had never played with a boy before and she fell in love with him. The little thing's actually pining away for him." She dropped the grapes and gave herself up to delicate mirth. "He was taken away and disappeared. Perhaps she fainted and fell into the wet flower bed and spoiled her frock, when she first realized that he wasn't coming."

"It did happen that morning," admitted Andrews, smiling a little also. "It does seem funny. But children take to each other in a queer way now and then. I've seen it upset them dreadful when they were parted."

"You must tell the doctor," laughed Feather. "Then he'll see there's nothing to be anxious about. She'll get over it in a week."

"It's five weeks since it happened, ma'am," remarked Andrews, with just a touch of seriousness.

"Five! Why, so it must be! I remember the day I spoke to Mrs. Muir. If she's that sort of child you had better keep her away from boys. HOW ridiculous! How Lord Coombe--how people will laugh when I tell them!"

She had paused a second because--for that second--she was not quite sure that Coombe WOULD laugh. Frequently she was of the opinion that he did not laugh at things when he should have done so. But she had had a brief furious moment when she had realized that the boy had actually been whisked away. She remembered the clearness of the fine eyes which had looked directly into hers. The woman had been deciding then that she would have nothing to do with her--or even with her child.

But the story of Robin worn by a bereft nursery passion for a little boy, whose mamma snatched him away as a brand from the burning, was far too edifying not to be related to those who would find it delicious.

It was on the occasion, a night or so later, of a gathering at dinner of exactly the few elect ones, whose power to find it delicious was the most highly developed, that she related it. It was a very little dinner--only four people. One was the long thin young man, with the good looking narrow face and dark eyes peering through a pince nez--the one who had said that Mrs. Gareth-Lawless "got her wondrous clothes from Helene" but that he couldn't. His name was Harrowby. Another was the Starling who was a Miss March who had, some years earlier, led the van of the girls who prostrated their relatives by becoming what was then called "emancipated"; the sign thereof being the demanding of latchkeys and the setting up of bachelor apartments. The relatives had astonishingly settled down, with the unmoved passage of time, and more modern emancipation had so far left latchkeys and bachelor apartments behind it that they began to seem almost old-fogeyish. Clara March, however, had progressed with her day. The third diner was an adored young actor with a low, veiled voice which, combining itself with almond eyes and a sentimental and emotional curve of cheek and chin, made the most commonplace "lines" sound yearningly impassioned. He was not impassioned at all--merely fond of his pleasures and comforts in a way which would end by his becoming stout. At present his figure was perfect--exactly the thing for the uniforms of royal persons of Ruritania and places of that ilk--and the name by which programmes presented him was Gerald Vesey.

Feather's house pleased him and she herself liked being spoken to in the veiled voice and gazed at by the almond eyes, as though insuperable obstacles alone prevented soul-stirring things from being said. That she knew this was not true did not interfere with her liking it. Besides he adored and understood her clothes.

Over coffee in the drawing-room, Coombe joined them. He had not known of the little dinner and arrived just as Feather was on the point of beginning her story.

"You are just in time," she greeted him, "I was going to tell them something to make them laugh."

"Will it make me laugh?" he inquired.

"It ought to. Robin is in love. She is five years old and she has been deserted, and Andrews came to tell me that she can neither eat nor sleep. The doctor says she has had a shock."

Coombe did not join in the ripple of amused laughter but, as he took his cup of coffee, he looked interested.

Harrowby was interested too. His dark eyes quite gleamed.

"I suppose she is in bed by now," he said. "If it were not so late, I should beg you to have her brought down so that we might have a look at her. I'm by way of taking a psychological interest."

"I'm psychological myself," said the Starling. "But what do you mean, Feather? Are you in earnest?"

"Andrews is," Feather answered. "She could manage measles but she could not be responsible for shock. But she didn't find out about the love affair. I found that out--by mere chance. Do you remember the day we got out of the victoria and went into the Gardens, Starling?"

"The time you spoke to Mrs. Muir?"

Coombe turned slightly towards them.

Feather nodded, with a lightly significant air.

"It was her boy," she said, and then she laughed and nodded at Coombe.

"He was quite as handsome as you said he was. No wonder poor Robin fell prostrate. He ought to be chained and muzzled by law when he grows up."

"But so ought Robin," threw in the Starling in her brusque, young mannish way.

"But Robin's only a girl and she's not a parti," laughed Feather. Her eyes, lifted to Coombe's, held a sort of childlike malice. "After his mother knew she was Miss Gareth-Lawless, he was not allowed to play in the Gardens again. Did she take him back to Scotland?"

"They went back to Scotland," answered Coombe, "and, of course, the boy was not left behind."

"Have YOU a child five years old?" asked Vesey in his low voice of Feather.

"You?"

"It seems absurd to ME," said Feather, "I never quite believe in her."

"I don't," said Vesey. "She's impossible."

"Robin is a stimulating name," put in Harrowby. "IS it too late to let us see her? If she's such a beauty as Starling hints, she ought to be looked at."

Feather actually touched the bell by the fireplace. A sudden caprice moved her. The love story had not gone off quite as well as she had thought it would. And, after all, the child was pretty enough to show off. She knew nothing in particular about her daughter's hours, but, if she was asleep, she could be wakened.

"Tell Andrews," she said to the footman when he appeared, "I wish Miss Robin to be brought downstairs."

"They usually go to bed at seven, I believe," remarked Coombe, "but, of course, I am not an authority."

Robin was not asleep though she had long been in bed. Because she kept her eyes shut Andrews had been deceived into carrying on a conversation with her sister Anne, who had come to see her. Robin had been lying listening to it. She had begun to listen because they had been talking about the day she had spoiled her rose-coloured smock and they had ended by being very frank about other things.

"As sure as you saw her speak to the boy's mother the day before, just so sure she whisked him back to Scotland the next morning," said Andrews. "She's one of the kind that's particular. Lord Coombe's the reason. She does not want her boy to see or speak to him, if it can be helped. She won't have it--and when she found out--"

"Is Lord Coombe as bad as they say?" put in Anne with bated breath. "He must be pretty bad if a boy that's eight years old has to be kept out of sight and sound of him."

So it was Lord Coombe who had somehow done it. He had made Donal's mother take him away. It was Lord Coombe. Who was Lord Coombe? It was because he was wicked that Donal's mother would not let him play with her--because he was wicked. All at once there came to her a memory of having heard his name before. She had heard it several times in the basement Servants' Hall and, though she had not understood what was said about him, she had felt the atmosphere of cynical disapproval of something. They had said "him" and "her" as if he somehow belonged to the house. On one occasion he had been "high" in the manner of some reproof to Jennings, who, being enraged, freely expressed his opinions of his lordship's character and general reputation. The impression made on Robin then had been that he was a person to be condemned severely. That the condemnation was the mere outcome of the temper of an impudent young footman had not conveyed itself to her, and it was the impression which came back to her now with a new significance. He was the cause--not Donal, not Donal's Mother--but this man who was so bad that servants were angry because he was somehow connected with the house.

"As to his badness," she heard Andrews answer, "there's some that can't say enough against him. Badness is smart these days. He's bad enough for the boy's mother to take him away from. It's what he is in this house that does it. She won't have her boy playing with a child like Robin."

Then--even as there flashed upon her bewilderment this strange revelation of her own unfitness for association with boys whose mothers took care of them-- Jennings, the young footman, came to the door.

"Is she awake, Miss Andrews?" he said, looking greatly edified by Andrews' astonished countenance.

"What on earth--?" began Andrews.

"If she is," Jennings winked humorously, "she's to be dressed up and taken down to the drawing-room to be shown off. I don't know whether it's Coombe's idea or not. He's there."

Robin's eyes flew wide open. She forgot to keep them shut. She was to go downstairs! Who wanted her--who?

Andrews had quite gasped.

"Here's a new break out!" she exclaimed. "I never heard such a thing in my life. She's been in bed over two hours. I'd like to know--"

She paused here because her glance at the bed met the dark liquidity of eyes wide open. She got up and walked across the room.

"You are awake!" she said. "You look as if you hadn't been asleep at all. You're to get up and have your frock put on. The Lady Downstairs wants you in the drawing-room."

Two months earlier such a piece of information would have awakened in the child a delirium of delight. But now her vitality was lowered because her previously unawakened little soul had soared so high and been so dashed down to cruel earth again. The brilliancy of the Lady Downstairs had been dimmed as a candle is dimmed by the light of the sun.

She felt only a vague wonder as she did as Andrews told her--wonder at the strangeness of getting up to be dressed, as it seemed to her, in the middle of the night.

"It's just the kind of thing that would happen in a house like this," grumbled Andrews, as she put on her frock. "Just anything that comes into their heads they think they've a right to do. I suppose they have, too. If you're rich and aristocratic enough to have your own way, why not take it? I would myself."

The big silk curls, all in a heap, fell almost to the child's hips. The frock Andrews chose for her was a fairy thing.

"She IS a bit thin, to be sure," said the girl Anne. "But it points her little face and makes her eyes look bigger."

"If her mother's got a Marquis, I wonder what she'll get," said Andrews. "She's got a lot before her: this one!"

When the child entered the drawing-room, Andrews made her go in alone, while she held herself, properly, a few paces back like a lady in waiting. The room was brilliantly lighted and seemed full of colour and people who were laughing. There were pretty things crowding each other everywhere, and there were flowers on all sides. The Lady Downstairs, in a sheathlike sparkling dress, and only a glittering strap seeming to hold it on over her fair undressed shoulders, was talking to a tall thin man standing before the fireplace with a gold cup of coffee in his hand.

As the little thing strayed in, with her rather rigid attendant behind her, suddenly the laughing ceased and everybody involuntarily drew a half startled breath--everybody but the tall thin man, who quietly turned and set his coffee cup down on the mantel piece behind him.

"Is THIS what you have been keeping up your sleeve!" said Harrowby, settling his pince nez.

"I told you!" said the Starling.

"You couldn't tell us," Vesey's veiled voice dropped in softly. "It must be seen to be believed. But still--" aside to Feather, "I don't believe it."

"Enter, my only child!" said Feather. "Come here, Robin. Come to your mother."

Now was the time! Robin went to her and took hold of a very small piece of her sparkling dress.

"ARE you my Mother?" she said. And then everybody burst into a peal of laughter, Feather with the rest.

"She calls me the Lady Downstairs," she said. "I really believe she doesn't know. She's rather a stupid little thing."

"Amazing lack of filial affection," said Lord Coombe.

He was not laughing like the rest and he was looking down at Robin. She thought him ugly and wicked looking. Vesey and Harrowby were beautiful by contrast. Before she knew who he was, she disliked him. She looked at him askance under her eyelashes, and he saw her do it before her mother spoke his name, taking her by the tips of her fingers and leading her to him.

"Come and let Lord Coombe look at you," she said. So it revealed itself to her that it was he--this ugly one--who had done it, and hatred surged up in her soul. It was actually in the eyes she raised to his face, and Coombe saw it as he had seen the sidelong glance and he wondered what it meant.

"Shake hands with Lord Coombe," Feather instructed.

"If you can make a curtsey, make one." She turned her head over her shoulders, "Have you taught her to curtsey, Andrews?"

But Andrews had not and secretly lost temper at finding herself made to figure as a nurse who had been capable of omission. Outwardly she preserved rigid calm.

"I'm afraid not, ma'am. I will at once, if you wish it."

Coombe was watching the inner abhorrence in the little face. Robin had put her hand behind her back--she who had never disobeyed since she was born! She had crossed a line of development when she had seen glimpses of the new world through Donal's eyes.

"What are you doing, you silly little thing," Feather reproved her. "Shake hands with Lord Coombe."

Robin shook her head fiercely.

"No! No! No! No!" she protested.

Feather was disgusted. This was not the kind of child to display.

"Rude little thing! Andrews, come and make her do it--or take her upstairs," she said.

Coombe took his gold coffee cup from the mantel.

"She regards me with marked antipathy, as she did when she first saw me," he summed the matter up. "Children and animals don't hate one without reason. It is some remote iniquity in my character which the rest of us have not yet detected." To Robin he said, "I do not want to shake hands with you if you object. I prefer to drink my coffee out of this beautiful cup."

But Andrews was seething. Having no conscience whatever, she had instead the pride of a female devil in her perfection in her professional duties. That the child she was responsible for should stamp her with ignominious fourth-ratedness by conducting herself with as small grace as an infant costermonger was more than her special order of flesh and blood could bear-and yet she must outwardly control the flesh and blood.

In obedience to her mistress' command, she crossed the room and bent down and whispered to Robin. She intended that her countenance should remain non-committal, but, when she lifted her head, she met Coombe's eyes and realized that perhaps it had not. She added to her whisper nursery instructions in a voice of sugar.

"Be pretty mannered, Miss Robin, my dear, and shake hands with his lord-ship."

Each person in the little drawing-room saw the queer flame in the child-face--Coombe himself was fantastically struck by the sudden thought that its expression might have been that of an obstinate young martyr staring at the stake. Robin shrilled out her words:

"Andrews will pinch me--Andrews will pinch me! But--No!--No!" and she kept her hand behind her back.

"Oh, Miss Robin, you naughty child!" cried Andrews, with pathos. "Your poor Andrews that takes such care of you!"

"Horrid little thing!" Feather pettishly exclaimed. "Take her upstairs, Andrews. She shall not come down again."

Harrowby, settling his pince nez a little excitedly in the spurred novelty of his interest, murmured,

"If she doesn't want to go, she will begin to shriek. This looks as if she were a little termagant."

But she did not shriek when Andrews led her towards the door. The ugly one with the wicked face was the one who had done it. He filled her with horror. To have touched him would have been like touching some wild beast of prey. That was all. She went with Andrews quite quietly.

"Will you shake hands with me?" said the Starling, goodnaturedly, as she passed, "I hope she won't snub me," she dropped aside to Harrowby.

Robin put out her hand prettily.

"Shake mine," suggested Harrowby, and she obeyed him.

"And mine?" smiled Vesey, with his best allure. She gave him her hand, and, as a result of the allure probably, a tiny smile flickered about the corners of her mouth. He did not look wicked.

"I remain an outcast," remarked Coombe, as the door closed behind the little figure.

"I detest an ill-mannered child," said Feather. "She ought to be slapped. We used to be slapped if we were rude."

"She said Andrews would pinch her. Is pinching the customary discipline?"

"It ought to be. She deserves it." Feather was quite out of temper. "But Andrews is too good to her. She is a perfect creature and conducts herself like a clock. There has never been the slightest trouble in the Nursery. You see how the child looks--though her face ISN'T quite as round as it was." She laughed disagreeably and shrugged her white undressed shoulders. "I think it's a little horrid, myself--a child of that age fretting herself thin about a boy."

CHAPTER XII

But though she had made no protest on being taken out of the drawing-room, Robin had known that what Andrews' soft-sounding whisper had promised would take place when she reached the Nursery. She was too young to feel more than terror which had no defense whatever. She had no more defense against Andrews than she had had against the man who had robbed her of Donal. They were both big and powerful, and she was nothing. But, out of the wonders she had begun to know, there had risen in her before almost inert little being a certain stirring. For a brief period she had learned happiness and love and woe, and, this evening, inchoate rebellion against an enemy. Andrews led by the hand up the narrow, top-story staircase something she had never led before. She was quite unaware of this and, as she mounted each step, her temper mounted also, and it was the temper of an incensed personal vanity abnormally strong in this particular woman. When they were inside the Nursery and the door was shut, she led Robin to the middle of the small and gloomy room and released her hand.

"Now, my lady," she said. "I'm going to pay you out for disgracing me before everybody in the drawing-room." She had taken the child below stairs for a few minutes before bringing her up for the night. She had stopped in the kitchen for something she wanted for herself. She laid her belongings on a chest of drawers and turned about.

"I'm going to teach you a lesson you won't forget," she said.

What happened next turned the woman quite sick with the shock of amazement. The child had, in the past, been a soft puppet. She had been automatic obedience and gentleness. Privately Andrews had somewhat looked down on her lack of spirit, though it had been her own best asset. The outbreak downstairs had been an abnormality.

And now she stood before her with hands clenched, her little face wild with defiant rage.

"I'll scream! I'll scream! I'll SCREAM!" she shrieked. Andrews actually heard herself gulp; but she sprang up and forward.

"You'll SCREAM!" she could scarcely believe her own feelings--not to mention the evidence of her ears, "YOU'LL scream!"

The next instant was more astonishing still. Robin threw herself on her knees and scrambled like a cat. She was under the bed and in the remotest corner against the wall. She was actually unreachable, and she lay on her back kicking madly, hammering her heels against the floor and uttering piercing shrieks. As something had seemed to let itself go when she writhed under the bushes in the Gardens, so did something let go now. In her overstrung little mind there ruled for this moment the feeling that if she was to be pinched, she would be pinched for a reason.

Andrews knelt by the side of the bed. She had a long, strong, thin arm and it darted beneath and clutched. But it was not long enough to attain the corner where the kicking and screaming was going on. Her temper became fury before her impotence and her hideous realization of being made ridiculous by this baby of six. Two floors below the afterglow of the little dinner was going on. Suppose even far echoes of the screams should be heard and make her more ridiculous still. She knew how they would laugh and her mistress would make some silly joke about Robin's being too much for her. Her fury rose so high that she had barely sense to realize that she must not let herself go too far when she got hold of the child. Get hold of her she would and pay her out--My word! She would pay her out!

"You little devil!" she said between her teeth, "Wait till I get hold of you." And Robin shrieked and hammered more insanely still.

The bed was rather a low one and it was difficult for any one larger than a child to find room beneath it. The correct and naturally rigid Andrews lay flat upon her stomach and wriggled herself partly under the edge. Just far enough for her long and strong arm, and equally long and strong clutching fingers to do their work. In her present state of mind, Andrews would have broken her back rather than not have reached the creature who so defied her. The strong fingers clenched a flying petticoat and dragged at it fiercely--the next moment they clutched a frantic foot, with a power which could not be broken away from. A jerk and a remorseless dragging over the carpet and Robin was out of the protecting darkness and in the gas light again, lying tumbled and in an untidy, torn little heap on the nursery floor. Andrews was panting, but she did not loose her hold as she scrambled, without a rag of professional dignity, to her feet.

"My word!" she breathlessly gave forth. "I've got you now! I've got you now."

She so looked that to Robin she seemed--like the ugly man downstairs--a sort of wicked wild beast, whose mere touch would have been horror even if it did not hurt. And the child knew what was coming. She felt herself dragged up from the floor and also dragged between Andrew's knees, which felt bony and hard as iron. There was no getting away from them. Andrews had seated herself firmly on a chair.

Holding her between the iron knees, she put her large hand over her mouth. It was a hand large enough to cover more than her mouth. Only the panic-stricken eyes seemed to flare wide and lustrous above it.

"YOU'LL scream!" she said, "YOU'LL hammer on the floor with your heels! YOU'LL behave like a wildcat--you that's been like a kitten! You've never done it before and you'll never do it again! If it takes me three days, I'll make you remember!"

And then her hand dropped--and her jaw dropped, and she sat staring with a furious, sick, white face at the open door--which she had shut as she came in. The top floor had always been so safe. The Nursery had been her own autocratic domain. There had been no human creature to whom it would have occurred to interfere. That was it. She had been actually SAFE.

Unheard in the midst of the struggle, the door had been opened without a knock. There on the threshold, as stiff as a ramrod, and with his hateful eyes uncovering their gleam, Lord Coombe was standing--no other than Lord Coombe.

Having a sharp working knowledge of her world, Andrews knew that it was all up. He had come upstairs deliberately. She knew what he had come for. He was as clever as he was bad, and he had seen something when he glanced at her in the drawing-room. Now he had heard and seen her as she dragged Robin from under the bed. He'd come up for that--for some queer evil reason of his own. The promptings of a remote gutter training made her feel a desire to use language such as she still had wisdom enough to restrain.

"You are a very great fool, young woman," he said. "You have nothing but your character as a nurse to live on. A scene in a police court would ruin you. There is a Society which interferes with nursery torture."

Robin, freed from the iron grasp, had slunk behind a chair. He was there again.

Andrews' body, automatically responsive to rule and habit, rose from its seat and stood before this member of a class which required an upright position. She knew better than to attempt to excuse or explain. She had heard about the Society and she knew publicity would spell ruin and starvation. She had got herself into an appalling mess. Being caught--there you were. But that this evil-reputationed swell should actually have been awakened by some whim to notice and follow her up was "past her," as she would have put it.

"You were going to pinch her--by instalments, I suppose," he said. "You inferred that it might last three days. When she said you would--in the drawing-room--it occurred to me to look into it. What are your wages?"

"Thirty pounds a year, my lord."

"Go tomorrow morning to Benby, who engaged you for Mrs. Gareth-Lawless. He will be at his office by nine and will pay you what is owed to you--and a month's wages in lieu of notice."

"The mistress--" began Andrews.

"I have spoken to Mrs. Gareth-Lawless." It was a lie, serenely told. Feather was doing a new skirt dance in the drawing-room. "She is engaged. Pack your box. Jennings will call a cab."

It was the utter idiotic hopelessness of saying anything to him which finished her. You might as well talk to a front door or a street lamp. Any silly thing you might try wouldn't even reach his ears. He had no ears for you. You didn't matter enough.

"Shall I leave her here--as she is?" she said, denoting Robin.

"Undress her and put her to bed before you pack your box," absolutely certain, fine cold modulations in the voice, which stood for his special plane of breeding, had their effect on her grovelling though raging soul. He was so exactly what he was and what she was not and could never attain. "I will stay here while you do it. Then go."

No vocabulary of the Servants' Hall could have encompassed the fine phrase grand seigneur, but, when Mrs. Blayne and the rest talked of him in their least resentful and more amiable moods, they unconsciously made efforts to express the quality in him which these two words convey. He had ways of his own. Men that paid a pretty woman's bills and kept her going in luxury, Jennings and Mrs. Blayne and the others knew something about. They sometimes began well enough but, as time went on, they forgot themselves and got into the way of being familiar and showing they realized that they paid for things and had their rights. Most of them began to be almost like husbands--speak slighting and sharp and be a bit stiff about accounts--even before servants. They ran in and out or--after a while--began to stay away and not show up for weeks. "He" was different--so different that it was queer. Queer it certainly was that he really came to the place very seldom. Wherever they met, it didn't noticeably often happen in the slice of a house. He came as if he were a visitor. He took no liberties. Everything was punctiliously referred to Mrs. Gareth-Lawless. Mr. Benby, who did everything, conducted himself outwardly as if he were a sort of man of business in Mrs. Gareth-Lawless' employ. It was open to the lenient to believe that she depended on some mysterious private income. There were people who preferred to try to believe this, but there were those who, in some occult way, knew exactly where her income came from. There were, in fact, hypercritical persons who did not know or notice her, but she had quite an entertaining, smart circle which neither suspicions nor beliefs prevented from placing her in their visiting lists. Coombe DID keep it up in the most perfect manner, some of them said admiringly among themselves. He showed extraordinarily perfect taste. Many fashionable open secrets, accepted by a brilliant world, were not half so fastidiously managed. Andrews knew he had unswervingly lied when he said he had "spoken to Mrs. Gareth-Lawless." But he never failed to place her in the position of authority. That he should have presented himself on the nursery floor was amazingly abnormal enough to mean some state of mind unregulated by all natural rules. "Him," Andrews thought, "that never steps out of a visitor's place in the drawing-room turning up on the third floor without a word!" One thing she knew, and that came first. Behind all the polite show he was the head of everything. And he was one that you'd better not give back a sound to if you knew what was good for yourself. Whatever people said against his character, he was one of the grand and high ones. A word from him--ever so quiet--and you'd be done for.

She was shaking with fear inwardly, but she undressed Robin and put her in bed, laying everything away and making things tidy for the night.

"This is the Night Nursery, I suppose," Coombe had said when she began. He put up his glasses and looked the uninviting little room over. He scrutinized it and she wondered what his opinion of it might be.

"Yes, my lord. The Day Nursery is through that door." He walked through the door in question and she could see that he moved slowly about it, examining the few pieces of furniture curiously, still with his glass in his eye. She had finished undressing Robin and had put her in her bed before he came back into the sleeping apartment. By that time, exhausted by the unknown tempest she had passed through, the child had dropped asleep in spite of herself. She was too tired to remember that her enemy was in the next room.

"I have seen the child with you several times when you have not been aware of it," Coombe said to her before he went downstairs. "She has evidently been well taken care of as far as her body is concerned. If you were not venomous--if you had merely struck her, when you lost your temper, you might have had another trial. I know nothing about children, but I know something about the devil, and if ever the devil was in a woman's face and voice the devil was in yours when you dragged the little creature from under the bed. If you had dared, you would have killed her. Look after that temper, young woman. Benby shall keep an eye on you if you take another place as nurse, and I shall know where you are."

"My lord!" Andrews gasped. "You wouldn't overlook a woman and take her living from her and send her to starvation!"

"I would take her living from her and send her to starvation without a shadow of compunction," was the reply made in the fine gentleman's cultivated voice, "--if she were capable of what you were capable of tonight. You are, I judge, about forty, and, though you are lean, you are a powerful woman; the child is, I believe, barely six." And then, looking down at her through his glass, he added--to her quite shuddering astonishment--in a tone whose very softness made it really awful to her, "Damn you! Damn you!"

"I'll--I swear I'll never let myself go again, my lord!" the woman broke out devoutly.

"I don't think you will. It would cost you too much," he said.

Then he went down the steep, crooked little staircase quite soundlessly and Andrews, rather white and breathless, went and packed her trunk. Robin--tired baby as she was--slept warm and deeply.

CHAPTER XIII

It was no custom of his to outstay other people; in fact, he usually went away comparatively early. Feather could not imagine what his reason could be, but she was sure there was a reason. She was often disturbed by his reasons, and found it difficult to adjust herself to them. How--even if one had a logically brilliant mind--could one calculate on a male being, who seemed not exactly to belong to the race of men.

As a result of the skirt dancing, the furniture of the empty drawing-room was a little scattered and untidy, but Feather had found a suitable corner among cushions on a sofa, after everyone had gone leaving Coombe alone with her. She wished he would sit down, but he preferred to stand in his still, uncomfortable way.

"I know you are going to tell me something," she broke the silence.

"I am. When I went out of the room, I did not drive round to my club as I said I found myself obliged to. I went upstairs to the third floor--to the Nursery."

Feather sat quite upright.

"YOU went up to the Nursery!" If this was the reason for his staying, what on earth had he come upon in the region of the third floor, and how ridiculously unlike him to allow himself to interfere. Could it be Andrews and Jennings? Surely Andrews was too old.--This passed across her mind in a flash.

"You called Andrews to use her authority with the child when she would not shake hands with me. The little creature, for some reason of her own, evidently feels an antipathy to me. That interested me and I watched her as Andrews whispered in her ear. The woman's vanity was stung. I realized that she whispered a threat. A hint of actual ferocity showed in her eyes in spite of herself. Robin turned pale."

"Andrews was quite right. Children must be punished when they are rude." Feather felt this at once silly and boring. What did he know about such matters?

"The child said, 'Andrews will pinch me!' and I caught Andrews' eye and knew it was true--also that she had done it before. I looked at the woman's long, thin, strong fingers. They were cruel fingers. I do not take liberties, as a rule, but I took a liberty. I excused myself and climbed three flights of stairs."

Never had Feather been so surprised in her life. She looked like a bewildered child.

"But--what COULD it matter to YOU?" she said in soft amaze.

"I don't know," his answer came after a moment's pause. "I have caprices of mood. Certain mental images made my temperature rise. Momentarily it did matter. One is like that at times. Andrews' feline face and her muscular fingers--and the child's extraordinarily exquisite flesh--gave me a second's furious shudder."

Feather quite broke in upon him.

"Are you--are you FOND of children?"

"No," he was really abrupt. "I never thought of such a thing in my life--as being FOND of things."

"That was what--I mean I thought so." Feather faltered, as if in polite acquiescence with a quite natural fact.

Coombe proceeded:

"As I went up the stairs I heard screams and I thought that the pinching had begun. I got up quickly and opened the door and found the woman lying flat on the floor by the bed, dragging out the child who had hidden under it. The woman's face was devilish, and so was her voice. I heard her threats. She got on her feet and dragged the child up and held her between her knees. She clapped her hand over mouth to stifle her shrieks. There I stopped her. She had a fright at sight of me which taught her something." He ended rather slowly. "I took the great liberty of ordering her to pack her box and leave the house--course," with a slight bow, "using you as my authority."

"Andrews!" cried Feather, aghast. "Has she--gone?"

"Would you have kept her?" he inquired.

"It's true that--that PINCHING" Feather's voice almost held tears, "--really HARD pinching is--is not proper. But Andrews has been invaluable. Everyone says Robin is better dressed and better kept than other children. And she is never allowed to make the least noise--"

"One wouldn't if one were pinched by those devilish, sinewy fingers every time one raised one's voice. Yes. She has gone. I ordered her to put her charge to bed before she packed. I did not leave her alone with Robin. In fact, I walked about the two nurseries and looked them over."

He had walked about the Night Nursery and the Day Nursery! He--the Head of the House of Coombe, whose finely acrid summing up of things, they were all secretly afraid of, if the truth were known. "They" stood for her smart, feverishly pleasure-chasing set. In their way, they half unconsciously tried to propitiate something in him, always without producing the least effect. Her mental vision presented to her his image as he had walked about the horrid little rooms, his somewhat stiffly held head not much below the low ceilings. He had taken in shabby carpets, furniture, faded walls, general dim dinginess.

"It's an unholy den for anything to spend its days in--that third floor," he made the statement detachedly, in a way. "If she's six, she has lived six years there--and known nothing else."

"All London top floors are like it," said Feather, "and they are all nurseries and school rooms--where there are children."

His faintly smiling glance took in her girl-child slimness in its glittering sheath--the zephyr scarf floating from the snow of her bared loveliness--her delicate soft chin deliciously lifted as she looked up at him.

"How would YOU like it?" he asked.

"But I am not a child," in pretty protest. "Children are--are different!"

"You look like a child," he suddenly said, queerly--as if the aspect of her caught him for an instant and made him absent-minded. "Sometimes--a woman does. Not often."

She bloomed into a kind of delighted radiance.

"You don't often pay me compliments," she said. "That is a beautiful one. Robin--makes it more beautiful."

"It isn't a compliment," he answered, still watching her in the slightly absent manner. "It is--a tragic truth."

He passed his hand lightly across his eyes as if he swept something away, and then both looked and spoke exactly as before.

"I have decided to buy the long lease of this house. It is for sale," he said, casually. "I shall buy it for the child."

"For Robin!" said Feather, helplessly.

"Yes, for Robin."

"It--it would be an income--whatever happened. It is in the very heart of May-fair," she said, because, in her astonishment--almost consternation--she could think of nothing else. He would not buy it for her. He thought her too silly to trust. But, if it were Robin's--it would be hers also. A girl couldn't turn her own mother into the street. Amid the folds of her narrow being hid just one spark of shrewdness which came to life where she herself was concerned.

"Two or three rooms--not large ones--can be added at the back," he went on. "I glanced out of a window to see if it could be done."

Incomprehensible as he was, one might always be sure of a certain princeliness in his inexplicable methods. He never was personal or mean. An addition to the slice of a house! That really WAS generous! Entrancement filled her.

"That really is kind of you," she murmured, gratefully. "It seems too much to ask!"

"You did not ask it," was his answer.

"But I shall benefit by it. Nothing COULD BE nicer. These rooms are so much too small," glancing about her in flushed rapture, "And my bedroom is dreadful. I'm obliged to use Rob's for a dressing-room."

"The new rooms will be for Robin," he said. An excellent method he had discovered, of entirely detaching himself from the excitements and emotions of other persons, removed the usual difficulties in the way of disappointing--speaking truths to--or embarrassing people who deserved it. It was this method which had utterly cast down the defences of Andrews. Feather was so wholly left out of the situation that she was actually almost saved from its awkwardness. "When one is six," he explained, "one will soon be seven--nine--twelve. Then the teens begin to loom up and one cannot be concealed in cupboards on a top floor. Even before that time a governess is necessary, and, even from the abyss of my ignorance, I see that no respectable woman would stand either the Night or the Day Nursery. Your daughter--"

"Oh, don't call her THAT!" cried Feather. "My daughter! It sounds as if she were eighteen!" She felt as if she had a sudden hideous little shock. Six years HAD passed since Bob died! A daughter! A school girl with long hair and long legs to keep out of the way. A grown-up girl to drag about with one. Never would she do it!

"Three sixes are eighteen," Coombe continued, "as was impressed upon one in early years by the multiplication table."

"I never saw you so interested in anything before," Feather faltered. "Climbing steep, narrow, horrid stairs to her nursery! Dismissing her nurse!" She paused a second, because a very ugly little idea had clutched at her. It arose from and was complicated with many fantastic, half formed, secret resentments of the past. It made her laugh a shade hysterical.

"Are you going to see that she is properly brought up and educated, so that if--anyone important falls in love with her she can make a good match?"

Hers was quite a hideous little mind, he was telling himself--fearful in its latter day casting aside of all such small matters as taste and feeling. People stripped the garments from things in these days. He laughed inwardly at himself and his unwitting "these days." Senile severity mouthed just such phrases. Were they not his own days and the outcome of a past which had considered itself so much more decorous? Had not boldly questionable attitudes been held in those other days? How long was it since the Prince Regent himself had flourished? It was only that these days brought it all close against one's eyes. But this exquisite creature had a hideous little mind of her own whatsoever her day.

Later, he confessed to himself that he was unprepared to see her spring to her feet and stand before him absurdly, fantastically near being impassioned.

"You think I as too silly to SEE anything," she broke forth. "But I do see--a long way sometimes. I can't bear it but I do--I do! I shall have a grown-up daughter. She will be the kind of girl everyone will look at--and someone--important--may want to marry her. But, Oh!--" He was reminded of the day when she had fallen at his feet, and clasped his rigid and reluctant knees. This was something of the same feeble desperation of mood. "Oh, WHY couldn't someone like that have wanted to marry ME! See!" she was like a pathetic fairy as she spread her nymphlike arms, "how PRETTY I am!"

His gaze held her a moment in the singular fashion with which she had become actually familiar, because--at long intervals--she kept seeing it again. He quite gently took her fingers and returned her to her sofa.

"Please sit down again," he requested. "It will be better."

She sat down without another imbecile word to say. As for him, he changed the subject.

"With your permission, Benby will undertake the business of the lease and the building," he explained. "The plans will be brought to you. We will go over them together, if you wish. There will be decent rooms for Robin and her governess. The two nurseries can be made fit for human beings to live in and used for other purposes. The house will be greatly improved."

It was nearly three o'clock when Feather went upstairs to her dozing maid, because, after he had left her, she sat some time in the empty, untidy little drawing-room and gazed straight before her at a painted screen on which shepherdesses and swains were dancing in a Watteau glade infested by flocks of little Loves.

CHAPTER XIV

When, from Robin's embarrassed young consciousness, there had welled up the hesitating confession, "She--doesn't like me," she could not, of course, have found words in which to make the reasons for her knowledge clear, but they had for herself no obscurity. The fair being who, at rare intervals, fluttered on the threshold of her world had a way of looking at her with a shade of aloof distaste in her always transient gaze.

The unadorned fact was that Feather did NOT like her. She had been outraged by her advent. A baby was absurdly "out of the picture." So far as her mind encompassed a future, she saw herself flitting from flower to flower of "smart" pleasures and successes, somehow, with more money and more exalted invitations--"something" vaguely--having happened to the entire Lawdor progeny, and she, therefore, occupying a position in which it was herself who could gracefully condescend to others. There was nothing so "stodgy" as children in the vision. When the worst came to the worst, she had been consoled by the thought that she had really managed the whole thing very cleverly. It was easier, of course, to so arrange such things in modern days and in town. The Day Nursery and the Night Nursery on the third floor, a smart-looking young woman who knew her business, who even knew what to buy for a child and where to buy it, without troubling any one simplified the situation. Andrews had been quite wonderful. Nobody can bother one about a healthy, handsome child who is seen meticulously cared for and beautifully dressed, being pushed or led or carried out in the open air every day.

But there had arrived the special morning when she had seen a child who so stood out among a dozen children that she had been startled when she recognized that it was Robin. Andrews had taken her charge to Hyde Park that day and Feather was driving through the Row on her way to a Knightsbridge shop. First her glance had been caught by the hair hanging to the little hips--extraordinary hair in which Andrews herself had a pride. Then she had seen the slender, exquisitely modeled legs, and the dancing sway of the small body. A wonderfully cut, stitched, and fagotted smock and hat she had, of course, taken in at a flash. When the child suddenly turned to look at some little girls in a pony cart, the amazing damask of her colour, and form and depth of eye had given her another slight shock. She realized that what she had thrust lightly away in a corner of her third floor produced an unmistakable effect when turned out into the light of a gay world. The creature was tall too--for six years old. Was she really six? It seemed incredible. Ten more years and she would be sixteen.

Mrs. Heppel-Bevill had a girl of fifteen, who was a perfect catastrophe. She read things and had begun to talk about her "right to be a woman." Emily Heppel-Bevill was only thirty-seven--three years from forty. Feather had reached the stage of softening in her disdain of the women in their thirties. She had found herself admitting that--in these days--there were women of forty who had not wholly passed beyond the pale into that outer darkness where there was weeping and wailing and gnashing of teeth. But there was no denying that this six year old baby, with the dancing step, gave one--almost hysterically--"to think." Her imagination could not--never had and never would she have allowed it to--grasp any belief that she herself could change. A Feather, No! But a creature of sixteen, eighteen--with eyes that shape--with lashes an inch long--with yards of hair--standing by one's side in ten years! It was ghastly!

Coombe, in his cold perfunctory way, climbing the crooked, narrow stairs, dismissing Andrews--looking over the rooms--dismissing them, so to speak, and then remaining after the rest had gone to reveal to her a new abnormal mood--that, in itself alone, was actually horrible. It was abnormal and yet he had always been more or less like that in all things. Despite everything--everything--he had never been in love with her at all. At first she had believed he was--then she had tried to make him care for her. He had never failed her, he had done everything in his grand seigneur fashion. Nobody dare make gross comment upon her, but, while he saw her loveliness as only such a man could--she had gradually realized that she had never had even a chance with him. She could not even think that if she had not been so silly and frightened that awful day six years ago, and had not lost her head, he might have admired her more and more and in the end asked her to marry him. He had said there must be no mistakes, and she had not been allowed to fall into making one. The fact that she had not, had, finally, made her feel the power of a certain fascination in him. She thought it was a result of his special type of looks, his breeding, the wonderful clothes he wore--but it was, in truth, his varieties of inaccessibility.

"A girl might like him," she had said to herself that night--she sat up late after he left her. "A girl who--who had up-to-date sense might. Modern people don't grow old as they used to. At fifty-five he won't be fat, or bald and he won't have lost his teeth. People have found out they needn't. He will be as thin and straight as he is today--and nothing can alter his nose. He will be ten years cleverer than he is now. Buying the house for a child of that age--building additional rooms for her!"

In the fevered, rapid, deep-dipping whirl of the life which was the only one she knew, she had often seen rather trying things happen--almost unnatural changes in situations. People had overcome the folly of being afraid to alter their minds and their views about what they had temporarily believed were permanent bonds and emotions. Bonds had become old fogeyish. Marriages went to pieces, the parties in love affairs engaged in a sort of "dance down the middle" and turn other people's partners. The rearrangement of figures sometimes made for great witticism. Occasionally people laughed at themselves as at each other. The admirers of engaging matrons had been known to renew their youth at the coming-out balls of lovely daughters in their early teens, and to end by assuming the flowery chains of a new allegiance. Time had, of course, been when such a volte face would have aroused condemnation and indignant discussion, but a humorous leniency spent but little time in selecting terms of severity. Feather had known of several such contretemps ending in quite brilliant matches. The enchanting mothers usually consoled themselves with great ease, and, if the party of each part was occasionally wittily pungent in her comments on the other, everybody laughed and nobody had time to criticize. A man who had had much to bestow and who preferred in youth to bestow it upon himself was not infrequently more in the mood for the sharing of marriage when years had revealed to him the distressing fact that he was not, and had never been, the centre of the universe, which distressing fact is one so unfairly concealed from youth in bloom.

It was, of course, but as a vaguely outlined vision that these recognitions floated through what could only be alleged to be Feather's mind because there was no other name for it. The dark little staircase, the rejected and despised third floor, and Coombe detachedly announcing his plans for the house, had set the--so to speak--rather malarious mist flowing around her. A trying thing was that it did not really dispel itself altogether, but continued to hang about the atmosphere surrounding other and more cheerful things. Almost impalpably it added to the familiar feeling--or lack of feeling--with regard to Robin. She had not at all hated the little thing; it had merely been quite true that, in an inactive way, she had not LIKED her. In the folds of the vague mist quietly floated the truth that she now liked her less.

Benby came to see and talk to her on the business of the structural changes to be made. He conducted himself precisely as though her views on the matter were of value and could not, in fact, be dispensed with. He brought the architect's plans with him and explained them with care. They were clever plans which made the most of a limited area. He did not even faintly smile when it revealed itself to him, as it unconsciously did, that Mrs. Gareth-Lawless regarded their adroit arrangement as a singular misuse of space which could have been much better employed for necessities of her own. She was much depressed by the ground floor addition which might have enlarged her dining-room, but which was made into a sitting-room for Robin and her future governess.

"And that is in ADDITION to her schoolroom which might have been thrown into the drawing-room--besides the new bedrooms which I needed so much," she said.

"The new nurse, who is a highly respectable person," explained Benby, "could not have been secured if she had not known that improvements were being made. The reconstruction of the third floor will provide suitable accommodations."

The special forte of Dowson, the new nurse, was a sublimated respectability far superior to smartness. She had been mystically produced by Benby and her bonnets and jackets alone would have revealed her selection from almost occult treasures. She wore bonnets and "jackets," not hats and coats.

"In the calm days of Her Majesty, nurses dressed as she does. I do not mean in the riotous later years of her reign--but earlier--when England dreamed in terms of Crystal Palaces and Great Exhibitions. She can only be the result of excavation,"

Coombe said of her.

She was as proud of her respectability as Andrews had been of her smartness. This had, in fact, proved an almost insuperable obstacle to her engagement. The slice of a house, with its flocking in and out of chattering, smart people in marvellous clothes was not the place for her, nor was Mrs. Gareth-Lawless the mistress of her dreams. But her husband had met with an accident and must be kept in a hospital, and an invalid daughter must live by the seaside--and suddenly, when things were at their worst with her, had come Benby with a firm determination to secure her with wages such as no other place would offer. Besides which she had observed as she had lived.

"Things have changed," she reflected soberly. "You've got to resign yourself and not be too particular."

She accepted the third floor, as Benby had said, because it was to be rearranged and the Night and Day Nurseries, being thrown into one, repainted and papered would make a decent place to live in. At the beautiful little girl given into her charge she often looked in a puzzled way, because she knew a good deal about children, and about this one there was something odd. Her examination of opened drawers and closets revealed piles of exquisite garments of all varieties, all perfectly kept. In these dingy holes, which called themselves nurseries, she found evidence that money had been spent like water so that the child, when she was seen, might look like a small princess. But she found no plaything--no dolls or toys, and only one picture book, and that had "Donal" written on the fly leaf and evidently belonged to someone else.

What exactly she would have done when she had had time to think the matter over, she never knew, because, a few days after her arrival, a tall, thin gentleman, coming up the front steps as she was going out with Robin, stopped and spoke to her as if he knew who she was.

"You know the kind of things children like to play with, nurse?" he said.

She respectfully replied that she had had long experience with young desires. She did not know as yet who he was, but there was that about him which made her feel that, while there was no knowing what height his particular exaltation in the matter of rank might reach, one would be safe in setting it high.

"Please go to one of the toy shops and choose for the child what she will like best. Dolls--games--you will know what to select. Send the bill to me at Coombe House. I am Lord Coombe."

"Thank you, my lord," Dowson answered, with a sketch of a curtsey, "Miss Robin, you must hold out your little hand and say 'thank you' to his lordship for being so kind. He's told Dowson to buy you some beautiful dolls and picture books as a present."

Robin's eyelashes curled against her under brows in her wide, still glance upward at him. Here was "the one" again! She shut her hand tightly into a fist behind her back.

Lord Coombe smiled a little--not much.

"She does not like me," he said. "It is not necessary that she should give me her hand. I prefer that she shouldn't, if she doesn't want to. Good morning, Dowson."

To the well-regulated mind of Dowson, this seemed treating too lightly a matter as serious as juvenile incivility. She remonstrated gravely and at length with Robin.

"Little girls must behave prettily to kind gentlemen who are friends of their mammas. It is dreadful to be rude and not say 'thank you'," she said.

But as she talked she was vaguely aware that her words passed by the child's ears as the summer wind passed. Perhaps it was all a bit of temper and would disappear and leave no trace behind. At the same time, there WAS something queer about the little thing. She had a listless way of sitting staring out of the window and seeming to have no desire to amuse herself. She was too young to be listless and she did not care for her food. Dowson asked permission to send for the doctor and, when he came, he ordered sea air.

"Of course, you can take her away for a few weeks," Mrs. Gareth-Lawless said. Here she smiled satirically and added, "But I can tell you what it is all about. The little minx actually fell in love with a small boy she met in the Square Gardens and, when his mother took him from London, she began to mope like a tiresome girl in her teens. It's ridiculous, but is the real trouble."

"Oh!" said Dowson, the low and respectful interjection expressing a shade of disapproval, "Children do have fancies, ma'am. She'll get over it if we give her something else to think of."

The good woman went to one of the large toy shops and bought a beautiful doll, a doll's house, and some picture books. When they were brought up to the Day Nursery, Robin was asleep after a rather long walk, which Dowson had decided would be good for her. When she came later into the room, after the things had been unpacked, she regarded them with an expression of actual dislike.

"Isn't that a beautiful doll?" said Dowson, good-humouredly. "And did you ever see such a lovely house? It was kind Lord Coombe who gave them to you. Just you look at the picture books."

Robin put her hands behind her back and would not touch them. Dowson, who was a motherly creature with a great deal of commonsense, was set thinking. She began to make guesses, though she was not yet sufficiently familiar with the household to guess from any firm foundation of knowledge of small things.

"Come here, dear," she said, and drew the small thing to her knee. "Is it because you don't love Lord Coombe?" she asked.

"Yes," she answered.

"But why?" said Dowson. "When he is such a kind gentleman?"

But Robin would not tell her why and never did. She never told any one, until years had passed, how this had been the beginning of a hatred. The toys were left behind when she was taken to the seaside. Dowson tried to persuade her to play with them several times, but she would not touch them, so they were put away. Feeling that she was dealing with something unusual, and, being a kindly person, Dowson bought her some playthings on her own account. They were simple things, but Robin was ready enough to like them.

"Did YOU give them to me?" she asked.

"Yes, I did, Miss Robin."

The child drew near her after a full minute of hesitation.

"I will KISS you!" she said solemnly, and performed the rite as whole-souledly as Donal had done.

"Dear little mite!" exclaimed the surprised Dowson. "Dear me!" And there was actual moisture in her eyes as she squeezed the small body in her arms.

"She's the strangest mite I ever nursed," was her comment to Mrs. Blayne below stairs. "It was so sudden, and she did it as if she'd never done it before. I'd actually been thinking she hadn't any feeling at all."

"No reason why she should have. She's been taken care of by the clock and dressed like a puppet, but she's not been treated human!" broke forth Mrs. Blayne.

Then the whole story was told--the "upstairs" story with much vivid description, and the mentioning of many names and the dotting of many "i's". Dowson had heard certain things only through vague rumour, but now she knew and began to see her way. She had not heard names before, and the definite inclusion of Lord Coombe's suggested something to her.

"Do you think the child could be JEALOUS of his lordship?" she suggested.

"She might if she knew anything about him--but she never saw him until the night she was taken down into the drawing-room. She's lived upstairs like a little dog in its kennel."

"Well," Dowson reflected aloud, "it sounds almost silly to talk of a child's hating any one, but that bit of a thing's eyes had fair hate in them when she looked up at him where he stood. That was what puzzled me."

CHAPTER XV

Before Robin had been taken to the seaside to be helped by the bracing air of the Norfolk coast to recover her lost appetite and forget her small tragedy, she had observed that unaccustomed things were taking place in the house. Workmen came in and out through the mews at the back and brought ladders with them and tools in queer bags. She heard hammerings which began very early in the morning and went on all day. As Andrews had trained her not to ask tiresome questions, she only crept now and then to a back window and peeped out. But in a few days Dowson took her away.

When she came back to London, she was not taken up the steep dark stairs to the third floor. Dowson led her into some rooms she had never seen before. They were light and airy and had pretty walls and furniture. A sitting-room on the ground floor had even a round window with plants in it and a canary bird singing in a cage.

"May we stay here?" she asked Dowson in a whisper.

"We are going to live here," was the answer.

And so they did.

At first Feather occasionally took her intimates to see the additional apartments.

"In perfect splendour is the creature put up, and I with a bedroom like a coal-hole and such drawing-rooms as you see each time you enter the house!" she broke forth spitefully one day when she forgot herself.

She said it to the Starling and Harrowby, who had been simply gazing about them in fevered mystification, because the new development was a thing which must invoke some more or less interesting explanation. At her outbreak, all they could do was to gaze at her with impartial eyes, which suggested question, and

Feather shrugged pettish shoulders.

"You knew *I* didn't do it. How could I?" she said. "It is a queer whim of Coombe's. Of course, it is not the least like him. I call it morbid."

After which people knew about the matter and found it a subject for edifying and quite stimulating discussion. There was something fantastic in the situation. Coombe was the last man on earth to have taken the slightest notice of the child's existence! It was believed that he had never seen her--except in long clothes--until she had glared at him and put her hand behind her back the night she was brought into the drawing-room. She had been adroitly kept tucked away in an attic somewhere. And now behold an addition of several wonderful, small rooms built, furnished and decorated for her alone, where she was to live as in a miniature palace attended by servitors! Coombe, as a purveyor of nursery appurtenances, was regarded with humour, the general opinion being that the eruption of a volcano beneath his feet alone could have awakened his somewhat chill self-absorption to the recognition of any child's existence.

"To be exact we none of us really know anything in particular about his mental processes." Harrowby pondered aloud. "He's capable of any number of things we might not understand, if he condescended to tell us about them--which he would never attempt. He has a remote, brilliantly stored, cynical mind. He owns that he is of an inhuman selfishness. I haven't a suggestion to make, but it sets one searching through the purlieus of one's mind for an approximately reasonable explanation."

"Why 'purlieus'?" was the Starling's inquiry. Harrowby shrugged his shoulders ever so lightly.

"Well, one isn't searching for reasons founded on copy-book axioms," he shook his head. "Coombe? No."

There was a silence given to occult thought.

"Feather is really in a rage and is too Feathery to be able to conceal it," said Starling.

"Feather would be--inevitably," Harrowby lifted his near-sighted eyes to her curiously. "Can you see Feather in the future--when Robin is ten years older?"

"I can," the Starling answered.

*   *   *   *   *

The years which followed were changing years--growing years. Life and entertainment went on fast and furiously in all parts of London, and in no part more rapidly than in the slice of a house whose front always presented an air of having been freshly decorated, in spite of summer rain and winter soot and fog. The plants in the window boxes seemed always in bloom, being magically replaced in the early morning hours when they dared to hint at flagging. Mrs. Gareth-Lawless, it was said, must be renewed in some such mysterious morning way, as she merely grew prettier as she neared thirty and passed it. Women did in these days! Which last phrase had always been a useful one, probably from the time of the Flood. Old fogeys, male and female, had used it in the past as a means of scathingly unfavourable comparison, growing flushed and almost gobbling like turkey cocks in their indignation. Now, as a phrase, it was a support and a mollifier. "In these days" one knew better how to amuse oneself, was more free to snatch at agreeable opportunity, less in bondage to old fancies which had called themselves beliefs; everything whirled faster and more lightly--danced, two-stepped, instead of marching.

Robin vaguely connected certain changes in her existence with the changes which took place in the fashion of sleeves and skirts which appeared to produce radical effects in the world she caught glimpses of. Sometimes sleeves were closely fitted to people's arms, then puffs sprang from them and grew until they were enormous and required delicate manipulation when coats were put on; then their lavishness of material fell from the shoulder to the wrists and hung there swaying until some sudden development of skirt seemed to distract their attention from themselves and they shrank into unimportance and skirts changed instead. Afterwards, sometimes figures were slim and encased in sheathlike draperies, sometimes folds rippled about feet, "fullness" crept here or there or disappeared altogether, trains grew longer or shorter or wider or narrower, cashmeres, grosgrain silks and heavy satins were suddenly gone and chiffon wreathed itself about the world and took possession of it. Bonnets ceased to exist and hats were immense or tiny, tall or flat, tilted at the back, at the side, at the front, worn over the face or dashingly rolled back from it; feathers drooped or stood upright at heights which rose and fell and changed position with the changing seasons. No garment or individual wore the same aspect for more than a month's time. It was necessary to change all things with a rapidity matching the change of moods and fancies which altered at the rate of the automobiles which dashed here and there and everywhere, through country roads, through town, through remote places with an unsparing swiftness which set a new pace for the world.

"I cannot hark back regretfully to stage coaches," said Lord Coombe. "Even I was not born early enough for that. But in the days of my youth and innocence express trains seemed almost supernatural. One could drive a pair of horses twenty miles to make a country visit, but one could not drive back the same day. One's circle had its limitations and degrees of intimacy. Now it is possible motor fifty miles to lunch and home to dine with guests from the remotest corners of the earth. Oceans are crossed in six days, and the eager flit from continent to continent. Engagements can be made by cable and the truly enterprising can accept an invitation to dine in America on a fortnight's notice. Telephones communicate in a few seconds and no one is secure from social intercourse for fifteen minutes. Acquaintances and correspondence have no limitations because all the inhabitants of the globe can reach one by motor or electricity. In moments of fatigue I revert to the days of Queen Anne with pleasure."

While these changes went on, Robin lived in her own world in her own quarters at the rear of the slice of a house. During the early years spent with Dowson, she learned gradually that life was a better thing than she had known in the dreary gloom of the third floor Day and Night Nurseries. She was no longer left to spend hours alone, nor was she taken below stairs to listen blankly to servants talking to each other of mysterious things with which she herself and the Lady Downstairs and "him" were somehow connected, her discovery of this fact being based on the dropping of voices and sidelong glances at her and sudden warning sounds from Andrews. She realized that Dowson would never pinch her, and the rooms she lived in were pretty and bright.

Gradually playthings and picture books appeared in them, which she gathered Dowson presented her with. She gathered this from Dowson herself.

She had never played with the doll, and, by chance a day arriving when Lord

Coombe encountered Dowson in the street without her charge, he stopped her again and spoke as before.

"Is the little girl well and happy, Nurse?" he asked.

"Quite well, my lord, and much happier than she used to be."

"Did she," he hesitated slightly, "like the playthings you bought her?"

Dowson hesitated more than slightly but, being a sensible woman and at the same time curious about the matter, she spoke the truth.

"She wouldn't play with them at all, my lord. I couldn't persuade her to. What her child's fancy was I don't know."

"Neither do I--except that it is founded on a distinct dislike," said Coombe. There was a brief pause. "Are you fond of toys yourself, Dowson?" he inquired coldly.

"I am that--and I know how to choose them, your lordship," replied Dowson, with a large, shrewd intelligence.

"Then oblige me by throwing away the doll and its accompaniments and buying some toys for yourself, at my expense. You can present them to Miss Robin as a personal gift. She will accept them from you."

He passed on his way and Dowson looked after him interestedly.

"If she was his," she thought, "I shouldn't be puzzled. But she's not--that I've ever heard of. He's got some fancy of his own the same as Robin has, though you wouldn't think it to look at him. I'd like to know what it is."

It was a fancy--an old, old fancy--it harked back nearly thirty years--to the dark days of youth and passion and unending tragedy whose anguish, as it then seemed, could never pass--but which, nevertheless, had faded with the years as they flowed by. And yet left him as he was and had been. He was not sentimental about it, he smiled at himself drearily--though never at the memory--when it rose again and, through its vague power, led him to do strange things curiously verging on the emotional and eccentric. But even the child--who quite loathed him for some fantastic infant reason of her own--even the child had her part in it. His soul oddly withdrew itself into a far remoteness as he walked away and Piccadilly became a shadow and a dream.

Dowson went home and began to pack neatly in a box the neglected doll and the toys which had accompanied her. Robin seeing her doing it, asked a question.

"Are they going back to the shop?"

"No. Lord Coombe is letting me give them to a little girl who is very poor and has to lie in bed because her back hurts her. His lordship is so kind he does not want you to be troubled with them. He is not angry. He is too good to be angry."

That was not true, thought Robin. He had done THAT THING she remembered! Goodness could not have done it. Only badness.

When Dowson brought in a new doll and other wonderful things, a little hand enclosed her wrist quite tightly as she was unpacking the boxes. It was Robin's and the small creature looked at her with a questioning, half appealing, half fierce.

"Did he send them, Dowson?"

"They are a present from me," Dowson answered comfortably, and Robin said again,

"I want to kiss you. I like to kiss you. I do."

To those given to psychical interests and speculations, it might have suggested itself that, on the night when the creature who had seemed to Andrews a soft tissued puppet had suddenly burst forth into defiance and fearless shrillness, some cerebral change had taken place in her. From that hour her softness had become a thing of the past. Dowson had not found a baby, but a brooding, little, passionate being. She was neither insubordinate nor irritable, but Dowson was conscious of a certain intensity of temperament in her. She knew that she was always thinking of things of which she said almost nothing. Only a sensible motherly curiosity, such as Dowson's could have made discoveries, but a rare question put by the child at long intervals sometimes threw a faint light. There were questions chiefly concerning mothers and their habits and customs. They were such as, in their very unconsciousness, revealed a strange past history. Lights were most unconsciously thrown by Mrs. Gareth-Lawless herself. Her quite amiable detachment from all shadow of responsibility, her brilliantly unending occupations, her goings in and out, the flocks of light, almost noisy, intimates who came in and out with her revealed much to a respectable person who had soberly watched the world.

"The Lady Downstairs is my mother, isn't she?" Robin inquired gravely once.

"Yes, my dear," was Dowson's answer.

A pause for consideration of the matter and then from Robin:

"All mothers are not alike, Dowson, are they?"

"No, my dear," with wisdom.

Though she was not yet seven, life had so changed for her that it was a far cry back to the Spring days in the Square Gardens. She went back, however, back into that remote ecstatic past.

"The Lady Downstairs is not--alike," she said at last, "Donal's mother loved him. She let him sit in the same chair with her and read in picture books. She kissed him when he was in bed."

Jennings, the young footman who was a humourist, had, of course, heard witty references to Robin's love affair while in attendance, and he had equally, of course, repeated them below stairs. Therefore,

Dowson had heard vague rumours but had tactfully refrained from mentioning the subject to her charge.

"Who was Donal?" she said now, but quite quietly. Robin did not know that a confidante would have made her first agony easier to bear. She was not really being confidential now, but, realizing Dowson's comfortable kindliness, she knew that it would be safe to speak to her.

"He was a big boy," she answered keeping her eyes on Dowson's face. "He laughed and ran and jumped. His eyes--" she stopped there because she could not explain what she had wanted to say about these joyous young eyes, which were the first friendly human ones she had known.

"He lives in Scotland," she began again. "His mother loved him. He kissed me. He went away. Lord Coombe sent him."

Dawson could not help her start.

"Lord Coombe!" she exclaimed.

Robin came close to her and ground her little fist into her knee, until its plumpness felt almost bruised.

"He is bad--bad--bad!" and she looked like a little demon.

Being a wise woman, Dowson knew at once that she had come upon a hidden child volcano, and it would be well to let it seethe into silence. She was not a clever person, but long experience had taught her that there were occasions when it was well to leave a child alone. This one would not answer if she were questioned. She would only become stubborn and furious, and no child should be goaded into fury. Dowson had, of course, learned that the boy was a relative of his lordship's and had a strict Scottish mother who did not approve of the slice of a house. His lordship might have been concerned in the matter--or he might not. But at least Dowson had gained a side light. And how the little thing had cared! Actually as if she had been a grown girl, Dowson found herself thinking uneasily.

She was rendered even a trifle more uneasy a few days later when she came upon Robin sitting in a corner on a footstool with a picture book on her knee, and she recognized it as the one she had discovered during her first exploitation of the resources of the third floor nursery. It was inscribed "Donal" and Robin was not looking at it alone, but at something she held in her hand--something folded in a crumpled, untidy bit of paper.

Making a reason for nearing her corner, Dowson saw what the paper held. The contents looked like the broken fragments of some dried leaves. The child was gazing at them with a piteous, bewildered face--so piteous that Dowson was sorry.

"Do you want to keep those?" she asked.

"Yes," with a caught breath. "Yes."

"I will make you a little silk bag to hold them in," Dowson said, actually feeling rather piteous herself. The poor, little lamb with her picture book and her bits of broken dry leaves--almost like senna.

She sat down near her and Robin left her footstool and came to her. She laid the picture book on her lap and the senna like fragments of leaves on its open page.

"Donal brought it to show me," she quavered. "He made pretty things on the leaves--with his dirk." She recalled too much--too much all at once. Her eyes grew rounder and larger with inescapable woe; "Donal did! Donal!" And suddenly she hid her face deep in Dowson's skirts and the tempest broke. She was so small a thing--so inarticulate--and these were her dead! Dowson could only catch her in her arms, drag her up on her knee, and rock her to and fro.

"Good Lord! Good Lord!" was her inward ejaculation. "And she not seven! What'll she do when she's seventeen! She's one of them there's no help for!"

It was the beginning of an affection. After this, when Dowson tucked Robin in bed each night, she kissed her. She told her stories and taught her to sew and to know her letters. Using some discretion she found certain little playmates for her in the Gardens. But there were occasions when all did not go well, and some pretty, friendly child, who had played with Robin for a few days, suddenly seemed to be kept strictly by her nurse's side. Once, when she was about ten years old, a newcomer, a dramatic and too richly dressed little person, after a day of wonderful imaginative playing appeared in the Gardens the morning following to turn an ostentatious cold shoulder.

"What is the matter?" asked Robin.

"Oh, we can't play with you any more," with quite a flounce superiority.

"Why not?" said Robin, becoming haughty herself.

"We can't. It's because of Lord Coombe." The little person had really no definite knowledge of how Lord Coombe was concerned, but certain servants' whisperings of names and mysterious phrases had conveyed quite an enjoyable effect of unknown iniquity connected with his lordship.

Robin said nothing to Dowson, but walked up and down the paths reflecting and building a slow fire which would continue to burn in her young heart. She had by then passed the round, soft baby period and had entered into that phase when bodies and legs grow long and slender and small faces lose their first curves and begin to show sharper modeling.

Accepting the situation in its entirety, Dowson had seen that it was well to first reach Lord Coombe with any need of the child's. Afterwards, the form of presenting it to Mrs. Gareth-Lawless must be gone through, but if she were first spoken to any suggestion might be forgotten or intentionally ignored.

Dowson became clever in her calculations as to when his lordship might be encountered and where--as if by chance, and therefore, quite respectfully. Sometimes she remotely wondered if he himself did not make such encounters easy for her. But his manner never altered in its somewhat stiff, expressionless chill of indifference. He never was kindly in his manner to the child if he met her. Dowson felt him at once casual and "lofty." Robin might have been a bit of unconsidered rubbish, the sight of which slightly bored him. Yet the singular fact remained that it was to him one must carefully appeal.

One afternoon Feather swept him, with one or two others, into the sitting-room with the round window in which flowers grew. Robin was sitting at a low table making pothooks with a lead pencil on a piece of paper Dowson had given her. Dowson had, in fact, set her at the task, having heard from Jennings that his lordship and the other afternoon tea drinkers were to be brought into the "Palace" as Feather ironically chose to call it. Jennings rather liked Dowson, and often told her little things she wanted to know. It was because Lord Coombe would probably come in with the rest that Dowson had set the low, white table in the round windows and suggested the pothooks.

In course of time there was a fluttering and a chatter in the corridor. Feather was bringing some new guests, who had not seen the place before.

"This is where my daughter lives. She is much grander than I am," she said.

"Stand up, Miss Robin, and make your curtsey," whispered Dowson. Robin did as she was told, and Mrs. Gareth-Lawless' pretty brows ran up.

"Look at her legs," she said. "She's growing like Jack and the Bean Stalk--though, I suppose, it was only the Bean Stalk that grew. She'll stick through the top of the house soon. Look at her legs, I ask you."

She always spoke as if the child were an inanimate object and she had, by this time and by this means, managed to sweep from Robin's mind all the old, babyish worship of her loveliness and had planted in its place another feeling. At this moment the other feeling surged and burned.

"They are beautiful legs," remarked a laughing young man jocularly, "but perhaps she does not particularly want us to look at them. Wait until she begins skirt dancing." And everybody laughed at once and the child stood rigid--the object of their light ridicule--not herself knowing that her whole little being was cursing them aloud.

Coombe stepped to the little table and bestowed a casual glance on the pencil marks.

"What is she doing?" he asked as casually of Dowson.

"She is learning to make pothooks, my lord," Dowson answered. "She's a child that wants to be learning things. I've taught her her letters and to spell little words. She's quick--and old enough, your lordship."

"Learning to read and write!" exclaimed Feather.

"Presumption, I call it. I don't know how to read and write--least I don't know how to spell. Do you know how to spell, Collie?" to the young man, whose name was Colin. "Do you, Genevieve? Do you, Artie?"

"You can't betray me into vulgar boasting," said Collie. "Who does in these days? Nobody but clerks at Peter Robinson's."

"Lord Coombe does--but that's his tiresome superior way," said Feather.

"He's nearly forty years older than most of you. That is the reason," Coombe commented. "Don't deplore your youth and innocence."

They swept through the rooms and examined everything in them. The truth was that the--by this time well known--fact that the unexplainable Coombe had built them made them a curiosity, and a sort of secret source of jokes. The party even mounted to the upper story to go through the bedrooms, and, it was while they were doing this, that Coombe chose to linger behind with Dowson.

He remained entirely expressionless for a few moments. Dowson did not in the least gather whether he meant to speak to her or not. But he did.

"You meant," he scarcely glanced at her, "that she was old enough for a governess."

"Yes, my lord," rather breathless in her hurry to speak before she heard the high heels tapping on the staircase again. "And one that's a good woman as well as clever, if I may take the liberty. A good one if--"

"If a good one would take the place?"

Dowson did not attempt refutation or apology. She knew better.

He said no more, but sauntered out of the room.

As he did so, Robin stood up and made the little "charity bob" of a curtsey which had been part of her nursery education. She was too old now to have refused him her hand, but he never made any advances to her. He acknowledged her curtsey with the briefest nod.

Not three minutes later the high heels came tapping down the staircase and the small gust of visitors swept away also.

CHAPTER XVI

The interview which took place between Feather and Lord Coombe a few days later had its own special character.

"A governess will come here tomorrow at eleven o'clock," he said. "She is a Mademoiselle Valle. She is accustomed to the educating of young children. She will present herself for your approval. Benby has done all the rest."

Feather flushed to her fine-spun ash-gold hair.

"What on earth can it matter!" she cried.

"It does not matter to you," he answered; "it chances--for the time being--to matter to ME."

"Chances!" she flamed forth--it was really a queer little flame of feeling. "That's it. You don't really care! It's a caprice--just because you see she is going to be pretty."

"I'll own," he admitted, "that has a great deal to do with it."

"It has everything to do with it," she threw out. "If she had a snub nose and thick legs you wouldn't care for her at all."

"I don't say that I do care for her," without emotion. "The situation interests me. Here is an extraordinary little being thrown into the world. She belongs to nobody. She will have to fight for her own hand. And she will have to FIGHT, by God! With that dewy lure in her eyes and her curved pomegranate mouth! She will not know, but she will draw disaster!"

"Then she had better not be taught anything at all," said Feather. "It would be an amusing thing to let her grow up without learning to read or write at all. I know numbers of men who would like the novelty of it. Girls who know so much are a bore."

"There are a few minor chances she ought to have," said Coombe. "A governess is one. Mademoiselle Valle will be here at eleven."

"I can't see that she promises to be such a beauty," fretted Feather. "She's the kind of good looking child who might grow up into a fat girl with staring black eyes like a barmaid."

"Occasionally pretty women do abhor their growing up daughters," commented Coombe letting his eyes rest on her interestedly.

"I don't abhor her," with pathos touched with venom. "But a big, lumping girl hanging about ogling and wanting to be ogled when she is passing through that silly age! And sometimes you speak to me as a man speaks to his wife when he is tired of her."

"I beg your pardon," Coombe said. "You make me feel like a person who lives over a shop at Knightsbridge, or in bijou mansion off Regent's Park."

But he was deeply aware that, as an outcome of the anomalous position he occupied, he not infrequently felt exactly this.

That a governess chosen by Coombe--though he would seem not to appear in the matter--would preside over the new rooms, Feather knew without a shadow of doubt.

A certain almost silent and always high-bred dominance over her existence she accepted as the inevitable, even while she fretted helplessly. Without him, she would be tossed, a broken butterfly, into the gutter. She knew her London. No one would pick her up unless to break her into smaller atoms and toss her away again. The freedom he allowed her after all was wonderful. It was because he disdained interference.

But there was a line not to be crossed--there must not even be an attempt at crossing it. Why he cared about that she did not know.

"You must be like Caesar's wife," he said rather grimly, after an interview in which he had given her a certain unsparing warning.

"And I am nobody's wife. What did Caesar's wife do?" she asked.

"Nothing." And he told her the story and, when she had heard him tell it, she understood certain things clearly.

Mademoiselle Valle was an intelligent, mature Frenchwoman. She presented herself to Mrs. Gareth-Lawless for inspection and, in ten minutes, realized that the power to inspect and sum up existed only on her own side. This pretty woman neither knew what inquiries to make nor cared for such replies as were given. Being swift to reason and practical in deduction, Mademoiselle Valle did not make the blunder of deciding that this light presence argued that she would be under no supervision more serious. The excellent Benby, one was made aware, acted and the excellent Benby, one was made aware, acted under clearly defined orders. Milord Coombe--among other things the best dressed and perhaps the least comprehended man in London--was concerned in this, though on what grounds practical persons could not explain to themselves. His connection with the narrow house on the right side of the right street was entirely comprehensible. The lenient felt nothing blatant or objectionable about it. Mademoiselle Valle herself was not disturbed by mere rumour. The education, manner and morals of the little girl she could account for. These alone were to be her affair, and she was competent to undertake their superintendence.

Therefore, she sat and listened with respectful intelligence to the birdlike chatter of Mrs. Gareth-Lawless. (What a pretty woman! The silhouette of a jeune fille!)

Mrs. Gareth-Lawless felt that, on her part, she had done all that was required of her.

"I'm afraid she's rather a dull child, Mademoiselle," she said in farewell. "You know children's ways and you'll understand what I mean. She has a trick of staring and saying nothing. I confess I wish she wasn't dull."

"It is impossible, madame, that she should be dull," said Mademoiselle, with an agreeably implicating smile. "Oh, but quite impossible! We shall see."

Not many days had passed before she had seen much. At the outset, she recognized the effect of the little girl with the slender legs and feet and the dozen or so of points which go to make a beauty. The intense eyes first and the deeps of them. They gave one furiously to think before making up one's mind. Then she noted the perfection of the rooms added to the smartly inconvenient little house. Where had the child lived before the addition had been built? Thought and actual architectural genius only could have done this. Light and even as much sunshine as London will vouchsafe, had been arranged for. Comfort, convenience, luxury, had been provided. Perfect colour and excellent texture had evoked actual charm. Its utter unlikeness to the quarters London usually gives to children, even of the fortunate class, struck Mademoiselle Valle at once. Madame Gareth-Lawless had not done this. Who then, had?

The good Dowson she at once affiliated with. She knew the excellence of her type as it had revealed itself to her in the best peasant class. Trustworthy, simple, but of kindly, shrewd good sense and with the power to observe. Dowson was not a chatterer or given to gossip, but, as a silent observer, she would know many things and, in time, when they had become friendly enough to be fully aware that each might trust the other, gentle and careful talk would end in unconscious revelation being made by Dowson.

That the little girl was almost singularly attached to her nurse, she had marked early. There was something unusual in her manifestations of her feeling. The intense eyes followed the woman often, as if making sure of her presence and reality. The first day of Mademoiselle's residence in the place she saw the little thing suddenly stop playing with her doll and look at Dowson earnestly for several moments. Then she left her seat and went to the kind creature's side.

"I want to KISS you, Dowie," she said.

"To be sure, my lamb," answered Dowson, and, laying down her mending, she gave her a motherly hug. After which Robin went back contentedly to her play.

The Frenchwoman thought it a pretty bit of childish affectionateness. But it happened more than once during the day, and at night Mademoiselle commented upon it.

"She has an affectionate heart, the little one," she remarked. "Madame, her mother, is so pretty and full of gaieties and pleasures that I should not have imagined she had much time for caresses and the nursery."

Even by this time Dowson had realized that with Mademoiselle she was upon safe ground and was in no danger of betraying herself to a gossip. She quietly laid down her sewing and looked at her companion with grave eyes.

"Her mother has never kissed her in her life that I am aware of," she said.

"Has never--!" Mademoiselle ejaculated. "Never!"

"Just as you see her, she is, Mademoiselle," Dowson said. "Any sensible woman would know, when she heard her talk about her child. I found it all out bit by bit when first I came here. I'm going to talk plain and have done with it. Her first six years she spent in a sort of dog kennel on the top floor of this house. No sun, no real fresh air. Two little holes that were dingy and gloomy to dull a child's senses. Not a toy or a bit of colour or a picture, but clothes fine enough for Buckingham Palace children--and enough for six. Fed and washed and taken out every day to be shown off. And a bad nurse, Miss--a bad one that kept her quiet by pinching her black and blue."

"Mon Dieu! Mon Dieu! That little angel!" cried Mademoiselle, covering her eyes.

Dowson hastily wiped her own eyes. She had shed many a motherly tear over the child. It was a relief to her to open her heart to a sympathizer.

"Black and blue!" she repeated. "And laughing and dancing and all sorts of fast fun going on in the drawing-rooms." She put out her hand and touched Mademoiselle's arm quite fiercely. "The little thing didn't know she HAD a mother! She didn't know what the word meant. I found that out by her innocent talk. She used to call HER 'The Lady Downstairs'."

"Mon Dieu!" cried the Frenchwoman again. "What a woman!"

"She first heard of mothers from a little boy she met in the Square Gardens. He was the first child she had been allowed to play with. He was a nice child and he had a good mother. I only got it bit by bit when she didn't know how much she was telling me. He told her about mothers and he kissed her--for the first time in her life. She didn't understand but it warmed her little heart. She's never forgotten."

Mademoiselle even started slightly in her chair. Being a clever Frenchwoman she felt drama and all its subtle accompaniments.

"Is that why----" she began.

"It is," answered Dowson, stoutly. "A kiss isn't an ordinary thing to her. It means something wonderful. She's got into the way of loving me, bless her, and every now and then, it's my opinion, she suddenly remembers her lonely days when she didn't know what love was. And it just wells up in her little heart and she wants to kiss me. She always says it that way, 'Dowie, I want to KISS you,' as if it was something strange and, so to say, sacred. She doesn't know it means almost nothing to most people. That's why I always lay down my work and hug her close."

"You have a good heart--a GOOD one!" said Mademoiselle with strong feeling.

Then she put a question:

"Who was the little boy?"

"He was a relation of--his lordship's."

"His lordship's?" cautiously.

"The Marquis. Lord Coombe."

There was a few minutes' silence. Both women were thinking of a number of things and each was asking herself how much it would be wise to say.

It was Dowson who made her decision first, and this time, as before, she laid down her work. What she had to convey was the thing which, above all others, the Frenchwoman must understand if she was to be able to use her power to its best effect.

"A woman in my place hears enough talk," was her beginning. "Servants are given to it. The Servants' Hall is their theatre. It doesn't matter whether tales are true or not, so that they're spicy. But it's been my way to credit just as much as I see and know and to say little about that. If a woman takes a place in a house, let her go or stay as suits her best, but don't let her stay and either complain or gossip. My business here is Miss Robin, and I've found out for myself that there's just one person that, in a queer, unfeeling way of his own, has a fancy for looking after her. I say 'unfeeling' because he never shows any human signs of caring for the child himself. But if there's a thing that ought to be done for her and a body can contrive to let him know it's needed, it'll be done. Downstairs' talk that I've seemed to pay no attention to has let out that it was him that walked quietly upstairs to the Nursery, where he'd never set foot before, and opened the door on Andrews pinching the child. She packed her box and left that night. He inspected the nurseries and, in a few days, an architect was planning these rooms,--for Miss Robin and for no one else, though there was others wanted them. It was him that told me to order her books and playthings--and not let her know it because she hates him. It was him I told she needed a governess. And he found you."

Mademoiselle Valle had listened with profound attention. Here she spoke.

"You say continually 'he' or 'him'. He is--?"

"Lord Coombe. I'm not saying I've seen much of him. Considering--" Dowson paused--"it's queer how seldom he comes here. He goes abroad a good deal. He's mixed up with the highest and it's said he's in favour because he's satirical and clever. He's one that's gossiped about and he cares nothing for what's said. What business of mine is it whether or not he has all sorts of dens on the Continent where he goes to racket. He might be a bishop for all I see. And he's the only creature in this world of the Almighty's that remembers that child's a human being. Just him-- Lord Coombe. There, Mademoiselle,--I've said a good deal."

More and more interestedly had the Frenchwoman listened and with an increasing hint of curiosity in her intelligent eyes. She pressed Dowson's needle-roughened fingers warmly.

"You have not said too much. It is well that I should know this of this gentleman. As you say, he is a man who is much discussed. I myself have heard much of him--but of things connected with another part of his character. It is true that he is in favour with great personages. It is because they are aware that he has observed much for many years. He is light and ironic, but he tells truths which sometimes startle those who hear them."

"Jennings tells below stairs that he says things it's queer for a lord to say. Jennings is a sharp young snip and likes to pick up things to repeat. He believes that his lordship's idea is that there's a time coming when the high ones will lose their places and thrones and kings will be done away with. I wouldn't like to go that far myself," said Dowson, gravely, "but I must say that there's not that serious respect paid to Royalty that there was in my young days. My word! When Queen Victoria was in her prime, with all her young family around her,--their little Royal Highnesses that were princes in their Highland kilts and the princesses in their crinolines and hats with drooping ostrich feathers and broad satin streamers--the people just went wild when she went to a place to unveil anything!"

"When the Empress Eugenie and the Prince Imperial appeared, it was the same thing," said Mademoiselle, a trifle sadly. "One recalls it now as a dream passed away--the Champs Elysees in the afternoon sunlight--the imperial carriage and the glittering escort trotting gaily--the beautiful woman with the always beautiful costumes--her charming smile--the Emperor, with his waxed moustache and saturnine face! It meant so much and it went so quickly. One moment," she made a little gesture, "and it is gone--forever! An Empire and all the splendour of it! Two centuries ago it could not have disappeared so quickly. But now the world is older. It does not need toys so much. A Republic is the people--and there are more people than kings."

"It's things like that his lordship says, according to Jennings," said Dowson.

"Jennings is never quite sure he's in earnest. He has a satirical way--And the company always laugh."

Mademoiselle had spoken thoughtfully and as if half to her inner self instead of to Dowson. She added something even more thoughtfully now.

"The same kind of people laughed before the French Revolution," she murmured.

"I'm not scholar enough to know much about that--that was a long time ago, wasn't it?" Dowson remarked.

"A long time ago," said Mademoiselle.

Dowson's reply was quite free from tragic reminiscence.

"Well, I must say, I like a respectable Royal Family myself," she observed. "There's something solid and comfortable about it--besides the coronations and weddings and procession with all the pictures in the Illustrated London News. Give me a nice, well-behaved Royal Family."

CHAPTER XVII

A nice, well-behaved Royal Family." There had been several of them in Europe for some time. An appreciable number of them had prided themselves, even a shade ostentatiously, upon their domesticity. The moral views of a few had been believed to border upon the high principles inscribed in copy books. Some, however, had not. A more important power or so had veered from the exact following of these commendable axioms--had high-handedly behaved according to their royal will and tastes. But what would you? With a nation making proper obeisance before one from infancy; with trumpets blaring forth joyous strains upon one's mere appearance on any scene; with the proudest necks bowed and the most superb curtseys swept on one's mere passing by, with all the splendour of the Opera on gala night rising to its feet to salute one's mere entry into the royal or imperial box, while the national anthem bursts forth with adulatory and triumphant strains, only a keen and subtle sense of humour, surely, could curb errors of judgment arising from naturally mistaken views of one's own importance and value to the entire Universe. Still there remained the fact that a number of them WERE well-behaved and could not be complained of as bearing any likeness to the bloodthirsty tyrants and oppressors of past centuries.

The Head of the House of Coombe had attended the Court Functions and been received at the palaces and castles of most of them. For in that aspect of his character of which Mademoiselle Valle had heard more than Dowson, he was intimate with well-known and much-observed personages and places. A man born among those whose daily life builds, as it passes, at least a part of that which makes history and so records itself, must needs find companions, acquaintances, enemies, friends of varied character, and if he be, by chance, a keen observer of passing panoramas, can lack no material for private reflection and the accumulation of important facts.

That part of his existence which connected itself with the slice of a house on the right side of the Mayfair street was but a small one. A feature of the untranslatableness of his character was that he was seen there but seldom. His early habit of crossing the Channel frequently had gradually reestablished itself as years passed. Among his acquaintances his "Saturday to Monday visits" to continental cities remote or unremote were discussed with humour. Possibly, upon these discussions, were finally founded the rumours of which Dowson had heard but which she had impartially declined to "credit". Lively conjecture inevitably figured largely in their arguments and, when persons of unrestrained wit devote their attention to airy persiflage, much may be included in their points of view.

Of these conjectural discussions no one was more clearly aware than Coombe himself, and the finished facility--even felicity--of his evasion of any attempt at delicately valued cross examination was felt to be inhumanly exasperating.

In one of the older Squares which still remained stately, through the splendour of modern fashion had waned in its neighbourhood, there was among the gloomy, though imposing, houses one in particular upon whose broad doorsteps--years before the Gareth-Lawlesses had appeared in London--Lord Coombe stood oftener than upon any other. At times his brougham waited before it for hours, and, at others, he appeared on foot and lifted the heavy knocker with a special accustomed knock recognized at once by any footman in waiting in the hall, who, hearing it, knew that his mistress--the old Dowager Duchess of Darte--would receive this visitor, if no other.

The interior of the house was of the type which, having from the first been massive and richly sombre, had mellowed into a darker sombreness and richness as it had stood unmoved amid London years and fogs. The grandeur of decoration and furnishing had been too solid to depreciate through decay, and its owner had been of no fickle mind led to waver in taste by whims of fashion. The rooms were huge and lofty, the halls and stairways spacious, the fireplaces furnished with immense grates of glittering steel, which held in winter beds of scarlet glowing coal, kept scarlet glowing by a special footman whose being, so to speak, depended on his fidelity to his task.

There were many rooms whose doors were kept closed because they were apparently never used; there were others as little used but thrown open, warmed and brightened with flowers each day, because the Duchess chose to catch glimpses of their cheerfulness as she passed them on her way up or downstairs. The house was her own property, and, after her widowhood, when it was emptied of her children by their admirable marriages, and she herself became Dowager and, later, a confirmed rheumatic invalid, it became doubly her home and was governed by her slightest whim. She was not indeed an old woman of caprices, but her tastes, not being those of the later day in which she now lived, were regarded as a shade eccentric being firmly defined.

"I will not have my house glaring with electricity as if it were a shop. In my own rooms I will be lighted by wax candles. Large ones--as many as you please," she said. "I will not be 'rung up' by telephone. My servants may if they like. It is not my affair to deprive them of the modern inconveniences, if they find them convenient. My senility does not take the form of insisting that the world shall cease to revolve upon its axis. It formed that habit without my assistance, and it is to be feared that it would continue it in the face of my protests."

It was, in fact, solely that portion of the world affecting herself alone which she preferred to retain as it had been in the brilliant early years of her life. She had been a great beauty and also a wit in the Court over which Queen Victoria had reigned. She had possessed the delicate high nose, the soft full eyes, the "polished forehead," the sloping white shoulders from which scarves floated or India shawls gracefully drooped in the Books of Beauty of the day. Her carriage had been noble, her bloom perfect, and, when she had driven through the streets "in attendance" on her Royal Mistress, the populace had always chosen her as "the pick of 'em all". Young as she had then been, elderly statesmen had found her worth talking to, not as a mere beauty in her teens, but as a creature of singular brilliance and clarity of outlook upon a world which might have dazzled her youth. The most renowned among them had said of her, before she was twenty, that she would live to be one of the cleverest women in Europe, and that she had already the logical outlook of a just man of fifty.

She married early and was widowed in middle life. In her later years rheumatic fever so far disabled her as to confine her to her chair almost entirely. Her sons and daughter had homes and families of their own to engage them. She would not allow them to sacrifice themselves to her because her life had altered its aspect.

"I have money, friends, good servants and a house I particularly like," she summed the matter up; "I may be condemned to sit by the fire, but I am not condemned to be a bore to my inoffensive family. I can still talk and read, and I shall train myself to become a professional listener. This will attract. I shall not only read myself, but I will be read to. A strong young man with a nice voice shall bring magazines and books to me every day, and shall read the best things aloud. Delightful people will drop in to see me and will be amazed by my fund of information."

It was during the first years of her enforced seclusion that Coombe's intimacy with her began. He had known her during certain black days of his youth, and she had comprehended things he did not tell her. She had not spoken of them to him but she had silently given him of something which vaguely drew him to her side when darkness seemed to overwhelm him. The occupations of her life left her in those earlier days little leisure for close intimacies, but, when she began to sit by her fire letting the busy world pass by, he gradually became one of those who "dropped in".

In one of the huge rooms she had chosen for her own daily use, by the well-tended fire in its shining grate, she had created an agreeable corner where she sat in a chair marvellous for ease and comfort, enclosed from draughts by a fire screen of antique Chinese lacquer, a table by her side and all she required within her reach. Upon the table stood a silver bell and, at its sound, her companion, her reader, her maid or her personally trained footman, came and went quietly and promptly as if summoned by magic. Her life itself was simple, but a certain almost royal dignity surrounded her loneliness. Her companion, Miss Brent, an intelligent, mature woman who had known a hard and pinched life, found at once comfort and savour in it.

"It is not I who am expensive,"--this in one of her talks with Coombe, "but to live in a house of this size, well kept by excellent servants who are satisfied with their lot, is not a frugal thing. A cap of tea for those of my friends who run in to warm themselves by my fire in the afternoon; a dinner or so when I am well enough to sit at the head of my table, represent almost all I now do for the world. Naturally, I must see that my tea is good and that my dinners cannot be objected to. Nevertheless, I sit here in my chair and save money--for what?"

Among those who "warmed themselves by her fire" this man had singularly become her friend and intimate. When they had time to explore each other's minds, they came upon curious discoveries of hidden sympathies and mutual comprehensions which were rich treasures. They talked of absorbing things with frankness. He came to sit with her when others were not admitted because she was in pain or fatigued. He added to neither her fatigue nor her pain, but rather helped her to forget them.

"For what?" he answered on this day. "Why not for your grandchildren?"

"They will have too much money. There are only four of them. They will make great marriages as their parents did," she said. She paused a second before she added, "Unless our World Revolution has broken into flame by that time--And there are no longer any great marriages to make."

For among the many things they dwelt on in their talks along, was the Chessboard, which was the Map of Europe, over which he had watched for many years certain hands hover in tentative experimenting as to the possibilities of the removal of the pieces from one square to another. She, too, from her youth had watched the game with an interest which had not waned in her maturity, and which, in her days of sitting by the fire, had increased with every move the hovering hands made. She had been familiar with political parties and their leaders, she had met heroes and statesmen; she had seen an unimportant prince become an emperor, who, from his green and boastful youth, aspired to rule the world and whose theatrical obsession had been the sly jest of unwary nations, too carelessly sure of the advance of civilization and too indifferently self-indulgent to realize that a monomaniac, even if treated as a source of humour, is a perilous thing to leave unwatched. She had known France in all the glitter of its showy Empire, and had seen its imperial glories dispersed as mist. Russia she had watched with curiosity and dread. On the day when the ruler, who had bestowed freedom on millions of his people, met his reward in the shattering bomb which tore him to fragments, she had been in St. Petersburg. A king, who had been assassinated, she had known well and had well liked; an empress, whom a frenzied madman had stabbed to the heart, had been her friend.

Her years had been richly full of varied events, giving a strong and far-seeing mind reason for much unspoken thought of the kind which leaps in advance of its day's experience and exact knowledge. She had learned when to speak and when to be silent, and she oftener chose silence. But she had never ceased gazing on the world with keen eyes, and reflecting upon its virtues and vagaries, its depths and its shallows, with the help of a clear and temperate brain.

By her fire she sat, an attracting presence, though only fine, strong lines remained of beauty ravaged by illness and years. The "polished forehead" was furrowed by the chisel of suffering; the delicate high nose springing from her waxen, sunken face seemed somewhat eaglelike, but the face was still brilliant in its intensity of meaning and the carriage of her head was still noble. Not able to walk except with the assistance of a cane, her once exquisite hands stiffened almost to uselessness, she held her court from her throne of mere power and strong charm. On the afternoons when people "ran in to warm themselves" by her fire, the talk was never dull and was often wonderful. There were those who came quietly into the room fresh from important scenes where subjects of weight to nations were being argued closely--perhaps almost fiercely. Sometimes the argument was continued over cups of perfect tea near the chair of the Duchess, and, howsoever far it led, she was able brilliantly to follow. With the aid of books and pamphlets and magazines, and the strong young man with the nice voice, who was her reader, she kept pace with each step of the march of the world.

It was, however, the modern note in her recollections of her world's march in days long past, in which Coombe found mental food and fine flavour. The phrase, "in these days" expressed in her utterance neither disparagement nor regret. She who sat in state in a drawing-room lighted by wax candles did so as an affair of personal preference, and denied no claim of higher brilliance to electric illumination. Driving slowly through Hyde Park on sunny days when she was able to go out, her high-swung barouche hinted at no lofty disdain of petrol and motor power. At the close of her youth's century, she looked forward with thrilled curiosity to the dawning wonders of the next.

"If the past had not held so much, one might not have learned to expect more," was her summing up on a certain afternoon, when he came to report himself after one of his absences from England. "The most important discovery of the last fifty years has been the revelation that no man may any longer assume to speak the last word on any subject. The next man--almost any next man--may evolve more. Before that period all elderly persons were final in their dictum. They said to each other--and particularly to the young--'It has not been done in my time--it was not done in my grandfather's time. It has never been done. It never can be done'."

"The note of today is 'Since it has never been done, it will surely be done soon'," said Coombe.

"Ah! we who began life in the most assured and respectable of reigns and centuries," she answered him, "have seen much. But these others will see more. Crinolines, mushroom hats and large families seemed to promise a decorum peaceful to dullness; but there have been battles, murders and sudden deaths; there have been almost supernatural inventions and discoveries--there have been marvels of new doubts and faiths. When one sits and counts upon one's fingers the amazements the 19th century has provided, one gasps and gazes with wide eyes into the future. I, for one, feel rather as though I had seen a calm milch cow sauntering--at first slowly--along a path, gradually evolve into a tiger--a genie with a hundred heads containing all the marvels of the world--a flying dragon with a thousand eyes! Oh, we have gone fast and far!"

"And we shall go faster and farther," Coombe added.

"That is it," she answered. "Are we going too fast?"

"At least so fast that we forget things it would be well for us to remember." He had come in that day with a certain preoccupied grimness of expression which was not unknown to her. It was generally after one of his absences that he looked a shade grim.

"Such as--?" she inquired.

"Such as catastrophes in the history of the world, which forethought and wisdom might have prevented. The French Revolution is the obvious type of figure which lies close at hand so one picks it up. The French Revolution--its Reign of Terror--the orgies of carnage--the cataclysms of agony--need not have been, but they WERE. To put it in words of one syllable."

"What!" was her involuntary exclamation. "You are seeking such similes as the French Revolution!"

"Who knows how far a madness may reach and what Reign of Terror may take form?" He sat down and drew an atlas towards him. It always lay upon the table on which all the Duchess desired was within reach. It was fat, convenient of form, and agreeable to look at in its cover of dull, green leather. Coombe's gesture of drawing it towards him was a familiar one. It was frequently used as reference.

"The atlas again?" she said.

"Yes. Just now I can think of little else. I have realized too much."

The continental journey had lasted a month. He had visited more countries than one in his pursuit of a study he was making of the way in which the wind was blowing particular straws. For long he had found much to give thought to in the trend of movement in one special portion of the Chessboard. It was that portion of it dominated by the ruler of whose obsession too careless nations made sly jest. This man he had known from his arrogant and unendearing youth. He had looked on with unbiassed curiosity at his development into arrogance so much greater than its proportions touched the grotesque. The rest of the world had looked on also, but apparently, merely in the casual way which good-naturedly smiles and leaves to every man--even an emperor--the privilege of his own eccentricities. Coombe had looked on with a difference, so also had his friend by her fireside. This man's square of the Chessboard had long been the subject of their private talks and a cause for the drawing towards them of the green atlas. The moves he made, the methods of his ruling, the significance of these methods were the evidence they collected in their frequent arguments. Coombe had early begun to see the whole thing as a process--a life-long labour which was a means to a monstrous end.

There was a certain thing he believed of which they often spoke as "It". He spoke of it now.

"Through three weeks I have been marking how It grows," he said; "a whole nation with the entire power of its commerce, its education, its science, its religion, guided towards one aim is a curious study. The very babes are born and bred and taught only that one thought may become an integral part of their being. The most innocent and blue eyed of them knows, without a shadow of doubt, that the world has but one reason for existence--that it may be conquered and ravaged by the country that gave them birth."

"I have both heard and seen it," she said. "One has smiled in spite of oneself, in listening to their simple, everyday talk."

"In little schools--in large ones--in little churches, and in imposing ones, their Faith is taught and preached," Coombe answered. "Sometimes one cannot believe one's hearing. It is all so ingenuously and frankly unashamed--the mouthing, boasting, and threats of their piety. There exists for them no God who is not the modest henchman of their emperor, and whose attention is not rivetted on their prowess with admiration and awe. Apparently, they are His business, and He is well paid by being allowed to retain their confidence."

"A lack of any sense of humour is a disastrous thing," commented the Duchess. "The people of other nations may be fools--doubtless we all are--but there is no other which proclaims the fact abroad with such guileless outbursts of raucous exultation."

"And even we--you and I who have thought more than others" he said, restlessly, "even we forget and half smile. There been too much smiling."

She picked up an illustrated paper and opened it at a page filled by an ornate picture.

"See!" she said. "It is because he himself has made it so easy, with his amazing portraits of his big boots, and swords, and eruption of dangling orders. How can one help but smile when one finds him glaring at one from a newspaper in his superwarlike attitude, defying the Universe, with his comic moustachios and their ferocious waxed and bristling ends. No! One can scarcely believe that a man can be stupid enough not to realize that he looks as if he had deliberately made himself up to represent a sort of terrific military bogey intimating that, at he may pounce and say 'Boo?'"

"There lies the peril. His pretensions seem too grotesque to be treated seriously. And, while he should be watched as a madman is watched, he is given a lifetime to we attack on a world that has ceased to believe in the sole thing which is real to himself."

"You are fresh from observation." There was new alertness in her eyes, though she had listened before.

"I tell you it GROWS!" he gave back and lightly struck the table in emphasis. "Do you remember Carlyle--?"

"The French Revolution again?"

"Yes. Do you recall this? 'Do not fires, fevers, seeds, chemical mixtures, GO ON GROWING. Observe, too, that EACH GROWS with a rapidity proportioned to the madness and unhealthiness there is in it.' A ruler who, in an unaggressive age such as this, can concentrate his life and his people's on the one ambition of plunging the world in an ocean of blood, in which his own monomania can bathe in triumph--Good God! there is madness and unhealthiness to flourish in!"

"The world!" she said. "Yes--it will be the world."

"See," he said, with a curve of the finger which included most of the Map of Europe. "Here are countries engaged--like the Bandarlog--in their own affairs. Quarrelling, snatching things from each other, blustering or amusing themselves with transitory pomps and displays of power. Here is a huge empire whose immense, half-savage population has seethed for centuries in its hidden, boiling cauldron of rebellion. Oh! it has seethed! And only cruelties have repressed it. Now and then it has boiled over in assassination in high places, and one has wondered how long its autocratic splendour could hold its own. Here are small, fierce, helpless nations overrun and outraged into a chronic state of secret ever-ready hatred. Here are innocent, small countries, defenceless through their position and size. Here is France rich, careless, super-modern and cynic. Here is England comfortable to stolidity, prosperous and secure to dullness in her own half belief in a world civilization, which no longer argues in terms of blood and steel. And here--in a well-entrenched position in the midst of it all--within but a few hundreds of miles of weakness, complicity, disastrous unreadiness and panic-stricken uncertainty of purpose, sits this Man of One Dream--who believes God Himself his vassal. Here he sits."

"Yes his One Dream. He has had no other." The Duchess was poring over the map also. They were as people pondering over a strange and terrible game.

"It is his monomania. It possessed him when he was a boy. What Napoleon hoped to accomplish he has BELIEVED he could attain by concentrating all the power of people upon preparation for it--and by not flinching from pouring forth their blood as if it were the refuse water of his gutters."

"Yes--the blood--the blood!" the Duchess shuddered. "He would pour it forth without a qualm."

Coombe touched the map first at one point and then at another.

"See!" he said again, and this time savagely. "This empire flattered and entangled by cunning, this country irritated, this deceived, this drawn into argument, this and this and this treated with professed friendship, these tricked and juggled with--And then, when his plans are ripe and he is made drunk with belief in himself--just one sodden insult or monstrous breach of faith, which all humanity must leap to resent--And there is our World Revolution."

The Duchess sat upright in her chair.

"Why did you let your youth pass?" she said. "If you had begun early enough, you could hare made the country listen to you. Why did you do it?"

"For the same reason that all selfish grief and pleasure and indifference let the world go by. And I am not sure they would have listened. I speak freely enough now in some quarters. They listen, but they do nothing. There is a warning in the fact that, as he has seen his youth leave him without giving him his opportunity, he has been a disappointed man inflamed and made desperate. At the outset, he felt that he must provide the world with some fiction of excuse. As his obsession and arrogance have swollen, he sees himself and his ambition as reason enough. No excuse is needed. Deutschland uber alles--is sufficient."

He pushed the map away and his fire died down. He spoke almost in his usual manner.

"The conquest of the world," he said. "He is a great fool. What would he DO with his continents if he got them?"

"What, indeed," pondered her grace. "Continents--even kingdoms are not like kittens in a basket, or puppies to be trained to come to heel."

"It is part of his monomania that he can persuade himself that they are little more." Coombe's eye-glasses had been slowly swaying from the ribbon in his fingers. He let them continue to sway a moment and then closed them with a snap.

"He is a great fool," he said. "But we,--oh, my friend--and by 'we' I mean the rest of the Map of Europe--we are much greater fools. A mad dog loose among us and we sit--and smile."

And this was in the days before the house with the cream-coloured front had put forth its first geraniums and lobelias in Feather's window boxes. Robin was not born.

CHAPTER XVIII

In the added suite of rooms at the back of the house, Robin grew through the years in which It was growing also. On the occasion when her mother saw her, she realized that she was not at least going to look like a barmaid. At no period of her least refulgent moment did she verge upon this type. Dowie took care of her and Mademoiselle Valle educated her with the assistance of certain masters who came to give lessons in German and Italian.

"Why only German and Italian and French," said Feather, "why not Latin and Greek, as well, if she is to be so accomplished?"

"It is modern languages one needs at this period. They ought to be taught in the Board Schools," Coombe replied. "They are not accomplishments but workman's tools. Nationalities are not separated as they once were. To be familiar with the language of one's friends--and one's enemies--is a protective measure."

"What country need one protect oneself against? When all the kings and queens are either married to each other's daughters or cousins or take tea with each other every year or so. Just think of the friendliness of Germany for instance----"

"I do," said Coombe, "very often. That is one of the reasons I choose German rather than Latin and Greek. Julius Caesar and Nero are no longer reasons for alarm."

"Is the Kaiser with his seventeen children and his respectable Frau?" giggled Feather. "All that he cares about is that women shall be made to remember that they are born for nothing but to cook and go to church and have babies. One doesn't wonder at the clothes they wear."

It was not a month after this, however, when Lord Coombe, again warming himself at his old friend's fire, gave her a piece of information.

"The German teacher, Herr Wiese, has hastily returned to his own country," he said.

She lifted her eyebrows inquiringly.

"He found himself suspected of being a spy," was his answer. "With most excellent reason. Some first-rate sketches of fortifications were found in a box he left behind him in his haste. The country--all countries--are sown with those like him. Mild spectacled students and clerks in warehouses and manufactories are weighing and measuring resources; round-faced, middle-aged governesses are making notes of conversation and of any other thing which may be useful. In time of war--if they were caught at what are now their simple daily occupations--they would be placed against a wall and shot. As it is, they are allowed to play about among us and slip away when some fellow worker's hint suggests it is time."

"German young men are much given to spending a year or so here in business positions," the Duchess wore a thoughtful air. "That has been going on for a decade or so. One recognizes their Teuton type in shops and in the streets. They say they come to learn the language and commercial methods."

"Not long ago a pompous person, who is the owner of a big shop, pointed out to me three of them among his salesmen," Coombe said. "He plumed himself on his astuteness in employing them. Said they worked for low wages and cared for very little else but finding out how things were done in England. It wasn't only business knowledge they were after, he said; they went about everywhere--into factories and dock yards, and public buildings, and made funny little notes and sketches of things they didn't understand--so that they could explain them in Germany. In his fatuous, insular way, it pleased him to regard them rather as a species of aborigines benefiting by English civilization. The English Ass and the German Ass are touchingly alike. The shade of difference is that the English Ass's sublime self-satisfaction is in the German Ass self-glorification. The English Ass smirks and plumes himself; the German Ass blusters and bullies and defies."

"Do you think of engaging another German Master for the little girl?" the Duchess asked the question casually.

"I have heard of a quiet young woman who has shown herself thorough and well-behaved in a certain family for three years. Perhaps she also will disappear some day, but, for the present, she will serve the purpose."

As he had not put into words to others any explanation of the story of the small, smart establishment in the Mayfair street, so he had put into words no explanation to her. That she was aware of its existence he knew, but what she thought of it, or imagined he himself thought of it, he had not at any period inquired. Whatsoever her point of view might be, he knew it would be unbiassed, clear minded and wholly just. She had asked no question and made no comment. The rapid, whirligig existence of the well-known fashionable groups, including in their circles varieties of the Mrs. Gareth-Lawless type, were to be seen at smart functions and to be read of in newspapers and fashion reports, if one's taste lay in the direction of a desire to follow their movements. The time had passed when pretty women of her kind were cut off by severities of opinion from the delights of a world they had thrown their dice daringly to gain. The worldly old axiom, "Be virtuous and you will be happy," had been ironically paraphrased too often. "Please yourself and you will be much happier than if you were virtuous," was a practical reading.

But for a certain secret which she alone knew and which no one would in the least have believed, if she had proclaimed it from the housetops, Feather would really have been entirely happy. And, after all, the fly in her ointment was merely an odd sting a fantastic Fate had inflicted on her vanity and did not in any degree affect her pleasures. So many people lived in glass houses that the habit of throwing stones had fallen out of fashion as an exercise. There were those, too, whose houses of glass, adroitly given the air of being respectable conservatories, engendered in the dwellers therein a leniency towards other vitreous constructions. As a result of this last circumstance, there were times when quite stately equipages drew up before Mrs. Gareth-Lawless' door and visiting cards bearing the names of acquaintances much to be desired were left upon the salver presented by Jennings. Again, as a result of this circumstance, Feather employed some laudable effort in her desire to give her own glass house the conservatory aspect. Her little parties became less noisy, if they still remained lively. She gave an "afternoon" now and then to which literary people and artists, and persons who "did things" were invited. She was pretty enough to allure an occasional musician to "do something", some new poet to read or recite. Fashionable people were asked to come and hear and talk to them, and, in this way, she threw out delicate fishing lines here and there, and again and again drew up a desirable fish of substantial size. Sometimes the vague rumour connected with the name of the Head of the House of Coombe was quite forgotten and she was referred to amiably as "That beautiful creature, Mrs. Gareth-Lawless." She was left a widow when she was nothing but a girl. If she hadn't had a little money of her own, and if her husband's relatives hadn't taken care of her, she would have had a hard time of it. She is amazingly clever at managing her, small income, they added. Her tiny house is one of the jolliest little places in London--always full of good looking people and amusing things.

But, before Robin was fourteen, she had found out that the house she lived in was built of glass and that any chance stone would break its panes, even if cast without particular skill in aiming. She found it out in various ways, but the seed from which all things sprang to the fruition of actual knowledge was the child tragedy through which she had learned that Donal had been taken from her--because his mother would not let him love and play with a little girl whose mother let Lord Coombe come to her house--because Lord Coombe was so bad that even servants whispered secrets about him. Her first interpretation of this had been that of a mere baby, but it had filled her being with detestation of him, and curious doubts of her mother. Donal's mother, who was good and beautiful, would not let him come to see her and kept Donal away from him. If the Lady Downstairs was good, too, then why did laugh and talk to him and seem to like him? She had thought this over for hours--sometimes wakening in the night to lie and puzzle over it feverishly. Then, as time went by, she had begun to remember that she had never played with any of the children in the Square Gardens. It had seemed as though this had been because Andrews would not let her. But, if she was not fit to play with Donal, perhaps the nurses and governesses and mothers of the other children knew about it and would not trust their little girls and boys to her damaging society. She did not know what she could have done to harm them--and Oh! how COULD she have harmed Donal!--but there must be something dreadful about a child whose mother knew bad people--something which other children could "catch" like scarlet fever. From this seed other thoughts had grown. She did not remain a baby long. A fervid little brain worked for her, picked up hints and developed suggestions, set her to singularly alert reasoning which quickly became too mature for her age. The quite horrid little girl, who flouncingly announced that she could not be played with any more "because of Lord Coombe" set a spark to a train. After that time she used to ask occasional carefully considered questions of Dowson and Mademoiselle Valle, which puzzled them by their vagueness. The two women were mutually troubled by a moody habit she developed of sitting absorbed in her own thoughts, and with a concentrated little frown drawing her brows together. They did not know that she was silently planning a subtle cross examination of them both, whose form would be such that neither of them could suspect it of being anything but innocent. She felt that she was growing cunning and deceitful, but she did not care very much. She possessed a clever and determined, though very young brain. She loved both Dowson and Mademoiselle, but she must find out about things for herself, and she was not going to harm or trouble them. They would never know she had found out: Whatsoever she discovered, she would keep to herself.

But one does not remain a baby long, and one is a little girl only a few years, and, even during the few years, one is growing and hearing and seeing all the time. After that, one is beginning to be a rather big girl and one has seen books and newspapers, and overheard scraps of things from servants. If one is brought up in a convent and allowed to read nothing but literature selected by nuns, a degree of aloofness from knowledge may be counted upon--though even convent schools, it is said, encounter their difficulties in perfect discipline.

Robin, in her small "Palace" was well taken care of but her library was not selected by nuns. It was chosen with thought, but it was the library of modern youth. Mademoiselle Valle's theories of a girl's education were not founded on a belief that, until marriage, she should be led about by a string blindfolded, and with ears stopped with wax.

"That results in a bleating lamb's being turned out of its fold to make its way through a jungle full of wild creatures and pitfalls it has never heard of," she said in discussing the point with Dowson. She had learned that Lord Coombe agreed with her. He, as well as she, chose the books and his taste was admirable. Its inclusion of an unobtrusive care for girlhood did not preclude the exercise of the intellect. An early developed passion for reading led the child far and wide. Fiction, history, poetry, biography, opened up vistas to a naturally quick and eager mind. Mademoiselle found her a clever pupil and an affection-inspiring little being even from the first.

She always felt, however, that in the depths of her something held itself hidden--something she did not speak of. It was some thought which perhaps bewildered her, but which something prevented her making clear to herself by the asking of questions. Mademoiselle Valle finally became convinced that she never would ask the questions.

Arrived a day when Feather swept into the Palace with some visitors. They were two fair and handsome little girls of thirteen and fourteen, whose mother, having taken them shopping, found it would suit her extremely well to drop then somewhere for an hour while she went to her dressmaker. Feather was quite willing that they should be left with Robin and Mademoiselle until their own governess called for them.

"Here are Eileen and Winifred Erwyn, Robin," she said, bringing them in. "Talk to them and show them your books and things until the governess comes. Dowson, give them some cakes and tea."

Mrs. Erwyn was one of the most treasured of Feather's circle. Her little girls' governess was a young Frenchwoman, entirely unlike Mademoiselle Valle. Eileen and Winifred saw Life from their schoolroom windows as an open book. Why not, since their governess and their mother's French maid conversed freely, and had rather penetrating voices even when they were under the impression that they lowered them out of deference to blameless youth. Eileen and Winifred liked to remain awake to listen as long as they could after they went to bed. They themselves had large curious eyes and were given to whispering and giggling.

They talked a good deal to Robin and assumed fashionable little grown up airs. They felt themselves mature creatures as compared to her, since she was not yet thirteen. They were so familiar with personages and functions that Robin felt that they must have committed to memory every morning the column in the Daily Telegraph known as "London Day by Day." She sometimes read it herself, because it was amusing to her to read about parties and weddings and engagements. But it did not seem easy to remember. Winifred and Eileen were delighted to display themselves in the character of instructresses. They entertained Robin for a short time, but, after that, she began to dislike the shared giggles which so often broke out after their introduction of a name or an incident. It seemed to hint that they were full of amusing information which they held back. Then they were curious and made remarks and asked questions. She began to think them rather horrid.

"We saw Lord Coombe yesterday," said Winifred at last, and the unnecessary giggle followed.

"We think he wears the most beautiful clothes we ever saw! You remember his overcoat, Winnie?" said Eileen. "He MATCHES so--and yet you don't know exactly how he matches," and she giggled also.

"He is the best dressed man in London," Winifred stated quite grandly. "I think he is handsome. So do Mademoiselle and Florine."

Robin said nothing at all. What Dowson privately called "her secret look" made her face very still. Winifred saw the look and, not understanding it or her, became curious.

"Don't you?" she said.

"No," Robin answered. "He has a wicked face. And he's old, too."

"You think he's old because you're only about twelve," inserted Eileen. "Children think everybody who is grown-up must be old. I used to. But now people don't talk and think about age as they used to. Mademoiselle says that when a man has distinction he is always young--and nicer than boys."

Winifred, who was persistent, broke in.

"As to his looking wicked, I daresay he IS wicked in a sort of interesting way. Of course, people say all sorts of things about him. When he was quite young, he was in love with a beautiful little royal Princess--or she was in love with him--and her husband either killed her or she died of a broken heart--I don't know which."

Mademoiselle Valle had left them for a short time feeling that they were safe with their tea and cakes and would feel more at ease relieved of her presence. She was not long absent, but Eileen and Winifred, being avid of gossip and generally eliminated subjects, "got in their work" with quite fevered haste. They liked the idea of astonishing Robin.

Eileen bent forward and lowered her voice.

"They do say that once Captain Thorpe was fearfully jealous of him and people wonder that he wasn't among the co-respondents." The word "co-respondent" filled her with self-gratulation even though she only whispered it.

"Co-respondents?" said Robin.

They both began to whisper at once--quite shrilly in their haste. They knew Mademoiselle might return at any moment.

"The great divorce case, you know! The Thorpe divorce case the papers are so full of. We get the under housemaid to bring it to us after Mademoiselle has done with it. It's so exciting! Haven't you been reading it? Oh!"

"No, I haven't," answered Robin. "And I don't know about co-respondents, but, if they are anything horrid, I daresay he WAS one of them."

And at that instant Mademoiselle returned and Dowson brought in fresh cakes. The governess, who was to call for her charges, presented herself not long afterwards and the two enterprising little persons were taken away.

"I believe she's JEALOUS of Lord Coombe," Eileen whispered to Winifred, after they reached home.

"So do I," said Winifred wisely. "She can't help but know how he ADORES Mrs. Gareth-Lawless because she's so lovely. He pays for all her pretty clothes. It's silly of her to be jealous--like a baby."

Robin sometimes read newspapers, though she liked books better. Newspapers were not forbidden her. She been reading an enthralling book and had not seen a paper for some days. She at once searched for one and, finding it, sat down and found also the Thorpe Divorce Case. It was not difficult of discovery, as it filled the principal pages with dramatic evidence and amazing revelations.

Dowson saw her bending over the spread sheets, hot-eyed and intense in her concentration.

"What are you reading, my love?" she asked.

The little flaming face lifted itself. It was unhappy, obstinate, resenting. It wore no accustomed child look and Dowson felt rather startled.

"I'm reading the Thorpe Divorce Case, Dowie," she answered deliberately and distinctly.

Dowie came close to her.

"It's an ugly thing to read, my lamb," she faltered. "Don't you read it. Such things oughtn't to be allowed in newspapers. And you're a little girl, my own dear." Robin's elbow rested firmly on the table and her chin firmly in her hand. Her eyes were not like a bird's.

"I'm nearly thirteen," she said. "I'm growing up. Nobody can stop themselves when they begin to grow up. It makes them begin to find out things. I want to ask you something, Dowie."

"Now, lovey--!" Dowie began with tremor. Both she and Mademoiselle had been watching the innocent "growing up" and fearing a time would come when the widening gaze would see too much. Had it come as soon as this?

Robin suddenly caught the kind woman's wrists in her hands and held them while she fixed her eyes on her. The childish passion of dread and shyness in them broke Dowson's heart because it was so ignorant and young.

"I'm growing up. There's something--I MUST know something! I never knew how to ask about it before." It was so plain to Dowson that she did not know how to ask about it now. "Someone said that Lord Coombe might have been a co-respondent in the Thorpe case----"

"These wicked children!" gasped Dowie. "They're not children at all!"

"Everybody's horrid but you and Mademoiselle," cried Robin, brokenly. She held the wrists harder and ended in a sort of outburst. "If my father were alive--could he bring a divorce suit----And would Lord Coombe----"

Dowson burst into open tears. And then, so did Robin. She dropped Dowson's wrists and threw her arms around her waist, clinging to it in piteous repentance.

"No, I won't!" she cried out. "I oughtn't to try to make you tell me. You can't. I'm wicked to you. Poor Dowie--darling Dowie! I want to KISS you, Dowie! Let me--let me!"

She sobbed childishly on the comfortable breast and Dowie hugged her close and murmured in a choked voice,

"My lamb! My pet lamb!"

CHAPTER XIX

Mademoiselle Valle and Dowson together realized that after this the growing up process was more rapid. It always seems incredibly rapid to lookers on, after thirteen. But these two watchers felt that, in Robin's case, it seemed unusually so. Robin had always been interested in her studies and clever at them, but, suddenly, she developed a new concentration and it was of an order which her governess felt denoted the secret holding of some object in view. She devoted herself to her lessons with a quality of determination which was new. She had previously been absorbed, but not determined. She made amazing strides and seemed to aspire to a thoroughness and perfection girls did not commonly aim at--especially at the frequently rather preoccupied hour of blossoming. Mademoiselle encountered in her an eagerness that she--who knew girls--would have felt it optimistic to expect in most cases. She wanted to work over hours; she would have read too much if she had not been watched and gently coerced.

She was not distracted by the society of young people of her own age. She, indeed, showed a definite desire to avoid such companionship. What she said to Mademoiselle Valle one afternoon during a long walk they took together, held its own revelation for the older woman.

They had come upon the two Erwyns walking with their attendant in Kensington Gardens, and, seeing them at some distance, Robin asked her companion to turn into another walk.

"I don't want to meet them," she said, hurriedly. "I don't think I like girls. Perhaps it's horrid of me--but I don't. I don't like those two." A few minutes later, after they had walked in an opposite direction, she said thoughtfully.

"Perhaps the kind of girls I should like to know would not like to know me."

From the earliest days of her knowledge of Lord Coombe, Mademoiselle Valle had seen that she had no cause to fear lack of comprehension on his part. With a perfection of method, they searched each other's intelligence. It had become understood that on such occasions as there was anything she wished to communicate or inquire concerning, Mr. Benby, in his private room, was at Mademoiselle's service, and there his lordship could also be met personally by appointment.

"There have been no explanations," Mademoiselle Valle said to Dowson. "He does not ask to know why I turn to him and I do not ask to know why he cares about this particular child. It is taken for granted that is his affair and not mine. I am paid well to take care of Robin, and he knows that all I say and do is part of my taking care of her."

After the visit of the Erwyn children, she had a brief interview with Coombe, in which she made for him a clear sketch. It was a sketch of unpleasant little minds, avid and curious on somewhat exotic subjects, little minds, awake to rather common claptrap and gossipy pinchbeck interests.

"Yes--unpleasant, luckless, little persons. I quite understand. They never appeared before. They will not appear again. Thank you, Mademoiselle," he said.

The little girls did not appear again; neither did any others of their type, and the fact that Feather knew little of other types was a sufficient reason for Robin's growing up without companions of her own age.

"She's a lonely child, after all," Mademoiselle said.

"She always was," answered Dowie. "But she's fond of us, bless her heart, and it isn't loneliness like it was before we came."

"She is not unhappy. She is too blooming and full of life," Mademoiselle reflected. "We adore her and she has many interests. It is only that she does not know the companionship most young people enjoy. Perhaps, as she has never known it, she does not miss it."

The truth was that if the absence of intercourse with youth produced its subtle effect on her, she was not aware of any lack, and a certain uncompanioned habit of mind, which gave her much time for dreams and thought, was accepted by her as a natural condition as simply as her babyhood had accepted the limitations of the Day and Night Nurseries.

She was not a self-conscious creature, but the time came when she became rather disturbed by the fact that people looked at her very often, as she walked in the streets. Sometimes they turned their heads to look after her; occasionally one person walking with another would say something quietly to his or her companion, and they even paused a moment to turn quite round and look. The first few times she noticed this she flushed prettily and said nothing to Mademoiselle Valle who was generally with her. But, after her attention had been attracted by the same thing on several different days, she said uneasily:

"Am I quite tidy, Mademoiselle?"

"Quite," Mademoiselle answered--just a shade uneasy herself.

"I began to think that perhaps something had come undone or my hat was crooked," she explained. "Those two women stared so. Then two men in a hansom leaned forward and one said something to the other, and they both laughed a little, Mademoiselle!" hurriedly, "Now, there are three young men!" quite indignantly. "Don't let them see you notice them--but I think it RUDE!"

They were carelessly joyous and not strictly well-bred youths, who were taking a holiday together, and their rudeness was quite unintentional and without guile. They merely stared and obviously muttered comments to each other as they passed, each giving the hasty, unconscious touch to his young moustache, which is the automatic sign of pleasurable observation in the human male.

"If she had had companions of her own age she would have known all about it long ago," Mademoiselle was thinking.

Her intelligent view of such circumstances was that the simple fact they arose from could--with perfect taste--only be treated simply. It was a mere fact; therefore, why be prudish and affected about it.

"They did not intend any rudeness," she said, after they had gone by. "They are not much more than boys and not perfectly behaved. People often stare when they see a very pretty girl. I am afraid I do it myself. You are very pretty," quite calmly, and as one speaking without prejudice.

Robin turned and looked at her, and the colour, which was like a Jacqueminot rose, flooded her face. She was at the flushing age. Her gaze was interested, speculative, and a shade startled--merely a shade.

"Oh," she said briefly--not in exclamation exactly, but in a sort of acceptance. Then she looked straight before her and went on walking, with the lovely, slightly swaying, buoyant step which in itself drew attracted eyes after her.

"If I were a model governess, such as one read of long before you were born," Mademoiselle Valle continued, "I should feel it my duty to tell you that beauty counts for nothing. But that is nonsense. It counts a great deal--with some women it counts for everything. Such women are not lucky. One should thank Heaven for it and make the best of it, without exaggerated anxiety. Both Dowie and I, who love you, are GRATEFUL to le bon Dieu that you are pretty."

"I have sometimes thought I was pretty, when I saw myself in the glass," said Robin, with unexcited interest. "It seemed to me that I LOOKED pretty. But, at the same time, I couldn't help knowing that everything is a matter of taste and that it might be because I was conceited."

"You are not conceited," answered the Frenchwoman.

"I don't want to be," said Robin. "I want to be--a serious person with--with a strong character."

Mademoiselle's smile was touched with affectionate doubt. It had not occurred to her to view this lovely thing in the light of a "strong" character. Though, after all, what exactly was strength? She was a warm, intensely loving, love compelling, tender being. Having seen much of the world, and of humanity and inhumanity, Mademoiselle Valle had had moments of being afraid for her--particularly when, by chance, she recalled the story Dowson had told her of the bits of crushed and broken leaves.

"A serious person," she said, "and strong?"

"Because I must earn my own living," said Robin. "I must be strong enough to take care of myself. I am going to be a governess--or something."

Here, it was revealed to Mademoiselle as in a flash, was the reason why she had applied herself with determination to her studies. This had been the object in view. For reasons of her own, she intended to earn her living. With touched inter-est, Mademoiselle Valle waited, wondering if she would be frank about the reason. She merely said aloud:

"A governess?"

"Perhaps there may be something else I can do. I might be a secretary or some-thing like that. Girls and women are beginning to do so many new things," her charge explained herself. "I do not want to be--supported and given money. I mean

I do not want--other people--to buy my clothes and food--and things. The newspapers are full of advertisements. I could teach children. I could translate business letters. Very soon I shall be old enough to begin. Girls in their teens do it."

She had laid some of her cards on the table, but not all, poor child. She was not going into the matter of her really impelling reasons. But Mademoiselle Valle was not dull, and her affection added keenness to her mental observations. Also she had naturally heard the story of the Thorpe lawsuit from Dowson. Inevitably several points suggested themselves to her.

"Mrs. Gareth-Lawless----" she began, reasonably.

But Robin stopped her by turning her face full upon her once more, and this time her eyes were full of clear significance.

"She will let me go," she said. "You KNOW she will let me go, Mademoiselle, darling. You KNOW she will." There was a frank comprehension and finality in the words which made a full revelation of facts Mademoiselle herself had disliked even to allow to form themselves into thoughts. The child knew all sorts of things and felt all sorts of things. She would probably never go into details, but she was extraordinarily, harrowingly, AWARE. She had been learning to be aware for years. This had been the secret she had always kept to herself.

"If you are planning this," Mademoiselle said, as reasonably as before, "we must work very seriously for the news few years."

"How long do you think it will take?" asked Robin. She was nearing sixteen--bursting into glowing blossom--a radiant, touching thing whom one only could visualize in flowering gardens, in charming, enclosing rooms, figuratively embraced by every mature and kind arm within reach of her. This presented itself before Mademoiselle Valle with such vividness that it was necessary for her to control a sigh.

"When I feel that you are ready, I will tell you," she answered. "And I will do all I can to help you--before I leave you."

"Oh!" Robin gasped, in an involuntarily childish way, "I--hadn't thought of that! How could I LIVE without you--and Dowie?"

"I know you had not thought of it," said Mademoiselle, affectionately. "You are only a dear child yet. But that will be part of it, you know. A governess or a secretary, or a young lady in an office translating letters cannot take her governess and maid with her."

"Oh!" said Robin again, and her eyes became suddenly so dewy that the person who passed her at the moment thought he had never seen such wonderful eyes in his life. So much of her was still child that the shock of this sudden practical realization thrust the mature and determined part of her being momentarily into the background, and she could scarcely bear her alarmed pain. It was true that she had been too young to face her plan as she must.

But, after the long walk was over and she found herself in her bedroom again, she was conscious of a sense of being relieved of a burden. She had been wondering when she could tell Mademoiselle and Dowie of her determination. She had not liked to keep it a secret from them as if she did not love them, but it had been difficult to think of a way in which to begin without seeming as if she thought she was quite grown up--which would have been silly. She had not thought of speaking today, but it had all come about quite naturally, as a result of Mademoiselle's having told her that she was really very pretty--so pretty that it made people turn to look at her in the street. She had heard of girls and women who were like that, but she had never thought it possible that she----! She had, of course, been looked at when she was very little, but she had heard Andrews say that people looked because she had so much hair and it was like curled silk.

She went to the dressing table and looked at herself in the glass, leaning forward that she might see herself closely. The face which drew nearer and nearer had the effect of some tropic flower, because it was so alive with colour which seemed to palpitate instead of standing still. Her soft mouth was warm and brilliant with it, and the darkness of her eyes was--as it had always been--like dew. Her brow were a slender black velvet line, and her lashes made a thick, softening shadow. She saw they were becoming. She cupped her round chin in her hands and studied herself with a desire to be sure of the truth without prejudice or self conceit. The whole effect of her was glowing, and she felt the glow as others did. She put up a finger to touch the velvet petal texture of her skin, and she saw how prettily pointed and slim her hand was. Yes, that was pretty--and her hair--the way it grew about her forehead and ears and the back of her neck. She gazed at her young curve and colour and flame of life's first beauty with deep curiosity, singularly impersonal for her years.

She liked it; she began to be grateful as Mademoiselle had said she and Dowie were. Yes, if other people liked it, there was no use in pretending it would not count.

"If I am going to earn my living," she thought, with entire gravity, "it may be good for me. If I am a governess, it will be useful because children like pretty people. And if I am a secretary and work in an office, I daresay men like one to be pretty because it is more cheerful."

She mentioned this to Mademoiselle Valle, who was very kind about it, though she looked thoughtful afterwards. When, a few days later, Mademoiselle had an interview with Coombe in Benby's comfortable room, he appeared thoughtful also as he listened to her recital of the incidents of the long walk during which her charge had revealed her future plans.

"She is a nice child," he said. "I wish she did not dislike me so much. I understand her, villain as she thinks me. I am not a genuine villain," he added, with his cold smile. But he was saying it to himself, not to Mademoiselle.

This, she saw, but--singularly, perhaps--she spoke as if in reply.

"Of that I am aware."

He turned his head slightly, with a quick, unprepared movement.

"Yes?" he said.

"Would your lordship pardon me if I should say that otherwise I should not ask your advice concerning a very young girl?"

He slightly waved his hand.

"I should have known that--if I had thought of it. I do know it."

Mademoiselle Valle bowed.

"The fact," she said, "that she seriously thinks that perhaps beauty may be an advantage to a young person who applies for work in the office of a man of business because it may seem bright and cheerful to him when he is tired and out of spirits--that gives one furiously to think. Yes, to me she said it, milord--with the eyes of a little dove brooding over her young. I could see her--lifting them like an angel to some elderly vaurien, who would merely think her a born cocotte."

Here Coombe's rigid face showed thought indeed.

"Good God!" he muttered, quite to himself, "Good God!" in a low, breathless voice. Villain or saint, he knew not one world but many.

"We must take care of her," he said next. "She is not an insubordinate child. She will do nothing yet?"

"I have told her she is not yet ready," Mademoiselle Valle answered. "I have also promised to tell her when she is--And to help her."

"God help her if we do not!" he said. "She is, on the whole, as ignorant as a little sheep--and butchers are on the lookout for such as she is. They suit them even better than the little things whose tendencies are perverse from birth. An old man with an evil character may be able to watch over her from a distance."

Mademoiselle regarded him with grave eyes, which took in his tall, thin erectness of figure, his bearing, the perfection of his attire with its unfailing freshness, which was not newness.

"Do you call yourself an old man, milord?" she asked.

"I am not decrepit--years need not bring that," was his answer. "But I believe I became an old man before I was thirty. I have grown no older--in that which is really age--since then."

In the moment's silence which followed, his glance met Mademoiselle Valle's and fixed itself.

"I am not old enough--or young enough--to be enamoured of Mrs. Gareth-Lawless' little daughter," he said. "YOU need not be told that. But you have heard that there are those who amuse themselves by choosing to believe that I am."

"A few light and not too clean-minded fools," she admitted without flinching.

"No man can do worse for himself than to explain and deny," he responded with a smile at once hard and fine. "Let them continue to believe it."

CHAPTER XX

Sixteen passed by with many other things much more disturbing and important to the world than a girl's birthday; seventeen was gone, with passing events more complicated still and increasingly significant, but even the owners of the hands hovering over the Chessboard, which was the Map of Europe, did not keep a watch on all of them as close as might have been kept with advantage. Girls in their teens are seldom interested in political and diplomatic conditions, and Robin was not fond of newspapers. She worked well and steadily under Mademoiselle's guidance, and her governess realized that she was not losing sight of her plans for self support. She was made aware of this by an occasional word or so, and also by a certain telepathic union between them. Little as she cared for the papers, the child had a habit of closely examining the advertisements every day. She read faithfully the columns devoted to those who "Want" employment or are "Wanted" by employers.

"I look at all the paragraphs which begin 'Wanted, a young lady' or a 'young woman' or a 'young person,' and those which say that 'A young person' or 'a young woman' or 'a young lady' desires a position. I want to find out what is oftenest needed."

She had ceased to be disturbed by the eyes which followed her, or opened a little as she passed. She knew that nothing had come undone or was crooked and that untidiness had nothing to do with the matter. She accepted being looked at as a part of everyday life. A certain friendliness and pleasure in most of the glances she liked and was glad of. Sometimes men of the flushed, middle-aged or elderly type displeased her by a sort of boldness of manner and gaze, bet she thought that they were only silly, giddy, old things who ought to go home to their families and stay with than. Mademoiselle or Dowie was nearly always with her, but, as she was not a French jemme fille, this was not because it was supposed that she could not be trusted out alone, but because she enjoyed their affectionate companionship.

There was one man, however, whom she greatly disliked, as young girls will occasionally dislike a member of the opposite sex for no special reason they can wholly explain to themselves.

He was an occasional visitor of her mother's--a personable young Prussian officer of high rank and title. He was blonde and military and good-looking; he brought his bearing and manner from the Court at Berlin, and the click of his heels as he brought them smartly together, when he made his perfect automatic bow, was one of the things Robin knew she was reasonless in feeling she detested in him.

"It makes me feel as if he was not merely bowing as a a man who is a gentleman does," she confided to Mademoiselle Valle, "but as if he had been taught to do it and to call attention to it as if no one had ever known how to do it properly before. It is so flourishing in its stiff way that it's rather vulgar."

"That is only personal fancy on your part," commented Mademoiselle.

"I know it is," admitted Robin. "But--" uneasily, "--but that isn't what I dislike in him most. It's his eyes, I suppose they are handsome eyes. They are blue and full--rather too full. They have a queer, swift stare--as if they plunged into other people's eyes and tried to hold them and say something secret, all in one second. You find yourself getting red and trying to look away."

"I don't," said Mademoiselle astutely--because she wanted to hear the rest, without asking too many questions.

Robin laughed just a little.

"You have not seen him do it. I have not seen him do it myself very often. He comes to call on--Mamma"--she never said "Mother"--"when he is in London. He has been coming for two or three seasons. The first time I saw him I was going out with Dowie and he was just going upstairs. Because the hall is so small, we almost knocked against each other, and he jumped back and made his bow, and he stared so that I felt silly and half frightened. I was only fifteen then."

"And since then?" Mademoiselle Valle inquired.

"When he is here it seems as if I always meet him somewhere. Twice, when Fraulein Hirsch was with me in the Square Gardens, he came and spoke to us. I think he must know her. He was very grand and condescendingly polite to her, as if he did not forget she was only a German teacher and I was only a little girl whose mamma he knew. But he kept looking at me until I began to hate him."

"You must not dislike people without reason. You dislike Lord Coombe."

"They both make me creep. Lord Coombe doesn't plunge his eyes into mine, but he makes me creep with his fishy coldness. I feel as if he were like Satan in his still way."

"That is childish prejudice and nonsense."

"Perhaps the other is, too," said Robin. "But they both make me creep, nevertheless. I would rather DIE than be obliged to let one of them touch me. That was why I would never shake hands with Lord Coombe when I was a little child."

"You think Fraulein Hirsch knows the Baron?" Mademoiselle inquired further.

"I am sure she does. Several times, when she has gone out to walk with me, we have met him. Sometimes he only passes us and salutes, but sometimes he stops and says a few words in a stiff, magnificent way. But he always bores his eyes into mine, as if he were finding out things about me which I don't know myself. He has passed several times when you have been with me, but you may not remember."

Mademoiselle Valle chanced, however, to recall having observed the salute of a somewhat haughty, masculine person, whose military bearing in itself was sufficient to attract attention, so markedly did it suggest the clanking of spurs and accoutrements, and the high lift of a breast bearing orders.

"He is Count von Hillern, and I wish he would stay in Germany," said Robin.

Fraulein Hirsch had not been one of those who returned hastily to her own country, giving no warning of her intention to her employers. She had remained in London and given her lessons faithfully. She was a plain young woman with a large nose and pimpled, colourless face and shy eyes and manner. Robin had felt sure that she stood in awe of the rank and military grandeur of her fellow countryman. She looked shyer than ever when he condescended to halt and address her and her charge--so shy, indeed, that her glances seemed furtive. Robin guessed that she admired him but was too humble to be at ease when he was near her. More than once she had started and turned red and pale when she saw him approaching, which had caused Robin to wonder if she herself would feel as timid and overpowered by her superiors, if she became a governess. Clearly, a man like Count von Hillern would then be counted among her superiors, and she must conduct herself becomingly, even if it led to her looking almost stealthy. She had, on several occasions, asked Fraulein certain questions about governesses. She had inquired as to the age at which one could apply for a place as instructress to children or young girls. Fraulein Hirsch had begun her career in Germany at the age of eighteen. She had lived a serious life, full of responsibilities at home as one of a large family, and she had perhaps been rather mature for her age. In England young women who wished for situations answered advertisements and went to see the people who had inserted them in the newspapers, she explained. Sometimes, the results were very satisfactory. Fraulein Hirsch was very amiable in her readiness to supply information. Robin did not tell her of her intention to find work of some sort--probably governessing-- but the young German woman was possessed of a mind "made in Germany" and was quite well aware of innumerable things her charge did not suspect her of knowing. One of the things she knew best was that the girl was a child. She was not a child herself, and she was an abjectly bitter and wretched creature who had no reason for hope. She lived in small lodgings in a street off Abbey Road, and, in a drawer in her dressing table, she kept hidden a photograph of a Prussian officer with cropped blond head, and handsome prominent blue eyes, arrogantly gazing from beneath heavy lids which drooped. He was of the type the German woman, young and slim, or mature and stout, privately worships as a god whose relation to any woman can only be that of a modern Jove stooping to command service. In his teens he had become accustomed to the female eye which lifts itself adoringly or casts the furtively excited glance of admiration or appeal. It was the way of mere nature that it should be so--the wise provision of a masculine God, whose world was created for the supply and pleasure of males, especially males of the Prussian Army, whose fixed intention it was to dominate the world and teach it obedience.

To such a man, so thoroughly well trained in the comprehension of the power of his own rank and values, a young woman such as Fraulein Hirsch--subservient and without beauty--was an unconsidered object to be as little regarded as the pavement upon which one walks. The pavement had its uses, and such women had theirs. They could, at least, obey the orders of those Heaven had placed above them, and, if they showed docility and intelligence, might be re warded by a certain degree of approval.

A presumption, which would have dared to acknowledge to the existence of the hidden photograph, could not have been encompassed by the being of Fraulein Hirsch. She was, in truth, secretly enslaved by a burning, secret, heart-wringing passion which, sometimes, as she lay on her hard bed at night, forced from her thin chest hopeless sobs which she smothered under the bedclothes.

Figuratively, she would have licked the boots of her conquering god, if he would have looked at her--just looked-as if she were human. But such a thing could not have occurred to him. He did not even think of her as she thought of herself, torturingly--as not young, not in any degree good-looking, not geboren, not even female. He did not think of her at all, except as one of those born to serve in such manner as their superiors commanded. She was in England under orders, because she was unobtrusive looking enough to be a safe person to carry on the work she had been given to do. She was cleverer than she looked and could accomplish certain things without attracting any attention whatsoever.

Von Hillern had given her instructions now and then, which had made it necessary for him to see and talk to her in various places. The fact that she had before her the remote chance of seeing him by some chance, gave her an object in life. It was enough to be allowed to stand or sit for a short time near enough to have been able to touch his sleeve, if she had had the mad audacity to do it; to quail before his magnificent glance, to hear his voice, to ALMOST touch his strong, white hand when she gave him papers, to see that he deigned, sometimes, to approve of what she had done, to assure him of her continued obedience, with servile politeness.

She was not a nice woman, or a good one, and she had, from her birth, accepted her place in her world with such finality that her desires could not, at any time, have been of an elevated nature. If he had raised a haughty hand and beckoned to her, she would have followed him like a dog under any conditions he chose to impose. But he did not raise his hand, and never would, because she had no attractions whatsoever. And this she knew, so smothered her sobs in her bed at night or lay awake, fevered with anticipation when there was a vague chance that he might need her for some reason and command her presence in some deserted park or country road or cheap hotel, where she could take rooms for the night as if she were a passing visitor to London.

One night--she had taken cheap lodgings for a week in a side street, in obedience to orders--he came in about nine o'clock dressed in a manner whose object was to dull the effect of his grandeur and cause him to look as much like an ordinary Englishman as possible.

But, when the door was closed and he stood alone in the room with her, she saw, with the blissful pangs of an abjectly adoring woman, that he automatically resumed his magnificence of bearing. His badly fitting overcoat removed, he stood erect and drawn to his full height, so dominating the small place and her idolatrously cringing being that her heart quaked within her. Oh! to dare to cast her unloveliness at his feet, if it were only to be trampled upon and die there! No small sense of humour existed in her brain to save her from her pathetic idiocy. Romantic humility and touching sacrifice to the worshipped one were the ideals she had read of in verse and song all her life. Only through such servitude and sacrifice could woman gain man's love--and even then only if she had beauty and the gifts worthy of her idol's acceptance.

It was really his unmitigated arrogance she worshipped and crawled upon her poor, large-jointed knees to adore. Her education, her very religion itself had taught that it was the sign of his nobility and martial high breeding. Even the women of his own class believed something of the same sort--the more romantic and sentimental of them rather enjoying being mastered by it. To Fraulein Hirsch's mental vision, he was a sublimated and more dazzling German Rochester, and she herself a more worthy, because more submissive, Jane Eyre. Ach Gott! His high-held, cropped head--his so beautiful white hands--his proud eyes which deigned to look at her from their drooping lids! His presence filled the shabby room with the atmosphere of a Palace.

He asked her a few questions; he required from her certain notes she had made; without wasting a word or glance he gave her in detail certain further orders.

He stood by the table, and it was, therefore, necessary that she should approach him--should even stand quite near that she might see clearly a sketch he made hastily--immediately afterwards tearing it into fragments and burning it with a match. She was obliged to stand so near him that her skirt brushed his trouser leg. His nearness, and a vague scent of cigar smoke, mingled with the suggestion of some masculine soap or essence, were so poignant in their effect that she trembled and water rose in her eyes. In fact--and despite her terrified effort to control it, a miserable tear fell on her cheek and stood there because she dared not wipe it away.

Because he realized, with annoyance, that she was trembling, he cast a cold, inquiring glance at her and saw the tear. Then he turned away and resumed his examination of her notes. He was not here to make inquiries as to whether a sheep of a woman was crying or had merely a cold in her head. "Ach!" grovelled poor Hirsch in her secret soul,--his patrician control of outward expression and his indifference to all small and paltry things! It was part, not only of his aristocratic breeding, but of the splendour of his military training.

It was his usual custom to leave her at once, when the necessary formula had been gone through. Tonight--she scarcely dared to believe it--he seemed to have some reason for slight delay. He did not sit down or ask Fraulein Hirsch to do so-- but he did not at once leave the room. He lighted a quite marvellous cigar--deigning a slight wave of the admired hand which held it, designating that he asked permission. Oh! if she dared have darted to him with a match! He stood upon the hearth and asked a casual-sounding question or so regarding her employer, her household, her acquaintances, her habits.

The sole link between them was the asking of questions and the giving of private information, and, therefore, the matter of taste in such matters did not count as a factor. He might ask anything and she must answer. Perhaps it was necessary for her to seek some special knowledge among the guests Mrs. Gareth-Lawless received. But training, having developed in her alertness of mind, led her presently to see that it was not Mrs. Gareth-Lawless he was chiefly interested in--but a member of her family--the very small family which consisted of herself and her daughter.

It was Robin he was enclosing in his network of questions. And she had seen him look at Robin when he had passed or spoken to them. An illuminating flash brought back to her that he had cleverly found out from her when they were to walk together, and where they were to go. She had not been quick enough to detect this before, but she saw it now. Girls who looked like that--yes! But it could not be--serious. An English girl of such family--with such a mother! A momentary caprice, such as all young men of his class amused themselves with and forgot--but nothing permanent. It would not, indeed, be approved in those High Places where obedience was the first commandment of the Decalogue.

But he did not go. He even descended a shade from his inaccessible plane. It was not difficult for him to obtain details of the odd loneliness of the girl's position. Fraulein Hirsch was quite ready to explain that, in spite of the easy morals and leniency of rank and fashion in England, she was a sort of little outcast from sacred inner circles. There were points she burned to make clear to him, and she made them so. She was in secret fiercely desirous that he should realize to the utmost, that, whatsoever rashness this young flame of loveliness inspired in him, it was NOT possible that he could regard it with any shadow of serious intention. She had always disliked the girl, and now her weak mildness and humility suddenly transformed themselves into something else--a sort of maternal wolfishness. It did not matter what happened to the girl--and whatsoever befell or did not befall her, she--Mathilde Hirsch--could neither gain nor lose hope through it. But, if she did not displease him and yet saved him from final disaster, he would, perhaps, be grateful to her--and perhaps, speak with approval--or remember it--and his Noble Mother most certainly would--if she ever knew. But behind and under and through all these specious reasonings, was the hot choking burn of the mad jealousy only her type of luckless woman can know--and of whose colour she dare not show the palest hint.

"I have found out that, for some reason, she thinks of taking a place as governess," she said.

"Suggest that she go to Berlin. There are good places there," was his answer.

"If she should go, her mother will not feel any anxiety about her," returned Fraulein Hirsch.

"If, then, some young man she meets in the street makes love to her and they run away together, she will not be pursued by her relatives."

Fraulein Hirsch's flat mouth looked rather malicious.

"Her mother is too busy to pursue her, and there is no one else--unless it were Lord Coombe, who is said to want her himself."

Von Hillern shrugged his fine shoulders.

"At his age! After the mother! That is like an Englishman!"

Upon this, Fraulein Hirsch drew a step nearer and fixed her eyes upon his, as she had never had the joy of fixing them before in her life. She dared it now because she had an interesting story to tell him which he would like to hear. It WAS like an Englishman. Lord Coombe had the character of being one of the worst among them, but was too subtle and clever to openly offend people. It was actually said that he was educating the girl and keeping her in seclusion and that it was probably his colossal intention to marry her when she was old enough. He had no heir of his own--and he must have beauty and innocence. Innocence and beauty his viciousness would have.

"Pah!" exclaimed von Hillern. "It is youth which requires such things--and takes them. That is all imbecile London gossip. No, he would not run after her if she ran away. He is a proud man and he knows he would be laughed at. And he could not get her back from a young man--who was her lover."

Her lover! How it thrilled the burning heart her poor, flat chest panted above. With what triumphant knowledge of such things he said it.

"No, he could not," she answered, her eyes still on his. "No one could."

He laughed a little, confidently, but almost with light indifference.

"If she were missing, no particular search would be made then," he said. "She is pretty enough to suit Berlin."

He seemed to think pleasantly of something as he stood still for a moment, his eyes on the floor. When he lifted them, there was in their blue a hint of ugly exulting, though Mathilde Hirsch did not think it ugly. He spoke in a low voice.

"It will be an exciting--a colossal day when we come to London--as we shall. It will be as if an ocean had collected itself into one huge mountain of a wave and swept in and overwhelmed everything. There will be confusion then and the rushing up of untrained soldiers--and shouts--and yells----"

"And Zeppelins dropping bombs," she so far forgot herself as to pant out, "and buildings crashing and pavements and people smashed! Westminster and the Palaces rocking, and fat fools running before bayonets."

He interrupted her with a short laugh uglier than the gleam in his eyes. He was a trifle excited.

"And all the women running about screaming and trying to hide and being pulled out. We can take any of their pretty, little, high nosed women we choose--any of them."

"Yes," she answered, biting her lip. No one would take her, she knew.

He put on his overcoat and prepared to leave her. As he stood at the door before opening it, he spoke in his usual tone of mere command.

"Take her to Kensington Gardens tomorrow afternoon," he said. "Sit in one of the seats near the Round Pond and watch the children sailing their boats. I shall not be there but you will find yourself near a quiet, elegant woman in mourning who will speak to you. You are to appear to recognize her as an old acquaintance. Follow her suggestions in everything."

After this he was gone and she sat down to think it over.

CHAPTER XXI

She saw him again during the following week and was obliged to tell him that she had not been able to take her charge to Kensington Gardens on the morning that he had appointed but that, as the girl was fond of the place and took pleasure in watching the children sailing their boats on the Round Pond, it would be easy to lead her there. He showed her a photograph of the woman she would find sitting on a particular bench, and he required she should look at it long enough to commit the face to memory. It was that of a quietly elegant woman with gentle eyes.

"She will call herself Lady Etynge," he said. "You are to remember that you once taught her little girl in Paris. There must be no haste and no mistakes. It be well for them to meet--by accident--several times."

Later he aid to her:

"When Lady Etynge invites her to go to her house, you will, of course, go with her. You will not stay. Lady Etynge will tell you what to do."

In words, he did not involve himself by giving any hint of his intentions. So far as expression went, he might have had none, whatever. Her secret conclusion was that he knew, if he could see the girl under propitious circumstances--at the house of a clever and sympathetic acquaintance, he need have no shadow of a doubt as to the result of his efforts to please her. He knew she was a lonely, romantic creature, who had doubtless read sentimental books and been allured by their heroes. She was, of course, just ripe for young peerings into the land of love making. His had been no peerings, thought the pale Hirsch sadly. What girl--or woman--could resist the alluring demand of his drooping eyes, if he chose to allow warmth to fill them? Thinking of it, she almost gnashed her teeth. Did she not see how he would look, bending his high head and murmuring to a woman who shook with joy under his gaze? Had she not seen it in her own forlorn, hopeless dreams?

What did it matter if what the world calls disaster befell the girl? Fraulein Hirsch would not have called it disaster. Any woman would have been paid a thousand times over. His fancy might last a few months. Perhaps he would take her to Berlin--or to some lovely secret spot in the mountains where he could visit her. What heaven--what heaven! She wept, hiding her face on her hot, dry hands.

But it would not last long--and he would again think only of the immense work--the august Machine, of which he was a mechanical part--and he would be obliged to see and talk to her, Mathilde Hirsch, having forgotten the rest. She could only hold herself decently in check by telling herself again and again that it was only natural that such things should come and go in his magnificent life, and that the sooner it began the sooner it would end.

It was a lovely morning when her pupil walked with her in Kensington Gardens, and, quite naturally, strolled towards the Round Pond. Robin was happy because there were flutings of birds in the air, gardeners were stuffing crocuses and hyacinths into the flower beds, there were little sweet scents floating about and so it was Spring. She pulled a bare looking branch of a lilac bush towards her and stooped and kissed the tiny brown buttons upon it, half shyly.

"I can't help it when I see the first ones swelling on the twigs. They are working so hard to break out into green," she said. "One loves everything at this time--everything! Look at the children round the pond. That fat, little boy in a reefer and brown leather leggings is bursting with joy. Let us go and praise his boat, Fraulein."

They went and Robin praised the boat until its owner was breathless with rapture. Fraulein Hirsch, standing near her, looked furtively at all the benches round the circle, giving no incautiously interested glance to any one of them in particular. Presently, however, she said:

"I think that is Lady Etynge sitting on the third bench from here. I said to you that I had heard she was in London. I wonder if her daughter is still in the Convent at Tours?"

When Robin returned, she saw a quiet woman in perfect mourning recognize Fraulein Hirsch with a a bow and smile which seemed to require nearer approach.

"We must go and speak to her." Fraulein Hirsch said. "I know she wil wish me to present you. She is fond of young girls--because of Helene."

Robin went forward prettily. The woman was gentle looking and attracting. She had a sweet manner and was very kind to Fraulein Hirsch. She seemed to know her well and to like her. Her daughter, Helene, was still in the Convent at Tours but was expected home very shortly. She would be glad to find that Fraulein Hirsch was in London.

"I have turned the entire top story of my big house into a pretty suite for her. She has a fancy for living high above the street," smiled Lady Etynge, indulgently. Perhaps she was a "Mother" person, Robin thought.

Both her looks and talk were kind, and she was very nice in her sympathetic interest in the boats and the children's efforts to sail them.

"I often bring my book here and forget to read, because I find I am watching them," she said. "They are so eager and so triumphant when a boat gets across the Pond."

She went away very soon and Robin watched her out of sight with interest.

They saw her again a few days later and talked a little more. She was not always near the Pond when they came, and they naturally did not go there each time they walked together, though Fraulein Hirsch was fond of sitting and watching the children.

She had been to take tea with her former employer, she told Robin one day, and she was mildly excited by the preparations for Helene, who had been educated entirely in a French convent and was not like an English girl at all. She had always been very delicate and the nuns seemed to know how to take care of her and calm her nerves with their quiet ways.

"Her mother is rather anxious about her coming to London. She has, of course, no young friends here and she is so used to the quiet of convent life," the Fraulein explained. "That is why the rooms at the top of the house have been arranged for her. She will hear so little sound. I confess I am anxious about her myself. Lady Etynge is wondering if she can find a suitable young companion to live in the house with her. She must be a young lady and perfectly educated--and with brightness and charm. Not a person like myself, but one who can be treated as an equal and a friend--almost a playmate."

"It would be an agreeable position," commented Robin, thoughtfully.

"Extremely so," answered Fraulein Hirsch. "Helene is a most lovable and af-fectionate girl. And Lady Etynge is rich enough to pay a large salary. Helene is her idol. The suite of rooms is perfect. In Germany, girls are not spoiled in that way. It is not considered good for them."

It was quite natural, since she felt an interest in Helene, that, on their next meeting, Robin should find pleasure in sitting on the green bench near the girl's mother and hear her speak of her daughter. She was not diffuse or intimate in her manner. Helene first appeared in the talk as a result of a polite inquiry made by Fraulein Hirsch. Robin gathered, as she listened, that this particular girl was a ten-derly loved and cared for creature and was herself gentle and intelligent and loving. She sounded like the kind of a girl one would be glad to have for a friend. Robin wondered and wondered--if she would "do." Perhaps, out of tactful consideration for the feelings of Fraulein Hirsch who would not "do"--because she was neither bright, nor pretty, nor a girl--Lady Etynge touched but lightly on her idea that she might find a sort of sublimated young companion for her daughter.

"It would be difficult to advertise for what one wants," she said.

"Yes. To state that a girl must be clever and pretty and graceful, and attractive, would make it difficult for a modest young lady to write a suitable reply," said Frau-lein Hirsch grimly, and both Lady Etynge and Robin smiled.

"Among your own friends," Lady Etynge said to Robin, a little pathetically in her yearning, "do you know of anyone--who might know of anyone who would fit in? Sometimes there are poor little cousins, you know?"

"Or girls who have an independent spirit and would like to support them-selves," said the Fraulein. "There are such girls in these advanced times."

"I am afraid I don't know anyone," answered Robin. Modesty also prevented her from saying that she thought she did. She herself was well educated, she was good tempered and well bred, and she had known for some time that she was pret-ty.

"Perhaps Fraulein Hirsch may bring you in to have tea with me some after-noon when you are out," Lady Etynge said kindly before she left them. "I think you would like to see Helene's rooms. I should be glad to hear what another girl thinks of them."

Robin was delighted. Perhaps this was a way opening to her. She talked to Mademoiselle Valle about it and so glowed with hope that Mademoiselle's heart was moved.

"Do you think I might go?" she said. "Do you think there is any chance that I might be the right person? AM I nice enough--and well enough educated, and ARE my manners good?"

She did not know exactly where Lady Etynge lived, but believed it was one of those big houses in a certain dignified "Place" they both knew--a corner house, she was sure, because--by mere chance--she had one day seen Lady Etynge go into such a house as if it were her own. She did not know the number, but they could ask Fraulein.

Fraulein Hirsch was quite ready with detail concerning her former patroness and her daughter. She obviously admired them very much. Her manner held a touch of respectful reverence. She described Helene's disposition and delicate nerves and the perfection of the nuns' treatment of her.

She described the beauty of the interior of the house, its luxury and convenience, and the charms of the suite of apartments prepared for Helene. She thought the number of the house was No. 97 A. Lady Etynge was the kindest employer she had ever had. She believed that Miss Gareth-Lawless and Helene would be delighted with each other, if they met, and her impression was that Lady Etynge privately hoped they would become friends.

Her mild, flat face was so modestly amiable that Mademoiselle Valle, who always felt her unattractive femininity pathetic, was a little moved by her evident pleasure in having been the humble means of providing Robin with acquaintances of an advantageous kind.

No special day had been fixed upon for the visit and the cup of tea. Robin was eager in secret and hoped Lady Etynge would not forget to remind them of her invitation.

She did not forget. One afternoon--they had not seen her for several days and had not really expected to meet her, because they took their walk later than usual--they found her just rising from her seat to go home as they appeared.

"Our little encounters almost assume the air of appointments," she said. "This is very nice, but I am just going away, I am sorry to say. I wonder--" she paused a moment, and then looked at Fraulein Hirsch pleasantly; "I wonder if, in about an hour, you would bring Miss Gareth-Lawless to me to have tea and tell me if she thinks Helene will like her new rooms. You said you would like to see them," brightly to Robin.

"You are very kind. I should like it so much," was Robin's answer.

Fraulein Hirsch was correctly appreciative of the condescension shown to her. Her manner was the perfection of the exact shade of unobtrusive chaperonship. There was no improper suggestion of a mistaken idea that she was herself a guest, or, indeed, anything, in fact, but a proper appendage to her charge. Robin had never been fond of Fraulein as she was fond of Mademoiselle and Dowie, still she was not only an efficient teacher, but also a good walker and very fond of long tramps, which Mademoiselle was really not strong enough for, but which Robin's slender young legs rejoiced in.

The two never took cabs or buses, but always walked everywhere. They walked on this occasion, and, about an hour later, arrived at a large, corner house in Berford Place. A tall and magnificently built footman opened the door for them, and they were handed into a drawing room much grander than the one Robin sometimes glanced into as she passed it, when she was at home. A quite beautiful tea equipage awaited them on a small table, but Lady Etynge was not in the room.

"What a beautiful house to live in," said Robin, "but, do you know, the number ISN'T 97 A. I looked as we came in, and it is No. 25."

"Is it? I ought to have been more careful," answered Fraulein Hirsch. "It is wrong to be careless even in small matters."

Almost immediately Lady Etynge came in and greeted them, with a sort of gentle delight. She drew Robin down on to a sofa beside her and took her hand and gave it a light pat which was a caress.

"Now you really ARE here," she said, "I have been so busy that I have been afraid I should not have time to show you the rooms before it was too late to make a change, if you thought anything might be improved."

"I am sure nothing can improve them," said Robin, more dewy-eyed than usual and even a thought breathless, because this was really a sort of adventure, and she longed to ask if, by any chance, she would "do." And she was so afraid that she might lose this amazingly good opportunity, merely because she was too young and inexperienced to know how she ought to broach the subject. She had not thought yet of asking Mademoiselle Valle how it should be done.

She was not aware that she looked at Lady Etynge with a heavenly, little un-conscious appeal, which made her enchanting. Lady Etynge looked at her quite fixedly for an instant.

"What a child you are! And what a colour your cheeks and lips are!" she said. "You are much--much prettier than Helene, my dear."

She got up and brought a picture from a side table to show it to her.

"I think she is lovely," she said. "Is it became I am her mother?"

"Oh, no! Not because you are her mother!" exclaimed Robin. "She is angelic!"

She was rather angelic, with her delicate uplifted face and her communion veil framing it mistily.

The picture was placed near them and Robin looked at is many times as they took their tea. To be a companion to a girl with a face like that would be almost too much to ask of one's luck. There was actual yearning in Robin's heart. Suddenly she realized that she had missed something all her life, without knowing that she missed it. It was the friendly nearness of youth like her own. How she hoped that she might make Lady Etynge like her. After tea was over, Lady Etynge spoke pleas-antly to Fraulein Hirsch.

"I know that you wanted to register a letter. There is a post-office just around the corner. Would you like to go and register it while I take Miss Gareth-Lawless upstairs? You have seen the rooms. You will only be away a few minutes."

Fraulein Hirsch was respectfully appreciative again. The letter really was im-portant. It contained money which she sent monthly to her parents. This month she was rather late, and she would be very glad to be allowed to attend to the matter without losing a post.

So she went out of the drawing-room and down the stairs, and Robin heard the front door close behind her with a slight thud. She had evidently opened and closed it herself without waiting for the footman.

The upper rooms in London houses--even in the large ones--are usually given up to servants' bedrooms, nurseries, and school rooms. Stately staircases become narrower as they mount, and the climber gets glimpses of apartments which are frequently bare, whatsoever their use, and, if not grubby in aspect, are dull and uninteresting.

But, in Lady Etynge's house, it was plain that a good deal had been done. Stairs had been altered and widened, walls had been given fresh and delicate tints, and one laid one's hand on cream white balustrades and trod on soft carpets. A good architect had taken interest in the problems presented to him, and the result was admirable. Partitions must have been removed to make rooms larger and of better shape.

"Nothing could be altered without spoiling it!" exclaimed Robin, standing in the middle of a sitting room, all freshness and exquisite colour--the very pictures on the wall being part of the harmony.

All that a girl would want or love was there. There was nothing left undone--unremembered. The soft Chesterfield lounge, which was not too big and was placed near the fire, the writing table, the books, the piano of satinwood inlaid with garlands; the lamp to sit and read by.

"How glad she must be to come back to anyone who loves her so," said Robin.

Here was a quilted basket with three Persian kittens purring in it, and she knelt and stroked their fluffiness, bending her slim neck and showing how prettily the dark hair grew up from it. It was, perhaps, that at which Lady Etynge was looking as she stood behind her and watched her. The girl-nymph slenderness and flexibility of her leaning body was almost touchingly lovely.

There were several other rooms and each one was, in its way, more charming than the other. A library in Dresden blue and white, and with peculiarly pretty windows struck the last note of cosiness. All the rooms had pretty windows with rather small square panes enclosed in white frames.

It was when she was in this room that Robin took her courage in her hands. She must not let her chance go by. Lady Etynge was so kind. She wondered if it would seem gauche and too informal to speak now.

She stood quite upright and still, though her voice was not quite steady when she began.

"Lady Etynge," she said, "you remember what Fraulein Hirsch said about girls who wish to support themselves? I--I am one of them. I want very much to earn my own living. I think I am well educated. I have been allowed to read a good deal and my teachers, Mademoiselle Valle and Fraulein Hirsch, say I speak and write French and German well for an English girl. If you thought I could be a suitable companion for Miss Etynge, I--should be very happy."

How curiously Lady Etynge watched her as she spoke. She did not look displeased, but there was something in her face which made Robin afraid that she was, perhaps, after all, not the girl who was fortunate enough to quite "do."

She felt her hopes raised a degree, however, when Lady Etynge smiled at her.

"Do you know, I feel that is very pretty of you!" she said. "It quite delights me--as I am an idolizing mother--that my mere talk of Helene should have made you like her well enough to think you might care to live with her. And I confess I am modern enough to be pleased with your wishing to earn your own living."

"I must," said Robin. "I MUST! I could not bear not to earn it!" She spoke a little suddenly, and a flag of new colour fluttered in her cheek.

"When Helene comes, you must meet. If you like each other, as I feel sure you will, and if Mrs. Gareth-Lawless does not object--if it remains only a matter of being suitable--you are suitable, my dear--you are suitable."

She touched Robin's hand with the light pat which was a caress, and the child was radiant.

"Oh, you are kind to me!" The words broke from her involuntarily. "And it is such GOOD fortune! Thank you, thank you, Lady Etynge."

The flush of her joy and relief had not died out before the footman, who had opened the door, appeared on the threshold. He was a handsome young fellow, whose eyes were not as professionally impassive as his face. A footman had no right to dart a swift side look at one as people did in the street. He did dart such a glance. Robin saw, and she was momentarily struck by its being one of those she sometimes objected to.

Otherwise his manner was without flaw. He had only come to announce to his mistress the arrival of a caller.

When Lady Etynge took the card from the salver, her expression changed. She even looked slightly disturbed.

"Oh, I am sorry," she murmured, "I must see her," lifting her eyes to Robin. "It is an old friend merely passing through London. How wicked of me to forget that she wrote to say that she might dash in at any hour."

"Please!" pled Robin, prettily. "I can run away at once. Fraulein Hirsch must have come back. Please--"

"The lady asked me particularly to say that she has only a few minutes to stay, as she is catching a train," the footman decorously ventured.

"If that is the case," Lady Etynge said, even relievedly, "I will leave you here to look at things until I come back. I really want to talk to you a little more about yourself and Helene. I can't let you go." She looked back from the door before she passed through it. "Amuse yourself, my dear," and then she added hastily to the man.

"Have you remembered that there was something wrong with the latch, William? See if it needs a locksmith."

"Very good, my lady."

She was gone and Robin stood by the sofa thrilled with happiness and relief. How wonderful it was that, through mere lucky chance, she had gone to watch the children sailing their boats! And that Fraulein Hirsch had seen Lady Etynge! What good luck and how grateful she was! The thought which passed through her mind was like a little prayer of thanks. How strange it would be to be really intimate with a girl like herself--or rather like Helene. It made her heart beat to think of it. How wonderful it would be if Helene actually loved her, and she loved Helene. Something sprang out of some depths of her being where past things were hidden. The something was a deadly little memory. Donal! Donal! It would be--if she loved Helene and Helene loved her--as new a revelation as Donal. Oh! she remembered.

She heard the footman doing something to the latch of the door, which caused it to make a clicking sound. He was obeying orders and examining it. As she involuntarily glanced at him, he--bending over the door handle--raised his eyes sideways and glanced at her. It was an inexcusable glance from a domestic, because it was actually as if he were taking the liberty of privately summing her up--taking her points in for his own entertainment. She so resented the unprofessional bad manners of it, that she turned away and sauntered into the Dresden blue and white library and sat down with a book.

She was quite relieved, when, only a few minutes later, he went away having evidently done what he could.

The book she had picked up was a new novel and opened with an attention-arresting agreeableness, which led her on. In fact it led her on further and, for a longer time than she was aware of. It was her way to become wholly absorbed in books when they allured her; she forgot her surroundings and forgot the passing of time. This was a new book by a strong man with the gift which makes alive people, places, things. The ones whose lives had taken possession of his being in this story were throbbing with vital truth.

She read on and on because, from the first page, she knew them as actual pulsating human creatures. They looked into her face, they laughed, she heard their voices, she CARED for every trivial thing that happened to them--to any of them. If one of them picked a flower, she saw how he or she held it and its scent was in the air.

Having been so drawn on into a sort of unconsciousness of all else, it was inevitable that, when she suddenly became aware that she did not see her page quite clearly, she should withdraw her eyes from her page and look about her. As she did so, she started from her comfortable chair in amazement and some alarm. The room had become so much darker that it must be getting late. How careless and silly she had been. Where was Fraulein Hirsch?

"I am only a strange girl and Lady Etynge might so easily have forgotten me," passed through her mind. "Her friend may have stayed and they may have had so much to talk about, that, of coarse, I was forgotten. But Fraulein Hirsch--how could she!"

Then, remembering the subservient humility of the Fraulein's mind, she wondered if it could have been possible that she had been too timid to do more than sit waiting--in the hall, perhaps--afraid to allow the footman to disturb Lady Etynge by asking her where her pupil was. The poor, meek, silly thing.

"I must get away without disturbing anyone," she thought, "I will slip downstairs and snatch Fraulein Hirsch from her seat and we will go quietly out. I can write a nice note to Lady Etynge tomorrow, and explain. I HOPE she won't mind having forgotten me. I must make her feel sure that it did not matter in the least. I'll tell her about the book."

She replaced the book on the shelf from which she had taken it and passed through into the delightful sitting room. The kittens were playing together on the hearth, having deserted their basket. One of them gave a soft, airy pounce after her and caught at her dress with tiny claws, rolling over and over after his ineffectual snatch.

She had not heard the footman close the door when he left the room, but she found he must have done so, as it was now shut. When she turned the handle it did not seem to work well, because the door did not open as it ought to have done. She turned it again and gave it a little pull, but it still remained tightly shut. She turned it again, still with no result, and then she tried the small latch. Perhaps the man had done some blundering thing when he had been examining it. She remembered hearing several clicks. She turned the handle again and again. There was no key in the keyhole, so he could not have bungled with the key. She was quite aghast at the embarrassment of the situation.

"How CAN I get out without disturbing anyone, if I cannot open the door!" she said. "How stupid I shall seem to Lady Etynge! She won't like it. A girl who could forget where she was--and then not be able to open a door and be obliged to bang until people come!"

Suddenly she remembered that there had been a door in the bedroom which had seemed to lead out into the hall. She ran into the room in such a hurry that all three kittens ran frisking after her. She saw she had not been mistaken. There was a door. She went to it and turned the handle, breathless with excitement and relief. But the handle of that door also would not open it. Neither would the latch. And there was no key.

"Oh!" she gasped. "Oh!"

Then she remembered the electric bell near the fireplace in the sitting room. There was one by the fireplace here, also. No, she would ring the one in the sitting room. She went to it and pressed the button. She could not hear the ghost of a sound and one could generally hear SOMETHING like one. She rang again and waited. The room was getting darker. Oh, how COULD Fraulein Hirsch--how could she?

She waited--she waited. Fifteen minutes by her little watch--twenty minutes--and, in their passing, she rang again. She rang the bell in the library and the one in the bedroom--even the one in the bathroom, lest some might be out of order. She slowly ceased to be embarrassed and self-reproachful and began to feel afraid, though she did not know quite what she was afraid of. She went to one of the windows to look at her watch again in the vanishing light, and saw that she had been ringing the bells for an hour. She automatically put up a hand and leaned against the white frame of one of the decorative small panes of glass. As she touched it, she vaguely realized that it was of such a solidity that it felt, not like wood but iron. She drew her hand away quickly, feeling a sweep of unexplainable fear--yes, it was FEAR. And why should she so suddenly feel it? She went back to the door and tried again to open it--as ineffectively as before. Then she began to feel a little cold and sick. She returned to the Chesterfield and sat down on it helplessly.

"It seems as if--I had been locked in!" she broke out, in a faint, bewildered wail of a whisper. "Oh, WHY--did they lock the doors!"

CHAPTER XXII

She had known none of the absolute horrors of life which were possible in that underworld which was not likely to touch her own existence in any form.

"Why," had argued Mademoiselle Valle, "should one fill a white young mind with ugly images which would deface with dark marks and smears, and could only produce unhappiness and, perhaps, morbid broodings? One does not feel it is wise to give a girl an education in crime. One would not permit her to read the Newgate Calendar for choice. She will be protected by those who love her and what she must discover she will discover. That is Life."

Which was why her first discovery that neither door could be opened, did not at once fill her with horror. Her first arguments were merely those of a girl who, though her brain was not inactive pulp, had still a protected girl's outlook. She had been overwhelmed by a sense of the awkwardness of her position and by the dread that she would be obliged to disturb and, almost inevitably, embarrass and annoy Lady Etynge. Of course, there had been some bungling on the part of the impudent footman--perhaps actually at the moment when he had given his sidelong leer at herself instead of properly attending to what he was trying to do. That the bedroom was locked might be the result of a dozen ordinary reasons.

The first hint of an abnormality of conditions came after she had rung the bells and had waited in vain for response to her summons. There were servants whose business it was to answer bells at once. If ALL the bells were out of order, why were they out of order when Helene was to return in a few days and her apartment was supposed to be complete? Even to the kittens--even to the kittens!

"It seems as if I had been locked in," she had whispered to the silence of the room. "Why did they lock the doors?"

Then she said, and her heart began to thump and race in her side:

"It has been done on purpose. They don't intend to let me out--for some HOR-RIBLE reason!"

Perhaps even her own growing panic was not so appalling as a sudden rushing memory of Lady Etynge, which, at this moment, overthrew her. Lady Etynge! Lady Etynge! She saw her gentle face and almost affectionately watching eyes. She heard her voice as she spoke of Helene; she felt the light pat which was a caress.

"No! No!" she gasped it, because her breath had almost left her. "No! No! She couldn't! No one could! There is NOTHING as wicked--as that!"

Bat, even as she cried out, the overthrow was utter, and she threw herself forward on the arm of the couch and sobbed--sobbed with the passion she had only known on the day long ago when she had crawled into the shrubs and groveled in the earth. It was the same kind of passion--the shaken and heart-riven woe of a creature who has trusted and hoped joyously and has been forever betrayed. The face and eyes had been so kind. The voice so friendly! Oh, how could even the wickedest girl in the world have doubted their sincerity. Unfortunately--or fortunately--she knew nothing whatever of the mental processes of the wicked girls of the world, which was why she lay broken to pieces, sobbing--sobbing, not at the moment because she was a trapped thing, but because Lady Etynge had a face in whose gentleness her heart had trusted and rejoiced.

When she sat upright again, her own face, as she lifted it, would have struck a perceptive onlooker as being, as it were, the face of another girl. It was tear-stained and wild, but this was not the cause of its change. The soft, bird eyes were different--suddenly, amazingly older than they had been when she had believed in Helene.

She had no experience which could reveal to her in a moment the monstrousness of her danger, but all she had ever read, or vaguely gathered, of law breakers and marauders of society, collected itself into an advancing tidal wave of horror.

She rose and went to the window and tried to open it, but it was not intended to open. The decorative panes were of small size and of thick glass. Her first startled impression that the white framework seemed to be a painted metal was apparently founded on fact. A strong person might have bent it with a hammer, but he could not have broken it. She examined the windows in the other rooms and they were of the same structure.

"They are made like that," she said to herself stonily, "to prevent people from getting OUT."

She stood at the front one and looked down into the broad, stately "Place." It was a long way to look down, and, even if the window could be opened, one's voice would not be heard. The street lamps were lighted and a few people were to be seen walking past unhurriedly.

"In the big house almost opposite they are going to give a party. There is a red carpet rolled out. Carriages are beginning to drive up. And here on the top floor, there is a girl locked up--And they don't know!"

She said it aloud, and her voice sounded as though it were not her own. It was a dreadful voice, and, as she heard it, panic seized her.

Nobody knew--nobody! Her mother never either knew or cared where she was, but Dowie and Mademoiselle always knew. They would be terrified. Fraulein Hirsch had, perhaps, been told that her pupil had taken a cab and gone home and she would return to her lodgings thinking she was safe.

Then--only at this moment, and with a suddenness which produced a sense of shock--she recalled that it was Fraulein Hirsch who had presented her to Lady Etynge. Fraulein Hirsch herself! It was she who had said she had been in her employ and had taught Helene--Helene! It was she who had related anecdotes about the Convent at Tours and the nuns who were so wise and kind! Robin's hand went up to her forehead with a panic-stricken gesture. Fraulein Hirsch had made an excuse for leaving her with Lady Etynge--to be brought up to the top of the house quite alone--and locked in. Fraulein Hirsch had KNOWN! And there came back to her the memory of the furtive eyes whose sly, adoring sidelooks at Count Von Hillern had always--though she had tried not to feel it--been, somehow, glances she had disliked--yes, DISLIKED!

It was here--by the thread of Fraulein Hirsch--that Count Von Hillern was drawn into her mind. Once there, it was as if he stood near her--quite close--looking down under his heavy, drooping lids with stealthy, plunging eyes. It had always been when Fraulein Hirsch had walked with her that they had met him--almost as if by arrangement.

There were only two people in the world who might--because she herself had so hated them--dislike and choose in some way to punish her. One was Count Von

Hillern. The other was Lord Coombe. Lord Coombe, she knew, was bad, vicious, did the things people only hinted at without speaking of them plainly. A sense of instinctive revolt in the strength of her antipathy to Von Hillern made her feel that he must be of the same order.

"If either of them came into this room now and locked the door behind him, I could not get out."

She heard herself say it aloud in the strange girl's dreadful voice, as she had heard herself speak of the party in the big house opposite. She put her soft, slim hand up to her soft, slim throat.

"I could not get out," she repeated.

She ran to the door and began to beat on its panels. By this time, she knew it would be no use and yet she beat with her hands until they were bruised and then she snatched up a book and beat with that. She thought she must have been beating half an hour when she realized that someone was standing outside in the corridor, and the someone said, in a voice she recognized as belonging to the leering foot-man,

"May as well keep still, Miss. You can't hammer it down and no one's going to bother taking any notice," and then his footsteps retired down the stairs. She involuntarily clenched her hurt hands and the shuddering began again though she stood in the middle of the room with a rigid body and her head thrown fiercely back.

"If there are people in the world as hideous--and monstrous as THIS--let them kill me if they want to. I would rather be killed than live! They would HAVE to kill me!" and she said it in a frenzy of defiance of all mad and base things on earth.

Her peril seemed to force her thought to delve into unknown dark places in her memory and dig up horrors she had forgotten--newspaper stories of crime, old melodramas and mystery romances, in which people disappeared and were long afterwards found buried under floors or in cellars. It was said that the Berford Place houses, winch were old ones, had enormous cellars under them.

"Perhaps other girls have disappeared and now are buried in the cellars," she thought.

And the dreadful young voice added aloud.

"Because they would HAVE to kill me."

One of the Persian kittens curled up in the basket wakened because he heard it and stretched a sleepy paw and mewed at her.

Coombe House was one of the old ones, wearing somewhat the aspect of a stately barrack with a fine entrance. Its court was enclosed at the front by a stone wall, outside which passing London roared in low tumult. The court was surrounded by a belt of shrubs strong enough to defy the rain of soot which fell quietly upon them day and night.

The streets were already lighted for the evening when Mademoiselle Valle presented herself at the massive front door and asked for Lord Coombe. The expression of her face, and a certain intensity of manner, caused the serious-looking head servant, who wore no livery, to come forward instead of leaving her to the footmen.

"His lordship engaged with--a business person--and must not be disturbed," he said. "He is also going out."

"He will see me," replied Mademoiselle Valle. "If you give him this card he will see me."

She was a plainly dressed woman, but she had a manner which removed her entirely from the class of those who merely came to importune. There was absolute certainty in the eyes she fixed with steadiness on the man's face. He took her card, though he hesitated.

"If he does not see me," she added, "he will be very much displeased."

"Will you come in, ma'am, and take a seat for a moment?" he ventured. "I will inquire."

The great hall was one of London's most celebrated. A magnificent staircase swept up from it to landings whose walls were hung with tapestries the world knew. In a gilded chair, like a throne, Mademoiselle Valle sat and waited.

But she did not wait long. The serious-looking man without livery returned almost immediately. He led Mademoiselle into a room like a sort of study or apartment given up to business matters. Mademoiselle Valle had never seen Lord Coombe's ceremonial evening effect more flawless. Tall, thin and finely straight, he waited in the centre of the room. He was evidently on the point of going out, and the light-textured satin-lined overcoat he had already thrown on revealed, through a suggestion of being winged, that he wore in his lapel a delicately fresh, cream-coloured carnation.

A respectable, middle-class looking man with a steady, blunt-featured face, had been talking to him and stepped quietly aside as Mademoiselle entered. There seemed to be no question of his leaving the room.

Coombe met his visitor half way:

"Something has alarmed you very much?" he said.

"Robin went out with Fraulein Hirsch this afternoon," she said quickly. "They went to Kensington Gardens. They have not come back--and it is nine o'clock. They are always at home by six."

"Will you sit down," he said. The man with the steady face was listening intently, and she realized he was doing so and that, somehow, it was well that he should.

"I do not think there is time for any one to sit down," she said, speaking more quickly than before. "It is not only that she has not come back. Fraulein Hirsch has presented her to one of her old employers-a Lady Etynge. Robin was delighted with her. She has a daughter who is in France--,"

"Marguerite staying with her aunt in Paris," suddenly put in the voice of the blunt-featured man from his side of the room.

"Helene at a Covent in Tours," corrected Mademoiselle, turning a paling countenance towards him and then upon Coombe. "Lady Etynge spoke of wanting to engage some nice girl as a companion to her daughter, who is coming home. Robin thought she might have the good fortune to please her. She was to go to Lady Etynge's house to tea sine afternoon and be shown the rooms prepared for Helene. She thought the mother charming."

"Did she mention the address?" Coombe asked at once.

"The house was in Berford Place-a large house at a corner. She chanced to see Lady Etynge go into it one day or we should not have known. She did not notice the number. Fraulein Hirsch thought it was 97A. I have the Blue Book, Lord Coombe--through the Peerage--through the Directory! There is no Lady Etynge and there is no 97A in Berford Place! That is why I came here."

The man who had stood aside, stepped forward again. It was as if he answered some sign, though Lord Coombe at the moment crossed the hearth and rang the bell.

"Scotland Yard knows that, ma'am," said the man. "We've had our eyes on that house for two weeks, and this kind of thing is what we want."

"The double brougham," was Coombe's order to the servant who answered his ring. Then he came back to Mademoiselle.

"Mr. Barkstow is a detective," he said. "Among the other things he has done for me, he has, for some time, kept a casual eye on Robin. She is too lovely a child and too friendless to be quite safe. There are blackguards who know when a girl has not the usual family protection. He came here to tell me that she had been seen sitting in Kensington Gardens with a woman Scotland Yard has reason to suspect."

"A black 'un!" said Barkstow savagely. "If she's the one we think she is-a black, poisonous, sly one with a face that no girl could suspect."

Coombe's still countenance was so deadly in the slow lividness, which Mademoiselle saw began to manifest itself, that she caught his sleeve with a shaking hand.

"She's nothing but a baby!" she said. "She doesn't know what a baby she is. I can see her eyes frantic with terror! She'd go mad."

"Good God!" he said, in a voice so low it scarcely audible.

He almost dragged her out of the room, though, as they passed through the hall, the servants only saw that he had given the lady his arm-and two of the younger footmen exchanged glances with each other which referred solely to the inimitableness of the cut of his evening overcoat.

When they entered the carriage, Barkstow entered with them and Mademoiselle Valle leaned forward with her elbows on her knees and her face clutched in her hands. She was trying to shut out from her mental vision a memory of Robin's eyes.

"If--if Fraulein Hirsch is--not true," she broke out once. "Count von Hillern is concerned. It has come upon me like a flash. Why did I not see before?"

The party at the big house, where the red carpet was rolled across the pavement, was at full height when they drove into the Place. Their brougham did not stop at the corner but at the end of the line of waiting carriages.

Coombe got out and looked up and down the thoroughfare.

"It must be done quietly. There must be no scandal," he said. "The policeman on the beat is an enormous fellow. You will attend to him, Barkstow," and Barkstow nodded and strolled away.

Coombe walked up the Place and down on the opposite side until he was within a few yards of the corner house. When he reached this point, he suddenly quickened his footsteps because he saw that someone else was approaching it with an air of intention. It was a man, not quite as tall as himself but of heavier build and with square held shoulders. As the man set his foot upon the step, Coombe touched him on the arm and said something in German.

The man started angrily and then suddenly stood quite still and erect.

"It will be better for us to walk up the Place together," Lord Coombe said, with perfect politeness.

If he could have been dashed down upon the pavement and his head hammered in with the handle of a sword, or if he could have been run through furiously again and again, either or both of these things would have been done. But neither was possible. It also was not possible to curse aloud in a fashionable London street. Such curses as one uttered must be held in one's foaming mouth between one's teeth. Count von Hillern knew this better than most men would have known it. Here was one of those English swine with whom Germany would deal in her own way later.

They walked back together as if they were acquaintances taking a casual stroll.

"There is nothing which would so infuriate your--Master-as a disgraceful scandal," Lord Coombe's highbred voice suggested undisturbedly. "The high honour of a German officer-the knightly bearing of a wearer of the uniform of the All Highest-that sort of thing you know. All that sort of thing!"

Von Hillern ground out some low spoken and quite awful German words. If he had not been trapped-if he had been in some quiet by-street!

"The man walking ahead of us is a detective from Scotland Yard. The particularly heavy and rather martial tread behind us is that of a policeman much more muscular than either of us. There is a ball going on in the large house with the red carpet spread across the pavement. I know the people who are giving it. There are a good many coachmen and footmen about. Most of them would probably recognize me."

It became necessary for Count von Hillern actually to wipe away certain flecks of foam from his lips, as he ground forth again more varied and awful sentiments in his native tongue.

"You are going back to Berlin," said Coombe, coldly. "If we English were not such fools, you would not be here. You are, of course, not going into that house."

Von Hillern burst into a derisive laugh.

"You are going yourself," he said. "You are a worn-out old ROUE, but you are mad about her yourself in your senile way."

"You should respect my age and decrepitude," answered Coombe. "A certain pity for my gray hairs would become your youth. Shall we turn here or will you return to your hotel by some other way?" He felt as if the man might a burst a blood vessel if he were obliged to further restrain himself.

Von Hillern wheeled at the corner and confronted him.

"There will come a day--" he almost choked.

"Der Toy? Naturally," the chill of Coombe's voice was a sound to drive this particular man at this particular, damnably-thwarted moment, raving mad. And not to be able to go mad! Not to be able!

"Swine of a doddering Englishman! Who would envy you--trembling on your lean shanks--whatsoever you can buy for yourself. I spit on you-spit!"

"Don't," said Coombe. "You are sputtering to such an extent that you really ARE, you know."

Von Hillern whirled round the corner.

Coombe, left alone, stood still a moment.

"I was in time," he said to himself, feeling somewhat nauseated. "By extraordinary luck, I was in time. In earlier days one would have said something about 'Provadence'." And he at once walked back.

CHAPTER XXIII

It was not utterly dark in the room, though Robin, after passing her hands carefully over the walls, had found no electric buttons within reach nor any signs of candles or matches elsewhere. The night sky was clear and brilliant with many stars, and this gave her an unshadowed and lighted space to look at. She went to the window and sat down on the floor, huddled against the wall with her hands clasped round her knees, looking up. She did this in the effort to hold in check a rising tide of frenzy which threatened her. Perhaps, if she could fix her eyes on the vault full of stars, she could keep herself from going out of her mind. Though, perhaps, it would be better if she DID go out of her mind, she found herself thinking a few seconds later.

After her first entire acceptance of the hideous thing which had happened to her, she had passed through nerve breaking phases of terror-stricken imaginings. The old story of the drowning man across whose brain rush all the images of life, came back to her. She did not know where or when or how she had ever heard or read of the ghastly incidents which came trooping up to her and staring at her with dead or mad eyes and awful faces. Perhaps they were old nightmares-perhaps a kind of delirium had seized her. She tried to stop their coming by saying over and over again the prayers Dowie had taught her when she was a child. And then she thought, with a sob which choked her, that perhaps they were only prayers for a safe little creature kneeling by a white bed-and did not apply to a girl locked up in a top room, which nobody knew about. Only when she thought of Mademoiselle Valle and Dowie looking for her--with all London spread out before their helplessness--did she cry. After that, tears seemed impossible. The images trooped by too close to her. The passion hidden within her being--which had broken out when she tore the earth under the shrubbery, and which, with torture staring her in the face, had leaped in the child's soul and body and made her defy Andrews with shrieks--leaped up within her now. She became a young Fury, to whom a mad fight with monstrous death was nothing. She told herself that she was strong for a girl--that she could tear with her nails, she could clench her teeth in a flesh, she could shriek, she could battle like a young madwoman so that they would be FORCED to kill her. This was one of the images which rose op before her again yet again, A hideous-hideous thing, which would not remain away.

She had not had any food since the afternoon cap of tea and she began to feel the need of it. If she became faint-! She lifted her face desperately as she said it, and saw the immense blue darkness, powdered with millions of stars and curving over her--as it curved over the hideous house and all the rest of the world. How high--how immense--how fathomlessly still it was--how it seemed as if there could be nothing else--that nothing else could be real! Her hands were clenched together hard and fiercely, as she scrambled to her knees and uttered a of prayer--not a child's--rather the cry of a young Fury making a demand.

"Perhaps a girl is Nothing," she cried, "-a girl locked up in a room! But, perhaps, she is Something--she may he real too! Save me-save me! But if you won't save me, let me be killed!"

She knelt silent after it for a few minutes and then she sank down and lay on the floor with her face on her arm.

How it was possible that even young and worn-out as she was, such peace as sleep could overcome her at such a time, one cannot say. But in the midst of her torment she was asleep.

But it was not for long. She wakened with a start and sprang to her feet shivering. The carriages were still coming and going with guests for the big house opposite. It could not be late, though she seemed to have been in the place for years--long enough to feel that it was the hideous centre of the whole earth and all sane and honest memories were a dream. She thought she would begin to walk up and down the room.

But a sound she heard at this very instant made her stand stock still. She had known there would be a sound at last--she had waited for it all the time--she had known, of course, that it would come, but she had not even tried to guess whether she would hear it early or late. It would be the sound of the turning of the handle of the locked door. It had come. There it was! The click of the lock first and then the creak of the turned handle!

She went to the window again and stood with her back against it, so that her body was outlined against the faint light. Would the person come in the dark, or would he carry a light? Something began to whirl in her brain. What was the low, pumping thump she seemed to hear and feel at the same time? It was the awful thumping of her heart.

The door opened--not stealthily, but quite in the ordinary way. The person who came in did not move stealthily either. He came in as though he were making an evening call. How tall and straight his body was, with a devilish elegance of line against the background of light in the hall. She thought she saw a white flower on his lapel as his overcoat fell back. The leering footman had opened the for him.

"Turn on the lights." A voice she knew gave the order, the leering footman obeyed, touching a spot high on the wall.

She had vaguely and sickeningly felt almost sure that it would be either Count von Hillern or Lord Coombe--and it was not Count von Hillern! The cold wicked face--the ironic eyes which made her creep--the absurd, elderly perfection of dress--even the flawless flower-made her flash quake with repulsion. If Satan came into the room, he might look like that and make one's revolting being quake so.

"I thought--it might be you," the strange girl's voice said to him aloud.

"Robin," he said.

He was moving towards her and, as she threw out her madly clenched little hands, he stopped and drew back.

"Why did you think I might come?" he asked.

"Because you are the kind of a man who would do the things only devils would do. I have hated-hated-hated you since I was a baby. Come and kill me if you like. Call the footman back to help you, if yon like. I can't get away. Kill me--kill me--kill me!"

She was lost in her frenzy and looked as if she were mad.

One moment he hesitated, and then he pointed politely to the sofa.

"Go and sit down, please," he suggested. It was no more then a courteous suggestion. "I shall remain here. I have no desire to approach you--if you'll pardon my saying so."

But she would not leave the window.

"It is natural that you should be overwrought," he said.

"This is a damnable thing. You are too young to know the worst of it."

"You are the worst of it!" she cried. "You."

"No" as the chill of his even voice struck her, she wondered if he were really human. "Von Hillern would have been the worst of it. I stopped him at the front door and knew how to send him away. Now, listen, my good child. Hate me as ferociously as you like. That is a detail. You are in the house of a woman whose name stands for shame and infamy and crime."

"What are YOU doing in it--" she cried again, "--in a place where girls are trapped-and locked up in top rooms--to be killed?"

"I came to take you away. I wish to do it quietly. It would be rather horrible if the public discovered that you have spent some hours here. If I had not slipped in when they were expecting von Hillern, and if the servants were not accustomed to the quiet entrance of well dressed men, I could not have got in without an open row and the calling of the policemen,--which I wished to avoid. Also, the woman downstairs knows me and realized that I was not lying when I said the house was surrounded and she was on the point of being 'run in'. She is a woman of broad experience, and at once knew that she might as well keep quiet."

Despite his cold eyes and the bad smile she hated, despite his almost dandified meticulous attire and the festal note of his white flower, which she hated with the rest--he was, perhaps, not lying to her. Perhaps for the sake of her mother he had chosen to save her--and, being the man he was, he had been able to make use of his past experiences.

She began to creep away from the window, and she felt her legs, all at once, shaking under her. By the time she reached the Chesterfield sofa she fell down by it and began to cry. A sort of hysteria seized her, and she shook from head to foot and clutched at the upholstery with weak hands which clawed. She was, indeed, an awful, piteous sight. He was perhaps not lying, but she was afraid of him yet.

"I told the men who are waiting outside that if I did not bring you out in half an hour, they were to break into the house. I do not wish them to break in. We have not any time to spare. What you are doing is quite natural, but you must try and get up." He stood by her and said this looking down at her slender, wrung body and lovely groveling head.

He took a flask out of his overcoat pocket--and it was a gem of goldsmith's art. He poured some wine into its cup and bent forward to hold it out to her.

"Drink this and try to stand on your feet," he said. He knew better than to try to help her to rise--to touch her in any way. Seeing to what the past hours had reduced her, he knew better. There was mad fear in her eyes when she lifted her head and threw out her hand again.

"No! No!" she cried out. "No, I will drink nothing!" He understood at once and threw the wine into the grate.

"I see," he said. "You might think it might be drugged. You are right. It might be. I ought to have thought of that." He returned the flask to his pocket. "Listen again. You must. The time will soon be up and we must not let those fellows break in and make a row that will collect a crowd We must go at once. Mademoiselle Valle is waiting for you in my carriage outside. You will not be afraid to drink wine she gives you."

"Mademoiselle!" she stammered.

"Yes. In my carriage, which is not fifty yards from the house. Can you stand on your feet?" She got up and stood but she was still shuddering all over.

"Can you walk downstairs? If you cannot, will you let me carry you? I am strong enough-in spite of my years."

"I can walk," she whispered.

"Will you take my arm?"

She looked at him for a moment with awful, broken-spirited eyes.

"Yes. I will take your arm."

He offered it to her with rigid punctiliousness of manner. He did not even look at her. He led her out of the room and down the three flights of stairs. As they passed by the open drawing-room door, the lovely woman who had called herself Lady Etynge stood near it and watched them with eyes no longer gentle.

"I have something to say to you, Madam," he said; "When I place this young lady in the hands of her governess, I will come back and say it."

"Is her governess Fraulein Hirsch?" asked the woman lightly.

"No. She is doubtless on her way back to Berlin--and von Hillern will follow her."

There was only the first floor flight of stairs now. Robin could scarcely see her way. But Lord Coombe held her up firmly and, in a few moments more, the leering footman, grown pale, opened the large door, they crossed the pavement to the carriage, and she was helped in and fell, almost insensible, across Mademoiselle Valle's lap, and was caught in a strong arm which shook as she did.

"Ma cherie," she heard, "The Good God! Oh, the good--good God!--And Lord Coombe! Lord Coombe!"

Coombe had gone back to the house. Four men returned with him, two in plain clothes and two heavily-built policemen. They remained below, but Coombe went up the staircase with the swift lightness of a man of thirty.

He merely stood upon the threshold of the drawing-room. This was what he said, and his face was entirely white his eyes appalling.

"My coming back to speak to you is--superfluous--and the result of pure fury. I allow it to myself as mere shameless indulgence. More is known against you than this--things which have gone farther and fared worse. You are not young and you are facing years of life in prison. Your head will be shaved--your hands worn and blackened and your nails broken with the picking of oakum. You will writhe in hopeless degradation until you are done for. You will have time, in the night blackness if of your cell, to remember--to see faces--to hear cries. Women such as you should learn what hell on earth means. You will learn."

When he ended, the woman hung with her back to the wall she had staggered against, her mouth opening and shutting helplessly but letting forth no sound.

He took out an exquisitely fresh handkerchief and touched his forehead because it was damp. His eyes were still appalling, but his voice suddenly dropped and changed.

"I have allowed myself to feel like a madman," he said. "It has been a rich experience--good for such a soul as I own."

He went downstairs and walked home because his carriage had taken Robin and Mademoiselle back to the slice of a house.

CHAPTER XXIV

Von Hillern made no further calls on Mrs. Gareth-Lawless. His return to Berlin was immediate and Fraulein Hirsch came no more to give lessons in German. Later, Coombe learned from the mam with the steady, blunt-featured face, that she had crossed the Channel on a night boat not many hours after Von Hillern had walked away from Berford Place. The exact truth was that she had been miserably prowling about the adjacent streets, held in the neighbourhood by some self-torturing morbidness, half thwarted helpless passion, half triumphing hatred of the young thing she had betrayed. Up and down the streets she had gone, round and round, wringing her lean fingers together and tasting on her lips the salt of tears which rolled down her cheeks--tears of torment and rage.

There was the bitterness of death in what, by a mere trick of chance, came about. As she turned a corner telling herself for the hundredth time that she must go home, she found herself face to face with a splendid figure swinging furiously along. She staggered at the sight of the tigerish rage in the white face she recognized with a gasp. It was enough merely to behold it. He had met with some disastrous humiliation!

As for him, the direct intervention of that Heaven whose special care he was, had sent him a woman to punish--which, so far, was at least one thing arranged as it should be. He knew so well how he could punish her with his mere contempt and displeasure--as he could lash a spaniel crawling at his feet. He need not deign to tell her what had happened, and he did not. He merely drew back and stood in stiff magnificence looking down at her.

"It is through some folly of yours," he dropped in a voice of vitriol. "Women are always foolish. They cannot hold their tongues or think clearly. Return to Berlin at once. You are not of those whose conduct I can commend to be trusted in the future."

He was gone before she could have spoken even if she had dared. Sobbing gasps caught her breath as she stood and watched him striding pitilessly and superbly away with, what seemed to her abject soul, the swing and tread of a martial god. Her streaming tears tasted salt indeed. She might never see him again--even from a distance. She would be disgraced and flung aside as a blundering woman. She had obeyed his every word and done her straining best, as she had licked the dust at his feet--but he would never cast a glance at her in the future or utter to her the remotest word of his high commands. She so reeled as she went her wretched way that a good-natured policeman said to her as he passed,

"Steady on, my girl. Best get home and go to bed."

To Mrs. Gareth-Lawless, it was stated by Coombe that Fraulein Hirsch had been called back to Germany by family complications. That august orders should recall Count Von Hillern, was easily understood. Such magnificent persons never shone upon society for any length of time.

That Feather had been making a country home visit when her daughter had faced tragedy was considered by Lord Coombe as a fortunate thing.

"We will not alarm Mrs. Gareth-Lawless by telling her what has occurred," he said to Mademoiselle Valle. "What we most desire is that no one shall suspect that the hideous thing took place. A person who was forgetful or careless might, unintentionally, let some word escape which--"

What he meant, and what Mademoiselle Valle knew he meant--also what he knew she knew he meant--was that a woman, who was a heartless fool, without sympathy or perception, would not have the delicacy to feel that the girl must be shielded, and might actually see a sort of ghastly joke in a story of Mademoiselle Valle's sacrosanct charge simply walking out of her enshrining arms into such a "galere" as the most rackety and adventurous of pupils could scarcely have been led into. Such a point of view would have been quite possible for Feather--even probable, in the slightly spiteful attitude of her light mind.

"She was away from home. Only you and I and Dowie know," answered Mademoiselle.

"Let us remain the only persons who know," said Coombe. "Robin will say nothing."

They both knew that. She had been feverish and ill for several days and Dowie had kept her in bed saying that she had caught cold. Neither of the two women had felt it possible to talk to her. She had lain staring with a deadly quiet fixedness straight before her, saying next to nothing. Now and then she shuddered, and once she broke into a mad, heart-broken fit of crying which she seemed unable to control.

"Everything is changed," she said to Dowie and Mademoiselle who sat on either side of her bed, sometimes pressing her head down onto a kind shoulder, sometimes holding her hand and patting it. "I shall be afraid of everybody forever. People who have sweet faces and kind voices will make me shake all over. Oh! She seemed so kind--so kind!"

It was Dowie whose warm shoulder her face hidden on this time, and Dowie was choked with sobs she dared not let loose. She could only squeeze hard and kiss the "silk curls all in a heap"--poor, tumbled curls, no longer a child's!

"Aye, my lamb!" she managed to say. "Dowie's poor pet lamb!"

"It's the knowing that kind eyes--kind ones--!" she broke off, panting. "It's the KNOWING! I didn't know before! I knew nothing. Now, it's all over. I'm afraid of all the world!"

"Not all, cherie," breathed Mademoiselle.

She sat upright against her pillows. The mirror on a dressing table reflected her image--her blooming tear-wet youth, framed in the wonderful hair falling a shadow about her. She stared at the reflection hard and questioningly.

"I suppose," her voice was pathos itself in its helplessness, "it is because what you once told me about being pretty, is true. A girl who looks like THAT," pointing her finger at the glass, "need not think she can earn her own living. I loathe it," in fierce resentment at some bitter injustice. "It is like being a person under a curse!"

At this Dowie broke down openly and let her tears run fast. "No, no! You mustn't say it or think it, my dearie!" she wept. "It might call down a blight on it. You a young thing like a garden flower! And someone--somewhere--God bless him--that some day'll glory in it--and you'll glory too. Somewhere he is--somewhere!"

"Let none of them look at me!" cried Robin. "I loather them, too. I hate everything--and everybody--but you two--just you two."

Mademoiselle took her in her arms this time when she sobbed again. Mademoiselle knew how at this hour it seemed to her that all her world was laid bare forever more. When the worst of the weeping was over and she lay quiet, but for the deep catching breaths which lifted her breast in slow, childish shudders at intervals, she held Mademoiselle Valle's hand and looked at her with a faint, wry smile.

"You were too kind to tell me what a stupid little fool I was when I talked to you about taking a place in an office!" she said. "I know now that you would not have allowed me to do the things I was so sure I could do. It was only my ignorance and conceit. I can't answer advertisements. Any bad person can say what they choose in an advertisement. If that woman had advertised, she would have described Helene. And there was no Helene." One of the shuddering catches of her breath broke in here. After it, she said, with a pitiful girlishness of regret: "I--I could SEE Helene. I have known so few people well enough to love them. No girls at all. I though--perhaps--we should begin to LOVE each other. I can't bear to think of that--that she never was alive at all. It leaves a sort of empty place."

When she had sufficiently recovered herself to be up again, Mademoiselle Valle said to her that she wished her to express her gratitude to Lord Coombe.

"I will if you wish it," she answered.

"Don't you feel that it is proper that you should do it? Do you not wish it yourself?" inquired Mademoiselle. Robin looked down at the carpet for some seconds.

"I know," she at last admitted, "that it is proper. But I don't wish to do it."

"No?" said Mademoiselle Valle.

Robin raised her eyes from the carpet and fixed them on her.

"It is because of--reasons," she said. "It is part of the horror I want to forget. Even you mayn't know what it has done to me. Perhaps I am turning into a girl with a bad mind. Bad thoughts keep swooping down on me--like great black ravens. Lord Coombe saved me, but I think hideous things about him. I heard Andrews say he was bad when I was too little to know what it meant. Now, I KNOW, I remember that HE knew because he chose to know--of his own free will. He knew that woman and she knew him. HOW did he know her?" She took a forward step which brought her nearer to Mademoiselle. "I never told you but I will tell you now," she confessed, "When the door opened and I saw him standing against the light I--I did not think he had come to save me."

"MON DIEU!" breathed Mademoiselle in soft horror.

"He knows I am pretty. He is an old man but he knows. Fraulein Hirsch once made me feel actually sick by telling me, in her meek, sly, careful way, that he liked beautiful girls and the people said he wanted a young wife and had his eye on me. I was rude to her because it made me so furious. HOW did he know that woman so well? You see how bad I have been made!"

"He knows nearly all Europe. He has seen the dark corners as well as the bright places. Perhaps he has saved other girls from her. He brought her to punishment, and was able to do it because he has been on her track for some time. You are not bad--but unjust. You have had too great a shock to be able to reason sanely just yet."

"I think he will always make me creep a little," said Robin, "but I will say anything you think I ought to say."

On an occasion when Feather had gone again to make a visit in the country, Mademoiselle came into the sitting room with the round window in which plants grew, and Coombe followed her. Robin looked up from her book with a little start and then stood up.

"I have told Lord Coombe that you wish--that I wish you to thank him," Mademoiselle Valle said.

"I came on my own part to tell you that any expression of gratitude is entirely unnecessary," said Coombe.

"I MUST be grateful. I AM grateful." Robin's colour slowly faded as she said it. This was the first time she had seen him since he had supported her down the staircase which mounted to a place of hell.

"There is nothing to which I should object so much as being regarded as a benefactor," he answered definitely, but with entire lack of warmth. "The role does not suit me. Being an extremely bad man," he said it as one who speaks wholly without prejudice, "my experience is wide. I chance to know things. The woman who called herself Lady Etynge is of a class which--which does not count me among its clients. I had put certain authorities on her track--which was how I discovered your whereabouts when Mademoiselle Valle told me that you had gone to take tea with her. Mere chance you see. Don't be grateful to me, I beg of you, but to Mademoiselle Valle."

"Why," faltered Robin, vaguely repelled as much as ever, "did it matter to you?"

"Because," he answered--Oh, the cold inhumanness of his gray eye!--"you happened to live in--this house."

"I thought that was perhaps the reason," she said--and she felt that he made her "creep" even a shade more.

"I beg your pardon," she added, suddenly remembering, "Please sit down."

"Thank you," as he sat. "I will because I have something more to say to you."

Robin and Mademoiselle seated themselves also and listened.

"There are many hideous aspects of existence which are not considered necessary portions of a girl's education," he began.

"They ought to be," put in Robin, and her voice was as hard as it was young.

It was a long and penetrating look he gave her.

"I am not an instructor of Youth. I have not been called upon to decide. I do not feel it my duty to go even now into detail."

"You need not," broke in the hard young voice. "I know everything in the world. I'm BLACK with knowing."

"Mademoiselle will discuss that point with you. What you have, unfortunately, been forced to learn is that it is not safe for a girl--even a girl without beauty--to act independently of older people, unless she has found out how to guard herself against--devils." The words broke from him sharply, with a sudden incongruous hint of ferocity which was almost startling. "You have been frightened," he said next, "and you have discovered that there are devils, but you have not sufficient experience to guard yourself against them."

"I have been so frightened that I shall be a coward--a coward all my life. I shall be afraid of every face I see--the more to be trusted they look, the more I shall fear them. I hate every one in the world!"

Her quite wonderful eyes--so they struck Lord Coombe--flamed with a child's outraged anguish. A thunder shower of tears broke and rushed down her cheeks, and he rose and, walking quietly to the window full of flowers, stood with his back to her for a few moments. She neither cared nor knew whether it was because her hysteric emotion bored or annoyed him, or because he had the taste to realize that she would not wish to be looked at. Unhappy youth can feel no law but its own.

But all was over during the few moments, and he turned and walked back to his chair.

"You want very much to do some work which will insure your entire independence--to take some situation which will support you without aid from others? You are not yet prepared to go out and take the first place which offers. You have been--as you say--too hideously frightened, and you know there are dangers in wandering about unguided. Mademoiselle Valle," turning his head, "perhaps you will tell her what you know of the Duchess of Darte?"

Upon which, Mademoiselle Valle took hold of her hand and entered into a careful explanation.

"She is a great personage of whom there can be no doubt. She was a lady of the Court. She is of advanced years and an invalid and has a liking for those who are pretty and young. She desires a companion who is well educated and young and fresh of mind. The companion who had been with her for many years recently died. If you took her place you would live with her in her town house and go with her to the country after the season. Your salary would be liberal and no position could be more protected and dignified. I have seen and talked to her grace myself, and she will allow me to take you to her, if you desire to go."

"Do not permit the fact that she has known me for many years to prejudice you against the proposal," said Coombe. "You might perhaps regard it rather as a sort of guarantee of my conduct in the matter. She knows the worst of me and still allows me to retain her acquaintance. She was brilliant and full of charm when she was a young woman, and she is even more so now because she is--of a rarity! If I were a girl and might earn my living in her service, I should feel that fortune had been good to me--good."

Robin's eyes turned from one of them to the other--from Coombe to Mademoiselle Valle, and from Mademoiselle to Coombe pathetically.

"You--you see--what has been done to me," she said. "A few weeks ago I should have KNOWN that God was providing for me--taking care of me. And now--I am still afraid. I feel as if she would see that--that I am not young and fresh any more but black with evil. I am afraid of her--I am afraid of you," to Coombe, "and of myself."

Coombe rose, evidently to go away.

"But you are not afraid of Mademoiselle Valle," he put it to her. "She will provide the necessary references for the Duchess. I will leave her to help you to decide."

Robin rose also. She wondered if she ought not to hold out her hand. Perhaps he saw her slight movement. He himself made none.

"I remember you objected to shaking hands as a child," he said, with an impersonal civil smile, and the easy punctiliousness of his bow made it impossible for her to go further.

CHAPTER XXV

Some days before this the Duchess of Darte had driven out in the morning to make some purchases and as she had sat in her large landau she had greatly missed Miss Brent who had always gone with her when she had made necessary visits to the shops. She was not fond of shopping and Miss Brent had privately found pleasure in it which had made her a cheerful companion. To the quiet elderly woman whose life previous to her service with this great lady had been spent in struggles with poverty, the mere incident of entering shops and finding eager salesmen springing forward to meet her with bows and amiable offers of ministration, was to the end of her days an almost thrilling thing. The Duchess bought splendidly though quietly. Knowing always what she wanted, she merely required that it be produced, and after silently examining it gave orders that it should be sent to her. There was a dignity in her decision which was impressive. She never gave trouble or hesitated. The staffs of employees in the large shops knew and reveled in her while they figuratively bent the knee. Miss Brent had been a happy satisfied woman while she had lived. She had died peacefully after a brief and, as it seemed at first, unalarming illness at one of her employer's country houses to which she had been amiably sent down for a holiday. Every kindness and attention had been bestowed upon her and only a few moments before she fell into her last sleep she had been talking pleasantly of her mistress.

"She is a very great lady, Miss Hallam," she had said to her nurse. "She's the last of her kind I often think. Very great ladies seem to have gone out--if you know what I mean. They've gone out."

The Duchess had in fact said of Brent as she stood a few days later beside her coffin and looked down at her contentedly serene face, something not unlike what Brent had said of herself.

"You were a good friend, Brent, my dear," she murmured. "I shall always miss you. I am afraid there are no more like you left."

She was thinking of her all the morning as she drove slowly down to Bond Street and Piccadilly. As she got out of her carriage to go into a shop she was attracted by some photographs of beauties in a window and paused to glance at them. Many of them were beauties whom she knew, but among them were some of society's latest discoveries. The particular photographs which caught her eye were two which had evidently been purposely placed side by side for an interesting reason. The reason was that the two women, while obviously belonging to periods of some twenty years apart as the fashion of their dress proved, were in face and form so singularly alike that they bewilderingly suggested that they were the same person. Both were exquisitely nymphlike, fair and large eyed and both had the fine light hair which is capable of forming itself into a halo. The Duchess stood and looked at them for the moment spell-bound. She slightly caught her breath. She was borne back so swiftly and so far. Her errand in the next door shop was forgotten. She went into the one which displayed the photographs.

"I wish to look at the two photographs which are so much alike," she said to the man behind the counter.

He knew her as most people did and brought forth the photographs at once.

"Many people are interested in them, your grace," he said. "It was the amazing likeness which made me put them beside each other."

"Yes," she answered. "It is almost incredible." She looked up from the beautiful young being dressed in the mode of twenty years past.

"This is--WAS--?" she corrected herself and paused. The man replied in a somewhat dropped voice. He evidently had his reasons for feeling it discreet to do so.

"Yes--WAS. She died twenty years ago. The young Princess Alixe of X--" he said. "There was a sad story, your grace no doubt remembers. It was a good deal talked about."

"Yes," she replied and said no more, but took up the modern picture. It displayed the same almost floating airiness of type, but in this case the original wore diaphanous wisps of spangled tulle threatening to take wings and fly away leaving the girl slimness of arms and shoulders bereft of any covering whatsoever.

"This one is--?" she questioned.

"A Mrs. Gareth-Lawless. A widow with a daughter though she looks in her teens. She's older than the Princess was, but she's kept her beauty as ladies know how to in these days. It's wonderful to see them side by side. But it's only a few that saw her Highness as she was the season she came with the Prince to visit at Windsor in Queen Victoria's day. Did your grace--" he checked himself feeling that he was perhaps somewhat exceeding Bond Street limits.

"Yes. I saw her," said the Duchess. "If these are for sale I will take them both."

"I'm selling a good many of them. People buy them because the likeness makes them a sort of curiosity. Mrs. Gareth-Lawless is a very modern lady and she is quite amused."

The Duchess took the two photographs home with her and looked at them a great deal afterwards as she sat in her winged chair.

They were on her table when Coombe came to drink tea with her in the afternoon.

When he saw them he stood still and studied the two faces silently for several seconds.

"Did you ever see a likeness so wonderful?" he said at last.

"Never," she answered. "Or an unlikeness. That is the most wonderful of all-- the unlikeness. It is the same body inhabited by two souls from different spheres."

His next words were spoken very slowly.

"I should have been sure you would see that," he commented.

"I lost my breath for a second when I saw them side by side in the shop window--and the next moment I lost it again because I saw--what I speak of--the utter world wide apartness. It is in their eyes. She--," she touched the silver frame enclosing the young Princess, "was a little saint--a little spirit. There never was a young human thing so transparently pure."

The rigid modeling of his face expressed a thing which, himself recognizing its presence, he chose to turn aside as he moved towards the mantel and leaned on it. The same thing caused his voice to sound hoarse and low as he spoke in answer, saying something she had not expected him to say. Its unexpectedness in fact produced in her an effect of shock.

"And she was the possession of a brute incarnate, mad with unbridled lust and drink and abnormal furies. She was a child saint, and shook with terror before him.

He killed her."

"I believe he did," she said unsteadily after a breath space of pause. "Many people believed so though great effort was made to silence the stories. But there were too many stories and they were so unspeakable that even those in high places were made furiously indignant. He was not received here at Court afterwards. His own emperor could not condone what he did. Public opinion was too strong."

"The stories were true," answered the hoarse low voice. "I myself, by royal command, was a guest at the Schloss in the Bavarian Alps when it was known that he struck her repeatedly with a dog whip. She was going to have a child. One night I was wandering in the park in misery and I heard shrieks which sent me in mad search. I do not know what I should have done if I had succeeded, but I tried to force an entrance into the wing from which the shrieks came. I was met and stopped almost by open violence. The sounds ceased. She died a week later. But the most experienced lying could not hide some things. Even royal menials may have human blood in their veins. It was known that there were hideous marks on her little dead body."

"We heard. We heard," whispered the Duchess.

"He killed her. But she would have died of horror if he had not struck her a blow. She began to die from the hour the marriage was forced upon her. I saw that when she was with him at Windsor."

"You were in attendance on him," the Duchess said after a little silence. "That was when I first knew you."

"Yes." She had added the last sentence gravely and his reply was as grave though his voice was still hoarse. "You were sublime goodness and wisdom. When a woman through the sheer quality of her silence saves a man from slipping over the verge of madness he does not forget. While I was sane I dared scarcely utter her name. If I had gone mad I should have raved as madmen do. For that reason I was afraid."

"I knew. Speech was the greatest danger," she answered him. "She was a princess of a royal house--poor little angel--and she had a husband whose vileness and violence all Europe knew. How DARED they give her to him?"

"For reasons of their own and because she was too humbly innocent and obedient to rebel."

The Duchess did not ask questions. The sublime goodness of which he had spoken had revealed its perfection through the fact that in the long past days she had neither questioned nor commented. She had given her strong soul's secret support to him and in his unbearable hours he had known that when he came to her for refuge, while she understood his need to the uttermost, she would speak no word even to himself.

But today though she asked no question her eyes waited upon him as it were. This was because she saw that for some unknown reason a heavy veil had rolled back from the past he had chosen to keep hidden even from himself, as it were, more than from others.

"Speech is always the most dangerous thing," he said. "Only the silence of years piled one upon the other will bury unendurable things. Even thought must be silenced. I have lived a lifetime since--" his words began to come very slowly--as she listened she felt as if he were opening a grave and drawing from its depths long buried things, "--since the night when I met her alone in a wood in the park of the Schloss and--lost hold of myself--lost it utterly."

The Duchess' withered hands caught each other in a clasp which was almost like a passionate exclamation.

"There was such a night. And I was young--young--not an iron bound vieillard then. When one is young one's anguish is the Deluge which ends the world forever. I had lain down and risen up and spent every hour in growing torture for months. I had been forced to bind myself down with bands of iron. When I found myself, without warning, face to face with her, alone in the night stillness of the wood, the bands broke. She had dared to creep out in secret to hide herself and her heartbroken terror in the silence and darkness alone. I knew it without being told. I knew and I went quite mad for the time. I was only a boy. I threw myself face downward on the earth and sobbed, embracing her young feet."

Both of them were quite silent for a few moments before he went on.

"She was not afraid," he said, even with something which was like a curious smile of tender pity at the memory. "Afterwards--when I stood near her, trembling--she even took my hand and held it. Once she kissed it humbly like a little child while her tears rained down. Never before was there anything as innocently heartbreaking. She was so piteously grateful for love of any kind and so heart wrung by my misery."

He paused again and looked down at the carpet, thinking. Then he looked up at her directly.

"I need not explain to you. You will know. I was twenty-five. My heart was pounding in my side, my blood thudded through my veins. Every atom of natural generous manhood in my being was wild with fury at the brutal wrong done her exquisiteness. And she--"

"She was a young novice fresh from a convent and very pious," the Duchess' quiet voice put in.

"You understand," he answered. "She knelt down and prayed for her own soul as well as mine. She thanked God that I was kind and would forgive her and go away--and only remember her in my prayers. She believed it was possible. It was not, but I kissed the hem of her white dress and left her standing alone--a little saint in a woodland shrine. That was what I thought deliriously as I staggered off. It was the next night that I heard her shrieks. Then she died."

The Duchess knew what else had died--the high adventure of youth and joy of life in him, the brilliant spirit which had been himself and whose utter withdrawal from his being had left him as she had seen him on his return to London in those days which now seemed a memory of a past life in a world which had passed also. He had appeared before her late one afternoon and she had for a moment been afraid to look at him because she was struck to the depths of her being by a sense of seeing before her a body which had broken the link holding it to life and walked the earth, the crowded streets, the ordinary rooms where people gathered, a dead thing. Even while it moved it gazed out of dead eyes. And the years had passed and though they had been friends he had never spoken until now.

"Such a thing must be buried in a tomb covered with a heavy stone and with a seal set upon it. I am unsealing a tomb," he said. Then after a silence he added, "I have, of cause, a reason." She bent her head because she had known this must be the case.

"There is a thing I wish you to understand. Every woman could not."

"I shall understand."

"Because I know you will I need not enter into exact detail. You will not find what I say abnormal."

There had been several pauses during his relation. Once or twice he had stopped in the middle of a sentence as if for calmer breath or to draw himself back from a past which had suddenly become again a present of torment too great to face with modern steadiness. He took breath so to speak in this manner again.

"The years pass, the agony of being young passes. One slowly becomes another man," he resumed. "I am another man. I could not be called a creature of sentiment. I have given myself interests in existence--many of them. But the sealed tomb is under one's feet. Not to allow oneself to acknowledge its existence consciously is one's affair. But--the devil of chance sometimes chooses to play tricks. Such a trick was played on me."

He glanced down at the two pictures at which she herself was looking with grave eyes. It was the photograph of Feather he took up and set a strange questioning gaze upon.

"When I saw this," he said, "this--exquisitely smiling at me under a green tree in a sunny garden--the tomb opened under my feet, and I stood on the brink of it--twenty-five again."

"You cannot possibly put it into words," the Duchess said. "You need not. I know." For he had become for the moment almost livid. Even to her who so well knew him it was a singular thing to see him hastily set down the picture and touch his forehead with his handkerchief.

She knew he was about to tell her his reason for this unsealing of the tomb. When he sat down at her table he did so. He did not use many phrases, but in making clear his reasons he also made clear to her certain facts which most persons would have ironically disbelieved. But no shadow of a doubt passed through her mind because she had through a long life dwelt interestedly on the many variations in human type. She was extraordinarily interested when he ended with the story of Robin.

"I do not know exactly why 'it matters to me'--I am quoting her mother," he explained, "but it happens that I am determined to stand between the child and what would otherwise be the inevitable. It is not that she has the slightest resemblance to--to anyone--which might awaken memory. It is not that. She and her mother are of totally different types. And her detestation of me is unconquerable. She believes me to be the worst of men. When I entered the room into which the woman had trapped her, she thought that I came as one of the creature's damnable clients. You will acknowledge that my position presents difficulties in the way of explanation to a girl--to most adults in fact. Her childish frenzy of desire to support herself arises from her loathing of the position of accepting support from me. I sympathize with her entirely."

"Mademoiselle Valle is an intelligent woman," the Duchess said as though thinking the matter out. "Send her to me and we will talk the matter over. Then she can bring the child."

CHAPTER XXVI

A s a result of this, her grace saw Mademoiselle Valle alone a few mornings later and talked to her long and quietly. Their comprehension of each other was complete. Before their interview was at an end the Duchess' interest in the adventure she was about to enter into had become profound.

"The sooner she is surrounded by a new atmosphere, the better," was one of the things the Frenchwoman had said. "The prospect of an arrangement so perfect and so secure fills me with the profoundest gratitude. It is absolutely necessary that I return to my parents in Belgium. They are old and failing in health and need me greatly. I have been sad and anxious for months because I felt that it would be wickedness to desert this poor child. I have been torn in two. Now I can be at peace--thank the good God."

"Bring her to me tomorrow if possible," the Duchess said when they parted. "I foresee that I may have something to overcome in the fact that I am Lord Coombe's old friend, but I hope to be able to overcome it."

"She is a baby--she is of great beauty--she has a passionate little soul of which she knows nothing." Mademoiselle Valle said it with an anxious reflectiveness. "I have been afraid. If I were her mother----" her eyes sought those of the older woman.

"But she has no mother," her grace answered. Her own eyes were serious. She knew something of girls, of young things, of the rush and tumult of young life in them and of the outlet it demanded. A baby who was of great beauty and of a passionate soul was no trivial undertaking for a rheumatic old duchess, but--"Bring her to me," she said.

So was Robin brought to the tall Early Victorian mansion in the belatedly stately square. And the chief thought in her mind was that though mere good manners demanded under the circumstances that she should come to see the Dowager Duchess of Darte and be seen by her, if she found that she was like Lord Coombe, she would not be able to endure the prospect of a future spent in her service howsoever desirable such service might outwardly appear. This desirableness Mademoiselle Valle had made clear to her. She was to be the companion of a personage of great and mature charm and grace who desired not mere attendance, but something more, which something included the warmth and fresh brightness of happy youth and bloom. She would do for her employer the things a young relative might do. She would have a suite of rooms of her own and a freedom as to hours and actions which greater experience on her part would have taught was not the customary portion meted out to a paid companion. But she knew nothing of paid service and a preliminary talk of Coombe's with Mademoiselle Valle had warned her against allowing any suspicion that this "earning a living" had been too obviously ameliorated.

"Her life is unusual. She herself is unusual in a most dignified and beautiful way. You will, it might almost be said, hold the position of a young lady in waiting," was Mademoiselle's gracefully put explanation.

When, after they had been ushered into the room where her grace sat in her beautiful and mellow corner by the fire, Robin advanced towards the highbacked chair, what the old woman was chiefly conscious of was the eyes which seemed all lustrous iris. There was uncommon appeal and fear in them. The blackness of their setting of up-curled lashes made them look babyishly wide.

"Mademoiselle Valle has told me of your wish to take a position as companion," the Duchess said after they were seated.

"I want very much," said Robin, "to support myself and Mademoiselle thinks that I might fill such a place if I am not considered too young."

"You are not too young--for me. I want something young to come and befriend me. Am I too old for YOU?" Her smile had been celebrated fifty years earlier and it had not changed. A smile does not. She was not like Lord Coombe in any degree however remote. She did not belong to his world, Robin thought.

"If I can do well enough the things you require done," she answered blushing her Jacqueminot rose blush, "I shall be grateful if you will let me try to do them.

Mademoiselle will tell you that I have no experience, but that I am one who tries well."

"Mademoiselle has answered all my questions concerning your qualifications so satisfactorily that I need ask you very few."

Such questions as she asked were not of the order Robin had expected. She led her into talk and drew Mademoiselle Valle into the conversation. It was talk which included personal views of books, old gardens and old houses, people, pictures and even--lightly--politics. Robin found herself quite incidentally, as it were, reading aloud to her an Italian poem. She ceased to be afraid and was at ease. She forgot Lord Coombe. The Duchess listening and watching her warmed to her task of delicate investigation and saw reason for anticipating agreeably stimulating things. She was not taking upon herself a merely benevolent duty which might assume weight and become a fatigue. In fact she might trust Coombe for that. After all it was he who had virtually educated the child--little as she was aware of the singular fact. It was he who had dragged her forth from her dog kennel of a top floor nursery and quaintly incongruous as it seemed, had found her a respectable woman for a nurse and an intelligent person for a governess and companion as if he had been a domesticated middle class widower with a little girl to play mother to. She saw in the situation more than others would have seen in it, but she saw also the ironic humour of it. Coombe--with the renowned cut of his overcoat--the perfection of his line and scarcely to be divined suggestions of hue--Coombe!

She did not avoid all mention of his name during the interview, but she spoke of him only casually, and though the salary she offered was an excellent one, it was not inordinate. Robin could not feel that she was not being accepted as of the class of young persons who support themselves self-respectingly, though even the most modest earned income would have represented wealth to her ignorance.

Before they parted she had obtained the position so pleasantly described by Mademoiselle Valle as being something like that of a young lady in waiting. "But I am really a companion and I will do everything--everything I can so that I shall be worth keeping," she thought seriously. She felt that she should want to be kept. If Lord Coombe was a friend of her employer's it was because the Duchess did not know what others knew. And her house was not his house--and the hideous thing she had secretly loathed would be at an end. She would be supporting herself as decently and honestly as Mademoiselle or Dowie had supported themselves all their lives.

With an air of incidentally recalling a fact, the Duchess said after they had risen to leave her:

"Mademoiselle Valle tells me you have an elderly nurse you are very fond of. She seems to belong to a class of servants almost extinct."

"I love her," Robin faltered--because the sudden reminder brought back a pang to her. There was a look in her eyes which faltered also. "She loves me. I don't know how----" but there she stopped.

"Such women are very valuable to those who know the meaning of their type. I myself am always in search of it. My dear Miss Brent was of it, though of a different class."

"But most people do not know," said Robin. "It seems old-fashioned to them-- and it's beautiful! Dowie is an angel."

"I should like to secure your Dowie for my housekeeper and myself,"--one of the greatest powers of the celebrated smile was its power to convince. "A competent person is needed to take charge of the linen. If we can secure an angel we shall be fortunate."

A day or so later she said to Coombe in describing the visit.

"The child's face is wonderful. If you could but have seen her eyes when I said it. It is not the mere beauty of size and shape and colour which affect one. It is something else. She is a little flame of feeling."

The "something else" was in the sound of her voice as she answered.

"She will be in the same house with me! Sometimes perhaps I may see her and talk to her! Oh! how GRATEFUL I am!" She might even see and talk to her as often as she wished, it revealed itself and when she and Mademoiselle got into their hansom cab to drive away, she caught at the Frenchwoman's hand and clung to it, her eyelashes wet,

"It is as if there MUST be Goodness which takes care of one," she said. "I used to believe in it so--until I was afraid of all the world. Dowie means most of all. I did now know how I could bear to let her go away. And since her husband and her daughter died, she has no one but me. I should have had no one but her if you had gone back to Belgium, Mademoiselle. And now she will be safe in the same house with me. Perhaps the Duchess will keep her until she dies. I hope she will keep me until I die. I will be as good and faithful as Dowie and perhaps the Duchess will live until I am quite old--and not pretty any more. And I will make economies as you have made them, Mademoiselle, and save all my salary--and I might be able to end my days in a little cottage in the country."

Mademoiselle was conscious of an actual physical drag at her heartstrings. The pulsating glow of her young loveliness had never been more moving and oh! the sublime certainty of her unconsciousness that Life lay between this hour and that day when she was "quite old and not pretty any more" and having made economies could die in a little cottage in the country! She believed in her vision as she had believed that Donal would come to her in the garden.

Upon Feather the revelation that her daughter had elected to join the ranks of girls who were mysteriously determined to be responsible for themselves produced a curious combination of effects. It was presented to her by Lord Coombe in the form of a simple impersonal statement which had its air of needing no explanation. She heard it with eyes widening a little and a smile slowly growing. Having heard, she broke into a laugh, a rather high-pitched treble laugh.

"Really?" she said. "She is really going to do it? To take a situation! She wants to be independent and 'live her own life!' What a joke--for a girl of mine!" She was either really amused or chose to seem so.

"What do YOU think of it?" she asked when she stopped laughing. Her eyes had curiosity in them.

"I like it," he answered.

"Of course. I ought to have remembered that you helped her to an Early Victorian duchess. She's one without a flaw--the Dowager Duchess of Darte. The most conscientiously careful mother couldn't object. It's almost like entering into the kingdom of heaven--in a dull way." She began to laugh again as if amusing images rose suddenly before her. "And what does the Duchess think of it?" she said after her laughter had ceased again. "How does she reconcile herself to the idea of a companion whose mother she wouldn't have in her house?"

"We need not enter into that view of the case. You decided some years ago that it did not matter to you whether Early Victorian duchesses included you in their visiting lists or did not. More modern ones do I believe--quite beautiful and amusing ones."

"But for that reason I want this one and those like her. They would bore me, but I want them. I want them to come to my house and be polite to me in their stuffy way. I want to be invited to their hideous dinner parties and see them sitting round their tables in their awful family jewels 'talking of the sad deaths of kings.' That's Shakespeare, you know. I heard it last night at the theatre."

"Why do you want it?" Coombe inquired.

"When I ask you why you show your morbid interest in Robin, you say you don't know. I don't know--but I do want it."

She suddenly flushed, she even showed her small teeth. For an extraordinary moment she looked like a little cat.

"Robin will hare it," she cried, grinding a delicate fist into the palm on her knee. "She's not eighteen and she's a beauty and she's taken up by a perfectly decent old duchess. She'll have EVERYTHING! The Dowager will marry her to someone important. You'll help," she turned on him in a flame of temper. "You are capable of marrying her yourself!" There was a a brief but entire silence. It was broken by his saying,

"She is not capable of marrying ME."

There was brief but entire silence again, and it was he who again broke it, his manner at once cool and reasonable.

"It is better not to exhibit this kind of feeling. Let us be quite frank. There are few things you feel more strongly than that you do not want your daughter in the house. When she was a child you told me that you detested the prospect of having her on your hands. She is being disposed of in the most easily explained and enviable manner."

"It's true--it's true," Feather murmured. She began to see advantages and the look of a little cat died out, or at least modified itself into that of a little cat upon whom dawned prospects of cream. No mood ever held her very long. "She won't come back to stay," she said. "The Duchess won't let her. I can use her rooms and I shall be very glad to have them. There's at least some advantage in figuring as a sort of Dame Aux Camelias."

CHAPTER XXVII

The night before Robin went away as she sat alone in the dimness of one light, thinking as girls nearly always sit and think on the eve of a change, because to youth any change seems to mean the final closing as well as the opening of ways, the door of her room was opened and an exquisite and nymphlike figure in pale green stood exactly where the rays of the reading lamp seemed to concentrate themselves in an effort to reveal most purely its delicately startling effect. It was her mother in a dress whose spring-like tint made her a sort of slim dryad. She looked so pretty and young that Robin caught her breath as she rose and went forward.

"It is your aged parent come to give you her blessing," said Feather.

"I was wondering if I might come to your room in the morning," Robin answered.

Feather seated herself lightly. She was not intelligent enough to have any real comprehension of the mood which had impelled her to come. She had merely given way to a secret sense of resentment of something which annoyed her. She knew, however, why she had put on the spring-leaf green dress which made her look like a girl. She was not going to let Robin feel as if she were receiving a visit from her grandmother. She had got that far.

"We don't know each other at all, do we?" she said.

"No," answered Robin. She could not remove her eyes from her loveliness. She brought up such memories of the Lady Downstairs and the desolate child in the shabby nursery.

"Mothers are not as intimate with their daughters as they used to be when it was a sort of virtuous fashion to superintend their rice pudding and lecture them about their lessons. We have not seen each other often."

"No," said Robin.

Feather's laugh had again the rather high note Coombe had noticed.

"You haven't very much to say, have you?" she commented. "And you stare at me as if you were trying to explain me. I dare say you know that you have big eyes and that they're a good colour, but I may as well hint to you that men do not like to be stared at as if their deeps were being searched. Drop your eyelids."

Robin's lids dropped in spite of herself because she was startled, but immediately she was startled again by a note in her mother's voice--a note of added irritation.

"Don't make a habit of dropping them too often," it broke out, "or it will look as if you did it to show your eyelashes. Girls with tricks of that sort are always laughed at. Alison Carr LIVES sideways became she has a pretty profile."

Coombe would have recognized the little cat look, if he had been watching her as she leaned back in her chair and scrutinized her daughter. The fact was that she took in her every point, being an astute censor of other women's charms.

"Stand up," she said.

Robin stood up because she could not well refuse to do so, but she coloured because she was suddenly ashamed.

"You're not little, but you're not tall," her mother said. "That's against you. It's the fashion for women to be immensely tall now. Du Maurier's pictures in Punch and his idiotic Trilby did it. Clothes are made for giantesses. I don't care about it myself, but a girl's rather out of it if she's much less than six feet high. You can sit down."

A more singular interview between mother and daughter had assuredly rarely taken place. As she looked at the girl her resentment of her increased each moment. She actually felt as if she were beginning to lose her temper.

"You are what pious people call 'going out into the world'," she went on. "In moral books mothers always give advice and warnings to their girls when they're leaving them. I can give you some warnings. You think that because you have been taken up by a dowager duchess everything will be plain sailing. You're mistaken. You think because you are eighteen and pretty, men will fall at your feet."

"I would rather be hideous," cried suddenly passionate Robin. "I HATE men!"

The silly pretty thing who was responsible for her being, grew sillier as her irritation increased.

"That's what girls always pretend, but the youngest little idiot knows it isn't true. It's men who count. It makes me laugh when I think of them--and of you. You know nothing about them and they know everything about you. A clever man can do anything he pleases with a silly girl."

"Are they ALL bad?" Robin exclaimed furiously.

"They're none of them bad. They're only men. And that's my warning. Don't imagine that when they make love to you they do it as if you were the old Duchess' granddaughter. You will only be her paid companion and that's a different matter."

"I will not speak to one of them----" Robin actually began.

"You'll be obliged to do what the Duchess tells you to do," laughed Feather, as she realized her obvious power to dull the glitter and glow of things which she had felt the girl must be dazzled and uplifted unduly by. She was rather like a spiteful schoolgirl entertaining herself by spoiling an envied holiday for a companion. "Old men will run after you and you will have to be nice to them whether you like it or not." A queer light came into her eyes. "Lord Coombe is fond of girls just out of the schoolroom. But if he begins to make love to you don't allow yourself to feel too much flattered."

Robin sprang toward her.

"Do you think I don't ABHOR Lord Coombe!" she cried out forgetting herself in the desperate cruelty of the moment. "Haven't I reason----" but there she remembered and stopped.

But Feather was not shocked or alarmed. Years of looking things in the face had provided her with a mental surface from which tilings rebounded. On the whole it even amused her and "suited her book" that Robin should take this tone.

"Oh! I suppose you mean you know he admires me and pays bills for me. Where would you have been if he hadn't done it? He's been a sort of benefactor."

"I know nothing but that even when I was a little child I could not bear to touch his hand!" cried Robin. Then Feather remembered several things she had almost forgotten and she was still more entertained.

"I believe you've not forgotten through all these years that the boy you fell so indecently in love with was taken away by his mother because Lord Coombe was

YOUR mother's admirer and he was such a sinner that even a baby was contaminated by him! Donal Muir is a young man by this time. I wonder what his mother would do now if he turned up at your mistress' house--that's what she is, you know, your mistress--and began to make love to you." She laughed outright. "You'll get into all sorts of messes, but that would be the nicest one!"

Robin could only stand and gaze at her. Her moment's fire had died down. Without warning, out of the past a wave rose and overwhelmed her then and there. It bore with it the wild woe of the morning when a child had waited in the spring sun and her world had fallen into nothingness. It came back--the broken-hearted anguish, the utter helpless desolation, as if she stood in the midst of it again, as if it had never passed. It was a re-incarnation. She could not bear it.

"Do you hate me--as I hate Lord Coombe?" she cried out. "Do you WANT unhappy things to happen to me? Oh! Mother, why!" She had never said "Mother" before. Nature said it for her here. The piteous appeal of her youth and lonely young rush of tears was almost intolerably sweet. Through some subtle cause it added to the thing in her which Feather resented and longed to trouble and to hurt.

"You are a spiteful little cat!" she sprang up to exclaim, standing close and face to face with her. "You think I am an old thing and that I'm jealous of you! Because you're pretty and a girl you think women past thirty don't count. You'll find out. Mrs. Muir will count and she's forty if she's a day. Her son's such a beauty that people go mad over him. And he worships her--and he's her slave. I wish you WOULD get into some mess you couldn't get out of! Don't come to me if you do."

The wide beauty of Robin's gaze and her tear wet bloom were too much. Feather was quite close to her. The spiteful schoolgirl impulse got the better of her.

"Don't make eyes at me like that," she cried, and she actually gave the rose cheek nearest her a sounding little slap, "There!" she exclaimed hysterically and she turned about and ran out of the room crying herself.

Robin had parted from Mademoiselle Valle at Charing Cross Station on the afternoon of the same day, but the night before they had sat up late together and talked a long time. In effect Mademoiselle had said also, "You are going out into the world," but she had not approached the matter in Mrs. Gareth-Lawless' mood. One may have charge of a girl and be her daily companion for years, but there are certain things the very years themselves make it increasingly difficult to say to her.

And after all why should one state difficult things in exact phrases unless one lacks breeding and is curious. Anxious she had been at times, but not curious. So it was that even on this night of their parting it was not she who spoke.

It was after a few minutes of sitting in silence and looking at the fire that Robin broke in upon the quiet which had seemed to hold them both.

"I must learn to remember always that I am a sort of servant. I must be very careful. It will be easier for me to realize that I am not in my own house than it would be for other girls. I have not allowed Dowie to dress me for a good many weeks. I have learned how to do everything for myself quite well."

"But Dowie will be in the house with you and the Duchess is very kind."

"Every night I have begun my prayers by thanking God for leaving me Dowie," the girl said. "I have begun them and ended them with the same words." She looked about her and then broke out as if involuntarily. "I shall be away from here. I shall not wear anything or eat anything or sleep on any bed I have not paid for myself."

"These rooms are very pretty. We have been very comfortable here," Mademoiselle said. Suddenly she felt that if she waited a few moments she would know definitely things she had previously only guessed at. "Have you no little regrets?"

"No," answered Robin, "No."

She stood upon the hearth with her hands behind her. Mademoiselle felt as if her fingers were twisting themselves together and the Frenchwoman was peculiarly moved by the fact that she looked like a slim jeune fille of a creature saying a lesson. The lesson opened in this wise.

"I don't know when I first began to know that I was different from all other children," she said in a soft, hot voice--if a voice can express heat. "Perhaps a child who has nothing--nothing--is obliged to begin to THINK before it knows what thoughts are. If they play and are loved and amused they have no time for anything but growing and being happy. You never saw the dreadful little rooms up-stairs----"

"Dowie has told me of them," said Mademoiselle.

"Another child might have forgotten them. I never shall. I--I was so little and they were full of something awful. It was loneliness. The first time Andrews pinched me was one day when the thing frightened me and I suddenly began to cry quite loud. I used to stare out of the window and--I don't know when I noticed it first--I could see the children being taken out by their nurses. And there were always two or three of them and they laughed and talked and skipped. The nurses used to laugh and talk too. Andrews never did. When she took me to the gardens the other nurses sat together and chattered and their children played games with other children. Once a little girl began to talk to me and her nurse called her away. Andrews was very angry and jerked me by my arm and told me that if ever I spoke to a child again she would pinch me."

"Devil!" exclaimed the Frenchwoman.

"I used to think and think, but I could never understand. How could I?"

"A baby!" cried Mademoiselle Valle and she got up and took her in her arms and kissed her. "Chere petite ange!" she murmured. When she sat down again her cheeks were wet. Robin's were wet also, but she touched them with her handkerchief quickly and dried them. It was as if she had faltered for a moment in her lesson.

"Did Dowie ever tell you anything about Donal?" she asked hesitatingly.

"Something. He was the little boy you played with?"

"Yes. He was the first human creature," she said it very slowly as if trying to find the right words to express what she meant, "--the first HUMAN creature I had ever known. You see Mademoiselle, he--he knew everything. He had always been happy, he BELONGED to people and things. I belonged to nobody and nothing. If I had been like him he would not have seemed so wonderful to me. I was in a kind of delirium of joy. If a creature who had been deaf dumb and blind had suddenly awakened, and seeing on a summer day in a world full of flowers and sun--it might have seemed to them as it seemed to me."

"You have remembered it through all the years," said Mademoiselle, "like that?"

"It was the first time I became alive. One could not forget it. We only played as children play but--it WAS a delirium of joy. I could not bear to go to sleep at night and forget it for a moment. Yes, I remember it--like that. There is a dream I have every now and then and it is more real than--than this is--" with a wave of her hand about her. "I am always in a real garden playing with a real Donal. And his eyes--his eyes--" she paused and thought, "There is a look in them that is like--it is just like--that first morning."

The change which passed over her face the next moment might have been said to seem to obliterate all trace of the childish memory.

"He was taken away by his mother. That was the beginning of my finding out," she said. "I heard Andrews talking to her sister and in a baby way I gathered that Lord Coombe had sent him. I hated Lord Coombe for years before I found out that he hadn't--and that there was another reason. After that it took time to puzzle things out and piece them together. But at last I found out what the reason had been. Then I began to make plans. These are not my rooms," glancing about her again, "--these are not my clothes," with a little pull at her dress. "I'm not 'a strong character', Mademoiselle, as I wanted to be, but I haven't one little regret--not one." She kneeled down and put her arms round her old friend's waist, lifting her face. "I'm like a leaf blown about by the wind. I don't know what it will do with me. Where do leaves go? One never knows really."

She put her face down on Mademoiselle's knee then and cried with soft bitterness.

When she bade her good-bye at Charing Cross Station and stood and watched the train until it was quite out of sight, afterwards she went back to the rooms for which she felt no regrets. And before she went to bed that night Feather came and gave her farewell maternal advice and warning.

CHAPTER XXVIII

That a previously scarcely suspected daughter of Mrs. Gareth-Lawless had become a member of the household of the Dowager Duchess of Darte stirred but a passing wave of interest in a circle which was not that of Mrs. Gareth-Lawless herself and which upon the whole but casually acknowledged its curious existence as a modern abnormality. Also the attitude of the Duchess herself was composedly free from any admission of necessity for comment.

"I have no pretty young relative who can be spared to come and live with me. I am fond of things pretty and young and I am greatly pleased with what a kind chance put in my way," she said. In her discussion of the situation with Coombe she measured it with her customary fine acumen.

"Forty years ago it could not have been done. The girl would have been made uncomfortable and outside things could not have been prevented from dragging themselves in. Filial piety in the mass would have demanded that the mother should be accounted for. Now a genial knowledge of a variety in mothers leaves Mrs. Gareth-Lawless to play about with her own probably quite amusing set. Once poor Robin would have been held responsible for her and so should I. My position would have seemed to defy serious moral issues. But we have reached a sane habit of detaching people from their relations. A nice condition we should be in if we had not."

"You, of course, know that Henry died suddenly in some sort of fit at Ostend." Coombe said it as if in a form of reply. She had naturally become aware of it when the rest of the world did, but had not seen him since the event.

"One did not suppose his constitution would have lasted so long," she answered. "You are more fortunate in young Donal Muir. Have you seen him and his mother?"

"I made a special journey to Braemarnie and had a curious interview with Mrs. Muir. When I say 'curious' I don't mean to imply that it was not entirely dignified. It was curious only because I realize that secretly she regards with horror and dread the fact that her boy is the prospective Head of the House of Coombe. She does not make a jest of it as I have had the temerity to do. It's a cheap defense, this trick of making an eternal jest of things, but it IS a defense and one has formed the habit."

"She has never done it--Helen Muir," his friend said. "On the whole I believe she at times knows that she has been too grave. She was a beautiful creature passionately in love with her husband. When such a husband is taken away from such a woman and his child is left it often happens that the flood of her love is turned into one current and that it is almost overwhelming. She is too sane to have coddled the boy and made him effeminate--what has she done instead?"

"He is a splendid young Highlander. He would be too good-looking if he were not as strong and active as a young stag. All she has done is to so fill him with the power and sense of her charm that he has not seen enough of the world or learned to care for it. She is the one woman on earth for him and life with her at Braemarnie is all he asks for."

"Your difficulty will be that she will not be willing to trust him to your instructions."

"I have not as much personal vanity as I may seem to have," Coombe said. "I put all egotism modestly aside when I talked to her and tried to explain that I would endeavour to see that he came to no harm in my society. My heir presumptive and I must see something of each other and he must become intimate with the prospect of his responsibilities. More will be demanded of the next Marquis of Coombe than has been demanded of me. And it will be DEMANDED not merely hoped for or expected. And it will be the overwhelming forces of Fate which will demand it--not mere tenants or constituents or the general public."

"Have you any views as to WHAT will be demanded?" was her interested question.

"None. Neither has anyone else who shares my opinion. No one will have any until the readjustment comes. But before the readjustment there will be the pouring forth of blood--the blood of magnificent lads like Donal Muir--perhaps his own blood,--my God!"

"And there may be left no head of the house of Coombe," from the Duchess.

"There will be many a house left without its head--houses great and small. And if the peril of it were more generally foreseen at this date it would be less perilous than it is."

"Lads like that!" said the old Duchess bitterly. "Lads in their strength and joy and bloom! It is hideous."

"In all their young virility and promise for a next generation--the strong young fathers of forever unborn millions! It's damnable! And it will be so not only in England, but all over a blood drenched world."

It was in this way they talked to each other of the black tragedy for which they believed the world's stage already being set in secret, and though there were here and there others who felt the ominous inevitability of the raising of the curtain, the rest of the world looked on in careless indifference to the significance of the open training of its actors and even the resounding hammerings of its stage carpenters and builders. In these days the two discussed the matter more frequently and even in the tone of those who waited for the approach of a thing drawing nearer every day.

Each time the Head of the House of Coombe made one of his so-called "week end" visits to the parts an Englishman can reach only by crossing the Channel, he returned with new knowledge of the special direction in which the wind veered in the blowing of those straws he had so long observed with absorbed interest.

"Above all the common sounds of daily human life one hears in that one land the rattle and clash of arms and the unending thudding tread of marching feet," he said after one such visit. "Two generations of men creatures bred and born and trained to live as parts of a huge death dealing machine have resulted in a monstrous construction. Each man is a part of it and each part's greatest ambition is to respond to the shouted word of command as a mechanical puppet responds to the touch of a spring. To each unit of the millions, love of his own country means only hatred of all others and the belief that no other should be allowed existence. The sacred creed of each is that the immensity of Germany is such that there can be no room on the earth for another than itself. Blood and iron will clear the world of the inferior peoples. To the masses that is their God's will. Their God is an understudy of their Kaiser."

"You are not saying that as part of the trick of making a jest of things?"

"I wish to God I were. The poor huge inhuman thing he has built does not know that when he was a boy he did not play at war and battles as other boys do, but as a creature obsessed. He has played at soldiers with his people as his toys throughout all his morbid life--and he has hungered and thirsted as he has done it."

A Bible lay upon the table and the Duchess drew it towards her.

"There is a verse here--" she said "--I will find it." She turned the pages and found it. "Listen! 'Know this and lay it to thy heart this day. Jehovah is God in heaven above and on the earth beneath. There is none else.' That is a power which does not confine itself to Germany or to England or France or to the Map of Europe. It is the Law of the Universe--and even Wilhelm the Second cannot bend it to his almighty will. 'There is none else.'"

"'There is none else'," repeated Coombe slowly. "If there existed a human being with the power to drive that home as a truth into his delirious brain, I believe he would die raving mad. To him there is no First Cause which was not 'made in Germany.' And it is one of his most valuable theatrical assets. It is part of his paraphernalia--like the jangling of his sword and the glitter of his orders. He shakes it before his people to arrest the attention of the simple and honest ones as one jingles a rattle before a child. There are those among them who are not so readily attracted by terms of blood and iron."

"But they will be called upon to shed blood and to pour forth their own. There will be young things like Donal Muir--lads with ruddy cheeks and with white bodies to be torn to fragments." She shuddered as she said it. "I am afraid!" she said. "I am afraid!"

"So am I," Coombe answered. "Of what is coming. What a FOOL I have been!"

"How long will it be before other men awaken to say the same thing?"

"Each man's folly is his own shame." He drew himself stiffly upright as a man might who stood before a firing squad. "I had a life to live or to throw away. Because I was hideously wounded at the outset I threw it aside as done for. I said 'there is neither God nor devil, vice nor virtue, love nor hate. I will do and leave undone what I choose.' I had power and brain and money. A man who could see clearly and who had words to choose from might have stood firmly in the place to which he was born and have spoken in a voice which might have been listened to. He might have fought against folly and blindness and lassitude. I deliberately chose privately to sneer at the thought of lifting a hand to serve any thing but the cold fool who was myself. Life passes quickly. It does not turn back." He ended with a short harsh laugh. "This is Fear," he said. "Fear clears a man's mind of rubbish and non-essentials. It is because I am AFRAID that I accuse myself. And it is not for myself or you but for the whole world which before the end comes will seem to fall into fragments."

"You have been seeing ominous signs?" the Duchess said leaning forward and speaking low.

"There have been affectionate visits to Vienna. There is a certain thing in the air--in the arrogance of the bearing of men clanking their sabres as they stride through the streets. There is an exultant eagerness in their eyes. Things are said which hold scarcely concealed braggart threats. They have always been given to that sort of thing--but now it strikes one as a thing unleashed--or barely leashed at all. The background of the sound of clashing arms and the thudding of marching feet is more unendingly present. One cannot get away from it. The great munition factories are working night and day. In the streets, in private houses, in the shops, one hears and recognizes signs. They are signs which might not be clear to one who has not spent years in looking on with interested eyes. But I have watched too long to see only the surface of things. The nation is waiting for something--waiting."

"What will be the pretext--what," the Duchess pondered.

"Any pretext will do--or none--except that Germany must have what she wants and that she is strong enough to take it--after forty years of building her machine."

"And we others have built none. We almost deserve whatever comes to us." The old woman's face was darkly grave.

"In three villages where I chance to be lord of the manor I have, by means of my own, set lads drilling and training. It is supposed to be a form of amusement and an eccentric whim of mine and it is a change from eternal cricket. I have given prizes and made an occasional speech on the ground that English brawn is so envi-able a possession that it ought to develop itself to the utmost. When I once went to the length of adding that each Englishman should be muscle fit and ready in case of England's sudden need, I saw the lads grin cheerfully at the thought of England in any such un-English plight. Their innocent swaggering belief that the country is always ready for everything moved my heart of stone. And it is men like myself who are to blame--not merely men of my class, but men of my KIND. Those who have chosen to detach themselves from everything but the living of life as it best pleased their tastes or served their personal ambitions."

"Are we going to be taught that man cannot argue without including his fellow man? Are we going to be forced to learn it?" she said.

"Yes--forced. Nothing but force could reach us. The race is an undeveloped thing. A few centuries later it will have evolved another sense. This century may see the first huge step--because the power of a cataclysm sweeps it forward."

He turned his glance towards the opening door. Robin came in with some letters in her hand. He was vaguely aware that she wore an aspect he was unfamiliar with. The girl of Mrs. Gareth-Lawless had in the past, as it went without saying, expressed the final note of priceless simplicity and mode. The more finely simple she looked, the more priceless. The unfamiliarity in her outward seeming lay in the fact that her quiet dun tweed dress with its lines of white at neck and wrists was not priceless though it was well made. It, in fact, unobtrusively suggested that it was meant for service rather than for adornment. Her hair was dressed closely and her movements were very quiet. Coombe realized that her greeting of him was delicately respectful.

"I have finished the letters," she said to the Duchess. "I hope they are what you want. Sometimes I am afraid----"

"Don't be afraid," said the Duchess kindly. "You write very correct and graceful little letters. They are always what I want. Have you been out today?"

"Not yet." Robin hesitated a little. "Have I your permission to ask Mrs. James if it will be convenient to her to let Dowie go with me for an hour?"

"Yes," as kindly as before. "For two hours if you like. I shall not drive this afternoon."

"Thank you," said Robin and went out of the room as quietly as she had entered it.

When the door closed the Duchess was smiling at Lord Coombe.

"I understand her," she said. "She is sustained and comforted by her pretty air of servitude. She might use Dowie as her personal maid and do next to nothing, but she waits upon herself and punctiliously asks my permission to approach Mrs. James the housekeeper with any request for a favour. Her one desire is to be sure that she is earning her living as other young women do when they are paid for their work. I should really like to pet and indulge her, but it would only make her unhappy. I invent tasks for her which are quite unnecessary. For years the little shut-up soul has been yearning and praying for this opportunity to stand honestly on her own feet and she can scarcely persuade herself that it has been given to her. It must not be spoiled for her. I send her on errands my maid could perform. I have given her a little room with a serious business air. It is full of files and papers and she sits in it and copies things for me and even looks over accounts. She is clever at looking up references. I have let her sit up quite late once or twice searching for detail and dates for my use. It made her bloom with joy."

"You are quite the most delightful woman in the world," said Coombe. "Quite."

CHAPTER XXIX

In the serious little room the Duchess had given to her Robin built for herself a condition she called happiness. She drew the spiritual substance from which it was made from her pleasure in the books of reference closely fitted into their shelves, in the files for letters and more imposing documents, in the varieties of letter paper and envelopes of different sizes and materials which had been provided for her use in case of necessity.

"You may not use the more substantial ones often, but you must be prepared for any unexpected contingency," the Duchess had explained, thereby smoothing her pathway by the suggestion of responsibilities.

The girl did not know the extent of her employer's consideration for her, but she knew that she was kind with a special grace and comprehension. A subtle truth she also did not recognize was that the remote flame of her own being was fiercely alert in its readiness to leap upward at any suspicion that her duties were not worth the payment made for them and that for any reason which might include Lord Coombe she was occupying a position which was a sinecure. She kept her serious little room in order herself, dusting and almost polishing the reference books, arranging and re-arranging the files with such exactness of system that she could--as is the vaunt of the model of orderly perfection--lay her hand upon any document "in the dark." She was punctuality's self and held herself in readiness at any moment to appear at the Duchess' side as if a magician had instantaneously transported her there before the softly melodious private bell connected with her room had ceased to vibrate. The correctness of her to deference to the convenience of Mrs. James the housekeeper in her simplest communication with Dowie quite touched that respectable person's heart.

"She's a young lady," Mrs. James remarked to Dowie. "And a credit to you and her governess, Mrs. Dowson. Young ladies have gone almost out of fashion."

"Mademoiselle Valle had spent her governessing days among the highest. My own places were always with gentle-people. Nothing ever came near her that could spoil her manners. A good heart she was born with," was the civil reply of Dowie.

"Nothing ever came NEAR her--?" Mrs. James politely checked what she became conscious was a sort of unconscious exclamation.

"Nothing," said Dowie going on with her sheet hemming steadily.

Robin wrote letters and copied various documents for the Duchess, she went shopping with her and executed commissions to order. She was allowed to enter into correspondence with the village schoolmistress and the wife of the Vicar at Darte Norham and to buy prizes for notable decorum and scholarship in the school, and baby linen and blankets for the Maternity Bag and other benevolences. She liked buying prizes and the baby clothes very much because--though she was unaware of the fact--her youth delighted in youngness and the fulfilling of young desires. Even oftener and more significantly than ever did eyes turn towards her--try to hold hers--look after her eagerly when she walked in the streets or drove with the Duchess in the high-swung barouche. More and more she became used to it and gradually she ceased to be afraid of it and began to feel it nearly always--there were sometimes exceptions--a friendly thing.

She saw friendliness in it because when she caught sight as she so often did of young things like herself passing in pairs, laughing and talking and turning to look into each other's eyes, her being told her that it was sweet and human and inevitable. They always turned and looked at each other--these pairs--and then they smiled or laughed or flushed a little. As she had not known when first she recognized, as she looked down into the street from her nursery window, that the children nearly always passed in twos or threes and laughed and skipped and talked, so she did not know when she first began to notice these joyous young pairs and a certain touch of exultation in them and feel that it was sweet and quite a simple common natural thing. Her noting and being sometimes moved by it was as natural as her pleasure in the opening of spring flowers or the new thrill of spring birds--but she did not know that either.

The brain which has worked through many years in unison with the soul to which it was apportioned has evolved a knowledge which has deep cognizance of the universal law. The brain of the old Duchess had so worked, keeping pace always with its guide, never visualizing the possibility of working alone, also never falling into the abyss of that human folly whose conviction is that all that one sees and gives a special name to is all that exists--or that the names accepted by the world justly and clearly describe qualities, yearnings, moods, as they are. This had developed within her wide perception and a wisdom which was sane and kind to tenderness.

As she drove through the streets with Robin beside her she saw the following eyes, she saw the girl's soft friendly look at the young creatures who passed her glowing and uplifted by the joy of life, and she was moved and even disturbed.

After her return from one particular morning's outing she sent for Dowie.

"You have taken care of Miss Robin since she was a little child?" she began.

"She was not quite six when I first went to her, your grace."

"You are not of the women who only feed and bathe a child and keep her well dressed. You have been a sort of mother to her."

"I've tried to, your grace. I've loved her and watched over her and she's loved me, I do believe."

"That is why I want to talk to you about her, Dowie. If you were the woman who merely comes and goes in a child's life, I could not. She is--a very beautiful young thing, Dowie."

"From her little head to her slim bits of feet, your grace. No one knows better than I do."

The Duchess' renowned smile revealed itself.

"A beautiful young thing ought to see and know other beautiful young things and make friends with them. That is one of the reasons for their being put in the world. Since she has been with me she has spoken to no one under forty. Has she never had young friends?"

"Never, your grace. Once two--young baggages--were left to have tea with her and they talked to her about divorce scandals and corespondents. She never wanted to see them again." Dowie's face set itself in lines of perfectly correct inexpressiveness and she added, "They set her asking me questions I couldn't answer. And she broke down because she suddenly understood why. No, your grace, she's not known those of her own age."

"She is--of the ignorance of a child," the Duchess thought it out slowly.

"She thinks not, poor lamb, but she is," Dowie answered. The Duchess' eyes met hers and they looked at each other for a moment. Dowie tried to retain a non-committal steadiness and the Duchess observing the intention knew that she was free to speak.

"Lord Coombe confided to me that she had passed through a hideous danger which had made a lasting impression on her," she said in a low voice. "He told me because he felt it would explain certain reserves and fears in her."

"Sometimes she wakes up out of nightmares about it," said Dowie. "And she creeps into my room shivering and I take her into my bed and hold her in my arms until she's over the panic. She says the worst of it is that she keeps thinking that there may have been other girls trapped like her--and that they did not get away."

The Duchess was very thoughtful. She saw the complications in which such a horror would involve a girl's mind.

"If she consorted with other young things and talked nonsense with them and shared their pleasures she would forget it," she said.

"Ah!" exclaimed Dowie. "That's it."

The question in the Duchess' eyes when she lifted them required an answer and she gave it respectfully.

"The thing that happened was only the last touch put to what she'd gradually been finding out as she grew from child to young girl. The ones she would like to know--she said it in plain words once to Mademoiselle--might not want to know her. I must take the liberty of speaking plain, your grace, or it's no use me speaking at all. She holds it deep in her mind that she's a sort of young outcast."

"I must convince her that she is not--." It was the beginning of what the Duchess had meant to say, but she actually found herself pausing, held for the moment by Dowie's quiet, civil eye.

"Was your grace in your kindness thinking--?" was what the excellent woman said.

"Yes. That I would invite young people to meet her--help them to know each other and to make friends." And even as she said it she was conscious of being slightly under the influence of Dowie's wise gaze.

"Your grace only knows those young people she would like to know." It was a mere simple statement.

"People are not as censorious as they once were." Her grace's tone was intended to reply to the suggestion lying in the words which had worn the air of statement without comment.

"Some are not, but some are," Dowie answered. "There's two worlds in London now, your grace. One is your grace's and one is Mrs. Gareth-Lawless'. I HAVE heard say there are others between, but I only know those two."

The Duchess pondered again.

"You are thinking that what Miss Robin said to Mademoiselle Valle might be true--in mine. And perhaps you are not altogether wrong even if you are not altogether right."

"Until I went to take care of Miss Robin I had only had places in families Mrs. Gareth-Lawless' set didn't touch anywhere. What I'm remembering is that there was a--strictness--shown sometimes even when it seemed a bit harsh. Among the servants the older ones said that is was BECAUSE of the new sets and their fast wicked ways. One of my young ladies once met another young lady about her own age--she was just fifteen--at a charity bazaar and they made friends and liked each other very much. The young lady's mother was one there was a lot of talk about in connection with a person of very high station--the highest, your grace--and everyone knew. The girl was a lovely little creature and beautifully behaved. It was said her mother wanted to push her into the world she couldn't get into herself. The acquaintance was stopped, your grace--it was put a stop to at once. And my poor little young lady quite broke her heart over it, and I heard it was much worse for the other."

"I will think this over," the Duchess said. "It needs thinking over. I wished to talk to you because I have seen that she has fixed little ideas regarding what she thinks is suited to her position as a paid companion and she might not be prepared. I wish you to see that she has a pretty little frock or so which she could wear if she required them."

"She has two, your grace," Dowie smiled affectionately as she said it. "One for evening and one for special afternoon wear in case your grace needed her to attend you for some reason. They are as plain as she dare make them, but when she puts one on she can't help giving it A LOOK."

"Yes--she would give it all it needed," her grace said. "Thank you, Dowie. You may go."

With her sketch of a respectful curtsey Dowie went towards the door. As she approached it her step became slower; before she reached it she had stopped and there was a remarkable look on her face--a suddenly heroic look. She turned and made several steps backward and paused again which unexpected action caused the Duchess to turn to glance at her. When she glanced her grace recognized the heroic look and waited, with a consciousness of some slight new emotion within herself, for its explanation.

"Your grace," Dowie began, asking God himself to give courage if she was doing right and to check her if she was making a mistake, "When your grace was thinking of the parents of other young ladies and gentlemen--did it come to you to put it to yourself whether you'd be willing--" she caught her breath, but ended quite clearly, respectfully, reasonably. "Lady Kathryn--Lord Halwyn--" Lady Kathryn was the Duchess' young granddaughter, Lord Halwyn was her extremely good-looking grandson who was in the army.

The Duchess understood what the heroic look had meant, and her respect for it was great. Its intention had not been to suggest inclusion of George and Kathryn in her pun, it had only with pure justice put it to her to ask herself what her own personal decision in such a matter would be.

"You do feel as if you were her mother," she said. "And you are a practical, clear-minded woman. It is only if I myself am willing to take such a step that I have a right to ask it of other people. Lady Lothwell is the mother I must speak to first. Her children are mine though I am a mere grandmother."

Lady Lothwell was her daughter and though she was not regarded as Victorian either of the Early or the Middle periods, Dowie as she returned to her own comfortable quarters wondered what would happen.

CHAPTER XXX

What did occur was not at all complicated. It would not have been possible for a woman to have spent her girlhood with the cleverest mother of her day and have emerged from her training either obstinate or illogical. Lady Lothwell listened to as much of the history of Robin as her mother chose to tell her and plainly felt an amiable interest in it. She knew much more detail and gossip concerning Mrs. Gareth-Lawless than the Duchess herself did. She had heard of the child who was kept out of sight, and she had been somewhat disgusted by a vague story of Lord Coombe's abnormal interest in it and the ugly hint that he had an object in view. It was too unpleasantly morbid to be true of a man her mother had known for years.

"Of course you were not thinking of anything large or formal?" she said after a moment of smiling hesitation.

"No. I am not launching a girl into society. I only want to help her to know a few nice young people who are good-natured and well-mannered. She is not the ordinary old lady's companion and if she were not so strict with herself and with me, I confess I should behave towards her very much as I should behave to Kathryn if you could spare her to live with me. She is a heart-warming young thing. Because I am known to have one of my eccentric fancies for her and because after all her father WAS well connected, her present position will not be the obstacle. She is not the first modern girl who has chosen to support herself."

"But isn't she much too pretty?"

"Much. But she doesn't flaunt it."

"But heart-warming--and too pretty! Dearest mamma!" Lady Lothwell laughed again. "She can do no harm to Kathryn, but I own that if George were not at present quite madly in love with a darling being at least fifteen years older than himself

I should pause to reflect. Mrs. Stacy will keep him steady--Mrs. Alan Stacy, you know--the one with the magnificent henna hair, and the eyes that droop. No boy of twenty-two can resist her. They call her adorers 'The Infant School'."

"A small dinner and a small dance--and George and Kathryn may be the beginning of an interesting experiment. It would be pretty and kind of you to drop in during the course of the evening."

"Are you hoping to--perhaps--make a marriage for her?" Lady Lothwell asked the question a shade disturbedly. "You are so amazing, mamma darling, that I know you will do it, if you believe in it. You seem to be able to cause the things you really want, to evolve from the universe."

"She is the kind of girl whose place in the universe is in the home of some young man whose own place in the universe is in the heart and soul and life of her kind of girl. They ought to carry out the will of God by falling passionately in love with each other. They ought to marry each other and have a large number of children as beautiful and rapturously happy as themselves. They would assist in the evolution of the race."

"Oh! Mamma! how delightful you always are! For a really brilliant woman you are the most adorable dreamer in the world."

"Dreams are the only things which are true. The rest are nothing but visions."

"Angel!" her daughter laughed a little adoringly as she kissed her. "I will do whatever you want me to do. I always did, didn't I? It's your way of making one see what you see when you are talking that does it."

It was understood before they parted that Kathryn and George would be present at the small dinner and the small dance, and that a few other agreeable young persons might be trusted to join them, and that Lady Lothwell and perhaps her husband would drop in.

"It's your being almost Early Victorian, mamma, which makes it easy for you to initiate things. You will initiate little Miss Lawless. It was rather neat of her to prefer to drop the 'Gareth.' There has been less talk in late years of the different classes 'keeping their places'--'upper' and 'lower' classes really strikes one as vulgar."

"We may 'keep our places'," the Duchess said. "We may hold on to them as firmly as we please. It is the places themselves which are moving, my dear. It is not unlike the beginning of a landslide."

Robin went to Dowie's room the next evening and stood a moment in silence watching her sewing before she spoke. She looked anxious and even pale.

"Her grace is going to give a party to some young people, Dowie," she said. "She wishes me to be present. I--I don't know what to do."

"What you must do, my dear, is to put on your best evening frock and go downstairs and enjoy yourself as the other young people will. Her grace wants you to see someone your own age," was Dowie's answer.

"But I am not like the others. I am only a girl earning her living as a companion. How do I know--"

"Her grace knows," Dowie said. "And what she asks you to do it is your duty to do--and do it prettily."

Robin lost even a shade more colour.

"Do you realize that I have never been to a party in my life--not even to a children's party, Dowie? I shall not know how to behave myself."

"You know how to talk nicely to people, and you know how to sit down and rise from your chair and move about a room like a quiet young lady. You dance like a fairy. You won't be asked to do anything more."

"The Duchess," reflected Robin aloud slowly, "would not let me come downstairs if she did not know that people would--be kind."

"Lady Kathryn and Lord Halwyn are coming. They are her own grandchildren," Dowie said.

"How did you know that?" Robin inquired.

Robin's colour began to come back.

"It's not what usually happens to girls in situations," she said.

"Her grace herself isn't what usually happens," said Dowie. "There is no one like her for high wisdom and kindness."

Having herself awakened to the truth of this confidence-inspiring fact, Robin felt herself supported by it. One knew what far-sighted perception and clarity of experienced vision this one woman had gained during her many years of life. If she had elected to do this thing she had seen her path clear before her and was not offering a gift which awkward chance might spoil or snatch away from the hand held out to receive it. A curious slow warmth began to creep about Robin's heart and in its mounting gradually fill her being. It was true she had been taught to dance, to move about and speak prettily. She had been taught a great many things which seemed to be very carefully instilled into her mind and body without any special reason. She had not been aware that Lord Coombe and Mademoiselle Valle had directed and discussed her training as if it had been that of a young royal person whose equipment must be a flawless thing. If the Dowager Duchess of Darte had wished to present her at Court some fair morning she would have known the length of the train she must wear, where she must make her curtseys and to whom and to what depth, how to kiss the royal hand, and how to manage her train when she retired from the presence. When she had been taught this she had asked Mademoiselle Valle if the training was part of every girl's education and Mademoiselle had answered,

"It is best to know everything--even ceremonials which may or may not prove of use. It all forms part of a background and prevents one from feeling unfamiliar with customs."

When she had passed the young pairs in the streets she had found an added interest in them because of this background. She could imagine them dancing together in fairy ball rooms whose lights and colours her imagination was obliged to construct for her out of its own fabric; she knew what the girls would look like if they went to a Drawing Room and she often wondered if they would feel shy when the page spread out their lovely peacock tails for them and left them to their own devices. It was mere Nature that she should have pondered and pondered and sometimes unconsciously longed to feel herself part of the flood of being sweeping past her as she stood apart on the brink of the river.

The warmth about her heart made it beat a little faster. She opened the door of her wardrobe when she found herself in her bedroom. The dress hung modestly in its corner shrouded from the penetration of London fogs by clean sheeting. It was only white and as simple as she knew how to order it, but Mademoiselle had taken her to a young French person who knew exactly what she was doing in all cases, and because the girl had the supple lines of a wood nymph and the eyes of young antelope she had evolved that which expressed her as a petal expresses its rose. Robin locked her door and took the dress down and found the silk stockings and slippers which belonged to it. She put them all on standing before her long mirror and having left no ungiven last touch she fell a few steps backward and looked at herself, turning and balancing herself as a bird might have done. She turned lightly round and round.

"Yes. I AM--" she said. "I am--very!"

The next instant she laughed at herself outright.

"How silly! How silly!" she said. "Almost EVERYBODY is--more or less! I wonder if I remember the new steps." For she had been taught the new steps--the new walking and swayings and pauses and sudden swirls and swoops. And her new dress was as short as other fashionable girls' dresses were, but in her case revealed a haunting delicacy of contour and line.

So before her mirror she danced alone and as she danced her lips parted and her breast rose and fell charmingly, and her eyes lighted and glowed as any girl's might have done or as a joyous girl nymph's might have lighted as she danced by a pool in her forest seeing her loveliness mirrored there.

Something was awakening as something had awakened when Donal had kissed a child under the soot sprinkled London trees.

CHAPTER XXXI

The whole day before the party was secretly exciting to Robin. She knew how much more important it seemed to her than it really was. If she had been six years old she might have felt the same kind of uncertain thrills and tremulous wonders. She hid herself behind the window curtains in her room that she might see the men putting up the crimson and white awning from the door to the carriage step. The roll of red carpet they took from their van had a magic air. The ringing of the door bell which meant that things were being delivered, the extra moving about of servants, the florists' men who went into the drawing-rooms and brought flowers and big tropical plants to re-arrange the conservatory and fill corners which were not always decorated--each and every one of them quickened the beating of her pulses. If she had belonged in her past to the ordinary cheerful world of children, she would have felt by this time no such elation. But she had only known of the existence of such festivities as children's parties because once a juvenile ball had been given in a house opposite her mother's and she had crouched in an almost delirious little heap by the nursery window watching carriages drive up and deposit fluffy pink and white and blue children upon the strip of red carpet, and had seen them led or running into the house. She had caught sounds of strains of music and had shivered with rapture--but Oh! what worlds away from her the party had been.

She found her way into the drawing-rooms which were not usually thrown open. They were lofty and stately and seemed to her immense. There were splendid crystal-dropping chandeliers and side lights which she thought looked as if they would hold a thousand wax candles. There was a delightfully embowered corner for the musicians. It was all spacious and wonderful in its beautiful completeness--its preparedness for pleasure. She realized that all of it had always been waiting to be used for the happiness of people who knew each other and were young and ready for delight. When the young Lothwells had been children they had had dances and frolicking games with other children in the huge rooms and had kicked up their young heels on the polished floors at Christmas parties and on birthdays. How wonderful it must have been. But they had not known it was wonderful.

As Dowie dressed her the reflection she saw in the mirror gave back to her an intensified Robin whose curved lips almost quivered as they smiled. The soft silk of her hair looked like the night and the small rings on the back of her very slim white neck were things to ensnare the eye and hold it helpless.

"You look your best, my dear," Dowie said as she clasped her little necklace. "And it is a good best." Dowie was feeling tremulous herself though she could not have explained why. She thought that perhaps it was because she wished that Mademoiselle could have been with her.

Robin kissed her when the last touch had been given.

"I'm going to run down the staircase," she said. "If I let myself walk slowly I shall have time to feel queer and shy and I might seem to CREEP into the drawing-room. I mustn't creep in. I must walk in as if I had been to parties all my life."

She ran down and as she did so she looked like a white bird flying, but she was obliged to stop upon the landing before the drawing-room door to quiet a moment of excited breathing. Still when she entered the room she moved as she should and held her head poised with a delicately fearless air. The Duchess--who herself looked her best in her fine old ivory profiled way--gave her a pleased smile of welcome which was almost affectionate.

"What a perfect little frock!" she said. "You are delightfully pretty in it."

"Is it quite right?" said Robin. "Mademoiselle chose it for me."

"It is quite right. 'Frightfully right,' George would say. George will sit near you at dinner. He is my grandson--Lord Halwyn you know, and you will no doubt frequently hear him say things are 'frightfully' something or other during the evening. Kathryn will say things are 'deevy' or 'exquig'. I mention it because you may not know that she means 'exquisite' and 'divine.' Don't let it frighten you if you don't quite understand their language. They are dear handsome things sweeping along in the rush of their bit of century. I don't let it frighten me that their world seems to me an entirely new planet."

Robin drew a little nearer her. She felt something as she had felt years ago when she had said to Dowie. "I want to kiss you, Dowie." Her eyes were pools of childish tenderness because she so well understood the infinitude of the friendly tact which drew her within its own circle with the light humour of its "I don't let them frighten ME."

"You are kind--kind to me," she said. "And I am grateful--GRATEFUL."

The extremely good-looking young people who began very soon to drift into the brilliant big room--singly or in pairs of brother and sister--filled her with innocent delight. They were so well built and gaily at ease with each other and their surroundings, so perfectly dressed and finished. The filmy narrowness of delicate frocks, the shortness of skirts accentuated the youth and girlhood and added to it a sort of child fairy-likeness. Kathryn in exquisite wisps of silver-embroidered gauze looked fourteen instead of nearly twenty--aided by a dimple in her cheek and a small tilted nose. A girl in scarlet tulle was like a child out of a nursery ready to dance about a Christmas tree. Everyone seemed so young and so suggested supple dancing, perhaps because dancing was going on everywhere and all the world whether fashionable or unfashionable was driven by a passion for whirling, swooping and inventing new postures and fantastic steps. The young men had slim straight bodies and light movements. Their clothes fitted their suppleness to perfection. Robin thought they all looked as if they had had a great deal of delightful exercise and plenty of pleasure all their lives.

They were of that stream which had always seemed to be rushing past her in bright pursuit of alluring things which belonged to them as part of their existence, but which had had nothing to do with her own youth. Now the stream had paused as if she had for the moment some connection with it. The swift light she was used to seeing illuminate glancing eyes as she passed people in the street, she saw again and again as new arrivals appeared. Kathryn was quite excited by her eyes and eyelashes and George hovered about. There was a great deal of hovering. At the dinner table sleek young heads held themselves at an angle which allowed of their owners seeing through or around, or under floral decorations and alert young eyes showed an eager gleam. After dinner was over and dancing began the Duchess smiled shrewdly as she saw the gravitating masculine movement towards a certain point. It was the point where Robin stood with a small growing circle about her.

It was George who danced with her first. He was tall and slender and flexible and his good shoulders had a military squareness of build. He had also a nice square face, and a warmly blue eye and knew all the latest steps and curves and unexpected swirls. Robin was an ozier wand and there was no swoop or dart or sudden sway and change she was not alert at. The swing and lure of the music, the swift movement, the fluttering of airy draperies as slim sister nymphs flew past her, set her pulses beating with sweet young joy. A brief, uncontrollable ripple of laughter broke from her before she had circled the room twice.

"How heavenly it is!" she exclaimed and lifted her eyes to Halwyn's. "How heavenly!"

They were not safe eyes to lift in such a way to those of a very young man. They gave George a sudden enjoyable shock. He had heard of the girl who was a sort of sublimated companion to his grandmother. The Duchess herself had talked to him a little about her and he had come to the party intending to behave very amiably and help the little thing enjoy herself. He had also encountered before in houses where there were no daughters the smart well-born, young companion who was allowed all sorts of privileges because she knew how to assume tiresome little responsibilities and how to be entertaining enough to add cheer and spice to the life of the elderly and lonely. Sometimes she was a subtly appealing sort of girl and given to being sympathetic and to liking sympathy and quiet corners in conservatories or libraries, and sometimes she was capable of scientific flirtation and required scientific management. A man had to have his wits about him. This one as she flew like a blown leaf across the floor and laughed up into his face with wide eyes, produced a new effect and was a new kind.

"It's you who are heavenly," he answered with a boy's laugh. "You are like a feather--and a willow wand."

"You are light too," she laughed back, "and you are like steel as well."

Mrs. Alan Stacy, the lady with the magnificent henna hair, had recently given less time to him, being engaged in the preliminary instruction of a new member of the Infant Class. Such things will, of course, happen and though George had quite ingenuously raged in secret, the circumstances left him free to "hover" and hovering was a pastime he enjoyed.

"Let us go on like this forever and ever," he said sweeping half the length of the room with her and whirling her as if she were indeed a leaf in the wind, "Forever and ever."

"I wish we could. But the music will stop," she gave back.

"Music ought never to stop--never," he answered.

But the music did stop and when it began again almost immediately another tall, flexible young man made a lightning claim on her and carried her away only to hand her to another and he in his turn to another. She was not allowed more than a moment's rest and borne on the crest of the wave of young delight, she did not need more. Young eyes were always laughing into hers and elating her by a special look of pleasure in everything she did or said or inspired in themselves. How was she informed without phrases that for this exciting evening she was a creature without a flaw, that the loveliness of her eyes startled those who looked into them, that it was a thrilling experience to dance with her, that somehow she was new and apart and wonderful? No sleek-haired, slim and straight-backed youth said exactly any of these things to her, but somehow they were conveyed and filled her with a wondering realization of the fact that if they were true, they were no longer dreadful and maddening, since they only made people like and want to dance with one. To dance, to like people and be liked seemed so heavenly natural and right--to be only like air and sky and free, happy breathing. There was, it was true, a blissful little uplifted look about her which she herself was not aware of, but which was singularly stimulating to the masculine beholder. It only meant indeed that as she whirled and swayed and swooped laughing she was saying to herself at intervals,

"This is what other girls feel like. They are happy like this. I am laughing and talking to people just as other girls do. I am Robin Gareth-Lawless, but I am enjoying a party like this--a YOUNG party."

Lady Lothwell sitting near her mother watched the trend of affairs with an occasional queer interested smile.

"Well, mamma darling," she said at last as youth and beauty whirled by in a maelstrom of modern Terpsichorean liveliness, "she is a great success. I don't know whether it is quite what you intended or not."

The Duchess did not explain what she had intended. She was watching the trend also and thinking a good deal. On the whole Lady Lothwell had scarcely expected that she would explain. She rarely did. She seldom made mistakes, however.

Kathryn in her scant gauzy strips of white and silver having drifted towards them at the moment stood looking on with a funny little disturbed expression on her small, tip-tilted face.

"There's something ABOUT her, grandmamma," she said.

"All the girls see it and no one knows what it is. She's sitting out for a few minutes and just look at George--and Hal Brunton--and Captain Willys. They are all laughing, of course, and pretending to joke, but they would like to eat each other up. Perhaps it's her eyelashes. She looks out from under them as if they were a curtain."

Lady Lothwell's queer little smile became a queer little laugh.

"Yes. It gives her a look of being ecstatically happy and yet almost shy and appealing at the same time. Men can't stand it of course."

"None of them are trying to stand it," answered little Lady Kathryn somewhat in the tone of a retort.

"I don't believe she knows she does it," Lady Lothwell said quite reflectively.

"She does not know at all. That is the worst of it," commented the Duchess.

"Then you see that there IS a worst," said her daughter.

The Duchess glanced towards Kathryn, but fortunately the puzzled fret of the girl's forehead was even at the moment melting into a smile as a young man of much attraction descended upon her with smiles of his own and carried her into the Tango or Fox Trot or Antelope Galop, whichsoever it chanced to be.

"If she were really aware of it that would be 'the worst' for other people--for us probably. She could look out from under her lashes to sufficient purpose to call what she wanted and take and keep it. As she is not aware, it will make things less easy for herself--under the circumstances."

"The circumstance of being Mrs. Gareth-Lawless' daughter is not an agreeable one," said Lady Lothwell.

"It might give some adventurous boys ideas when they had time to realize all it means. Do you know I am rather sorry for her myself. I shouldn't be surprised if she were rather a dear little thing. She looks tender and cuddle-some. Perhaps she is like the heroine of a sentimental novel I read the other day. Her chief slave said of her 'She walks into a man's heart through his eyes and sits down there and makes a warm place which will never get cold again.' Rather nice, I thought."

The Duchess thought it rather nice also.

"'Never get cold again,'" she repeated. "What a heavenly thing to happen to a pair of creatures--if--" she paused and regarded Robin, who at the other side of the room was trying to decide some parlous question of dances to which there was more than one claimant. She was sweetly puckering her brow over her card and round her were youthful male faces looking eager and even a trifle tense with repressed anxiety for the victory of the moment.

"Oh!" Lady Lothwell laughed. "As Kitty says 'There's something about her' and it's not mere eyelashes. You have let loose a germ among us, mamma my sweet, and you can't do anything with a germ when you have let it loose. To quote Kitty again, 'Look at George!'"

The music which came from the bower behind which the musicians were hidden seemed to gain thrill and wildness as the hours went on. As the rooms grew warmer the flowers breathed out more reaching scent. Now and again Robin paused for a moment to listen to strange delightful chords and to inhale passing waves of something like mignonette and lilies, and apple blossoms in the sun. She thought there must be some flower which was like all three in one. The rushing stream was carrying her with it as it went--one of the happy petals on its surface. Could it ever cast her aside and leave her on the shore again? While the violins went singing on and the thousand wax candles shone on the faint or vivid colours which mingled into a sort of lovely haze, it did not seem possible that a thing so enchanting and so real could have an end at all. All the other things in her life seemed less real to-night.

In the conservatory there was a marble fountain which had long years ago been brought from a palace garden in Rome. It was not as large as it was beautiful and it had been placed among palms and tropic ferns whose leaves and fronds it splashed merrily among and kept deliciously cool and wet-looking. There was a quite intoxicating hot-house perfume of warm damp moss and massed flowers and it was the kind of corner any young man would feel it necessary to gravitate towards with a partner.

George led Robin to it and she naturally sat upon the edge of the marble basin and as naturally drew off a glove and dipped her hand into the water, splashing it a little because it felt deliciously cool. George stood near at first and looked down at her bent head. It was impossible not also to take in her small fine ear and the warm velvet white of the lovely little nape of her slim neck. He took them in with elated appreciation. He was not subtle minded enough to be aware that her reply to a casual remark he had made to her at dinner had had a remote effect upon him.

"One of the loveliest creatures I ever saw was a Mrs. Gareth-Lawless," he had said. "Are you related to her?"

"I am her daughter," Robin had answered and with a slightly startled sensation he had managed to slip into amiably deft generalities while he had secretly wondered how much his grandmother knew or did not know.

An involuntary thought of Feather had crossed his mind once or twice during the evening. This was the girl who, it was said, had actually been saved up for old Coombe. Ugly morbid sort of idea if it was true. How had the Duchess got hold of her and why and what was Coombe really up to? Could he have some elderly idea of wanting a youngster for a wife? Occasionally an old chap did. Serve him right if some young chap took the wind out of his sails. He was not a desperate character, but he had been very intimate with Mrs. Alan Stacy and her friends and it had made him careless. Also Robin had drawn him--drawn him more than he knew.

"Is it still heavenly?" he asked. (How pointed her fingers were and how soft and crushable her hand looked as it splashed like a child's.)

"More heavenly every minute," she answered. He laughed outright.

"The heavenly thing is the way you are enjoying it yourself. I never saw a girl light up a whole room before. You throw out stars as you dance."

"That's like a skyrocket," Robin laughed back. "And it's because in all my life I never went to a dance before."

"Never! You mean except to children's parties?"

"There were no children's parties. This is the first--first--first."

"Well, I don't see how that happened, but I am glad it did because it's been a great thing for me to see you at your first--first--first."

He sat down on the fountain's edge near her.

"I shall not forget it," he said.

"I shall remember it as long as I live," said Robin and she lifted her unsafe eyes again and smiled into his which made them still more unsafe.

Perhaps it was because he was extremely young, perhaps it was because he was immoral, perhaps because he had never held a tight rein on his fleeting emotions, even the next moment he felt that it was because he was an idiot--but suddenly he found he had let himself go and was kissing the warm velvet of the slim little nape--had kissed it twice.

He had not given himself time to think what would happen as a result, but what did happen was humiliating and ridiculous. One furious splash of the curled hand flung water into his face and eyes and mouth while Robin tore herself free from him and stood blazing with fury and woe--for it was not only fury he saw.

"You--You--!" she cried and actually would have swooped to the fountain again if he had not caught her arm.

He was furious himself--at himself and at her.

"You--little fool!" he gasped. "What did you do that for even if I WAS a jackass? There was nothing in it. You're so pretty----"

"You've spoiled everything!" she flamed, "everything--everything!"

"I've spoiled nothing. I've only been a fool--and it's your own fault for being so pretty."

"You've spoiled everything in the world! Now--" with a desolate horrible little sob, "now I can only go back--BACK!"

He had a queer idea that she spoke as if she were Cinderella and he had made the clock strike twelve. Her voice had such absolute grief in it that he involuntarily drew near her.

"I say," he was really breathless, "don't speak like that. I beg pardon. I'll grovel! Don't--Oh! Kathryn--COME here."

This last because at this difficult moment from between the banks of hot-house bloom and round the big palms his sister Kathryn suddenly appeared. She immediately stopped short and stared at them both--looking from one to the other.

"What is the matter?" she asked in a low voice.

"Oh! COME and talk to her," George broke forth. "I feel as if she might scream in a minute and call everybody in. I've been a lunatic and she has apparently never been kissed before. Tell her--tell her you've been kissed yourself."

A queer little look revealed itself in Kathryn's face. A delicate vein of her grandmother's wisdom made part of her outlook upon a rapidly moving and exciting world. She had never been hide-bound or dull and for a slight gauzy white and silver thing she was astute.

"Don't be impudent," she said to George as she walked up to Robin and put a cool hand on her arm. "He's only been silly. You'd better let him off," she said. She turned a glance on George who was wiping his sleeve with a handkerchief and she broke into a small laugh, "Did she push you into the fountain?" she asked cheerfully.

"She threw the fountain at me," grumbled George. "I shall have to dash off home and change."

"I would," replied Kathryn still cheerful. "You can apologize better when you're dry."

He slid through the palms like a snake and the two girls stood and gazed at each other. Robin's flame had died down and her face had settled itself into a sort of hardness. Kathryn did not know that she herself looked at her as the Duchess might have looked at another girl in the quite different days of her youth.

"I'll tell you something now he's gone," she said. "I HAVE been kissed myself and so have other girls I know. Boys like George don't really matter, though of course it's bad manners. But who has got good manners? Things rush so that there's scarcely time for manners at all. When an older man makes a snatch at you it's sometimes detestable. But to push him into the fountain was a good idea," and she laughed again.

"I didn't push him in."

"I wish you had," with a gleeful mischief. The next moment, however, the hint of a worried frown showed itself on her forehead. "You see," she said protestingly, "you are so FRIGHTFULLY pretty."

"I'd rather be a leper," Robin shot forth.

But Kathryn did not of course understand.

"What nonsense!" she answered. "What utter rubbish! You know you wouldn't. Come back to the ball room. I came here because my mother was asking for George."

She turned to lead the way through the banked flowers and as she did so added something.

"By the way, somebody important has been assassinated in one of the Balkan countries. They are always assassinating people. They like it. Lord Coombe has just come in and is talking it over with grandmamma. I can see they are quite excited in their quiet way."

As they neared the entrance to the ball room she paused a moment with a new kind of impish smile.

"Every girl in the room is absolutely shaky with thrills at this particular moment," she said. "And every man feels himself bristling a little. The very best looking boy in all England is dancing with Sara Studleigh. He dropped in by chance to call and the Duchess made him stay. He is a kind of miracle of good looks and takingness."

Robin said nothing. She had plainly not been interested in the Balkan tragedy and she as obviously did not care for the miracle.

"You don't ask who he is?" said Kathryn.

"I don't want to know."

"Oh! Come! You mustn't feel as sulky as that. You'll want to ask questions the moment you see him. I did. Everyone does. His name is Donal Muir. He's Lord Coombe's heir. He'll be the Head of the House of Coombe some day. Here he comes," quite excitedly, "Look!"

It was one of the tricks of Chance--or Fate--or whatever you will. The dance brought him within a few feet of them at that very moment and the slow walking steps he was taking held him--they were some of the queer stealthy almost stationary steps of the Argentine Tango. He was finely and smoothly fitted as the other youngsters were, his blond glossed head was set high on a heroic column of neck, he was broad of shoulder, but not too broad, slim of waist, but not too slim, long and strong of leg, but light and supple and firm. He had a fair open brow and a curved mouth laughing to show white teeth. Robin felt he ought to wear a kilt and plaid and that an eagle's feather ought to be standing up from a chieftain's bonnet on the fair hair which would have waved if it had been allowed length enough. He was scarcely two yards from her now and suddenly--almost as if he had been called--he turned his eyes away from Sara Studleigh who was the little thing in Christmas tree scarlet. They were blue like the clear water in a tarn when the sun shines on it and they were still laughing as his mouth was. Straight into hers they laughed--straight into hers.

CHAPTER XXXII

Through all aeons since all the worlds were made it is at least not unthinkable that in all the worlds of which our own atom is one, there has ruled a Force illimitable, unconquerable and inexplicable and whichsoever its world and whatsoever the sign denoting or the name given it, the Force--the Thing has been the same. Upon our own atom of the universe it is given the generic name of Love and its existence is that which the boldest need not defy, the most profound need not attempt to explain with clarity, the most brilliantly sophistical to argue away. Its forms of beauty, triviality, magnificence, imbecility, loveliness, stupidity, holiness, purity and bestiality neither detract from nor add to its unalterable power. As the earth revolves upon its axis and reveals night and day, Spring, Summer and Winter, so it reveals this ceaselessly working Force. Men who were as gods have been uplifted or broken by it, fools have trifled with it, brutes have sullied it, saints have worshipped, poets sung and wits derided it. As electricity is a force death dealing, or illuminating and power bestowing, so is this Great Impeller, and it is fatuous--howsoever worldly wise or moderately sardonic one would choose to be--to hint ironically that its proportions are less than the ages have proved them. Whether a world formed without a necessity for the presence and assistance of this psychological factor would have been a better or a worse one, it is--by good fortune--not here imperative that one should attempt to decide. What is--exists. None of us created it. Each one will deal with the Impeller as he himself either sanely or madly elects. He will also bear the consequences--and so also may others.

Of this force the Head of the House of Coombe and his old friend knew much and had often spoken to each other. They had both been accustomed to recognizing its signs subtle or crude, and watching their development. They had seen it in the eyes of creatures young enough to be called boys and girls, they had heard it in musical laughter and in silly giggles, they had seen it express itself in tragedy and comedy and watched it end in union or in a nothingness which melted away like a wisp of fog. But they knew it was a thing omnipresent and that no one passed through life untouched by it in some degree.

Years before this evening two children playing in a garden had not know that the Power--the Thing--drew them with its greatest strength because among myriads of atoms they two were created for oneness. Enraptured and unaware they played together, their souls and bodies drawn nearer each other every hour.

So it was that--without being portentous--one may say that when an unusually beautiful and unusually well dressed and perfectly fitted young man turned involuntarily in the particular London ball room in which Mrs. Gareth-Lawless' daughter watched the dancers, and looked unintentionally into the eyes of a girl standing for a moment near the wide entrance doors, the inexplicable and unconquerable Force reconnected its currents again.

Donal Muir's eyes only widened a little for a second's time. He had not known why he had suddenly looked around and he did not know why he was conscious of something which startled him a little. You could not actually stare at a girl because your eyes chanced to get entangled in hers for a second as you danced past her. It was true she was of a startling prettiness and there was something--. Yes, there was SOMETHING which drew the eye and--. He did not know what it was. It had actually given him a sort of electric shock. He laughed at himself a little and then his open brow looked puzzled for a moment.

"You saw Miss Lawless," said Sara Studleigh who was at the moment dancing prettily with him. She was guilty of something which might have been called a slight giggle, but it was good-natured. "I know, you saw Miss Lawless--the pretty one near the door."

"There are so many pretty ones near everything. You can't lift your eyes without seeing one," Donal answered. "What a lot of them!" (The sense of having received a slight electric shock made you feel that you must look again and find out what had caused it, he was thinking.)

"She is the one with the eyelashes."

"I have eyelashes--so have you," looking down at hers with a very taking expression. Hers were in fact nice ones.

"But ours are not two inches long and they don't make a big soft circle round our eyes when we look at anyone."

"Please look up and let me see," said Donal. "When I asked you to dance with me I thought--"

What a "way" he had, Sara Studleigh was thinking. But "perhaps it WAS the eyelashes" was passing through Donal's mind. Very noticeable eyelashes were rather arresting.

"I knew you saw her," said Sara Studleigh, "because I have happened to be near two or three people this evening when they caught their first sight of her."

"What happens to them?" asked Donal Muir.

"They forget where they are," she laughed, "and don't say anything for a few seconds."

"I should not want to forget where I am. It wouldn't be possible either," answered Donal. ("But that was it," he thought. "For a minute I forgot.")

One should not dance with one girl and talk to her about another. Wisely he led her to other subjects. The music was swinging through the air performing its everlasting miracle of swinging young souls and pulses with it, the warmed flowers breathed more perceptible scent, sweet chatter and laughter, swaying colour and glowing eyes concentrated in making magic. This beautiful young man's pulses only beat with the rest--as one with the pulse of the Universe. Lady Lothwell acting for the Duchess was very kind to him finding him another partner as soon as a new dance began--this time her own daughter, Lady Kathryn.

Even while he had been tangoing with Sara Studleigh he had seen the girl with the eyelashes, whirling about with someone, and when he began his dance with Kathryn, he caught a glimpse of her at the other end of the room. And almost immediately Kathryn spoke of her.

"I don't know when you will get a dance with Miss Lawless," she said. "She is obliged to work out mathematical problems on her programme."

"I have a setter who fixes his eyes on you and waits without moving until you look at him and then he makes a dart and you're obliged to pat him," he said. "Perhaps if I go and stand near her and do that she will take notice of me."

"Take notice of him, the enslaving thing!" thought Kathryn. "She'd jump--for all her talk about lepers--any girl would. He's TOO nice! There's something about HIM too."

Robin did not jump. She had no time to do it because one dance followed another so quickly and some of them were even divided in two or three pieces. But the thrill of the singing sound of the violins behind the greenery, the perfume and stately spaces and thousand candlelights had suddenly been lifted on to another plane though she had thought they could reach no higher one. Her whole being was a keen fine awareness. Every moment she was AWARE. After all the years--from the far away days--he had come back. No one had dreamed of the queer half abnormal secret she had always kept to herself as a child--as a little girl--as a bigger one when she would have died rather than divulge that in her loneliness there had been something she had remembered--something she had held on to--a memory which she had actually made a companion of, making pictures, telling herself stories in the dark, even inventing conversations which not for one moment had she thought would or could ever take place. But they had been living things to her and her one near warm comfort--closer, oh, so weirdly closer than kind, kind Dowie and dearly beloved Mademoiselle. She had wondered if the two would have disapproved if they had known--if Mademoiselle would have been shocked if she had realized that sometimes when they walked together there walked with them a growing, laughing boy in a swinging kilt and plaid and that he had a voice and eyes that drew the heart out of your breast for joy. At first he had only been a child like herself, but as she had grown he had grown with her--but always taller, grander, marvellously masculine and beyond compare. Yet never once had she dared to believe or hope that he could take form before her eyes--a living thing. He had only been the shadow she had loved and which could not be taken away from her because he was her secret and no one could ever know.

The music went swinging and singing with notes which were almost a pain. And he was in the very room with her! Donal! Donal! He had not known and did not know. He had laughed into her eyes without knowing--but he had come back. A young man now like all the rest, but more beautiful. What a laugh, what wonderful shoulders, what wonderful dancing, how long and strongly smooth and supple he was in the line fabric of his clothes! Though her mind did not form these things in words for her, it was only that her eyes saw all the charm of him from head to foot, and told her that he was only more than ever what he had been in the miraculous first days.

"Perhaps he will not find out at all," she thought, dancing all the while and trying to talk as well as think. "I was too little for him to remember. I only remembered because I had nothing else. Oh, if he should not find out!" She could not go and tell him. Even if a girl could do such a thing, perhaps he could not recall a childish incident of so long ago--such a small, small thing. It had only been immense to her and so much water had flowed under his bridge bearing so many flotillas. She had only stood and looked down at a thin trickling stream which carried no ships at all. It was very difficult to keep her eyes from stealing--even darting--about in search of him. His high fair head with the clipped wave in its hair could be followed if one dared be alert. He danced with an auburn haired girl, he spun down the room with a brown one, he paused for a moment to show the trick of a new step to a tall one with black coils. He was at the end of the room, he was tangoing towards her and she felt her heart beat and beat. He passed close by and his eyes turned upon her and after he had passed a queer little inner trembling would not cease. Oh! if he had looked a little longer--if her partner would only carry her past him! And how dreadful she was to let herself feel so excited when he could not be EXPECTED to remember such a little thing--just a baby playing with him in a garden. Oh!--her heart giving a leap--if he would look--if he would LOOK!

When did she first awaken to a realization--after what seemed years and years of waiting and not being able to conquer the inwardly trembling feeling--that he was BEGINNING to look--that somehow he had become aware of her presence and that it drew his eyes though there was no special recognition in them? Down the full length of the room they met hers first, and again as he passed with yet another partner. Then when he was resting between danced and being very gay indeed--though somehow he always seemed gay. He had been gay when they played in the Gardens. Yes, his eyes cane and found her. She thought he spoke of her to someone near him. Of course Robin looked away and tried not to look again too soon. But when in spite of intention and even determination, something forced her glance and made it a creeping, following glance--there were his eyes again. She was frightened each time it happened, but he was not. She began to know with new beatings of the pulse that he no longer looked by chance, but because he wanted to see her-

-and wished her to see him, as if he had begun to call to her with a gay Donal challenge. It was like that, though his demeanour was faultlessly correct.

The incident of their meeting was faultlessly correct, also, when after one of those endless lapses of time Lady Lothwell appeared and presented him as if the brief ceremony were one of the most ordinary in existence. The conventional grace of his bow said no more than George's had said to those looking on, but when he put his arm round her and they began to sway together in the dance, Robin wondered in terror if he could not feel the beating of her heart under his hand. If he could it would be horrible--but it would not stop. To be so near--to try to believe it--to try to make herself remember that she could mean nothing to him and that it was only she who was shaking--for nothing! But she could not help it. This was the disjointed kind of thing that flew past her mental vision. She was not a shy girl, but she could not speak. Curiously enough he also was quite silent for several moments. They danced for a space without a word and they did not notice that people began to watch them because they were an attracting pair to watch. And the truth was that neither of the two knew in the least what the other thought.

"That--is a beautiful waltz," he said at last. He said it in a low meaning voice as if it were a sort of emotional confidence. He had not actually meant to speak in such a tone, but when he realized what its sound had been he did not care in the least. What was the matter with him?

"Yes," Robin answered. (Only "Yes.")

He had not known when he glanced at her first, he was saying mentally. He could not, of course, swear to her now. But what an extraordinary thing that--! She was like a swallow--she was like any swift flying thing on a man's arm. One could go on to the end of time. Once round the great ball room, twice, and as the third round began he gave a little laugh and spoke again.

"I am going to ask you a question. May I?"

"Yes."

"Is your name Robin?"

"Yes," she could scarcely breathe it.

"I thought it was," in the voice in which he had spoken of the music. "I hoped it was--after I first began to suspect. I HOPED it was."

"It is--it is."

"Did we--" he had not indeed meant that his arm should hold her a shade closer, but--in spite of himself--it did because he was after all so little more than a boy, "--did we play together in a garden?"

"Yes--yes," breathed Robin. "We did." Surely she heard a sound as if he had caught a quick breath. But after it there were a few more steps and another brief space of silence.

"I knew," he said next, very low. "I KNEW that we played together in a garden."

"You did not know when you first looked at me tonight." Innocently revealing that even his first glance had been no casual thing to her.

But his answer revealed something too.

"You were near the door--just coming into the room. I didn't know why you startled me. I kept looking for you afterwards in the crowd."

"I didn't see you look," said Robin softly, revealing still more in her utter inexperience.

"No, because you wouldn't look at me--you were too much engaged. Do you like this step?"

"I like them all."

"Do you always dance like this? Do you always make your partner feel as if he had danced with you all his life?"

"It is--because we played together in the garden," said Robin and then was quite terrified at herself. Because after all--after all they were only two conventional young people meeting for the first time at a dance, not knowing each other in the least. It was really the first time. The meeting of two children could not count. But the beating and strange elated inward tremor would not stop.

As for him he felt abnormal also and he was usually a very normal creature. It was abnormal to be so excited that he found himself, as it were, upon another plane, because he had recognized and was dancing with a girl he had not seen since she was five or six. It was not normal that he should be possessed by a desire to keep near to her, overwhelmed by an impelling wish to talk to her--to ask her questions. About what--about herself--themselves--the years between--about the garden.

"It began to come back bit by bit after I had two fair looks. You passed me several times though you didn't know." (Oh! had she not known!) "I had been promised some dances by other people. But I went to Lady Lothwell. She's very kind."

Back swept the years and it had all begun again, the wonderful happiness--just as the anguish had swept back on the night her mother had come to talk to her. As he had brought it into her dreary little world then, he brought it now. He had the power. She was so happy that she seemed to be only waiting to hear what he would say--as if that were enough. There are phases like this--rare ones--and it was her fate that through such a phase she was passing.

It was indeed true that much more water had passed under his bridge than under hers, but now--! Memory reproduced for him with an acuteness like actual pain, a childish torment he thought he had forgotten. And it was as if it had been endured only yesterday--and as if the urge to speak and explain was as intense as it had been on the first day.

"She's very little and she won't understand," he had said to his mother. "She's very little, really--perhaps she'll cry."

How monstrous it had seemed! Had she cried--poor little soul! He looked down at her eyelashes. Her cheek had been of the same colour and texture then. That came back to him too. The impulse to tighten his arms was infernally powerful--almost automatic.

"She has no one but me to remember!" he heard his own child voice saying fiercely. Good Lord, it WAS as if it had been yesterday. He actually gulped something down in his throat.

"You haven't rested much," he said aloud. "There's a conservatory with marble seats and corners and a fountain going. Will you let me take you there when we stop dancing? I want to apologize to you."

The eyelashes lifted themselves and made round her eyes the big soft shadow of which Sara Studleigh had spoken. A strong and healthy valvular organ in his breast lifted itself curiously at the same time.

"To apologize?"

Was he speaking to her almost as if she were still four or five? It was to the helplessness of those years he was about to explain--and yet he did not feel as though he were still eight.

"I want to tell you why I never came back to the garden. It was a broken promise, wasn't it?"

The music had not ceased, but they stopped dancing.

"Will you come?" he said and she went with him like a child--just as she had followed in her babyhood. It seemed only natural to do what he asked.

The conservatory was like an inner Paradise now. The tropically scented warmth--the tiers on tiers of bloom above bloom--the softened swing of music--the splash of the fountain on water and leaves. Their plane had lifted itself too. They could hear the splashing water and sometimes feel it in the corner seat of marble he took her to. A crystal drop fell on her hand when she sat down. The blue of his eyes was vaguely troubled and he spoke as if he were not certain of himself.

"I was wakened up in what seemed to me the middle of the night," he said, as if indeed the thing had happened only the day before. "My mother was obliged to go back suddenly to Scotland. I was only a little chap, but it nearly finished me. Parents and guardians don't understand how gigantic such a thing can be. I had promised you--we had promised each other--hadn't we?"

"Yes," said Robin. Her eyes were fixed upon his face--open and unmoving. Such eyes! Such eyes! All the touchingness of the past was in their waiting on his words.

"Children--little boys especially--are taught that they must not cry out when they are hurt. As I sat in the train through the journey that day I thought my heart would burst in my small breast. I turned my back and stared out of the window for fear my mother would see my face. I'd always loved her. Do you know I think that just then I HATED her. I had never hated anything before. Good Lord! What a thing for a little chap to go through! My mother was an angel, but she didn't KNOW."

"No," said Robin in a small strange voice and without moving her gaze. "She didn't KNOW."

He had seated himself on a sort of low marble stool near her and he held a knee with clasped hands. They were hands which held each other for the moment with a sort of emotional clinch. His position made him look upward at her instead of down.

"It was YOU I was wild about," he said. "You see it was YOU. I could have stood it for myself. The trouble was that I felt I was such a big little chap. I thought I was years--ages older than you--and mountains bigger," his faint laugh was touched with pity for the smallness of the big little chap. "You seemed so tiny and pretty--

and lonely."

"I was as lonely as a new-born bird fallen out of its nest."

"You had told me you had 'nothing.' You said no one had ever kissed you. I'd been loved all my life. You had a wondering way of fixing your eyes on me as if I could give you everything--perhaps it was a coxy little chap's conceit that made me love you for it--but perhaps it wasn't."

"You WERE everything," Robin said--and the mere simpleness of the way in which she said it brought the garden so near that he smelt the warm hawthorn and heard the distant piano organ and it quickened his breath.

"It was because I kept seeing your eyes and hearing your laugh that I thought my heart was bursting. I knew you'd go and wait for me--and gradually your little face would begin to look different. I knew you'd believe I'd come. 'She's little'--that was what I kept saying to myself again and again. 'And she'll cry--awfully--and she'll think I did it. She'll never know.' There,"--he hesitated a moment--"there was a kind of mad shame in it. As if I'd BETRAYED your littleness and your belief, though I was too young to know what betraying was."

Just as she had looked at him before, "as if he could give her everything," she was looking at him now. In what other way could she look while he gave her this wonderful soothing, binding softly all the old wounds with unconscious, natural touch because he had really been all her child being had been irradiated and warmed by. There was no pose in his manner--no sentimental or flirtatious youth's affecting of a picturesque attitude. It was real and he told her this thing because he must for his own relief.

"Did you cry?" he said. "Did my little chap's conceit make too much of it? I suppose I ought to hope it did."

Robin put her hand softly against her heart.

"No," she answered. "I was only a baby, but I think it KILLED something--here."

He caught a big hard breath.

"Oh!" he said and for a few seconds simply sat and gazed at her.

"But it came to life again?" he said afterwards.

"I don't know. I don't know what it was. Perhaps it could only live in a very little creature. But it was killed."

"I say!" broke from him. "It was like wringing a canary's neck when it was singing in the sun!"

A sudden swelling of the music of a new dance swept in to them and he rose and stood up before her.

"Thank you for giving me my chance to tell you," he said. "This was the apology. You have been kind to listen."

"I wanted to listen," Robin said. "I am glad I didn't live a long time and grow old and die without your telling me. When I saw you tonight I almost said aloud, 'He's come back!'"

"I'm glad I came. It's queer how one can live a thing over again. There have been all the years between for us both. For me there's been all a lad's life--tutors and Eton and Oxford and people and lots of travel and amusement. But the minute I set eyes on you near the door something must have begun to drag me back. I'll own I've never liked to let myself dwell on that memory. It wasn't a good thing because it had a trick of taking me back in a fiendish way to the little chap with his heart bursting in the railway carriage--and the betrayal feeling. It's morbid to let yourself grouse over what can't be undone. So you faded away. But when I danced past you somehow I knew I'd come on SOMETHING. It made me restless. I couldn't keep my eyes away decently. Then all at once I KNEW! I couldn't tell you what the effect was. There you were again--I was as much obliged to tell you as I should have been if I'd found you at Braemarnie when I got there that night. Conventions had nothing to do with it. It would not have mattered even if you'd obviously thought I was a fool. You might have thought so, you know."

"No, I mightn't," answered Robin. "There have been no Eton and Oxford and amusements for me. This is my first party."

She rose as he had done and they stood for a second or so with their eyes resting on each other's--each with a young smile quivering into life which neither was conscious of. It was she who first wakened and came back. He saw a tiny pulse flutter in her throat and she lifted her hand with a delicate gesture.

"This dance was Lord Halwyn's and we've sat it out. We must go back to the ball room."

"I--suppose--we must," he answered with slow reluctance--but he could scarcely drag his eyes away from hers--even though he obeyed, and they turned and went.

In the shining ball room the music rose and fell and swelled again into ecstasy as he took her white young lightness in his arm and they swayed and darted and swooped like things of the air--while the old Duchess and Lord Coombe looked on almost unseeing and talked in murmurs of Sarajevo.

The Codes Of Hammurabi And Moses
W. W. Davies

QTY

The discovery of the Hammurabi Code is one of the greatest achievements of archaeology, and is of paramount interest, not only to the student of the Bible, but also to all those interested in ancient history...

Religion   ISBN: *1-59462-338-4*   **Pages:132**
MSRP $12.95

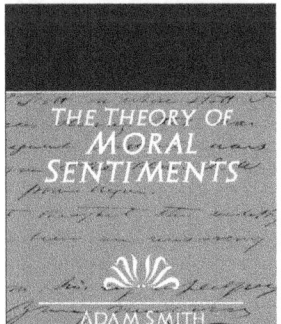

The Theory of Moral Sentiments
Adam Smith

QTY

This work from 1749. contains original theories of conscience amd moral judgment and it is the foundation for systemof morals.

Philosophy ISBN: *1-59462-777-0*   **Pages:536**
MSRP $19.95

Jessica's First Prayer
Hesba Stretton

QTY

In a screened and secluded corner of one of the many railway-bridges which span the streets of London there could be seen a few years ago, from five o'clock every morning until half past eight, a tidily set-out coffee-stall, consisting of a trestle and board, upon which stood two large tin cans, with a small fire of charcoal burning under each so as to keep the coffee boiling during the early hours of the morning when the work-people were thronging into the city on their way to their daily toil...

Childrens   ISBN: *1-59462-373-2*   **Pages:84**
MSRP $9.95

My Life and Work
Henry Ford

QTY

Henry Ford revolutionized the world with his implementation of mass production for the Model T automobile. Gain valuable business insight into his life and work with his own auto-biography... "We have only started on our development of our country we have not as yet, with all our talk of wonderful progress, done more than scratch the surface. The progress has been wonderful enough but..."

Biographies/   ISBN: *1-59462-198-5*   **Pages:300**
MSRP $21.95

www.bookjungle.com *email: sales@bookjungle.com fax: 630-214-0564 mail: Book Jungle PO Box 2226 Champaign, IL 61825*

The Art of Cross-Examination
Francis Wellman

QTY

I presume it is the experience of every author, after his first book is published upon an important subject, to be almost overwhelmed with a wealth of ideas and illustrations which could readily have been included in his book, and which to his own mind, at least, seem to make a second edition inevitable. Such certainly was the case with me; and when the first edition had reached its sixth impression in five months, I rejoiced to learn that it seemed to my publishers that the book had met with a sufficiently favorable reception to justify a second and considerably enlarged edition. ..

Pages:412

Reference   ISBN: *1-59462-647-2*   *MSRP $19.95*

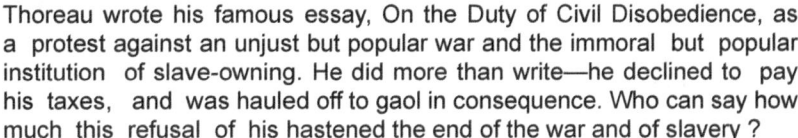

On the Duty of Civil Disobedience
Henry David Thoreau

QTY

Thoreau wrote his famous essay, On the Duty of Civil Disobedience, as a protest against an unjust but popular war and the immoral but popular institution of slave-owning. He did more than write—he declined to pay his taxes, and was hauled off to gaol in consequence. Who can say how much this refusal of his hastened the end of the war and of slavery ?

Law   ISBN: *1-59462-747-9*   **Pages:48**

MSRP $7.45

Dream Psychology Psychoanalysis for Beginners
Sigmund Freud

QTY

Sigmund Freud, born Sigismund Schlomo Freud (May 6, 1856 - September 23, 1939), was a Jewish-Austrian neurologist and psychiatrist who co-founded the psychoanalytic school of psychology. Freud is best known for his theories of the unconscious mind, especially involving the mechanism of repression; his redefinition of sexual desire as mobile and directed towards a wide variety of objects; and his therapeutic techniques, especially his understanding of transference in the therapeutic relationship and the presumed value of dreams as sources of insight into unconscious desires.

Pages:196

Psychology   ISBN: *1-59462-905-6*   *MSRP $15.45*

The Miracle of Right Thought
Orison Swett Marden

QTY

Believe with all of your heart that you will do what you were made to do. When the mind has once formed the habit of holding cheerful, happy, prosperous pictures, it will not be easy to form the opposite habit. It does not matter how improbable or how far away this realization may see, or how dark the prospects may be, if we visualize them as best we can, as vividly as possible, hold tenaciously to them and vigorously struggle to attain them, they will gradually become actualized, realized in the life. But a desire, a longing without endeavor, a yearning abandoned or held indifferently will vanish without realization.

Pages:360

Self Help   ISBN: *1-59462-644-8*   *MSRP $25.45*

www.bookjungle.com *email: sales@bookjungle.com fax: 630-214-0564 mail: Book Jungle PO Box 2226 Champaign, IL 61825*

QTY

The Rosicrucian Cosmo-Conception Mystic Christianity by *Max Heindel*   ISBN: *1-59462-188-8*   **$38.95**
The Rosicrucian Cosmo-conception is not dogmatic, neither does it appeal to any other authority than the reason of the student. It is: not controversial, but is: sent forth in the, hope that it may help to clear...   New Age/Religion 646

Abandonment To Divine Providence by *Jean-Pierre de Caussade*   ISBN: *1-59462-228-0*   **$25.95**
"The Rev. Jean Pierre de Caussade was one of the most remarkable spiritual writers of the Society of Jesus in France in the 18th Century. His death took place at Toulouse in 1751. His works have gone through many editions and have been republished...   Inspirational/Religion Pages 400

Mental Chemistry by *Charles Haanel*   ISBN: *1-59462-192-6*   **$23.95**
Mental Chemistry allows the change of material conditions by combining and appropriately utilizing the power of the mind. Much like applied chemistry creates something new and unique out of careful combinations of chemicals the mastery of mental chemistry...   New Age Pages 354

The Letters of Robert Browning and Elizabeth Barret Barrett 1845-1846 vol II   ISBN: *1-59462-193-4*   **$35.95**
by Robert Browning and Elizabeth Barrett   Biographies Pages 596

Gleanings In Genesis (volume I) by *Arthur W. Pink*   ISBN: *1-59462-130-6*   **$27.45**
Appropriately has Genesis been termed "the seed plot of the Bible" for in it we have, in germ form, almost all of the great doctrines which are afterwards fully developed in the books of Scripture which follow...   Religion/Inspirational Pages 420

The Master Key by *L. W. de Laurence*   ISBN: *1-59462-001-6*   **$30.95**
In no branch of human knowledge has there been a more lively increase of the spirit of research during the past few years than in the study of Psychology, Concentration and Mental Discipline. The requests for authentic lessons in Thought Control, Mental Discipline and...   New Age/Business Pages 422

The Lesser Key Of Solomon Goetia by *L. W. de Laurence*   ISBN: *1-59462-092-X*   **$9.95**
This translation of the first book of the "Lemegton" which is now for the first time made accessible to students of Talismanic Magic was done, after careful collation and edition, from numerous Ancient Manuscripts in Hebrew, Latin, and French...   New Age/Occult Pages 92

Rubaiyat Of Omar Khayyam by *Edward Fitzgerald*   ISBN:*1-59462-332-5*   **$13.95**
Edward Fitzgerald, whom the world has already learned, in spite of his own efforts to remain within the shadow of anonymity, to look upon as one of the rarest poets of the century, was born at Bredfield, in Suffolk, on the 31st of March, 1809. He was the third son of John Purcell...   Music Pages 172

Ancient Law by *Henry Maine*   ISBN: *1-59462-128-4*   **$29.95**
The chief object of the following pages is to indicate some of the earliest ideas of mankind, as they are reflected in Ancient Law, and to point out the relation of those ideas to modern thought.   Religion/History Pages 452

Far-Away Stories by *William J. Locke*   ISBN: *1-59462-129-2*   **$19.45**
"Good wine needs no bush, but a collection of mixed vintages does. And this book is just such a collection. Some of the stories I do not want to remain buried for ever in the museum files of dead magazine-numbers an author's not unpardonable vanity..."   Fiction Pages 272

Life of David Crockett by *David Crockett*   ISBN: *1-59462-250-7*   **$27.45**
"Colonel David Crockett was one of the most remarkable men of the times in which he lived. Born in humble life, but gifted with a strong will, an indomitable courage, and unremitting perseverance...   Biographies/New Age Pages 424

Lip-Reading by *Edward Nitchie*   ISBN: *1-59462-206-X*   **$25.95**
Edward B. Nitchie, founder of the New York School for the Hard of Hearing, now the Nitchie School of Lip-Reading, Inc, wrote "LIP-READING Principles and Practice". The development and perfecting of this meritorious work on lip-reading was an undertaking...   How-to Pages 400

A Handbook of Suggestive Therapeutics, Applied Hypnotism, Psychic Science   ISBN: *1-59462-214-0*   **$24.95**
by Henry Munro   Health/New Age/Health/Self-help Pages 376

A Doll's House: and Two Other Plays by *Henrik Ibsen*   ISBN: *1-59462-112-8*   **$19.95**
Henrik Ibsen created this classic when in revolutionary 1848 Rome. Introducing some striking concepts in playwriting for the realist genre, this play has been studied the world over.   Fiction/Classics/Plays 308

The Light of Asia by *sir Edwin Arnold*   ISBN: *1-59462-204-3*   **$13.95**
In this poetic masterpiece, Edwin Arnold describes the life and teachings of Buddha. The man who was to become known as Buddha to the world was born as Prince Gautama of India but he rejected the worldly riches and abandoned the reigns of power when... Religion/History/Biographies Pages 170

The Complete Works of Guy de Maupassant by *Guy de Maupassant*   ISBN: *1-59462-157-8*   **$16.95**
"For days and days, nights and nights, I had dreamed of that first kiss which was to consecrate our engagement, and I knew not on what spot I should put my lips..."   Fiction/Classics Pages 240

The Art of Cross-Examination by *Francis L. Wellman*   ISBN: *1-59462-309-0*   **$26.95**
Written by a renowned trial lawyer, Wellman imparts his experience and uses case studies to explain how to use psychology to extract desired information through questioning.   How-to/Science/Reference Pages 408

Answered or Unanswered? by *Louisa Vaughan*   ISBN: *1-59462-248-5*   **$10.95**
Miracles of Faith in China   Religion Pages 112

The Edinburgh Lectures on Mental Science (1909) by *Thomas*   ISBN: *1-59462-008-3*   **$11.95**
This book contains the substance of a course of lectures recently given by the writer in the Queen Street Hall, Edinburgh. Its purpose is to indicate the Natural Principles governing the relation between Mental Action and Material Conditions...   New Age/Psychology Pages 148

Ayesha by *H. Rider Haggard*   ISBN: *1-59462-301-5*   **$24.95**
Verily and indeed it is the unexpected that happens! Probably if there was one person upon the earth from whom the Editor of this, and of a certain previous history, did not expect to hear again...   Classics Pages 380

Ayala's Angel by *Anthony Trollope*   ISBN: *1-59462-352-X*   **$29.95**
The two girls were both pretty, but Lucy who was twenty-one who supposed to be simple and comparatively unattractive, whereas Ayala was credited, as her Bombwhat romantic name might show, with poetic charm and a taste for romance. Ayala when her father died was nineteen...   Fiction Pages 484

The American Commonwealth by *James Bryce*   ISBN: *1-59462-286-8*   **$34.45**
An interpretation of American democratic political theory. It examines political mechanics and society from the perspective of Scotsman James Bryce   Politics Pages 572

Stories of the Pilgrims by *Margaret P. Pumphrey*   ISBN: *1-59462-116-0*   **$17.95**
This book explores pilgrims religious oppression in England as well as their escape to Holland and eventual crossing to America on the Mayflower, and their early days in New England...   History Pages 268

www.bookjungle.com *email: sales@bookjungle.com fax: 630-214-0564 mail: Book Jungle PO Box 2226 Champaign, IL 61825*

QTY

The Fasting Cure *by Sinclair Upton*   ISBN: *1-59462-222-1* **$13.95**
In the Cosmopolitan Magazine for May, 1910, and in the Contemporary Review (London) for April, 1910, I published an article dealing with my experiences in fasting. I have written a great many magazine articles, but never one which attracted so much attention... New Age/Self Help/Health Pages 164

Hebrew Astrology *by Sepharial*   ISBN: *1-59462-308-2* **$13.45**
In these days of advanced thinking it is a matter of common observation that we have left many of the old landmarks behind and that we are now pressing forward to greater heights and to a wider horizon than that which represented the mind-content of our progenitors... Astrology Pages 144

Thought Vibration or The Law of Attraction in the Thought World   ISBN: *1-59462-127-6* **$12.95**

by William Walker Atkinson   *Psychology/Religion Pages 144*

Optimism *by Helen Keller*   ISBN: *1-59462-108-X* **$15.95**
Helen Keller was blind, deaf, and mute since 19 months old, yet famously learned how to overcome these handicaps, communicate with the world, and spread her lectures promoting optimism. An inspiring read for everyone... Biographies/Inspirational Pages 84

Sara Crewe *by Frances Burnett*   ISBN: *1-59462-360-0* **$9.45**
In the first place, Miss Minchin lived in London. Her home was a large, dull, tall one, in a large, dull square, where all the houses were alike, and all the sparrows were alike, and where all the door-knockers made the same heavy sound... Childrens/Classic Pages 88

The Autobiography of Benjamin Franklin *by Benjamin Franklin*   ISBN: *1-59462-135-7* **$24.95**
The Autobiography of Benjamin Franklin has probably been more extensively read than any other American historical work, and no other book of its kind has had such ups and downs of fortune. Franklin lived for many years in England, where he was agent... Biographies/History Pages 332

Name	
Email	
Telephone	
Address	
City, State ZIP	

☐ **Credit Card**   ☐ **Check / Money Order**

Credit Card Number	
Expiration Date	
Signature	

Please Mail to: Book Jungle
PO Box 2226
Champaign, IL 61825
or Fax to: 630-214-0564

ORDERING INFORMATION

web*: www.bookjungle.com*
email*: sales@bookjungle.com*
fax*: 630-214-0564*
mail*: Book Jungle PO Box 2226 Champaign, IL 61825*
or PayPal *to sales@bookjungle.com*

Please contact us for bulk discounts

DIRECT-ORDER TERMS

**20% Discount if You Order
Two or More Books**
Free Domestic Shipping!
Accepted: Master Card, Visa,
Discover, American Express